Swept Away

By Toni Blake

SWEPT AWAY

toni blake

Swept Away

AVON *red*

An Imprint of HarperCollinsPublishers
www.harpercollins.com

HarperCollins books may be purchased for educational, business, or sales promotional use. For information please write: Special Markets Department, HarperCollins Publishers Inc., 10 East 53rd Street, New York, NY 10022.

FIRST EDITION

Interior text designed by Diahann Sturge

Library of Congress Cataloging-in-Publication Data

Blake, Toni, 1965–
    Swept away / by Toni Blake.—1st ed.
        p. cm.
    ISBN-13: 978-0-06-113588-0
    ISBN-10: 0-06-113588-7
    I. Title.

PS3602. L349S94   2006
813'.6—dc22   2006006912

06 07 08 09 10   WBC/RRD   10 9 8 7 6 5 4 3 2 1

To Blair.
If I had to be stuck on a desert island with someone,
I'd pick you.

Acknowledgments

My utmost appreciation goes to:

Author Maggie Price and her husband, Bill, for answering my many FBI questions, as well as helping me figure out logical answers each time I wrote myself into a corner in the suspense portion of the story. I'm indebted.

Author Sue-Ellen Welfonder and her kind agent, Roberta Brown, for answering my questions about Naples, Florida, and helping me find just the right spots to set particular scenes.

Renee Norris and Lisa Koester for supplying pottery know-how and suggesting the sea glass ornamentation.

The good people on Ninclink for their feedback on cell phone reception and FBI agents.

Author J. R. Ward for fast feedback on the first thirty-five pages.

Renee Norris for fast feedback on the first one hundred pages, and for even more feedback on the finished manuscript. I would be lost without you.

Acknowledgments

Robin Zentmeyer, for early brainstorming sessions—so early she doesn't even remember them! And for listening to me talk about books and publishing ad nauseum for the last ten years or so.

And, finally, my fabulous agent, Meg Ruley, and my equally fabulous editor, Lucia Macro, both of whom saw something special in this story when it was only a two-page idea typed haphazardly into an e-mail, and who let me take the helm and sail this baby. I can't imagine two better captains for my ship!

The night of Kat's high-school graduation
Ten years ago

A thin rivulet of sweat rippled between her breasts as she shut the car door and walked toward him. The flirty skirt of her short dress flounced around her thighs, and her nipples rubbed against the fabric with each step. She'd never been so aware of her body.

Or of *his* body. He sat in a black bucket seat that had once resided in a car but now perched beside a swampy lake. A cigarette dangled from his mouth and a beer can rested between his legs, against the bulge in his worn blue jeans. His black T-shirt fit him just as well as the denim, molding to biceps, chest, and stomach, and messy hair hung too long over the ribbed neck of his shirt in back— one wayward lock dipped recklessly onto his forehead.

He looked as dangerous as the night. Exactly what she wanted, needed.

She stood before him, equal parts fear and excitement. She didn't know how to do this, at all—but she'd wanted him for so long, ever since he'd started working for her father at the gallery six months ago, lugging crates and making deliveries. Clean-cut high-school boys whose lives revolved around locker-room boasts and who had the fastest car? She didn't need 'em. She'd known the moment she set eyes on Brock Denton that she needed a *man*.

He was twenty-two and lived out here in the swamps with his grandpa. She knew the way because she'd ridden along with her dad once when Brock's car had broken down. She remembered the tense, quiet ride—how clear it had been that her father didn't like Brock even being in the same car with her, and she'd instinctively understood why. Because sex oozed from him like swamp mud if you picked it up in your hand and let it squeeze out between your fingers. One look from him and her whole body turned to liquid, something hot, bubbling from the inside out beneath the baking sun.

But now her father was nowhere around. And she was ready to become a woman with Brock, ready to learn all the secrets of passion, ready to sweat with him, ready to let him show her . . . everything.

His dark eyes burned right through her, tightening her nipples further. "What are you doing out here in that fancy car, kitten?" He didn't smile, but his gaze held exactly what she wanted it to—sex. Like always.

She tossed a vague glance over her shoulder at the shiny new red Mazda Miata. Really not so fancy in her world—a starter car, for college, her father had called it—but she guessed Brock saw it differently given the beat-up old Mustang he drove and talked about fixing up once he saved some money. "It's a graduation gift from my father," she said.

"Doesn't answer my question." His eyes pinned her in place so that she couldn't quite move—she'd been walking toward him, taking steady steps in her low heels over the uneven dirt drive, but now she stopped. "Your daddy know you're here?"

She gave her head a saucy tilt. "What do *you* think?"

The first hint of a smile quirked one side of his mouth, drawing her attention to the dark stubble that covered his chin—she wanted to touch it, feel its roughness against her fingertips. But just as quickly, his amusement faded back to serious. "I think this is an awful dangerous place for a pretty little thing like you." He hiked a thumb toward the marshy lake to his right. Moss covered much of the surface, thick cattails rimming the edge, and for the first time she noticed the fishing pole propped over a tackle box, the line sunk in the water nearby, waiting for a nibble. "Alligators out here, you know. They eat up kittens in one bite."

Why did even *that* make the juncture of her thighs tingle madly? "I'm not afraid."

"Maybe you *should* be. Maybe you don't know what you're getting yourself into. And maybe you better just tell me what you came here for, kitten."

She took a deep breath. *Now or never. Make it now. Get exactly what you want for graduation.* She took another step toward him, and the mere movement reminded her again of her body—and what she craved. A beat-up radio sat on the ground nearby, and the sexy strains of an old song, "Hot Child in the City," gave her the urge to sway. She let her hips begin to move, ever so slightly. "Since I graduated tonight, I want *you* to give me a present, too."

He flicked his cigarette aside, into the tall grass that edged the water, and crossed strong arms over his chest. His eyes narrowed into dark slits that should have warned her away but instead lured her nearer, especially when they followed the movement of her hips for a long, sultry moment before rising back to her face. "And just what do *I* have that *you* could want?"

She swallowed back the lump in her throat. "I want *you*."

Then, ignoring the heat that rose like flames to her cheeks, she reached up, hooked her thumbs into the thin shoulder straps of her dress, and let them fall—let the whole dress fall—skimming her curves until it dropped around her white graduation shoes, so that she stood before him in nothing but a pair of lacy pink Brazilian-cut panties bought just for this occasion.

God, she couldn't believe she'd done it. But she had, and this was it—she'd put her whole self out there, her whole soul, just for him.

A hot evening breeze wafted over her, as intense as his gaze, and there was no going slow now, no stopping. It had taken every ounce of courage within her to come this far, and she had to forge ahead. Never taking her eyes off his, which had grown blessedly lust-filled as he looked on her body, she stepped free of the dress pooled at her feet and took slow, steady strides toward him across the rough ground. *Be cool. Be seductive.* It suddenly wasn't as hard as she'd expected—the moves coming almost naturally now. Heat permeated her, both from the humid Florida night and the desire sizzling inside her. Without hesitation, she lifted one foot over the bucket seat and lowered herself onto his lap, straddling him.

Her crotch met the chilled beer can, so she reached deftly between them and tossed the aluminum aside, letting it spill foamy in the dirt. Neither looked toward it as she pressed herself to the mysterious bulge that had been the object of her fascination for so long. *Mmm, yes.* She was really doing this, really seducing Brock Denton.

"Jesus, kitten," he groaned at the connection.

She let out a hot, thready sigh, amazed—he was so hard. His rough hands closed loosely at her hips, and the mere touch—his flesh on hers—set off a whole new firestorm inside her. She started to move against him, not by plan but by pure, driving instinct, and the thick crease of his zipper abraded her through her panties to deliver the most delicious sensation she'd ever endured.

"I didn't know you were such a bad girl," he said in a low rumble. It was as if he were everywhere, all around her, consuming her.

"*Make* me a bad girl, Brock. Take me. Take my virginity right now." Not wanting to wait another second, she reached down to the button on his jeans—just as his grip tightened on her waist to lift her slightly away from him.

She knew intuitively that it wasn't a giving-her-better-access-to-the-zipper lift, but more of a *halting* lift. She jerked her gaze from bulge to eyes. They shone dark, delicious—but not inviting.

"I don't think so, kitten." His voice remained only slightly husky and as arrogant as ever.

She stopped breathing for a second at the hideous impact of his words, until finally she managed, "What?"

"Afraid I'm not into virgins. I like my girls with a little more experience."

Push down how much that hurts. Don't let yourself feel how clear he just made it that this is only sex. Make this happen—somehow. It was the overriding thought pummeling her—she'd come too far to fail now. *Convince him to want you.*

She leaned close to his ear, raking taut nipples against his T-shirt, and tried not to sound desperate as she purred, "Teach me. I'm an enthusiastic student."

And before giving him a chance to respond, she did what came naturally—raised her hands to bracket his face over that rough, delectable stubble, and sank her mouth onto his. God, Brock made even beer and a slight hint of smoke taste sexy, and she kissed him hard and long, pressing her tongue inward. His grip tightened, digging into her flesh as he began to knead, knead, in a way that heightened everything, the heaviness of her breasts, the yearning between her thighs.

When finally the long, languid kiss ended, their foreheads touched and she could smell the musky, manly scent of him, and she knew she had to have him or she'd die. *I love you.*

God, don't say that. *Even if it's what you've been thinking over and over each night in bed, trying to imagine what this would be like.*

"I want you," she said instead. "I'll do anything you want. Anything." *Anything to keep you from breaking my heart right now, crushing my soul.*

They both breathed heavily in the still air, which had turned dusky since her arrival, the dense tree lines surrounding them seeming to bring the night on with more intensity.

"Nice kiss, kitten," he rasped, his lips nearly touching hers—yet then he hauled her back from him again, to look her in the eye. "But I'm still not into it. You want to do it so bad, give it to some high-school boy who'll be more your speed."

It was like a blow to the gut. She was sitting in his lap nearly naked, and he was turning her down. And she'd been trying not to feel that, trying desperately to *change* that, but suddenly it was unavoidable—an impossible humiliation. Defeat crumbled through her in jagged, scarring pieces to settle low in her belly.

"You . . . really don't want me?" She didn't mean to ask—and she shut her eyes against the softness of her own voice as soon as the words left her lips.

"You don't belong here, kitten—you're out of your league. You need to get in that fancy car and go home now. Understand?" He pushed her still farther away, and when she gathered the courage to look back into his eyes, all she found was the usual grim, sexy conceit.

"You're an asshole."

He only shrugged, uncaring, and she rose up off him, dying inside, thinking—*Get out of here. Get out of here now.*

But she resisted running, scurrying, like a child. She only prayed he couldn't see her trembling as she plucked up her dress, struggled to find the opening, then slid it back over her head. One last ounce of defensiveness forced her to turn and say, "You don't know what you're missing."

Not one iota of emotion crossed his impossibly handsome face as he replied. "Go home, kitten. And don't come back."

Chapter One

*H*er whole world at the moment consisted of warm sun and cool sand, the gentle *shush* of the tide. Palm fronds rustled in the breeze behind her, and before her lay nothing but blue ocean and the calm, straight line of the horizon.

She'd come here to relax. Unwind. Escape.

No, wait—not escape. Where had *that* come from?

She'd come here to *prepare*. Yes, that was better. It was a . . . transitional period.

The period when she would transform from her normal, fun-loving self into someone's wife. But not just someone. A respected attorney. Who was also an investor—"gifted at it," her father said—and thus had more money than God.

She hadn't the faintest idea how she was going to be that kind of wife—the kind who hosted garden parties and Sunday brunches, the kind who could hold a glass of wine in her hand all evening at a cocktail party without ever getting tipsy and giggly. Kat was fairly *famous* among her friends for "tipsy and giggly."

But those days were behind her now—they had to be. Hence the transitional period, the sun and the sand. It truly *was* tranquil here. Her father had only bought the private island off the Gulf Coast of Florida last year, so they hadn't made any improvements yet, but once she and Ian were married, maybe she'd suggest they make a gift to her parents—perhaps a new beach house, a new dock for the boats. People said money couldn't buy happiness, but Kat knew better. Nothing would make her father happier than a shiny new beach house, courtesy of his daughter and new son-in-law. She could almost feel his smile beaming at her already.

A vision flashed in her mind—her, in a few years, as a mom, corralling a little boy and girl on this same beach. The children were adorable, exploring, occasionally picking up a sand dollar or a broken bit of shell. They all wore light colors, whites and pastels. She and the little girl sported straw hats and flowy sundresses. Somewhere in the distance, her father and Ian grilled steaks and drank martinis while her mother festooned a picnic table with brightly colored place mats and arranged peach-colored napkins in a fan shape to bloom from stemmed glasses.

Why did such a lovely image make her want to throw up?

She *liked* kids, after all. She spent each and every Saturday afternoon with kids at The Kiln, teaching them to throw pots. A messy and sometimes semidisastrous pastime, but pottery was her passion. She loved sharing it with children who weren't as fortunate as she'd been and who needed a distraction from the harsher realities of their lives.

And she liked steak and martinis and decorative napkins, too. Who didn't?

So what was wrong with this picture?

She sighed, thinking.

It wasn't that she didn't want to be married. She did—she always had. Sure, everyone thought of her as Crazy Kat, party girl extraordinaire—but deep inside, all she'd ever really wanted was commitment, someone to build a life with, a world with.

And she loved her parents, and she loved Ian's parents, and you really couldn't find a guy who was more respected or even better-looking than Ian. He was a catch—everyone said so.

So that settled it, once and for all. There was nothing wrong with the picture.

She was simply going to suffer a steep learning curve in terms of being a sophisticated wife, that was all. And really, it shouldn't be that much of a stretch—she'd been masquerading as a sophisticated daughter all her life and gotten by okay. And Ian didn't love her because she was sophisticated—he loved the *real* her, even the party her. He'd once told her that. So this was all going to be just fine.

A damn good thing given that the wedding was only seven days away.

The trill of her cell phone jarred her from her thoughts as she plucked it up from the sand next to her lounge chair, then mentally prepared herself to lie in case it was her mother, expecting to hear the sounds of slot machines behind her. "Hello?"

"Viva Las Vegas, baby!" No, just her lifelong best friend Nina—and it was *Kat* who heard the whirring sounds of electronic gambling in the background. "I'm coming to you live from Caesar's Palace!"

"So you guys made it in okay," Kat said, envisioning her five best buds partying without her in Sin City.

"Yeah, and—" Nina stopped, just briefly. "Oh. My. God. *The* hottest soldier in the entire Roman army just walked by!"

"Down, girl," Kat said dryly, at once sorry to be missing the fun but at the same time so removed from it that it didn't matter—she had bigger things on her mind.

"In a few minutes, we're going to walk over to Treasure Island and try to pick up some pirates. Swarthy ones, with scars. God, I can't believe you're missing this, Kat. Honestly, if I live to be a hundred, I still won't believe you actually bailed on your own bachelorette party." Nina let out a long, slow sigh, and then—if Kat wasn't mistaken—took a slurping sip from a beverage undoubtedly high in alcoholic content. "Are you sure you won't change your mind?"

"Too late now. I'm here, and you're there."

Nina's voice dropped so that Kat could barely hear her over the sounds of the slots. "No. I meant about the wedding."

Now it was Kat's turn to sigh as her stomach twisted. Why couldn't Nina just let this go? She was marrying Ian, and that was that. "Would you please drop it already?"

"You don't love him."

Here we go again. "Of course I love him. I've known him my whole life."

"I've known *you* my whole life, but that doesn't mean I'm marrying you. You know Ian's not pendant-worthy."

Kat took a deep breath. That was how they'd rated the guys in her life—always—by whether or not they lived up to the legend attached to the pendant her father had given her as a little girl, something he'd picked up on his "art travels." According to the old woman who'd sold her father the broken piece, the other half had been given to a young girl's lover when the two were separated. They never found each other again, and the legend said that bringing the pieces back together would unite their souls and that those who *brought* them back would unite for eternity, as well. The pendant hung behind glass, even now, in the rear of her father's gallery.

Kat and Nina hadn't, of course, judged guys by this *literally*—they knew no guy was magically going to produce the pendant's missing half. But it was their way of saying: *Is this guy a potential soulmate? A keeper for eternity?*

Although it suddenly seemed an adolescent way to size up a man, and Kat decided she wasn't going to deal with Nina's lectures any longer. "Listen, if you don't want to be kicked out as maid of honor, you'll stop bringing this up and accept the fact that I'm marrying Ian and am going to have a fabulous life with him. I'm going to wear straw hats and learn to sip instead of guzzle."

"What?"

"Nothing, never mind."

"I still say you should be in Vegas right now."

"I am. As far as the rest of the world knows. Don't forget that. Like in case my mother were to call."

"Got it. I'll tell her you can't come to the phone because you're getting a lap dance from a Chippendale."

"That's hysterical," Kat replied in her driest tone.

"Or I'll tell her you're riding a pirate." Nina giggled. "I mean, a pirate *ship*."

"Slow down on the fuzzy navels, girlfriend. It's early yet."

"They're rum twizzlers. Or fizzlers, or something," she said, sounding slightly confused. But then she sobered—as much as possible given the alcohol consumption. "This just isn't as much fun without you."

Kat reasoned with her. "Well, admittedly, a bachelorette party tends to suffer without the bachelorette. But I'm betting you'll muddle through and still manage to have a good time."

"Betting? Vegas? Ha!" She broke into peals of laughter.

And Kat sighed, disconcerted and slightly annoyed. Which was odd. Since when did Nina's silliness bring her down? "Listen, repeat after me. Kat is in the bathroom. Or Kat is sleeping. Or Kat is on a roll at the roulette wheel and cannot be disturbed. These are the types of things you say if anyone calls looking for me. Then you ring me and let me know so I can call them back."

"Got it. Kat is sleeping. With a pirate."

Sadly, for some reason, Kat couldn't even smile at that. Maybe she really wanted to be sleeping with a pirate? But this was all for the best—everybody had to grow up sometime. "I'm getting off the phone now. Go have fun. And be careful."

"I'm in Vegas. You should tell me to get lucky instead."

"Okay, get lucky. In a careful way."

After she hung up, she wondered when she'd turned into her mother—repeatedly telling people to be careful. And as she let her cell phone plunk gently back down into the sand, she couldn't deny some feelings of regret. Pirates were sounding pretty good right about now. She'd never done calm and serene well. What had she been thinking coming here?

You were thinking about relaxing and unwinding and preparing, she reminded herself. She'd likened it to starting a new pottery project— for which she always had to take some time to let the new piece come together in her mind before sitting down with her clay. She had to let her plans gel, develop, evolve. *This* was sort of like *that*, only the current project was a little bigger—starting her life as Ian's wife.

Not that her *whole* life would be different. She'd still go to work every day at her dad's gallery, helping him showcase local artists. By the time she'd graduated from college with a degree in art history, she'd realized the gallery had become much more to her than just a summer job over the years—it was a huge part of her life, so she'd chosen to stay there, expanding her position over time.

And she'd still have *her* art, her pottery. In fact, her first show was next month, not long after the honeymoon—featuring her Raku pots. She'd worked hard on developing her own unique style with the glazing technique over the past year, then started adding sea glass ornamentation. Everyone agreed the results were stunning, and her father had offered a showing—and not just because he loved her, either. Art was maybe the one thing Kat's dad cherished as much as his family—he didn't take it lightly, and he'd watched her work on her pots for years before finally extending the invitation just a few weeks ago.

So—this whole wife thing was just . . . a change. Which she needed to enter into reverently, humbly, with her whole heart. And coming here to help herself ease from one part of her life into another was an intelligent move, an act of true maturity, she thought.

Even so, the sight of a pirate ship on the horizon right now would have been just the pick-me-up she needed.

She probably should have gone to Vegas, kicked up her heels one last time. But as the trip had approached, it had stopped sounding fun. Mentally preparing for her future had seemed smarter. And the secluded island really *had* sounded relaxing after all the craziness of planning a huge wedding. She'd just had the overwhelming urge to get away, from everyone and everything, and just *be*.

Which was why her whereabouts were top secret. Naples was only fifteen short miles away, and relaxing would be impossible if her mother and father and Ian could all hop in a speedboat and head out here whenever they felt like it.

Now she realized she'd just cashed in her last chance to cut loose and party. And she wouldn't have done anything *too* heinous— she wouldn't *really* have slept with a pirate or ridden a Chippendale or vice versa—because if there was one thing Kat took seriously, it was *marriage*. She wanted a marriage like her parents had—stable and lasting and loving—and she wouldn't have sullied that notion by doing anything with another guy. But she still might have found some way to have a little fun, get a little wild, one last time.

Next week you'll be married. Next week, you'll be traveling down the road to sedate pastels and fanned napkins and motherhood.

It suddenly hit her that this, today, right now, was *it*, the last time she'd be *her*, herself, a single entity responsible to no one else—and that she had to do *something* totally for her, totally *about* her; she had to do something very Crazy-Kat-like that would make Nina hoot with laughter if she were here.

So—given that her options for wildness were limited under the circumstances—she did the only thing she could think of. She sat up in her lounge chair, reached behind her neck, and untied her bikini top. A moment later, she tossed it haphazardly into the sand, freeing her breasts to the world.

Of course, if a tree falls in the forest and there's no one around to hear, does it make a sound? And if you sunbathe topless in the middle of nowhere, are you really a girl gone wild?

She shrugged. Didn't matter. It was all she had right now.

And already it felt a bit . . . forbidden. And freeing.

Which was just what she needed.

Although shedding the top whisked her unexpectedly back to the past, for just the flash of a second, to the only other instance when she'd bared her breasts outdoors—that time for a guy, that loser Brock Denton. But she pushed the thought away quickly—it was among the most humiliating and debilitating of her existence and it had taken a long time to get over it.

Lying back in her lounge chair, she stretched her arms sensually overhead, soaking up the sun with freshly bared skin. Serene and tranquil in a decidedly much sexier way, and if this was her last hurrah, so be it.

Yet she couldn't resist opening one closed eye for just a peek, to make sure no pirate ships loomed on the horizon.

Damn—nothing.

Brock slid one arm around the hot blonde on his left, then slipped the other around the pretty brunette on his right. As the waters of the hot tub bubbled around them, he pulled both women closer, their bikini-clad breasts nestling against him. He briefly tried to recall their names but failed. Ah well, didn't matter. "When Carlos invited me along on the yacht today," he said, shifting his grin between them, "I didn't realize this was gonna be so much fun."

The blonde giggled. "We *love* when Carlos and Francisco bring friends on our little boat rides." She lifted one palm to his chest for a sensual caress, the touch tightening his groin just slightly.

"Especially hot ones like you, Jimmy," the brunette said, a mischievous spark in her gaze as she slipped her hand beneath the leg of his trunks to squeeze high on his thigh.

He flinched as the unexpected sensation shot upward, then flashed her a chiding look. Answering to the fake name didn't throw him at all, but the fondle did. "Whoa there, sweetheart. Let's save the real party for after the job, huh?" he said on a light laugh. Then he added a wink and spoke quietly, even though the other two men on the yacht were currently belowdecks. "Francisco can be a hardass about that kind of thing."

The brunette wrinkled her nose. "He's just jealous."

Brock shrugged. "But he's the boss." Lowering his voice again, he said, "Don't worry, though—there'll be plenty of me to go around later."

Both girls giggled, and Brock rewarded them each with a kiss on the cheek.

He couldn't deny it—The Morales brothers had a good thing

going here. Easy money, hot chicks, and life on a yacht sailing the clear Gulf waters, peppered with the occasional trip south through the Caribbean to their homeland of Guatemala. The only possible thing they were missing were servants and a crew, but given that it was a smallish yacht, the boys didn't seem to mind steering and serving themselves.

Yep, they had a good thing going, but they'd messed up by inviting *him* along. And not just because their girls wanted *him* now instead of them. In fact, part of him almost felt sorry for Carlos, who'd befriended him in a much tighter way than Francisco had. *Never should have trusted me, buddy,* he thought as Carlos ascended the spiral staircase from below. *Never should have let me in. But it's too late now.* By the end of the day, the Morales brothers' easy life would be nearing its demise.

When Carlos spied Brock between the two girls in the tub, he chuckled in his good-natured way, his thin, dark mustache curling upward at the corners of his mouth. "Moving in on our women, yes?" he asked in his thick Latin accent.

Brock returned the grin, then glanced back and forth between the girls. "How am I supposed to resist such beauty?" Actually, getting cozy with the girls hadn't been part of the plan, but Brock had learned to go with the flow in such situations. And if the flow happened to lead him in between two wet and willing women, who was he to complain?

Carlos raised his eyebrows. "Room for one more?"

The blonde—Brock couldn't remember if she belonged to Carlos or Francisco—spread her arms wide. "There's always room for you, baby."

Carlos flashed a lecherous grin and pushed black, slightly curly hair out of his face as he walked toward the bubbling tub.

But when Francisco appeared behind him—a bigger, broader,

badder version of his younger brother—his grim expression drew Brock's attention immediately. Something wasn't right here, he knew it that fast—a sixth sense that had nothing to do with seeing dead people.

"What's up, Francisco?" he asked easily. "You don't look happy." He could only hope something was amiss with the pickup—that it had been changed, or the mission had been scrapped for some reason—and that nothing more serious was going on.

"Come on into the water and let me make it all better," the blonde offered with pouting lips and inviting eyes. He *still* didn't know which guy was hers. Then it dawned on him that maybe they were interchangeable.

"Nothing like a little hot-tub party," the brunette said, shimmying her breasts suggestively within her red bikini top.

"Nice, honey," Carlos offered, dipping a foot into the water to join them.

"You ever know a man named Reyes?" Francisco asked, and Brock's eyes flew to his. Talk about a killjoy. How the hell had he found out Brock had known Reyes?

"Reyes?" Brock repeated, then pretended to be searching his memory for the name of the Miami drug runner he'd brought down three years ago. "Doesn't ring a bell. Why? Who is he?"

Francisco's eyes narrowed. "Friend of a friend," he said, his words a little too slow and his tone a little too threatening for Brock's liking. "He's dead now. But I happened to see a photo of him with some other guys taken not long before the FBI nailed him. And there was a guy in that photo who looked an awful lot like *you*, Jimmy."

Brock worked hard to keep a blank face and narrow eyes.

"So I said to my friend," Francisco went on, " 'that guy—he looks like a guy I know,' and so my friend put me in touch with *another* guy from the picture. And I just got an e-mail from that guy, and do you know what he said? He said the guy in the picture who looks like you was an undercover FBI agent. So—what do you think about that, *Jimmy*?"

I think I'm screwed.

But if Brock was well practiced at anything, it was getting out of a jam. And this operation had gone far too smoothly up to now. So this was just a snag—every job had at least one or two—and he could get out of it if he played it right.

"I think I'm pretty fucking upset—that's what I think!" he boomed, pushing to his feet with a bolt of adrenaline disguised as anger. Water sluiced off his body back into the tub. "Who the hell do you think you are, Morales? Accusing me of being a goddamn fed. I ought to rip your fucking head off, right here and now."

The two men squared off against each other, even though Brock remained in the hot tub with two suddenly cowering girls behind him.

Carlos, who had pulled his foot back out of the water when Francisco had started his diatribe, stepped up to intervene. "Look, guys, calm down. Francisco, I told you, Jimmy couldn't be the same guy you saw. Faces look alike. Jimmy is our friend, I'd stake my life on it." Then he shifted his gaze to Brock. "You know my brother's a hothead, always believes the worst. But I told him that you, an FBI agent—impossible, yes?"

Brock looked to Carlos, then locked a menacing gaze on Francisco. "Yes!" he bit off fiercely, a little dumbstruck by Carlos's blind trust in him. Of course, he'd given Carlos an extensive— even if false—history of his experience in burglary and smuggling. Claimed he'd gotten out of drug-running because it was too dangerous these days, saying he was willing to make a little less money for work that held a little less risk. But Carlos's loyalty, as well as the fact that he considered "Jimmy" a friend, came as a surprise.

"So this is settled now. Okay?" Carlos asked, directing the question to his brother.

Francisco took a long time answering as he and Brock stared each other down. Brock's heart beat like a hammer in his chest—his life depended on making Francisco believe he was just another smuggler like them. And it was in that still, tense moment that he noticed Francisco no longer wore around his neck the key that had dangled from a chain there earlier in the day. He hadn't asked what the key was for, but he had his suspicions, and its sudden absence was worth noting.

"Okay," Francisco finally said. "It's settled."

Brock gave a short nod and slowly eased his way back down into the hot tub, although the girls didn't fly back into his arms. He couldn't blame them.

For now, he was off the hook—but he'd have to think real carefully about how he wanted to play Francisco from this point forward. Did he act like this had never happened, like things really *were* cool between them? Or did he act like an asshole now, hold a grudge? That might give him the upper hand, make his charade more convincing.

Thankfully, time was on his side. The pickup was this afternoon. Five million dollars worth of Mayan artifacts looted from ancient cities in the Guatemalan wilderness and smuggled out of the country to be sold to wealthy collectors stateside. Late tonight they were scheduled to meet the head of the operation, code name Omega Man—a really *stupid* code name, in Brock's opinion, that made him picture the guy in a cape and tights—then as soon as he could get away and make a phone call, a team of agents would swoop in to seize the items and make the arrests. So all he had to do was keep Francisco in the dark for the rest of the day—and the night. Surely he could do *that*.

"Looks like the party's over, girls," Brock said apologetically. But not *too* apologetically—thugs didn't treat their women overly nice in his experience, and it was a good time to be sure he acted like enough of a thug.

"Doesn't have to be," Blondie said, curling up next to him anyway now that the tension had passed, pressing her ample cleavage against his arm as she slid one palm over his shoulder. "In fact, I think a party is *exactly* what we need right now." She flashed a scolding glance to Francisco, and Brock hoped it didn't get her slapped by the gruffer brother.

But Francisco only glared and said, "Pickup's in an hour. I don't care *what* you do 'til then—just be ready." After directing that last part specifically to Brock, he turned his back, peering out over the vast, empty waters that stretched before them.

As Blondie leaned near Brock's ear to say, "What's your pleasure, cowboy?" it occurred to him that maybe the best strategy was to continue going with the flow, to simply let the party commence. Francisco wouldn't expect a fed to do that. Especially right after the accusation.

He cast a cutting glance at Francisco for good measure, though—still acting pissed. "Why don't you surprise me," he said to Blondie, adding loudly enough for everyone to hear, "Do something to take my mind off all this *shit* being flung at me so I can concentrate on work in a little while."

"What about *me*?" the brunette asked.

Okay, this was getting a little sticky. Or good. Depending upon how he looked at it.

Go with the flow, dude—anything else and you look like the fed you are. "No reason you girls can't play nice and share," he said with a wink. Fact was, the girls were hot—and whatever happened, it wasn't exactly gonna be torture.

And when the brunette began raking her fingernails lightly down his chest, torture became the furthest thing from Brock's mind. He'd been working pretty much around the clock on this case for the last two months, with little time for play, and he didn't usually mix *this* kind of play with work—but it looked like that was about to change.

The brunette rained scintillating little kisses on his neck just as the blonde slid her slender hand down his stomach beneath the water, going lower, lower. She cupped him through his trunks, and he pulled in his breath. He peered down at her, eyelids heavy with arousal as his brain turned to a glob of mush and sex.

Don't get too caught up in this. And yet, how did he not? Sex was sex, and if he was gonna do it, he had to be into it. And if he *didn't* do it, he'd look pretty damn suspicious.

As the brunette rubbed her breasts against his arm, the blonde said, "Want more, baby?" and squeezed him lightly.

He was just about to tell her *exactly* what he wanted, when Francisco called over to him easily. "Hey, Brock."

He looked up from the sensual haze. "Yeah?"

And realized that trying to go with the flow had just distracted him—fatally. *Shit.*

"Who's Brock?" Carlos asked from somewhere to his right.

"*He* is," Francisco said, pinning Brock in place with eyes so sinister they could have belonged to the devil himself. "Brock Denton, FBI agent." The evil brother looked toward the less evil one. "See, bro, the guy who just e-mailed me knew the asshole fed's name. And the asshole fed just answered to it. And it's going to be the *last* fucking time he answers to *anything*."

Brock pushed to his feet beneath the hot sun, tensing for a fight—a fight for his life. But as lots of Spanish began flying back and forth between Carlos and Francisco, he slowly gathered that instead of shooting him, Francisco wanted to deliver him to Omega Man. "Let this scum see what they do to feds who try to screw us over."

Damn, he'd known when Carlos had insisted on swim trunks and the hot tub earlier that it had been a bad idea—because it meant his gun had stayed downstairs with his clothes—but there'd been no way to argue it without looking suspicious. Now, he stood helpless before them as Francisco snatched up a Colt .45 automatic, complete with silver grips, leveling it at Brock, then told Carlos where he could find some rope to tie up "your good friend, *Jimmy.*"

Brock tried not to see the wounded look in Carlos's eyes as he went to find the rope. Not that it mattered. This was his job, bringing down bad guys. And Carlos was a bad guy, so of course Brock had lied and pretended and gotten inside his world, same as always. He just never particularly enjoyed the part where the guys who trusted him found out the truth—at least when it was a guy like Carlos, whose biggest crime was going along with his bully of a brother.

Brock soon lay trussed like a pig belowdecks, alone in a small, tidy bedroom, listening to the boat's motor chug through the water—it was all he could hear, coming through the wall behind him. He lay on the floor, on rough carpet, his hands tied behind his back—in a sturdy knot from what he could tell. But he happened to be pretty skilled at getting loose from sturdy knots. Carlos never should have left him unguarded.

Twenty minutes and a lot of sweat later, he'd freed his hands and started working at the rope that bound his ankles. He should have been scared shitless—if they found him getting loose, they'd probably just shoot him to end the nuisance—but something about concentrating on that gentle chug of the engine calmed his breathing and helped him focus on the task at hand.

When he got to his feet, he looked around the room for anything he could use as a weapon. Nothing, of course—after bringing him down here, Francisco had ordered Carlos to take all the guns to the upper deck. So he was loose, but now what? He was on a goddamn boat in the middle of the ocean.

Well, no weapons, maybe, but there was still a missing key somewhere on this boat, which Francisco had likely shed with his clothes when he'd changed into swimwear. Not that Brock had time to waste—but he figured there was a pretty good chance that key might open a lock that guarded the Mayan treasures.

So giving a quick glance to the doorway, Brock quietly pulled open a dresser drawer. Then another. And another.

Until finally his eyes fell on the key and its thin silver chain, cradled in the fabric of Francisco's tropical print shirt. Whatever happened now, it couldn't hurt to make the key disappear and turn the Morales brothers' job a little more difficult—so he closed it in his fist, then tucked it into a zipper pocket in his trunks.

Next, he approached the room's one tiny porthole and looked out, more in search of inspiration than any tangible sort of help—but he nearly stopped breathing at the sight before him. *Land.* In the distance. A small island of some kind, sprouting the requisite groves of palm trees rimmed with a thin, sandy beach.

It was about half a mile away, and probably uninhabited, too.

Brock had no idea how far they were from the mainland, but they couldn't be *too* far—the pickup was soon and the delivery to Omega Man was tonight, so they had to be reasonably near the Florida coast. Which meant that a man, even on an uninhabited island, would be found. Maybe not tomorrow. Maybe not even next week. But on the other hand, there were such things as signal fires, and if he had nothing else to do all day, he could figure out how to start one. Yep, no question—getting to that island was a lot smarter than staying on this boat with a well-armed guy who was really pissed at him.

Taking a deep breath, Brock eased open the bedroom door and took a few steps toward the bow of the yacht. Above, voices—Carlos saying he still couldn't believe Jimmy was a fed, Francisco berating him for his ignorance.

"Stop, you two." It was one of the girls, he couldn't distinguish which. "Haven't you ever heard the saying, 'Make love, not war'? Why don't you boys calm down and let us make you feel better before your big pickup."

"No time," Francisco said. But then he let out a light moan that surprised the hell out of Brock—since up to this moment he'd thought Francisco was stronger than that.

Come on, Frankie, let her have her way with you. He knew from very recent experience that a little sexual distraction could be a man's downfall, and he needed the evil brother to start thinking about something besides business for a few minutes.

"Come on, baby, let's play," the same female voice pleaded. "Work can wait a little while."

"I don't think so," Francisco said, but he sounded weak, and another moan made Brock smile. *Give in, dude.*

"I can make you feel so good—you know I can. Let me show you."

"Later."

"Now."

And then . . . silence.

And another moan. From Francisco or Carlos?

Maybe it didn't matter, since other than the moans and a little rustling, and then a hot female sigh, everything else was quiet. The only sounds were sex and the boat puttering through the Gulf.

Brock eased back the narrow hallway toward the rear of the lower deck to another spiral staircase. He didn't think about the fact that each step brought him closer to death if he was heard—he just concentrated on being quiet and moving as quickly as possible. The current goal: get off the yacht without being noticed. With any luck, by the time they found out he'd escaped, they'd have no idea where he'd disappeared to. Being stranded on an island didn't hold a lot of appeal, but as long as they didn't know he was there, he'd be safe.

Once topside, he made his way to the boat's stern, where the engine was the loudest and would camouflage any other noise. Without looking back, he eased under the railing, dropped ten feet into the water, and hoped like hell he was as good a swimmer as he thought.

Kat felt herself slowly emerging from a delicious little nap in the sun, becoming pleasantly aware of the rushing tide and the tropical rays warming her skin. Ah, she'd been right—this was just what she needed. She couldn't remember the last time she'd felt so relaxed.

She thought she'd been dreaming . . . of pirates. Silly. But the truth was, it had been a rather steamy sort of dream—the pirates had been hot. As best she could recall—although it was sketchy, as dreams so often were—they'd anchored their ship offshore and shown up on the island, looking for plunder. She'd responded with something ridiculous like, "There's nothing here for you to take but little old me," and they hadn't really seemed too upset about that. Even though in real life pirates would be scary, the ethereal qualities surrounding this particular encounter had only added to her feelings of "ah, this is nice."

Sighing at the luxury of such dreamy comfort, she let her eyes flutter open. In the distance, she found the calming sight of the sea and its whitecapped waves rolling gently in to break on the shore, the clear blue sky dotted with an occasional cottony cloud—and a man, walking up out of the water, looking hot and wet and sexy as sin.

She closed her eyes again, quickly, because surely she was still dreaming.

There wasn't *really* a pirate coming to ravish her. There just wasn't.

Not that this guy had looked like a pirate exactly—but if you gave him longer hair and a big sword, maybe. She caught her breath and prepared to open her eyes again, yet she didn't—*couldn't*, actually.

Because as hot as he was, she didn't like the notion that maybe she was losing her mind. Right when she'd been so relaxed—and right when she'd *needed* to be relaxed. She suddenly thought she knew what it must feel like to spot a UFO or Bigfoot.

Open your eyes, idiot, and see that nothing's there. Then you can go back to sleep and dream about your pirates again.

When a drop of water hit her stomach, then her breast, her eyes automatically jerked open.

And, dear God, there *was* a guy! And he was hovering over her—blocking the sun so that it shone around his head in a blinding halo—and squinting down at her as if *she'd* just come walking up out of the ocean.

"Kitten? Is that you?"

That voice! She sucked in her breath so hard it hurt. Brock Denton? What the hell? She *was* dreaming. She had to be.

She simply stared up at the guy she still couldn't quite see and tried to make sense of it, of *him*. He dripped on her again.

"It *is* you," he said, shifting just enough that she could finally make out his face—his still drop-dead gorgeous and definitely all-grown-up-even-more-than-before face, as one side of his mouth quirked in amusement and his gaze fell to her chest. "Very nice, kitten, but I'm afraid you're gonna have a nasty sunburn."

Gasping, she slapped her hands over her bare breasts—yet he'd already turned to trudge past her through the sand as if they'd just bumped into each other on a public beach and he was headed for the snack bar.

Chapter Two

*W*here the hell had he come from? How could this be?

She bolted upright, then turned to look after him, bewildered. "Wh-where are you going? And what are you doing here? What the hell's going on?" She'd just woken up in the freaking Twilight Zone.

He stopped and peered back at her as she struggled to her feet, somehow needing to follow after him, or at least be on the same level with him—and she realized all over again just how incredible he was to look at. When they were younger, she'd never seen him with so few clothes on.

"Answer me," she demanded. "Where did you come from? What's happening here?"

His reply came crisp and dry. "I could tell you, kitten, but then I'd have to kill you."

Keeping her hands over her breasts, she trudged a few steps closer to him in the soft, warm sand. "What are you doing here? Tell me!"

"I could ask you the same question." Same arrogant tone as always, proving that some things never changed.

"My father happens to *own* this island," she informed him.

"Figures," he murmured, and it irritated her all the more.

"Which means you're trespassing."

He rolled his eyes. "Well, pardon me for the inconvenience, honey—I'll just turn around and swim on back to the mainland."

She narrowed her gaze on him, still as confused as the moment she'd woken up. "You really don't have a boat somewhere? You really just . . . swam here? How the hell is that possible?"

"Long story and no time to tell it," he said with a shrug. "But don't worry, I won't be in your hair long. Do cell phones work here?"

"Yeah. Most of the time, anyway."

"Then we're not far from shore?" He'd seemed to totally forget that he'd just washed up onto her island out of nowhere and still hadn't provided one iota of an explanation.

"Fifteen miles or so," she said, shaking her head as if to say— *Who cares? You still haven't told me what the hell you're doing here!*

"Great. Let me have your phone." When she just stood there for a second, he gave her an expectant look, adding, "Chop, chop, kitten—I'm in kind of a hurry."

Sheesh. Despite herself, she turned and dashed back to her lounge chair, snatching the phone up from the beach. She thrust it into his hand, then realized his dark gaze had fallen back to her breasts—because she'd dropped her palms to retrieve the phone, damn it!—so her next task was to turn away from him and scoop up the abandoned bikini top.

"Jesus, this is not my day," he growled behind her a few seconds later. "You don't have a signal. Is there electricity here? Where's your charger?"

Her bikini top suddenly seemed like an impossible twist of fabric and strings that made no sense. "Somewhere in my bag, I guess—I just got here a couple of hours ago."

"Get it."

Abandoning the top back to the sand, she turned to glare at him, hands planted at her hips and no longer caring about her state of undress. "For a guy who just washed up on my beach like a dead jellyfish, you're awfully demanding!"

He let out a sigh and ran his hands back through his hair— which she couldn't help noticing was a lot more kempt and stylish, even wet, than it had been ten years ago. "Look, kitten, believe it or not, I'm not trying to be an asshole. But there's a lot at stake here—which I can't explain right now—and I need that goddamn phone. Understand?"

What the hell was at stake? And how had he ended up on her is-land, for God's sake? She let out a frustrated breath in return, try-ing to decipher him, then grudgingly said, "Follow me," starting to march toward the small beach house fifty yards away.

And as she marched, and he followed, a most unsettling realiza-tion settled over her. She wanted him. Badly. As badly as ever. Maybe more. Because the way he kept looking at her breasts— between ordering her around—made her stomach curl with desire. And because all things considered, he was probably as close to a pi-rate as she was ever going to get. And because he was the one man she'd ever really wanted in a gut-wrenching sort of way, and sud-denly here he was, looking as hot and perfect as ever. And it was a little bit like a dream, him just floating onto her island out of nowhere, and it would be so easy to just take one more little shot at seduction . . .

"Can you hurry it up?"

. . . if he weren't such a prick.

Yanking open the bungalow's screen door, she stomped to the bed where she'd thrown her weekend bag and started digging through. As well as remembering that there were actually *lots* of reasons she couldn't have him, even besides the prick factor. For one, she was getting married in a week. Yeah, that was a *big* one. For another, she hated his guts and would never forgive him for what he'd done to her ten years ago. For a third, she had a weird feeling about all this—understandable, she supposed, the way he'd just shown up—but she was forced to wonder just what he'd been doing for the last ten years and if maybe he'd gotten into something bad.

"Come on, where is it?"

She turned to glare at him. "I can't seem to find it, you jerk."

He sighed. "Okay, never mind, I give up on the phone. How about a boat—do you have a boat?"

"Of course I have a boat."

"Great. You have to drive me to shore—now." He was looking at her chest again. "And as much as I enjoy you running around topless, kitten, you might want to put something on for the ride."

God, why hadn't she done that yet? For the moment, her arms would have to do—she crossed them over herself and tried to look more angry than sheepish.

"Give me the keys to the boat," he demanded, "tell me where to find it, and I'll get it running. Put on some clothes and meet me there."

She hesitated as a hint of distrust rippled through her. "You won't leave me here? Without transportation?"

"Not if you hurry." He held his hand out. "Now, the keys. And directions."

This seemed like a bad idea, but she was finding it hard to refuse him. He was so bossy. He'd claimed something was at stake. What if that was true and she stood in the way? Grabbing her sparkly flower key chain up off the bed, she thrust it at him, trying to cover both breasts with one arm. "Go to the left—there's a path through a wooded area that leads to the dock."

"Got it." He started toward the door, then, to her surprise, stopped and looked back. "Thanks, kitten."

She meant to nod—but instead only swallowed, hard. Because his eyes still dripped with all that was hot and sexual, and even given all the weirdness currently surrounding them, his gaze still possessed the ability to make the juncture of her thighs pulse.

"Hurry," he reminded her on the way out the door—and she wished she'd brought more actual clothes.

Kind of.

Brock jogged along the trail through junglelike woods. Nearing the water, he peered ahead through lush greenery to catch sight of a sexy little Stingray speedboat that had "kitten" written all over it, right down to the candy-apple red color that reminded him of that Miata she'd once had.

Jesus, he couldn't believe stumbling upon her like that. After all these years. She didn't look much different, just more grown-up, her long chestnut hair slightly lighter, her body more mature, curvier. And with those beautiful breasts on display, too—just as pretty as he remembered. Talk about distraction . . . Katrina Spencer could be a *way* worse distraction than those chicks on the boat—but that didn't matter because in half an hour she'd drop him off on the mainland and they'd go their separate ways. A hint of something like regret niggled inside him at the thought, yet he ignored it—no choice at the moment.

He bounded into the clearing above a lagoon that sported a small but serviceable dock, lifted his eyes—and found the Morales brothers' big white yacht floating quietly in his direction, the engine cut as the boat glided toward land.

Damn it. He'd have sworn he'd made a clean getaway, but they must have either seen him swimming to shore or found him missing quickly enough to figure out where he'd gone. He'd been in a rush to contact the Bureau and get someone else on the brothers' trail before the whole mission was lost, but this stopped him dead in his tracks. Both brothers stood on the bow staring back at him, and Francisco was pointing his big bad-ass gun in Brock's direction.

He could run, but *he* knew and *they* knew that they couldn't let him live—he was an FBI agent and he had too much information. If he ran, they'd just come onto the island, and then Kat would be involved, and they'd probably kill her, too, before it was over.

"Kiss your double-crossing ass good-bye, fed!" Francisco yelled, sounding too maniacal for comfort.

Brock had a split second to react, but no reaction to *make* that would solve anything.

So when Francisco pulled the trigger and the deafening shot blasted through the hot air, Brock followed a whim—he jerked backward, pretending he was hit, then clutched his gut and pitched forward into the dirt, where he lay still as a stone.

Damn, that was good—you still got it, Denton. So long as they bought it.

It was hard as hell to just lie there, facing away from them into a green island jungle, waiting to see if Francisco would shoot again just to make sure—and hit him this time. His heart beat like a drum against the ground, and a bead of sweat rolled ticklishly down the side of his face—but he couldn't reach to wipe it away.

And then the next urgent problem struck him—Kat. He'd told her to hurry. Which was exactly what he *didn't* need her to do now. *Don't rush, kitten—take your time. Put on some lipstick or something. Don't find me like this, don't see me and scream—and for God's sake, don't let* them *see* you.

"What the hell are you doing *now*?" Carlos's voice echoed, growing closer, which meant the yacht was getting closer, too. *Shit, don't come ashore.*

"Got to make sure the son of a bitch isn't breathing," Francisco said. *Shit, they're coming ashore.*

"He's dead already, for Christ's sake. You happy now? Let's go! There's a boat, somebody else here." *Listen to your brother, Francisco. Go the hell away.*

Silence pervaded then, and Brock could practically hear Francisco thinking it through. He prayed the evil brother made the wrong decision and just believed Brock was dead.

"Where could that key be?" Francisco muttered, a little lower, almost as if to himself but still loud enough for Brock to make out. "Where the hell could it be?"

"Don't look at me for this one, bro. *You* lost it. So I guess you can tell Omega it's *your* fault we got nothing to give him tonight."

"Maybe I wouldn't have lost it if I hadn't been dealing with the asshole fed you let into our business!"

Brock smiled, glad he was looking away from them and didn't have to hold it in. So the key *did* unlock the artifacts. Maybe today hadn't been so lousy, after all. He'd managed to keep the Morales boys away from the Mayan treasures—and he'd gotten to see an all-grown-up version of Katrina Spencer, something he'd wondered about more than once over the years. *Just get the hell out of here before Kat shows up*, he willed the brothers. *Then she can get me to shore, and I can get somebody following you guys before the whole operation is blown.*

He was almost on the verge of feeling confident until Francisco said, "Well, whoever else is on that island, they ain't getting off it anytime soon," then fired his .45 again—one, two, three, four gun blasts, apparently at the gas tank of Kat's boat judging from the earth-shattering *boom* of the explosion that followed and the ensuing fireball *whooshing* upward. *Shit!*

Heat scorched his skin as bits of wood, metal, and other boat debris rained down all around him, and it was all he could do to remain still and not follow the instinct to cover his head. *Just breathe evenly, dude. And don't move a muscle.*

When the air turned mostly quiet again, he heard one of the girls uttering, "Oh my God!" and Francisco laughing. Guy got a kick out of blowing things up, he guessed.

Carlos yelled, "Jesus Christ, sometimes I think you're crazy!"

"Just getting the job done," Francisco replied, then let out another peal of deep, bellowing laughter.

"Come on, man," Carlos urged, "let's get the hell out of here—now."

"You in a hurry to get somewhere, little brother?"

Carlos sounded troubled, another indicator that the younger Morales wasn't cut out for a life of crime. "I just want to get away from all this shit—clear my head. Maybe then we can figure out where you left the key."

Just then, Brock heard a twig snap, spotted a flash of pink among the green leaves and palm fronds before him—getting closer fast, and he knew Kat had come running to see what the hell had just happened.

"Stay where you are," he bit off, praying it was enough to stop her but *not* enough for anyone on the yacht to hear.

She flinched to a halt just before breaking through to the clearing, then caught sight of him and gasped.

"Don't come out of the woods. Don't make a sound."

She remained motionless, but her eyes looked frightened. Not that he could blame her. He'd just brought a world of trouble down on her and had no idea what the hell would happen next.

Time held still as his eyes met hers, as he willed her to heed his warning, and as he waited, praying the Morales brothers would decide they'd done enough damage and leave.

They were blue, her eyes. Had he ever noticed that when they were young? Probably not—he'd been a little self-absorbed then. Hell, he was self-absorbed *now*. But he still noticed when a shaft of sunlight shone down through the green canopy where she stood, turning her gaze almost the color of the Caribbean, complete with a sparkle or two. He concentrated on those sparkles and wondered if she hated him and worried how he was going to explain all this to her without giving away top secret information.

And then he took in what she wore. Not a tank top and shorts, or maybe some sort of beach cover-up—no, not his kitten. She'd topped the scant white bikini bottoms with a tiny, strappy pink top, no bra. On her dainty feet, matching flip-flops with little pink rhinestones lining the vee that met between her toes. After a long, leisurely perusal, he lifted his eyes back to hers. Damn, she was hot. Then. And now.

"They're gone," she said quietly—and he realized that in the back of his mind he had indeed heard the yacht's motor hum to life and then fade with distance. And that he'd just somehow forgotten he was in the middle of a life-or-death situation because of Kat's nipples jutting through her little top and those long, tan legs stretching all the way from heaven to earth.

"Completely out of sight?" he asked before daring to move.

She nodded shortly.

Cautiously, Brock braced his hands on the ground beneath him and pushed to a sitting position to look around at the debris. A small blaze still burned in what remained of Kat's boat, popping and crackling in the distance like an autumn bonfire. Jesus.

But she didn't even seem to notice, instead rushing from the cover of the trees to drop to her knees beside him. "My God, are you hurt?" He'd never seen such genuine worry on her face, her eyes glassy with emotion, the corners of her mouth turning jaggedly down.

"No," he said, shaking his head, sitting up a little straighter, getting his bearings back. "No, I'm fine."

"Good," she said on a heavy sigh—and her relieved demeanor vanished instantly, to be replaced with something much more cutting. "Now, what the hell's going on here?"

He shifted his gaze to hers, finding her closer than he'd realized. Even with the scent of gas and burning wood in the air, he could smell the light fruity scent of her suntan lotion. He meant to answer brusquely, but his words came out gentler than intended. "I already explained—I could tell you, but then I'd have to kill you."

Her angry expression slowly softened into something more like . . . sadness. "And that wasn't funny the first time you said it. Seriously, Brock. Are you . . ." Another long, pretty sigh, and a hint of . . . was that *fear* in her eyes? "Should I be afraid of you? Because something really serious is going on here, and I have no idea if you're a good guy or a bad one."

Maybe she *was* scared—but she hadn't moved away from him. So he lifted one hand to her slightly pinkened cheek, and leaned in closer, close enough to kiss her if he wanted. "I'm good, kitten, I promise you that much."

And he did want to kiss her. He wanted to kiss that bit of fear away. But this was no time for kissing. He'd been right about one thing—Kat Spencer equaled major distraction.

Which was probably what led his gaze down to her cute little top. "So this is what you put on to cover up? Not that I'm complaining."

She pulled back slightly, as if suddenly remembering to be mad at him. "I didn't exactly bring a lot of clothes on this trip. Because I thought I'd be alone. As opposed to having a nightmare from my past wash up on the beach, then having my boat blown to bits, thereby stranding me with said nightmare."

He knowingly arched one brow. "You didn't think I was such a nightmare *then*."

She gave her head a typically saucy tilt. "I was young and stupid."

Impudent as ever, he thought, amused—but something a little more urgent needed exploring here. "You, uh, used the word 'stranded.' Care to explain that?"

Kat emitted yet another huge sigh, so God only knew what was coming. "I . . . think maybe I forgot to pack my phone charger."

"Okay." A minor problem, but not the end of the world. "And?"

"And . . . since I'd planned to stay here until Thursday, no one will be looking for me for a while."

It was Saturday. He was starting to see the scope of their dilemma. *Shit.* "So we're really stuck here."

"So it would appear." She cast a dejected gaze toward the remains of her Stingray before raising her eyes more hopefully. "But maybe we could build a big fire on the beach. We're not that far from shore—someone in a plane or boat would see it. I even have matches."

She suddenly sounded so enthusiastic. *Sorry to disappoint you, kitten, but . . .*

He sighed. "I was thinking the same thing as I swam here, only now I don't think it's a good idea. Wrong people might see it. As in my friends on the yacht." The last thing he wanted to do was draw Carlos and Francisco back to the island.

"Who are?" she demanded. "And if you threaten to kill me one more time, Brock, *I'll* kill *you*. I just saw my boat blown to smithereens—you owe me some kind of explanation."

He knew she had every right to be angry, but he also couldn't answer her questions. So he changed the subject. "Got anything to eat?"

"What?" she snapped, eyes brimming with disbelief.

"You know, food? I'm hungry. I've had a hell of a day." He pushed to his feet, then grabbed her hand to pull her up next to him.

She failed to look appreciative. "Brock—tell me what's going on and who those madmen were. Now." She stomped one pink flip-flop in the dirt.

"I was thinking of doing that over dinner."

She remained incredulous. "*Dinner?* You actually think I'm going to eat *dinner* with you?"

He shrugged his shoulders, spread his arms, and pointed out to her what she clearly hadn't quite grasped yet. "We've got five days and nights together here, kitten. Looks like you're gonna be doing a *lot* of things with me you hadn't planned on."

Kat didn't like how she'd felt when she'd seen Brock lying on the ground after that explosion. Her heart had sunk to her stomach, and her whole body had gone weak—she could have collapsed on the spot. She stole a glance at him, standing at the grill now, flipping a steak with a long pair of tongs, as she set the picnic table outside the little island bungalow.

You'd react that way with anyone *in that situation. It has nothing to do with* him, *for God's sake.* He was a stranger to her now. He always had been, really, when she thought about it.

She couldn't believe someone had blown up her boat, that some stark, mysterious danger had come so close to her—and that she'd truly let Brock talk her into not discussing it until they sat down to dinner! They'd actually walked back here and gotten the steaks from the fridge and started cooking, like they were normal people on a normal beach preparing for a normal meal—and she still had no idea what had brought him here or why her boat had been obliterated. She could only attribute her acquiescence to the fact that she was utterly shell-shocked by the whole event.

Great, I'm probably going to end up with post-traumatic stress syndrome. She sneered at him behind his back. *And it's all your fault.*

Trying to think more pleasant thoughts, she retrieved two bright, flowered place mats from inside. Setting plastic plates of hot pink on the mats, she decided to pair them with lime green glasses from the multicolored picnic set her mother had brought out to the island last summer.

It wasn't until she caught herself folding a napkin to make it pretty that she dropped it to one of the plates, then gasped. Already it had begun. The transformation.

Only . . . maybe it didn't feel so awful. Which was good.

Until another glance up at the expanse of Brock's broad shoulders and tanned back told her that maybe, just maybe, it didn't feel so awful because she was with *him.* Stranger or not.

It was an unthinkable thought. Not to mention impossible.

So she decided to ignore it.

If it were Ian standing there grilling those steaks, I'd be anticipating this meal just as much. Because I'd still have a boat. And I wouldn't be stranded. With someone who might turn out to be a madman. A really hot *madman, but a potential madman just the same.*

A blip of memory flashed in her brain. She'd once been attracted to Brock because he'd seemed just a little bit dangerous. Now he seemed a *lot* dangerous.

But that does not *mean I'm a lot attracted to him.*

God, stop talking to yourself about him already. She needed a distraction that went beyond napkins and plates. "How are those steaks coming?" Of course, she took a few steps toward him as she spoke, and putting herself physically closer to the long-ago object of her desire made the distraction aspect of the question a little less than effective.

"Almost ready. You want to check the baked potatoes for me, kitten, and see if they're done?"

As she grabbed up a fork and leaned over the grill to poke into a foil-covered potato, she eyed the two juicy steaks sizzling alongside and voiced the thought in her head. "You realize you're eating one of my meals."

"One of your meals?" He didn't get it.

"I didn't exactly expect or *bring enough food* for company."

He shifted his eyes to hers, his generally jocular manner draining away instantly. "How much food don't we have? Because if this is a legitimate problem, I'll skip the steak and let you reheat it another day."

His response left her stunned. She hadn't anticipated him dropping into serious mode over this—more than anything, she'd just been trying to point out that he was an interloping nuisance. "What would *you* eat?"

"I could get by on a potato." She must have looked doubtful, since he added, "Trust me, I've gotten by on less." He sounded so matter-of-fact, like it was nothing, and she couldn't help wondering again just what he'd been up to for the last ten years. Or maybe he was talking about when he was younger—she knew he'd grown up poor.

Her voice came out smaller than she'd planned. "No, you can have the steak." She cleared her throat and tried to speak more normally. "We just . . . can't have a meal like this every night. But I have cold cuts and snack foods—and there might even be some canned stuff in one of the cabinets, I'll have to check."

"Only if you're really sure there's enough." He still sounded so serious. "The last thing I would want, kitten, is to leave you hungry."

She lifted her gaze to his, thinking he'd just said a mouthful, considering their past—even if he hadn't heard the double entendre in his own words. Despite herself, she could still *feel* just how very hungry he'd left her once upon a time.

Only the slow heat that invaded his eyes indicated that her look had drawn the double meaning to his attention. He leaned toward her ever so slightly, but enough that she could soak in the musky scent of him, as his voice came deep. "I wouldn't, you know. Leave you hungry. In *any* way. If I had it to do over again—that night— I'd make sure you left completely satisfied."

The burning warmth that rose to her cheeks wasn't from standing next to the grill because it was accompanied by a lump in her throat. "Oh," she said thinly, then forked the two potatoes onto a plate and walked away to the table as fast as she could.

"I'll be back in a minute," she added, then scurried into the house. While Brock had been starting up the grill and putting the food on, she'd taken a few minutes to unpack her bag, so at least now she knew where to find her clothes, scant bits of them that there were. Yanking open a bureau drawer, she drew out a long cotton sarong of fuchsia and white and tied it around her waist.

Because she found herself suddenly feeling a little naked. Because things were getting sexual here. Which shouldn't surprise her—things between her and Brock had *always* been sexual, from the very first moment she'd met him. She just wasn't prepared to be face-to-face with him again. And she wasn't used to him being *smooth*, or *seductive*. She *definitely* wasn't used to being trapped on an island with him all alone, where anything could happen. For five freaking days. And nights. Right before her wedding.

Deep breath. Deep breath. In. Out. You can do this.

Yet as she exited the bungalow, she glanced up at a dusky purple sky and sent a silent message to God: *You have rotten timing! Do you hear me? Rotten!*

Or maybe this was God's humorous way of paying her back for being . . . a little wild in her earlier days. And her later days, too, actually—until recently. Until she'd agreed to marry Ian last Christmas.

"Come and get it, kitten," Brock said, which in her current frame of mind forced her thoughts to the many things "it" could refer to, so she smirked heavenward once more before heading to the table.

"Looks good," she said, being sure to focus on the steaks and not him.

He eyed her sarong as she sat down. "What's with the skirt?"

"Nothing's *with* it," she said, dropping her gaze to the salt-shaker, then reaching for it. "I was . . . starting to get chilled." Not really, but the late May evening *had* cooled off the tropical air, so it wasn't inconceivable. Even if he looked amused by her answer.

"A little late for modesty," he said.

She cut into her steak, refused to let herself look into those darkly provocative eyes or to even notice that familiar lock of hair drooping carelessly onto his forehead, and decided to ignore the remark. But speaking of what she was wearing . . . "By the way, my friend Nina's boyfriend came out here with us for a weekend last summer and left some clothes behind that might fit you."

He arched one brow. "Why did he leave them?"

"Actually, he's her *ex*-boyfriend now. They had a nasty breakup that very weekend, and I think she's sort of holding them hostage, along with some other stuff."

He gave a short, dry nod. "Sounds the same as I remember her."

Kat was surprised he recalled Nina at all. "How do you remember her?"

"Erratic. Vindictive. Maybe slightly hysterical."

Unfortunately, Kat couldn't really dispute any of that. "But she's a lot of fun. Surprisingly sensible on her good days. And as loyal as the day is long," she said in her friend's defense. "Anyway, the clothes are in there, if you want to, uh"—she glanced at his bare chest, then motioned toward the house—"put something on."

"I'm fine for now, thanks."

Swell. That makes one of us.

Well, if she couldn't get him to cover up those muscles, she could at least force him to get down to business. "All right then. Start talking. About why my boat was blown up today. And who those scary men were. And why they wanted you dead and why you let them think you were."

"It's a long story." He offered up a light grin, as if this was fun, casual chitchat.

"As you pointed out earlier, we've got some time." No smiles from her, no way—she was getting the truth out of him if she had to beat it out. No more weak, flimsy, lusty Kat.

His grin faded as he released a long sigh. Looked like he was ready to start taking her questions seriously—and it was about time.

"All right, kitten." He met her gaze as a salty breeze wafted over them. "I didn't want to tell you this, not only because I'm not allowed to, but for your own safety. Yet you're right, I owe you an explanation. So here it is. I'm an FBI agent."

Kat raised her eyebrows, lowered her chin, and cast a you've-*got*-to-be-kidding look. "And I'm a nun." She forked a bite of steak into her mouth.

He leaned forward, eyes widening a bit, mouth hanging slightly open. "You don't believe me." Then he laughed, as if that were funny.

"I guess I don't blame you in a way, but sorry to tell you, Sister Katrina of the Tiny Bikini, it's true. Special Agent Brock Denton, Federal Bureau of Investigation, at your service."

She narrowed her gaze on him, trying to puzzle her way through what he'd just said. He couldn't be. Could he? She set down her fork, sat up straighter, and looked him in the eye. "Let's see a badge."

"Let's see a tiny bikini."

She smirked. "I'm serious."

He continued looking just as smug as usual. "No badge when you're working undercover, kitten. No ID at all, except a fake one—and I had to leave that on the yacht anyway. So you don't have much choice but to take my word for it, do you?"

"I can go right on not believing you," she argued.

"If it floats your boat, sure. You're the one who wanted answers, so I gave 'em to you."

"First of all, I no longer have a boat to float, thanks to you. And second, I need more." She propped her elbows on the table with a *plunk*. "If you want to convince me, tell me how the hell you got here."

He cut into his steak and took a big bite, then a sip of the wine she was suddenly glad she'd brought—because she thought she was going to need it. "Okay, here's the short version, which is all I can give you, and even that's too much. The guys on the boat are smugglers."

"What do they smuggle?"

"None of your business. I was trying to get to their superior when my cover was blown. They took my gun and tied me up."

She rolled her eyes and crossed her arms. "Boy, sounds like you're a really top-notch FBI agent."

To her surprise, he laughed, just softly. "I was having . . . an off-day. Anyway, I managed to get loose, slip off the yacht, and swim for the island. I didn't think they saw me, but I guess they did, and that's why they showed up here looking for me."

God, it sounded insane, but he spoke about it so easily that she was starting to think he was for real. "And you pretended to be shot because . . . ?"

"Because if they didn't think I was dead, they'd come after me. And then *you'd* be in danger, too." His gaze settled warm on hers. "And I couldn't have that."

Her stomach fluttered, but she tried not to feel it. "Why not?"

His eyes glittered beneath the soft light emitted from the security lamp mounted outside the bungalow, and for a long moment she thought he was going to say something gentle, or endearing, until finally a slow, calm expression took over his handsome face. "It's my job to protect civilians."

Oh. Well. That's all she was to him. A *civilian*. Fine. Who cared, anyway? She was getting married in a week.

He pushed another bite of steak into his mouth, chewed, swallowed. "So, do you believe me now?"

She kind of did, but it was hard to reconcile the Brock she'd once known with the guy who sat across from her. The guy who suddenly called other people *civilians*. "Why would *you* want to be an FBI agent?"

"Because I didn't want to waste my life. And that's exactly what I'd been doing until I applied at the Bureau."

To her surprise, he sounded honest. Frank. Real. Maybe like the guy she'd once hoped he could be. "Okay then," she said, even if it came out a bit hesitant, "I guess I believe you." She sat up a bit straighter and remembered how miffed she remained about various things that had happened over the last few hours. "It shocks the hell out of me to think of you in law enforcement of any kind, and this doesn't mean I *trust* you—but I *believe* you."

"Good," he said shortly. "Now, you know what *I'm* doing here—what are *you* doing here?"

As if *she* owed *him* an explanation. Besides, the answer was a little too complicated and none of his business. "Vacationing, sort of." She looked down, cleared her throat, shoveled some baked potato into her mouth.

"By yourself? Doesn't sound like much fun."

She let out a sigh, realizing that as much as she didn't want to, it would probably just be easier to explain the situation. After all, unless a miracle occurred, they had five agonizing days ahead of them, and she doubted she could withhold it that long, never having been an especially skilled liar or a particularly quiet person.

"I'm getting married," she said, lifting her gaze to look for a reaction but then dropping it just as quickly because she didn't want him to think she cared if he cared. "And my bachelorette party is in Las Vegas—right now, in fact. Only I'm not at it, because I'm here." Which didn't make much sense, judging from the look he gave her. So she pressed on. "Because marriage is a big step, and I just decided that I'd rather—you know—unwind, relax. By myself. Planning a wedding is a lot of work. Very stressful. And going from single girl to wife is a big transition. So I decided that some time alone would be the exact thing I needed right now. You know?" God, *of course* he didn't know—why was she babbling so incoherently? Slowly, she found the courage to raise her gaze from her plate to the man across from her. "Any questions?"

She couldn't read his expression—his face was a blank slate. Okay, a *gorgeous* blank slate. "Who are you marrying?"

"Ian Zeller. Do you remember him?"

He shook his head. "Should I?"

"I'm not sure if you knew my dad's best friend back then—Walt Zeller? He's also my dad's lawyer."

The light of recognition shone in Brock's eyes. "Oh. Yeah, now that you mention it, I did meet old Walt once. So, let me guess— this Ian guy is Walt's son."

"Right. He is." She nodded. Twice. "So you see how well this all works out. My family. His family. It's really perfect. For everyone." *Shut up. You sound like you're trying too hard to convince him.*

He squinted at her doubtfully, lowering his chin, then spoke slowly. "So let me get this straight—you blew off your own bach-elorette party to come sit here on an island by yourself?"

She nodded. "Yes, and don't act like it's weird."

"It *is* weird." She flashed a nasty look, to which he replied, "Sorry, but it is." He took another sip of wine. "When's the wedding?"

"Saturday."

His eyes flew open a little wider, and she liked having finally caught him off guard. "*Next* Saturday? As in seven days from now?"

She nodded. Only once this time, thank goodness.

His gaze narrowed on her slightly. "So, kitten, why are you marry-ing this guy?"

Why? What the hell kind of question was that? *Maybe the kind someone asks when you've just sounded like you're working too hard to persuade them everything's wonderful.* But it *was* wonderful. "Well," she said pointedly, "only for a *million* reasons. I mean, our families are close, I've known him my whole life. And he's a *great* guy—everyone thinks so. He'd do anything for me, and he's wild about me, of course—and not just the country club me, but even the sick me or the drunk me, so I know he really loves me for me. And he's an at-torney, too—did I mention that? And he's great with money—he has a lot of lucrative investments. So . . ." She feared she'd been bab-bling again—very recklessly. "So . . . that's why."

Across from her, Brock gave his handsome head a slight tilt. "You leave anything out?"

What was he getting at? "Not that I can think of. Why?"

"You love the guy?"

She rolled her eyes as her stomach pitched slightly. Somewhere nearby, palm fronds rustled in the evening breeze, and she really did feel chilled now. "Of *course* I love him. That . . . goes without saying. Which is why I didn't bother saying it."

He lifted an elbow to the table and propped his chin on one fist. "I'm not buying, kitten."

His words settled like a knot in her stomach, and she tried her best to cast a death glare. *This is your own fault, for trying too hard to make it all sound so fabulous.* But she decided to take it out on him, just the same. "As if I care what *you* think. I would hardly consider you an expert on love anyway."

He tilted his head to the other side, looking slightly mysterious. "Why not? For all you know, I left Naples, fell in love, and settled down. For all you know, I have a houseful of kids and a little missus waiting for me somewhere."

All the blood drained from her face, leaving her light-headed. "Did you? Do you?"

He grinned, sexy as ever. "No."

Thank you, God.

"But I know *one* thing about love."

"What's that?"

The grin faded. "That you damn well oughta be in it before you marry somebody."

Damn it, she was getting tired of defending herself. It was bad enough with Nina, but Brock didn't even know her anymore—if he ever had. She spoke slowly, firmly. "*I told you, I love my fiancé.*"

"Cutting it awfully close, aren't you?"

She narrowed her gaze. "Cutting *what* awfully close?"

"Staying here 'til Thursday, then getting married on Saturday? Seems like you'd want to be doing all that bride stuff girls do—getting ready for your big day, trying on your dress twenty times—rather than camping out on an island in the middle of nowhere."

Her stomach fluttered with the fear that his observation might hold a hint of truth. But she said, "There'll still be plenty of time for bride stuff when I get back. And given the change of circumstances out here, I'd go back right now if I could."

"So you think someone will come looking for you on Thursday, huh?"

She nodded. "When my parents figure out I'm not home when expected, they'll call Nina, and she'll be forced to come clean and tell them where I am." She drew in a deep breath, still feeling the desperate need to convince him everything was fine between her and Ian. "Then I can get back to the man I love."

He stayed silent for a minute, never taking his eyes off her. In fact, they somehow felt even more *on* her—as if he were peering into her soul and knew every thought and feeling he aroused in her. "Well, if you do love the guy, kitten," he finally said, "that's a real shame."

She blinked. "Oh?"

"Otherwise, we could take care of some unfinished business."

She swallowed nervously, unable to tear her gaze away. "Unfinished business?"

His eyes took on a wicked glimmer that melted all through her. "You remember. Me, you, a hot night, and the sexiest panties I'd ever seen. We've got five nights here—and, the way I see it, a lot of lost time to make up for."

Chapter Three

Kat worked hard not to let her eyes go wide as she tried to absorb his words. Although her breasts and the juncture of her thighs seemed to be absorbing them just fine, going maddeningly hot and tingly without a moment's delay. It was her heart and head that were having a more difficult time believing he'd just tossed out a major sexual proposition like it was typical dinner conversation.

"After all," Brock went on, speaking in that slow, sure, and all-too-hot way of his, "the last time I saw you, you wanted to give me your virginity."

She held in her gasp, but cringed inside at having that particularly humiliating reminder tossed out on the table like an unappetizing side dish. "Well," she said, trying to act cool and ignore the nervous lump that had grown in her throat, "I'm afraid it's already taken."

"Good," he said on a short laugh.

She couldn't help rolling her eyes. As different as he seemed, some parts of Brock Denton had stayed exactly the same. "Of course you'd say good. Since you don't like inexperienced girls."

He offered up a leisurely, knowing grin, and she felt them both remembering the heat of that night oozing warm and consuming all around them. Even if he ultimately hadn't wanted her, he'd felt the heat—that had never been in question. She tried to break their gaze but couldn't quite do it.

He spoke in a low timbre. "You have a good memory, kitten."

Her reply came just as soft. "That's a hard thing to forget."

He crossed his arms and tilted his head, his look going mischievously seductive. "So since you're more experienced now, there's nothing holding us back."

This time it was she who laughed. Not that what he'd said was funny—more like brutally tempting—but a laugh had seemed a smart way to respond. "Sorry, buddy, you missed your chance."

He looked doubtful, and arrogant as ever. "Did I?"

She drew her answer from deep down inside, and it came out sounding surprisingly firm and decisive. "Yes." *Very good, Kat. Keep it up and maybe you'll get through this without throwing yourself in his lap again.*

"You sound so sure." And he sounded skeptical. Arrogant bastard.

But his astonishment to find out he couldn't have her with a mere snap of his fingers pleased her—and brought out her next words with even more confidence. "I *am* sure. I'm getting married, Brock. Nothing can happen between you and me. End of story."

"My loss then," he said, but it still managed to piss her off—because his expression still dripped with unerring confidence. And when he raked his gaze suggestively over her breasts, it felt almost as if she'd been touched there.

This was clearly going to be the most difficult test of willpower she'd ever endured. Brock Denton. On her island. *Why, God, why?*

Debra Spencer watched all the world's tragedies on CNN and MSNBC. Wars, terrorists, and storms of biblical proportion. She watched them every day and every night, letting them break her heart—and forcing her to be thankful. Because her life really wasn't so bad; CNN reminded her of that almost constantly. And she'd needed the reminder a *lot* lately.

She sat in creamy satin lounging pants flipping back and forth between the channels, barely aware of the lush surroundings of her home. She almost didn't notice it anymore, and had stopped believing it mattered. And if she could ever get her *husband* to stop believing, life might change for the better. *If we didn't have so much, I might be a happier person.* It made no sense—yet she knew it was true.

Even now, Clark slaved away at the gallery—doing God knew what, but definitely something he thought would bring in more money. Or maybe Ian was there with him tonight, schooling him on which stocks to buy, and which to dump, and exactly when to execute the trades—he and Ian had been hunkered over desks together working on investment strategies since soon after his engagement to Kat almost six months ago.

She tried to appreciate Clark's work ethic, his determination to keep them living in the manner to which they were accustomed—yet it was Saturday, for heaven's sake, and Richard, the young man he'd hired especially for Saturdays, was perfectly capable of handling things at the gallery on his own. Still, Clark had gone in this afternoon, saying he'd be there "for a couple of hours. But we can go out to dinner tonight if you want. Someplace on the water?"

He knew Debra loved the water. He hadn't built the house

there, fearing hurricanes, storm surges, but he *had* bought the island last summer—for her forty-eighth birthday. A too-extravagant gift she hadn't needed and they hadn't really been able to afford, yet that was Clark's way, and something about it had touched her heart when she'd been feeling most neglected.

Now she was feeling neglected again, and nothing much was touching her heart. There had been no dinner over the water, no dinner at all, just a phone call saying he'd ended up in the middle of some work he didn't want to leave until tomorrow. "Especially since Kat's out for the next few weeks." As if there was so much traffic in the gallery that he'd be chained to the front door the whole time Kat was off on her girls' getaway, then her honeymoon.

Thinking of Kat, Debra pushed the mute button on the remote and grabbed up the phone, dialing her daughter's cell. When the message played saying Kat was unavailable, she knew Kat had either forgotten her charger again or was in the middle of some loud casino where she couldn't hear the phone. "Hi, sweetie," she said at the beep. "Just calling to check on you, but I guess you're having too much fun to answer. I hope so. Just be careful, Kat. And call when you can—I miss you."

She hung up feeling silly—Kat had left only this morning, but already she was saying she missed her. *I'm such a typical mom.*

Once upon a time she'd sworn to herself she'd be a cool mom, a hip mom, the fun mom all the kids wanted to have drive them around to shopping malls and movie theaters. In ways, she thought she'd lived up to that, but in the end, a mom was a mom—and somewhere along the way, she'd done what so many moms did: She'd started replacing her own hopes and dreams with Kat's dreams until she didn't really have any left of her own. Now Kat's happiness was the biggest part of her life—Kat's wedding next week felt as important to her as her own had twenty-nine years ago—and she supposed that was okay, the way life went, how things were meant to be. She just—immaturely, she supposed—wished she'd gotten to go out to dinner with Clark this evening, so that her life might feel like it was a little bit her own tonight.

In boredom, she left the TV quiet and padded from the large, plush family room down a wide hall to her office. She didn't exactly *need* an office—but Clark had insisted she have one, and it was a nice luxury when it came to her charity work and, more recently, her articles for her Booklovers' newsletter. Lately, the ever-growing book club had become a big part of her world—she'd made new friends there, and it gave her someplace to go once a week that was completely her own, about no one but her.

Easing into the big leather chair on wheels—Clark's motto in life was "only the best," even when it came to a chair she only spent a couple of hours a week in—she hit the e-mail button on her keyboard. A message appeared from Tansy, a friend from the country club, and then another from Michael Quinn—which made her pulse kick up a bit.

The local literary author had kindly come to speak to the Booklovers last month, and afterward, being a huge fan of his novels, she had gathered the courage to ask him for an interview, explaining that she was writing features for their new newsletter and that she knew the club members would be thrilled to learn more about him. To her amazement, he'd readily agreed, and they'd recently shared a lovely lunch at Bice, on Fifth Avenue, where, over an appetizer of beef carpaccio with arugula salad and hearts of palm, it had suddenly occurred to her how very handsome he was.

Odd, but she supposed that somewhere along the way she'd stopped really seeing that in men. Okay, Pierce Brosnan, George Clooney—she knew *they* were handsome, but as for the men who passed in and out of her daily life, she didn't really see them. Until it had struck her that Michael Quinn had the kindest blue eyes she'd looked into in a while. And he possessed those little crinkles around the eyes that somehow managed to make middle-aged men look rugged instead of old. Along with a strong jawline and light brown hair that had not yet become sprinkled with gray, even at forty-five.

She doubled-clicked to open his message.

Debra,

Thanks so much for sending the article. I had no idea you were such a talented writer—I'm impressed.

And now . . . I have a huge favor to ask.

I have a few trusted readers who look over my manuscripts before I send them to my editor, and one has had to back out for personal reasons this time around. Could I convince you to take a look at my next release? It's AFTER THE RAIN, the book I talked about (ad nauseum, I fear) during the interview. My only rules are A) if you're not comfortable with this or don't have the time, no problem, we're still friends, and B) if you read it, be honest, tell me what works and what sucks. I know you've read all my previous work, and after hearing some of your insights on my earlier novels, I respect your opinion.

So, what do you say? Depending on your schedule, I could give you the manuscript over lunch one day this week.

Michael

Debra stared at the screen, her bottom lip crushed firmly between her teeth. Michael Quinn thought she was a talented writer. And considered her a friend. And he wanted her to read his new book. And to have lunch with her again. This week. Her heart felt like it would beat right through her chest.

She hit the reply button.

Michael,

I'm flattered by your faith in me and would be thrilled to read AFTER THE RAIN. You may have to forgive me if I gush a bit, since you know I love your work, but if I find anything that does indeed suck, I promise to tell you.

 How's Monday? Too short notice?

Debra

P.S. So pleased you liked the article!

After sending the message, she sat back in her chair and let out a breath she hadn't quite realized she was holding. "Whoa," she murmured. This felt . . . big.

Because an author—an author!—was asking her to read his un-published work and weigh in with an opinion.

And because . . . she enjoyed being around him. Just over the one lunch they'd shared, she'd come away with the impression that he'd really listened to her when she talked.

In all honesty, she'd gone into the lunch on guard for pomposity, expecting to depart feeling glad she'd done it but also glad it was over. Yet Michael had been nothing but genuine. Interesting. *Severely* intelligent. And clearly in love with the craft of storytelling. At the same time, he'd seemed interested in *her*, her life, her hus-band's gallery, her daughter's art—he'd even said maybe he'd come to the opening of Kat's show next month.

She'd left the lunch feeling strangely exhilarated, and then a little sad, because the exhilaration was all she had left. The lunch was over. Everything *about* him had felt a little over. As if she'd just found this wonderful, energizing connection—and poof, in a blink it was gone.

Only now it *wasn't* over. Now there was another lunch. And there would be discussion about his book. Maybe ongoing. It felt suddenly as if a whole new, fascinating world had just opened before her, like maybe she would somehow get a life of her own back again. Through Michael.

Walking back down the hall to the family room, she put the sound back on the TV, then hit the channel button, moving away from the tragedies, ready to look for something a little more lively.

Brock lay on the floor next to the bed, atop a few blankets Kat had tried to call a mattress. He wore a pair of dark gray gym shorts that must have belonged to Nina's clothing-deprived ex-boyfriend.

"I can't believe you don't even have a couch in this place," he muttered. He couldn't see her, because she'd insisted his "mattress" be arranged on the far side of the bed, opposite where she lay, so that he couldn't look at her while she slept. Like he was going to just lie there and stare at her. Maybe he'd been a little too bold with his advances.

"Believe it," she said through the darkness.

He was actually amazed by the whole bungalow—which was little more than a studio apartment plunked down in the sand. Sturdy enough, with a cinder-block foundation and solid construction above it, but it seemed way too modest a place for Clark Spencer, right down to the 1970s décor, complete with paneled walls and a Formica table and countertop. The only element with any style or heart to it was the antique armoire on the other side of the bed. But then, Kat had explained that they simply hadn't gotten around to making improvements yet. So he firmly expected the little dwelling would soon be bulldozed to the ground and replaced with something much more palatial, and was only sorry he'd landed here before it happened.

"I also can't believe you're gonna make me sleep on a hard tile floor when you have a nice big bed up there you could be sharing with me." The floor really *was* hard. But his work had led to sleeping in far worse places than this, and wanting to crawl into bed with Kat was admittedly about more than saving him a backache in the morning.

"What part of *engaged* don't you grasp?" she asked, her voice crisp and irritated, making him feel challenged. Because she sure liked shooting around that word, "engaged," but her eyes kept saying something a lot closer to "tempted." Or at least they had before she'd turned out the lights a few minutes ago. He wanted to find out what her *body* said in the dark.

"Don't worry, kitten, I grasp it all right. I just think that under the circumstances, the guy would understand."

He sensed her sitting up in the darkness to snap at him, "Then you're out of your mind. Go to sleep."

He couldn't resist a quiet chuckle. For a moment.

But then he turned more somber, listening to the sounds of island insects chirping in the dense junglelike area surrounding the little house and thinking about Kat getting married. He hadn't let it show, but he'd felt it in his gut when she'd told him. He wasn't sure why—hell, he hadn't seen the girl in ten years. Probably just that little niggling regret from not letting her have her way with him so long ago.

He'd been with plenty of women, most of them hot, built, and skilled in bed. But the truth was—whenever he was deep undercover on a mission and the danger started getting closer, creeping in around him, and he needed to escape to someplace better in his head for a few minutes just to wash away the fear, he often thought of Kat. He could still see her in his mind, nearly naked and riding him. Except when he used that memory to push the danger aside, there weren't any panties, and he wasn't wearing anything, either. They were back in that black bucket seat that had come from his brother's old Thunderbird, naked and moving together, him inside her.

He'd never questioned until this moment why she was who he thought of when he needed a good fantasy to sweep him away from real life. He could only figure it was because she was the one he'd never quite had and that it had left a big question mark in his mind.

And now she was getting married. And turning him down even though her eyes said yes. Unfortunately, eyes that said yes didn't count for much given that she was about to belong to someone else, which meant the two of them would *never* have sex. It wasn't exactly like he'd ever made a point of tracking her down once they'd gotten older, but he should have. He'd felt *that* in his gut, too—pretty much the moment he'd seen her nearly naked body again, stretched out so pretty over that lounge chair.

Which reminded him . . . "Was I right about that sunburn?"

She stayed quiet, but he didn't think she was asleep. He had the feeling she was wide-awake, just like him, and the more arrogant side of him suspected she was lying up there wrestling with herself, wanting to invite him into her bed just as much as he wanted to be there.

"Yes," she finally admitted, grudgingly.

"I don't know, being a guy, but I'm betting that's a lousy place for a burn."

"Only if I were wearing a bra. But I didn't even bring any, so I don't have to worry about that."

His groin tightened reflexively as a vision of her bared breasts came back to mind, and he did what came naturally—kept trying to seduce. And since he was tired, his words came out with unedited, full-on lust. "Do you have any idea how much I want you right now, kitten? How much I want to kiss those pretty breasts and make them feel better? How much I want to take what you wanted to give me that night?"

Above him, she stayed quiet. And that alone made him a little harder than he already was. Because she wasn't yelling at him, offended, angry—she wasn't saying, "How dare you!" or "Leave me alone!" or the host of other things a woman who really wasn't interested would probably be flinging at him right now. No, she was blessedly silent, weighing, considering . . . *wanting*. She would probably turn him down again, but he could still feel that *wanting* practically emanating from the bed, seeping from her pores.

Finally, her voice wafted softly through the stillness. "That night was a long time ago, Brock."

"*Too* long. And my fault," he added, his voice low, steady. "Why don't you let me make it up to you."

More silence. More wanting. The room pulsed with it.

That's when she cut through the silence with grating words. "I think I liked you better when you were the jerky silent type."

"And what am I now?"

"The jerky . . . more-talkative type."

He laughed quietly. "Sorry, kitten—just your bad luck my job forced me to learn to communicate." The truth was, his job had changed him in *bigger* ways, too. It had taught him to be less angry and rebellious, and it had made him grow up and face the world head-on. If he'd been more mature back when he'd known Kat, he'd have handled her differently. Hell, he'd have handled a lot of things differently.

He thought again of Clark Spencer and wondered if her father was pressuring her to marry this guy. It all sounded too . . . tidy, her marrying Spencer's best friend's son. A little too "all in the family." Especially given that Kat had a wild streak, which he'd seen firsthand and had sensed even long before that. She'd have been the last person he'd expect to marry some straitlaced lawyer who was probably a clone of her dad.

That notion made his stomach pinch. He knew Spencer loved Kat—and maybe Brock had once even been a little jealous that someone had a parent who loved them that much—but he also wondered if you could love *too* much. If that was possible, Clark Spencer was guilty as charged. And Kat didn't need yet *another* man smothering her.

And as for her plan to stay out here by herself right up until two days before her wedding, he couldn't help thinking it was sort of like running away, maybe wanting to avoid the wedding as much as possible for as long as she could. He just didn't believe Kat was really into hooking up with Mr. Family-Friend-and-Lawyer for life.

"This guy you're marrying," he said, his voice breaking through the darkness again.

"What about him?"

"Is he good in bed?"

"Why—do you want to sleep with him?"

He smiled. "Funny, kitten." When she didn't answer further, he said, "Well? Is he?"

"Is it any of your business?"

"You didn't say yes," he pointed out.

"So?"

"If he was, you'd have just said yes."

She stayed quiet and he figured she was probably concocting ways to kill him, until finally she replied, "If you must know . . . we, uh, haven't really . . . done it yet."

Now it was Brock who bolted upright to glare at her shadowy form across the bed, illuminated just slightly by the security bulb outside the window. "What do you mean, you haven't done it yet? You're actually marrying a guy you haven't even had sex with?"

She rolled to face him and he saw her eyes, made out more of her shadowy shape, and loved the sleepy, tousled look of her with a sheet pulled to her waist. Her hair lay messy around her shoulders, which were left silkily bare in another little strappy top he hadn't quite gotten a good look at before lights out. "For your info," she said, "there was a time when people in our culture *waited* until marriage. I know it's hardly the trend these days, but forgive me if I wanted to be a little . . . old-fashioned."

He flashed a wicked grin and stated the obvious. "Kitten. You're about the least old-fashioned girl I know."

The sound of her sigh carried over to him. "Well, maybe not in some ways, but in others . . ."

"Let's stick to sex," he insisted before she could go on. "You mentioned you're not a virgin anymore."

She raised her head with a start, her eyes going indignantly wide. "I'm twenty-seven years old! What do you expect?"

He held up his hands. "Hey, I'm not criticizing—"

"Of course you're not, because you dislike virgins so much."

Man, she remembered *everything*. It earned another laugh from him, but he had to get back on track and make his point, because it was important. "I'm just saying that what I know about you and sex kinda tells me that you . . ."

She propped up on her elbows, looking thoroughly pissed now. "That I what?"

Tread carefully here, dude. "That you, uh . . . well, don't hold sex to be a . . . sacred act or anything."

She shot back up, directly into the pale beam cast through the window by the security light. Her eyes blazed and her chest heaved within a thin top of light green, the ridges of her breasts bowing from the low neckline. *"How dare you!"*

So *now* he was getting the 'How dare you.' Feeling the instant need to calm her down, he made a swift move up onto the bed, grabbing her hands in his. "Honey, honey, honey—I'm not criticizing, really. *I* don't treat it like a sacred act, either. It is what it is—what two people do when they're attracted to each other. I'm just saying it sounds weird to me, if you've had sex with other guys, that you wouldn't just go ahead and do it with the guy you're marrying, too. Just to . . . take a test-drive, if nothing else—make sure everything goes okay."

With eyes narrowed venomously, she withdrew one hand from his to shove a wayward lock of hair behind her ear. She let him keep holding the other. "You seem to have an awfully vested interest in my impending marriage."

The words sank to his gut. He *did* seem to care an awful lot, now that she mentioned it. So he was honest with her. "I just don't want to see you end up unhappy."

She glowered at him, looking incredulous. "My God, are you listening to yourself? You haven't seen me for ten years, then you swim up onto my beach today and suddenly think you know enough about me to assume I'm making some sort of mistake?"

She was right about that. Logically. Only she couldn't see it from his angle. She couldn't see the doubt in her expression when she'd talked about this guy earlier; she couldn't hear the slightly flustered sound to her voice—then, and now. And she definitely couldn't see the *heat* that had flashed in her eyes when flirting with him over dinner, the same heat he'd once seen a long time ago. For him, not some other guy.

And from a different girl, he might buy some claim about waiting for marriage as a romantic gesture—but not from Kat. He'd never had sex with Kat, but one thing he knew about her instinctively— she *loved* sex. She was into sex, she wanted sex, she wasn't afraid of sex. So he just couldn't believe that if this guy was really the man of her dreams she wouldn't have hopped into bed with him by now.

Despite all that, though, he simply said, "Okay, you're right. It's none of my business. Forget I said anything." He didn't drop the hand he still held, though, and she didn't pull it away as he looked into her eyes and said, "But just tell me something, Kat. Just tell me, again, that you love the guy."

"I do," she said softly, with a quick nod and eyes trying hard to convince.

Only you don't, kitten. You look like a deer in headlights right now, and whether it's any of my business or not, I know you don't love him. I see it in your eyes, and I feel it in my bones.

Yet the expression on her face made him so sad for her, deep down inside, that he couldn't bring himself to keep pushing this right now; he couldn't be that mean. He forced a teasing smile instead. "So, now that I'm in bed with you, can I stay?"

She blinked, and finally drew her hand away. "No." Then she pointed. "Back to your mattress."

He cast a dry look. "Even the peasants had straw."

"Wash up onto a better-appointed island next time."

One last shot. It was late, and he was exhausted—but she looked too adorable in that little pajama top, and he had started wondering what she wore on the bottom now. And her face had softened just enough for him to detect that blessed little bit of temptation he'd been hoping to bring back into those blue eyes.

Brock lifted his hand to gently brush the hair out of her face and back behind her ear because it had fallen free again, then brought his palm to rest warmly on her cheek. He waited to hear her snap some objection or push his arm away, but it was clear she felt the touch as much as he did—sensation spiraled down through him as keenly as if he'd just pressed his whole body against hers. Damn, how was that even possible?

Their eyes met, held. The need inside him grew heavy, and if the room hadn't been bathed in darkness, she might have seen how hard he was for her through his shorts. *I want you, baby—so, so much.*

He kept looking at her, thankful for the shaft of light shining in from outside, just enough that he could see the anguished longing in her eyes and knew she could see the smoldering desire in his.

What do you want, kitten? He knew the answer, even if she refused to admit or give in to it.

He dropped his gaze to her lips, full and slightly parted. *Let me, kitten. Just let me.* And since she'd finally stopped arguing, he leaned in ever so slowly, drawn to her like a magnet, bringing their faces closer, their mouths closer still, until heaven was a mere inch away. She'd kissed him once, ten years ago, and they were long overdue for a repeat performance. In that moment, he needed her mouth beneath his like he needed to breathe.

She turned her head at the last second, leaving his kiss to land on her cheek.

The sound of her heated sigh wafted over him as he held in a groan of frustration. So near but yet so far.

When he drew back, her eyes were shut, her lower lip between her teeth. "Go," she whispered, pointing again toward the floor.

His heart beat too hard in his chest. He couldn't quite believe she still had the strength to resist. Waiting until she opened her eyes once more, he met them with his own, then backed very slowly across the bed, saying, "If you change your mind, kitten, I'm just a heartbeat away."

"Go to sleep, Brock," she said softly. But her eyes sparkled with a healthy dose of shared lust, so that would have to be enough for now.

Settling back down on the floor, he laced his fingers behind his head, peered at the ceiling, and listened to Kat breathe. It was a nice sound—like the hum of the boat engine earlier today, gradually starting to relax him. To his surprise, despite his lingering arousal, the gentle feminine breathing even brought an odd sense of peace over him.

Practically speaking, putting the moves on her was probably the last thing he should be doing—not just because she was getting married in less than a week but because he was technically on a mission here and should stay alert. Practically speaking, he should *never* feel completely at peace.

But for all intents and purposes, the mission was scrapped—he'd blown it. Which really sucked, yet once you blew it, you might as well take a few days and relax. And as luck would have it, he'd ended up on an island with a beautiful girl from his past who didn't have many clothes.

So maybe he *shouldn't* be trying to seduce Kat—but the truth was, he just didn't think he could help himself. And she might have resisted him tonight—but they had four more nights to go, and he planned to make the most of them.

"Sweet dreams, kitten," he whispered.

Chapter Four

Kat yawned, stretched, eased her eyes open—and spotted Brock standing with his back to her at the little kitchen counter across the room. He still wore only a pair of shorts, and the sight of that smooth tan male back made the juncture of her thighs tingle. How had this happened? How had Brock Denton, of all people, ended up back in her life, threatening to ruin her transformation into an upper-class Carol Brady?

Dinner with him last night, not to mention their little bedtime discussion and near kiss, had been pure torture. It had been as if her body were suddenly wired differently—or maybe she'd been wired this way all along and his unexpected presence had sort of . . . plugged her in and started the electricity flowing in a jarringly intense way.

So she'd made sure not to drink too much wine—despite the fact that she'd really wanted to guzzle. Because the tipsy, giggly version of herself she'd been ruminating on yesterday at the beach was not always the most reverent or in-control version. God knew *what* she'd have done last night if she'd gotten even remotely intoxicated. So she was impressed with her restraint.

And she'd thought of Ian. And her dad. And her mom. She'd thought of her bridesmaids, all of them in their pale yellow gowns and the too-expensive shoes she'd insisted they have. Then she'd jumped ahead in time and thought of her little children in their pastel beachwear. She'd reminded herself over and over that everything would be ruined if she made a reckless decision here.

Yet she'd kept being hammered with the inescapable notion that if the timing were different, if this had happened six months ago, last year sometime, she could have done whatever she'd had the urge to do with him. She could have gotten as tipsy and giggly as she wanted and fulfilled a long-ago dream whose lack of a conclusion had always left her feeling a little . . . incomplete.

And despite what her friends probably thought, she didn't sleep with just any guy who flipped her trigger. But this was Brock. *The* Brock. Of her youth. Of her fantasies. Of her heart.

The uncensored truth was—she'd wanted to. *Really* bad. And right now, her body ached just lying here watching him from behind.

The only thing keeping her clothes—what few she had—on her at the moment was knowing she simply *couldn't* be that kind of a person. Because even if her engagement to Ian hadn't set off bells and whistles inside her, even if his kisses failed to do the same, she wanted a good marriage. It was all that mattered.

And, of course, every time she traveled this trail of thought in her head, she inevitably arrived at the big "guilty" sign pointing toward Naples and Ian, reminding her how devastated he would be if he had any idea she wanted another guy so much.

"Found the donuts." Brock turned toward her, an open bakery box in his hand. A light stubble dusted his cheeks, reminding her of touching his face so many years ago, and of being so close to him, bringing their bodies together, their mouths, their . . . crotches.

She caught her breath, prayed her thoughts weren't written all over her face, and said, "Don't eat the ones with the sprinkles."

A marginally remorseful look crossed his face as he licked his lips. "Sorry."

Damn him. One more bit of torture—no sprinkles. She let out a disgusted sigh, then noticed that her nipples were pointing tautly through her thin top. She reached to flip the sheet over her—and he cast another of his provocative little smiles. "Going shy on me again, kitten?"

The words irritated her so badly that something inside her snapped—she flung the covers back and bounded out of bed in her thin top and matching cotton shorts with pale green cartoon frogs on them, striding toward the kitchen area where he stood. "Fine, you want to see? Look all you like! You've seen it all anyway."

She plopped down in a chair at the small table near the counter, reaching up to snatch the donut box from his hand. She peered inside, harboring a tiny bit of hope that he'd just been teasing her. "Damn it, you really did eat all the ones with sprinkles. Hog."

"I was hungry. And I didn't know certain donuts were special. You're not the only one in the world who likes sprinkles, you know." Amusement laced his voice. "Tell me what I can do to make it up to you, kitten."

She rolled her eyes, flashing a look designed to let him know he was on her blacklist. "Pour me a glass of milk."

He turned toward the refrigerator. "This rich guy you're marrying, does he have servants?"

Damn, his butt looked good through those shorts when he bent over, and his thigh muscles flexed a little, too. She bit her lower lip, and when he turned back around, milk carton in hand, jerked her eyes up to his. "Someone who cleans once a week and makes a few meals. Why?"

"Thought maybe you'd been practicing. You've got that 'lady of the manor' thing down."

She decided to ignore that comment altogether, since it struck at the heart of every conceivable difference between them. Her family had had money, his had been poor. Now, she was poised to be a wealthy wife and, even if his circumstances were much improved from his youth, there was still that certain earthy, gritty quality about him that reminded her they were worlds apart—and which drew her to him all the more.

After he found two glasses in a cabinet above the sink, then lowered himself into the seat across from her to start pouring, she found herself focusing on his upper body again—because she couldn't quite stop it, because his muscles looked so good shifting beneath all that smooth skin with every move he made.

It was when she felt his warm gaze that she, again, yanked her eyes to his face, and his look made it all too clear he knew exactly where her mind was. Not exactly in the gutter, but well on its way. Time to make conversation, before he accused her of wanting him.

"Didn't you used to have your name tattooed there?" She pointed toward his right biceps.

He took a drink from his glass, nodding. "Had it removed. Can't go undercover very well with your name on your arm. Besides, it wasn't exactly a work of art."

Yeah, she recalled that. As tattoos went, it had been beyond plain—very simple letters in a straight line. "Did you have an amateur do it or something?" She didn't mean it as an insult, but it had *looked* amateurish and she'd figured that was all he could afford.

"No, he was a professional. Just not a very good one. And he was drunk at the time."

She flinched and raised her eyebrows in question.

"It was my twenty-first birthday—we were *all* drunk," he explained. "Guy was a friend, so said he'd give me a free tattoo for my birthday. All things considered, though, I can't complain." He lowered his chin, as if about to confide in her. "Because my brother, on the other hand . . ."

She'd only met his older brother Bruno once—he'd struck her as a rougher version of Brock, and whereas the aura of danger surrounding Brock had lured her, with Bruno, it had left her instantly wary. "What? Did he get a bad tattoo?"

Brock met her gaze and the corners of his mouth quirked upward, although he was clearly trying not to smile. "Guy misspelled his name."

She blinked in disbelief. "What?"

"His arm says Burno. B-U-R-N-O."

Kat slapped her hand over her mouth, but a laugh leaked through. "Oh my God, are you serious? That's *awful*."

Brock finally let out a grin. "Yeah, I'm serious. And yeah, it's awful." Then his expression turned a little sad, almost wistful. "He beat the pulp out of the guy when he saw it the next day. It wasn't pretty."

She wondered where his thoughts had gone, since—suddenly—there was more taking place behind his eyes. *What have you been through, Brock?* She'd never asked about his family when they were young—their time around each other had been about attraction and flirtation and little else—but she'd always wondered, knowing instinctively that something had been terribly wrong in that area of his life.

"What ever happened to Bruno?" she asked softly. By the time Brock had left town, Bruno had been in jail and she'd never heard anything more about him.

"He's in prison." He said it matter-of-factly, but his eyes contradicted his easy tone.

"Still? After all this time?"

Brock sighed, sounded tired. "Every time he gets out, he steals a car or holds up a liquor store and goes right back in. He doesn't really know how to function outside jail anymore, I don't think."

God, what would that be like, to have a brother or sister who lived such a sad life? She was an only child, but she figured it had to hurt—even for a tough guy like Brock.

"Do you . . . see him?" It was none of her business, but as always, she wanted to know. Ten years later, she still wanted to find out more about Brock, get under his skin, inside his head—just a little.

He gave a short nod. "When I can. He's up at the Gainesville facility. But my job keeps me on the move, so time gets away from me."

His eyes were narrowed now, cloudy with . . . memories, maybe, or just regrets on his brother's behalf. More questions burned inside her, things she couldn't ask. *How did you and Bruno turn out so different? Where are your parents? How did you end up living with your grandpa?* But mostly, in that moment, she realized she also wanted to tell him how proud she was of him, how impressed she was with all he'd accomplished. Because it was just hitting her that he must have had to overcome a lot to turn into who he was today. He'd gone from hauling crates at her dad's gallery for minimum wage to being an FBI agent. An occupation which was still pretty shocking in itself.

But it wasn't actually *her* place to be proud of him. It was hardly as if she'd had any sway in his life. And if a miracle occurred and

Brock did let her inside his world a little, she'd only feel more attached to him—and that was the last thing she needed at the moment. So, all things considered, the smartest move seemed to be lightening things up. "So . . . I guess Bruno got his tattoo removed, too?"

Brock grinned, reached for a donut, and Kat was glad she'd made him smile, glad to see the muscles in his face relax. "Actually, no—too expensive. And hurts too much for him, anyway. For a convicted multiple felon, he can be a real wimp."

She tilted her head, finally reaching for her first donut, sneering only slightly at the fact that it was a plain glazed. "So it's really excruciating to have them removed?"

"Yep. But the job called for it."

"This job's pretty important to you, huh?" And only as the words left her mouth did she realize—it was probably *everything* to him. Because he had nothing else. No family that she knew of other than Bruno because his grandpa had died a long time ago. Nothing.

He answered with only a small nod, then added, "I gave up smoking for the Bureau, too."

She blinked in surprise. "They don't let you smoke in the FBI?"

A light laugh escaped him. "They *let* you, I just decided not to. Besides the fact that smoking killed my grandfather, it's one less thing to need when you get in a tight spot—like, say, stuck on an island for four or five days. Plus it's smart to stay in peak physical condition for this job."

And *that*, she thought, he most certainly had done. She had a feeling fatty yeast donuts weren't on his everyday menu. She couldn't imagine a man with a better body than the one she was looking at, which tightened her nipples just slightly, causing her to hunch her shoulders in an effort to bunch up her top in front so they wouldn't be so apparent. Even if he'd seen most of her—she didn't need to make it so clear that he was causing uncontrollable physical reactions in her just by sitting at a table eating breakfast.

"You've really changed a lot," she observed.

She wasn't expecting the slow, seductive grin the comment earned. "So, am I not enough of a bad boy for you anymore, Kat?"

The question at once embarrassed and aroused her. She couldn't deny her attraction to . . . well, less-than-straitlaced guys. Back in her previous life, of course—since it so happened she was marrying the straightest arrow ever to cross her path.

"That's not what I said," she replied, then realized it was the wrong answer, since it was sort of like flirting, like admitting she was attracted to him just fine as he was, and it was *definitely* like agreeing that his once-rough edges had certainly appealed to her.

He leaned slightly forward and pinned her in place with his dark gray gaze. "Trust me, kitten, I can still be bad when I want to."

What earlier had tingled inside her now burned. With heat. Unadulterated yearning. She suddenly wanted, more than anything in that moment, to let him show her just how bad he could be. And she wanted to tell him that—but she held her tongue, because she was *engaged*, damn it. Engaged, engaged, engaged. It was starting to sound like a very ugly word.

"And just so you know," he added with an alluring little grin, "when I got the name taken off, I got *another* tattoo in a less conspicuous place."

She tried not to show her interest, but knew her eyes had just widened. "Where?"

Slouching back in his chair, he glanced downward—toward his crotch.

Her eyes followed in horror, even though that part of him was actually under the table. "Good God, not on your . . ."

He let out a hardy laugh. "No. Don't worry, kitten, I never purposely subject myself to pain *there*."

"Then *where*? And what is it of?"

He raised his eyebrows, looking playfully mysterious. "It's a secret. But I'll let you look for it if you want."

Boy, did she want—with every naughty fiber of her being. But she caught her breath, remembered the ugly word, and instead just sneered at him, as if it were reprehensible that he would even suggest such a hideous thing.

He ignored the face she made, looking as cool and confident as usual. "I'm surprised *you* don't have a tattoo or two. Seems like you'd be a tattoo sorta girl."

Kat's instant, unplanned response was to tilt her head and try like hell to be just as provocative as he was. "Who says I don't?" *What are you doing? Stop it!*

"I haven't noticed one."

"Maybe it's where you can't see." Why on earth was she lying about this? She didn't *have* a tattoo. She kind of wanted one, but her father would have killed her. And given her parents' pool, she wore bathing suits in her dad's presence far too often to simply hope he wouldn't notice something like an ink engraving on her skin.

"That's real interesting," Brock said, "given that I've seen all but a very small portion of your body. Where?"

Good question. She'd forgotten for a vital second that he'd actually seen more of her than her father had. *Next time you fib, prepare a plan.* She simply shrugged. "It's a secret, too."

He cast a typically slow and devilish grin. "I'll show you mine if you show me yours."

If only I had one to show. But the fact that she didn't and had just told a really dumb lie was actually a good deterrent, a way to keep herself from doing anything stupid and regrettable. She tried to appear as if she'd lost interest in the conversation. "Nice try, but I'm not that curious."

He lowered his chin slightly. "Like hell you're not."

"Your arrogance knows no bounds, does it?"

"Not arrogance, kitten—just the way things are."

Oh, it was arrogance, all right. And it was also the way things were—since she was *dying* to see that tattoo, and other certain appendages in that area of his body—and at the moment, she was unable to deny it, so she simply rolled her eyes, ate her donut, and said, "This sucks without sprinkles."

"If you love sprinkles so much, why didn't you get the whole dozen with them?"

She flashed a cutting look in his direction. "At the time I thought a little variety might be nice, and I had no idea I'd be splitting my donut stash with an interloper."

God, did the man *ever* smile without it looking wholly sexual? She simply glanced away—since even the way he smiled at her when they were talking about donuts had the ability to reach down into her panties and make her yearn.

"So, about the food situation," he said, suddenly switching into business mode, which was a relief—kind of, "what do we have to eat?"

She briefly thought through it again. "I told you last night, a lot of snack foods, and some sandwich stuff."

"You said maybe some canned food, too, but I looked through the cabinets and didn't see any."

She shrugged. "I guess I was wrong."

"What's behind that locked door?" He pointed to a closet next to the bathroom. "Pantry?"

She shook her head. "It's just storage."

"Why's it locked?"

She rolled her eyes, annoyed with his persistence over something so trivial. Yet she searched her memory and drew up a vague recollection of a conversation about the closet with her father. "I think my dad said the previous owner had left paint stripper and varnish in there, and that it was just locked up to keep their kids from getting into it. And you can quit worrying—there's enough food." She glared at the next donut he was about to reach for. "If you'd stop eating it at record speed."

He pulled his hand back, appearing surprisingly contrite. "Didn't even realize I was doing that. Just haven't had anything like this in a while." He patted that hard washboard stomach and—as was becoming habit—she had to jerk her gaze upward when she felt his look.

She made a split-second decision to depart from the table and whisk into the bathroom. "I'll be back," she said, and left without giving him even one more glance. She needed a cool shower. And a change of scenery. She needed to see something besides that perfect male torso.

Great, she thought, shutting the door firmly behind her. *You've just made a spectacle of yourself. He either thinks you're having some sort of unpleasant bathroom emergency or that you can't even look at him without wanting to attack.* The second of which was all-too-tragically true.

She'd done so well yesterday, she lamented as she stripped off her nighties and stepped under the spray. The whole time he'd been flirting and provoking her over dinner, she'd held completely strong. Well, maybe not *completely*—she'd wanted him, of course. Sometimes she thought she'd been *born* wanting Brock Denton since it seemed like a constant in her life that, if she was honest, never completely faded away. But she'd resisted last night. Admirably. This morning, on the other hand, temptation was . . . lurking. Nearby. Creeping closer and closer.

Showering, however, she quickly learned, had been a rotten idea. It meant soaping up her body. Which sort of meant *touching* her body. Which made her think of wanting *him* to touch her body. *Nina was right, I should have gone to Vegas.* Riding a pirate, in the long run, would have been less sinful than what she had going on in her head about Brock.

Even as she donned her white bikini, she glanced in the mirror, seeing her body as *he* probably saw it, and couldn't deny feeling utterly sensual. Where was a good, dependable turtleneck sweater when you needed it?

After moisturizing her pottery-roughened hands and slapping some lotion on her arms and legs for good measure, she exited the bathroom with a silky white sarong draped about her hips and tied low on one side. She walked to the bedside table to snatch up a hair clip, secured her hair in a messy knot atop her head, then grabbed up the straw bag where her towel and sunscreen resided. She still needed that change of scenery.

"And just where do you think *you're* going?" Brock snapped as she started past him for the door.

She looked up, blinking. "To the beach. Where else?"

"I can't let you do that, kitten."

She sighed. He was sexy as sin itself, but his nerve never ceased to amaze her. "I wasn't asking your permission." No more flirting, she'd decided—and defying him seemed a good way to prevent that.

She headed for the door again—only to feel his large hand latch tight around her wrist. "Wait." She looked up to find his face—his whole body for that matter—close. She wanted to touch the stubble again. And despite herself, she liked how tightly he held on to her.

She could barely locate her voice, but managed to ask, "So what's the problem? Do you think the bad guys are coming back or something?"

"Not really. But it's not impossible—and *that's* the problem." He still held her arm, making her whole body hum with his nearness.

Which meant she'd better get away from him—now. "Well, I'm not sitting here with *you* all day."

He gave her a slow, scolding look. "Fine. Then I'll sit *there* with *you* all day."

"You're going to the beach with me?" She kept her face blank since she hadn't yet decided how to feel about that.

His reply was a short, all-business nod.

She flashed a dry expression. "So how are you going to protect me if they show up, Mr. FBI Agent? Squirt them with my sunscreen?"

"You really *are* hysterical," he said, looking completely un-amused. "You should take that on the road."

"Maybe I would, but I can't *get* to the road. Someone blew up my boat." With that, she jerked her arm free and turned to march toward the beach—but she missed his touch the whole way.

Tell me you love him, kitten. Tell me again.

Glancing over at her lounge chair, where she lay with eyes closed, looking like every teenage boy's tropical fantasy, he thought about asking her, one more time. But he wasn't sure if it was because he wanted to see something new in her eyes, something to tell him that she *was* doing the right thing, marrying the right guy—or if he didn't.

Because as long as nothing changed and he remained uncon-vinced, that made it A-okay to keep flirting, trying to seduce, try-ing to make her give in to what they both wanted.

No doubt in his mind that she wanted it, either. Last night, maybe there'd been some question. This morning, though, she hadn't been able to keep her eyes off him. He'd felt her gaze all *over* him, and it was a good thing he'd been sitting down or she would have seen exactly how much he liked that, evidenced by the tent in his pants.

He watched the sensual way she let her arm droop over the edge of the chair, her fingertips dragging lightly through the powdery sand, almost petting, caressing it.

The thing that surprised him was that Kat was the last girl to be pushed into something she didn't want to do. He'd only known her for six months or so when they were younger, but he'd watched her, wanted her, even then. He'd seen the fine way she balanced her life—the skill with which she played the prim daughter, enough to please her father, and yet at the same time remained her own person. And if Brock had ever doubted her ability to be something other than the perfect daughter, she'd proven it that night out at the swamp.

Ten years should have only made her sense of self stronger. So what the hell was she doing marrying a guy just to please her dad, for God's sake?

She still raked her fingers through the sand, deeper now, letting it sift between, then rubbing her thumb over the grains that remained on her fingertips like she was blind and they spelled out something in Braille. Why was that sexy as hell?

Forcing his eyes away, he turned his gaze out on the ocean where, thankfully, he found nothing more than a blank horizon, blue sky over blue water. He really *didn't* think the Morales boys had any reason to return for his dead body, but his job had taught him never to let his guard down completely.

And if he needed a reminder of that, he need only think back to yesterday on the boat. A few kisses and touches should have been an extremely minor distraction under the high-tension circumstances— yet he'd blown his cover. And if those two girls could distract him that much, where did Kat rate on the distraction scale? A lot higher.

Good thing *she* hadn't been on the boat. And a good thing he'd shifted into relax-and-recover mode, because apparently he *needed* to relax and recover from the undercover shit, take a break for a little while.

Reaching down next to the old lounge chair he'd found for himself in a storage shed behind the house, he grabbed the equally ancient radio he'd nabbed from atop the fridge. It had batteries and worked, but he hadn't had much luck getting reception in the bungalow and thought it might go better out on the beach.

No difference, though—no matter how he turned the dial, nothing but static except for one oldies station that played only seventies music. At the moment, The Electric Light Orchestra sang "Can't Get It Out of My Head." He glanced over at Kat, still looking swimsuit-model-stunning with her arms raised over her head, sand abandoned now, her breasts jutting upward behind two white triangles, her body long and lean and glistening just slightly from the sun. He swallowed—gulped actually.

Geez, dude, get hold of yourself. She's just a chick, man. Just a chick.

Just a chick he had some history with. Just a chick he thought about when he was in danger sometimes. Just a chick whose future happiness had suddenly taken on an unexplained importance in his life. Talk about not being able to get something out of your head.

He propped the radio in the sand next to him, adjusted the antenna slightly, and leaned back in the chair, soaking up the rays and letting the steady sound of the tide lull him. It didn't take long to understand why Kat came here to unwind. The raw, natural beauty of palm trees jutting at all angles, the bright sun and white sand, and the undiluted sense of isolation made him feel like he could be on some deserted isle far, far away—not just a few miles off the Florida coast.

And he found himself wondering what it might be like to be this guy—what had she said his name was? Ethan? No, Ian. What might it be like to lie here on this private island, glance over at Kat to see her touching the sand like it was velvet, and know she was yours, the woman you would spend the rest of your life with?

He looked at her. Let himself sink into that notion, just for a moment. Felt a strange warmth coil low in his belly. Then shook it off—because he sure as hell wasn't Ian, and he wasn't the marrying kind anyway. And even if he were . . .

His gaze settled on her again, closer now—easy since her eyes were shut—and he studied the flat plane of her tan belly, the tiny slit of her belly button, the shapely form of her leg, bent at the knee.

He and Kat were worlds apart, always had been, and they'd both always known it. So despite the attraction, no matter how feral, he thought they'd both always understood nothing could ever happen between them—nothing beyond the backseat of a car. Or the front seat, removed, sitting next to a swampy lake.

He dragged his gaze back out over the ocean, remembering that he liked his life the way it was—no commitments, no responsibilities to anyone besides himself and the U.S. government. That's how the FBI liked it, too—guys without family ties made the best agents, and he knew it was that particular attribute that had first made him seem like a not completely unreasonable candidate for the job.

This island, and Kat—it was all just a little vacation, nothing more.

A few oldies later, he heard movement to his left and glanced over to see her sit up, reach in the bag beside her for a tube of sunscreen, and begin to smooth the stuff over her arms—and then her legs. She used long, even strokes that kept his eyes riveted on her tan skin as it began to shimmer moistly.

Making leisurely work of the task, she finally moved on to her belly. *Damn, nice belly, kitten.* He was usually a breast man, but that pretty tummy kept drawing his attention. Next came her chest, including the lovely slopes of those breasts, and she worked diligently to massage the lotion right up to the edges of the fabric, which took some time and captured every ounce of his attention.

He couldn't believe she hadn't noticed him watching and shot some scathing remark in his direction. Or maybe she *had* noticed. And maybe she just liked it. A thought that warmed his pelvic region.

Just then, she reached around, trying to apply the sunscreen to her back—but she couldn't, of course, only covering the outer edges. He knew an opportunity when he saw one, so he wasted no time pushing to his feet, taking a few steps over the sun-heated sand, and plucking the tube from between her fingers. "Allow me."

She let out a heavy breath of annoyance. "Do I have a choice?"

"Not unless you want your back to look like your breasts."

She glared in disbelief, but he ignored that and settled behind her. He had to sit close, since there wasn't much room between her ass and the sloping back of the chair. And she didn't move away, even though his thigh pressed firmly into her round bottom.

Squeezing a glob of coconut-scented lotion onto his fingertips, he started at the top of her back, rubbing it into her skin in a deliberately slow, wide circle, letting the loop grow gradually bigger and bigger until he moved onto her shoulders, finally abandoning the tube on his lap so he could use both hands. He smoothed in the sunscreen, massaging lightly at first, then deeper, deeper, until a gentle sigh of pleasure escaped her.

His groin tightened as he leaned near her ear and spoke in a low voice. "Feel good, kitten?"

She turned to look at him, which put his mouth about three inches from hers. He noticed her studying it before lifting her gaze to his eyes. "*Any* massage feels good," she claimed, but her voice came breathy, which made him harder.

He knew instinctively that his hot little massage felt way better to her than anything she could get in a spa, but he wasn't going to argue with her right now. "Then let me keep going," he said instead, squirting more lotion into his hand.

Leisurely dragging his palms over her shoulder blades, he worked his way down until he found himself rubbing carefully around the thin string that crossed the center of her back, pushing his fingertips up under. He moved slow and thorough the whole time, wanting her to feel every nuance of his touch.

Without planning it, his fingers soon massaged their way around to her sides, beginning to graze the soft outer curves of her breasts. She didn't stop him, and that knowledge combined with the lush feel of the flesh beneath his fingers turned him still stiffer in his trunks. *So soft, kitten. Soft and hot and perfect.*

He wanted desperately to press into her from behind and kiss her neck. He fought the urge to cup her breasts. He yearned to close his teeth over her earlobe and rake them slowly downward.

Still rubbing, rubbing, flirting with the edges of her breasts, he wondered if she'd let this always-present attraction between them finally progress to its natural conclusion, if a little sunscreen on his hands could be the beginning of hot, slow sex on the beach. He'd leapt at the chance to rub sunscreen on her back, but he hadn't really expected her to let things get so heated so fast.

And it was all he could do not to rain a few little kisses over her neck, shoulder—but he didn't want to screw up and send her racing away from him. He wanted to play this slow, safe. He wanted to ease his way there until she couldn't resist what he wanted to give her. Her tender sigh said he was on the right track.

He didn't say a word, and neither did she, the only sounds coming from the sweeping tide and the rustling palms overhead. The sea breeze cooled them amid the blasting rays from above. Brock put more lotion in his hand and proceeded to massage it into her lower back, which she arched for him—instinctually, he thought. He kept the kneading motions slow, rhythmic, and took them all the way down to the edge of her bikini bottom, not breathing for the few seconds she let his hands linger there, just touching her, curving low over the flesh where her back met her ass. They both stayed still, so still—he'd never imagined that such stillness could be so arousing.

He finally eased his palms around the edge of her suit to her hips, fingers splaying onto her stomach from both sides, and let them glide slowly up, up, over baby-soft skin, until they rested just beneath her chest, the weight of her breasts brushing overtop his fingers.

His body nearly trembled with want. Her skin was so soft, slick, beckoning—and all he desired in that moment was to slide his hands up over her breasts and capture them, know them, explore them. Without those triangles getting in his way.

He didn't even consider her reaction—just followed an impulse. Never taking his hands off her, he leaned in, closed his teeth around one of the strings behind her neck, and slowly pulled.

When the top dropped away in front, she gasped gently, but when she turned to look at him, there was far more heat than surprise in her gaze.

Their eyes locked, close, and he whispered to her. "Let me, kitten."

He watched her pull in her breath; she looked weak, ready to give in to her desires. *Yes, honey. Good.*

As he slowly started to ease his hands upward, though, she grabbed on to them, pushing them down. She held them tight, at her waist. They both stayed very still, but now stillness meant tense, frozen, locked in a silent battle with temptation. Kat stared out at the ocean, and he wondered what she saw, felt. *Please, baby, let me.*

Yet he knew the moment was passing, that resistance was slowly winning. He released a heavy breath and leaned his forehead over to rest on her shoulder.

Finally, her voice small, she said, "I can't, Brock. You know why."

Yeah, he knew why. He hated it, didn't believe it was real, wanted to rip it to shreds—this engagement of hers—but he knew why. And he decided that if Kat could stop this now, the magnetic pull between them that was even more powerful and persuasive than he remembered, then she was a lot stronger than he'd ever given her credit for. "Couldn't you just pretend," he said low, near her ear, "that you really went to Vegas?"

She turned her head, again bringing their faces painfully close. He wanted to kiss her so bad it hurt. "Why?" she asked.

He delivered his reply without a smile, completely serious. "Because what happens in Vegas stays in Vegas. You get a free pass there."

"So you mean . . . what happens on the island stays on the island?"

"Something like that."

She let out a sigh, her voice still whispery, sad. "That's never made any sense to me. Whatever you do, you've done. It all counts."

He longed desperately to convince her. Because she was so close to giving in and they both knew it. And it would be *so* good—they both knew that, too. He'd make sure she didn't regret it—he'd make sure it was the best she'd ever had. Yet she was still managing to hold back somehow.

"Tell me something, honey," he said softly. "What exactly would happen that's so bad if you . . . let me have my way with you?"

She bit her lower lip, her eyes clouded with sorrow, her voice going a little shaky. "I wouldn't be able to live with myself. Despite what you may think, I'm not the kind of person who could have sex with one guy, then marry another a few days later. I can't think of anything that would feel more wrong."

He leaned slightly closer, so close their faces almost touched. She still held his hands tight at her sides. "But if *you* want it, and *I* want it," he said, "isn't there something at least a little bit *right* in that, too?"

Her voice came stronger this time. "If I wasn't engaged, sure. But I am."

And he knew the moment, the temptation, had really passed—and the suffering could recommence. He closed his eyes for a second, trying to blot out the frustration, then met her gaze again. "Does that mean I'm still sleeping on the floor tonight?"

Her nod was emphatic.

He let out another heavy sigh, then drew his hands away.

She hurriedly pulled her top back up and retied it behind her neck, then rushed to her feet. "I'm going for a swim," she announced with just a quick glance. "And don't come with me. I need a few minutes by myself."

"Okay," he said. Then, just automatically, "Be careful."

"Don't worry—I can take care of myself."

As he watched her go, her lovely body swaying toward the water, he thought, *Can you, kitten?* He'd always seen her as perfectly capable, but if she was marrying the wrong person for the wrong reasons . . . well, now he wasn't so sure.

He knew this was none of his business—he knew that in a few days he'd go back to *his* life and she'd go back to *hers*, and that meant he should sure as hell leave hers alone. But Kat *couldn't* marry a guy who didn't excite her, thrill her, make her crazy with passion. Like *he* just had. He'd have bet all the Mayan artifacts in the world that Ian whatever-his-name-was had never made her want the way *he'd* just made her want.

Brock strongly suspected Clark Spencer was behind this whole farce of a marriage somehow. He knew Spencer loved his daughter and that she loved him back, but they were two very different people, and Brock could easily envision the guy still trying to mold Kat in his image after all these years. Maybe he'd worn her down over time. And maybe she didn't even realize it.

All the more reason why Brock couldn't just sit idly by and let her marry the wrong guy. He couldn't watch her travel down the wrong path if he could possibly do something to turn her in the right direction.

And he could.

He could seduce her.

He could keep right on chipping away at her defenses until she gave in.

And then, if what she'd just told him was true—if she really *couldn't* have sex with one guy and then marry another—then she'd have to call off the wedding.

He plopped back down in his lounge chair as Blondie sang "One Way or Another" on the radio, and he vowed, just as the song said, that he would get her—right where he longed to have her. He still had four long island nights left for seduction.

Chapter Five

*C*lark Spencer backed his Jaguar XJR carefully from the five-car garage, then eased onto the circular brick drive that fronted his large stucco home. He never quite managed to make those particular moves in the car without being intensely *aware* of it all. The Jag's sleek comforts, the old-world charm of the brick he drove across, the way the house towered over him like a Mediterranean fortress as he rolled past. He glanced at the well-manicured lawn and ornamental trees, pleased the gardener had come on Friday. To know he'd given his family the best possible life was his greatest source of satisfaction.

Of course, Debra was miffed at him for working this afternoon. "On a *Sunday*, Clark—a freaking *Sunday*?"

Why couldn't she understand? This stuff didn't grow on trees.

Maybe she thought it did. She'd never wanted for much, even as a girl. Her family hadn't been wealthy, but they'd been comfortable. She didn't realize what it took to keep this kind of lifestyle afloat.

The last year had been the most trying of his life, and she didn't even know it. All that money from the early days in the art business was slowly dwindling. They were far from broke, but any fool could look at the calculations of his net worth over the last few years and see the downward trend.

"Do you realize the pressures I'm up against lately, Debra?" he'd snapped. "Do you have any idea what it takes to pay for all this?" He'd motioned around him—they'd been standing amid all the modern stainless steel of the recently remodeled kitchen, which happened to be about the size of a small apartment he'd once lived in.

"We don't need it all," she'd said.

And his heart had skipped a beat. What the hell was she talking about? "What?"

"I said we don't need it all. We'd have a perfectly lovely life with *half* of what we have, Clark. So what if we were to have to scale back a little, give a few things up? That wouldn't matter to me."

She didn't see it, he thought now, taking one last look back at their home as he exited the drive. She didn't see that every grain of stucco in that house, every blade of grass in that yard, everything they owned—was *him*. It was what he'd done with his life, what he'd made of himself from next to nothing, his legacy. When he died, it was what he had to leave behind.

It wounded him to realize she didn't understand that, and he'd tried to let her know. "Maybe you don't appreciate how hard I work, maybe you don't care about our life—but I do. *I* want all this, Debra, okay? *I* want it."

"I just don't understand what you're going to do in that gallery this afternoon that couldn't wait until tomorrow."

Of course she didn't. But why couldn't she just trust and respect him enough to admire his work ethic? The fact was, he had a lot of new business going on via his connection with Ian, and it was taking up a great deal of time. He'd even been neglecting the gallery—and when all was said and done, that was his first love. He'd had the gallery before Debra, before Kat—and he couldn't let *that* business crumble just because of the opportunities Ian had brought his way.

As the first melodic notes of Elton John's "Levon" came trickling from the car's speakers, he reached to turn it up. The intro made him picture a young Elton's hands flowing magically across the piano keys, a moving work of art. The song always had the uncanny ability to at once relax him and depress him just a little. But it was too beautiful not to absorb, even if it made him a little sad. Some art was like that.

Damn, the last year had been difficult, watching the money begin to slip away—like blood draining slowly from his body. He only wanted to give his family the best—was that so terrible?

But the worries would be over soon, thank God.

Kat's agreeing to marry Ian had changed everything. *Everything.* She had no idea of the impact the union would have—was *already* having—on all of them.

She'd been the light of Clark's life since the day she was born. Some men longed for a son—to pass their name to, to make into a junior version of themselves; maybe it gave them the illusion they'd never die. But he and Debra had agreed that one perfect child was enough, girl or boy. Kat was all he'd ever needed to satisfy him as a father. And soon she'd have the life he'd always wanted for her.

Funny, he'd thought *he'd* always be able to give her the best of everything. He'd earned so much money once upon a time that he'd never dreamed it could diminish. But now that she was marrying Ian, he wouldn't have to worry about that. She'd never want for anything from this point forward.

And maybe wanting that for her was setting her up to be like Debra in a way, someone who'd never done without and didn't know the real value of all they possessed. But Kat was his little girl. And she *should* have everything. What parent didn't want that for his child? What parent wouldn't move heaven and earth to make sure his child was happy, safe, and would never know what it was like to be hungry or cold.

Just knowing his girl's future was set, until the day she died, made his mission in life feel a little more complete.

So suddenly it was a noble mission Brock was on, seducing Kat. And if they happened to have some incredibly hot fun in the process, who was he to complain?

As he slapped together a couple of turkey sandwiches for them at the kitchen counter, "Cruel to Be Kind" by Nick Lowe echoed from the radio, perched precariously next to the sink in the only position that allowed the oldies station to come through.

A minute later, he pushed the front door open with his back, two plates balanced in his hands. "Dinner is served," he said, lowering her sandwich and chips in front of her. Glancing down, he saw that she still wore her bathing suit, but much to his irritation, she'd tied her skirty thing up over her breasts, concealing her curves.

Not that it made her any less pleasant to look at, he acknowledged, taking a seat across from her. Her eyes still glittered beneath the rising moon, her hair still fell in messy waves around her shoulders, and those shoulders—God, he didn't know when he'd developed a shoulder fetish, but Kat's were about the smoothest, tannest, prettiest ones he'd ever seen. Shoulders, stomachs—hell, she was making him notice all *sorts* of body parts that didn't usually capture his attention.

"Quit staring at my breasts," she said.

"I'm not staring at your breasts. I'm staring at your shoulders."

"Why?"

"Because you covered up your breasts."

She rolled her eyes, and he couldn't resist a grin—although he tried to make it more playful than wolfish. He wasn't sure why, but maybe he'd felt a little bad after what had happened earlier. He didn't regret trying to seduce her, especially now that it had a more gallant purpose—but she'd seemed shaken afterward, and he didn't like making her uncomfortable. On the contrary, he wanted her to realize just how *good* he could make her feel.

After crunching down on a potato chip, he looked her in the eye and said, "Maybe we should talk about what happened today at the beach, kitten."

She lifted that pretty gaze to his, although it was colored with distress. "Why? What's the point?"

He hoped she could see his sincere concern. "You seemed upset."

She wrapped one delicate hand around her sandwich, started to lift it to her mouth, but then stopped. Her blue gaze, shining on him, looked darker than usual. "Tell me something, Brock. Why are you doing this?"

"This?"

"Trying so hard to get in my bikini bottoms."

Lots of reasons, kitten. But he couldn't tell her the big one, that he was working desperately to save her from a bad marriage. So he kept it simple. "Because I screwed up ten years ago and want what I missed."

He watched her eyes—and like so many times in the last day since his arrival, he knew they were both thinking back to that night long ago.

"You know what I've learned in the FBI, kitten? That life is short. I've seen people die. Was forced to shoot a man once myself.

All any of us really have for sure is this moment, right now. So I've learned that I have to seize the day—or the night," he said, casting a glance to the half-moon shining white overhead in a star-speckled sky. He seldom got so serious and earnest with anyone—but suddenly he felt he owed it to her somehow. He couldn't tell her the *whole* truth, but he could at least let her know his attempts at seduction were about more than his just being a jerk who had no respect for marriage. "I've learned to take what good things, and what pleasure, is offered to me whenever I can, because it might not be there tomorrow. And I've learned to go after what I want because I might not get another chance."

She looked at him long and hard, her gaze soft, her lips gently parted, and he knew she was feeling it, too, that need to live in the moment, to seize it for all it was worth—with him.

Until she sucked in her breath and transformed her expression into something less yielding. Her voice came out low, tender—but strong. "Do you know what the difference is between you and me, Brock? We don't live the same life. If I were some danger-loving secret agent like you, facing death around every corner, sure—I'd fuck your brains out right now."

He blinked. She'd said it so matter-of-factly—like such words from his kitten wouldn't instantly produce a painful erection in his swim trunks, unbidden.

"But I'm not in danger," she went on, shaking her head. "I'm not going to die tomorrow. Unless a freak accident occurs, I have all the time in the world, and my actions have consequences. I'm getting married in less than a week. I've made a commitment to a man who loves me. I can't indulge my whims anymore. All that's changed. I'm somebody else now."

Her words were stalwart and admirable. But the longer she talked, the more he heard . . . that little tinge of sorrow, that acknowledgment that she was giving something up, and maybe she didn't want to. "I don't *want* you to be somebody else, honey. And I don't believe you really are. I don't believe you *can* be."

She took it the wrong way. "You don't believe I can change? You don't believe I can be a . . . a good girl? A good wife?"

He sighed. He had to make her get what he was trying to say. "This isn't about good or bad, Kat. It's about who you are. Shakespeare once wrote, 'There is nothing either good or bad, but thinking makes it so.' And I—"

She shot to her feet, expression bewildered and angry. "Jesus Christ! Brock Denton spouting Shakespeare to me? I am truly in the freaking Twilight Zone. And I want out." She shoved back the picnic table's bench and started to march away, but then stopped and turned back. "And do you know why *I* think you want in my pants?" Her eyes held accusation. "I think you want it so bad just because you can't have it. I think you somehow want to get *back* at me by seducing me."

He flinched, suddenly incredulous. "Get back at you for what?"

"For . . ." She looked flustered now, but pressed on. "For the same reason you turned me down that night at the swamp. For being rich when you were poor. For having a better life than you."

Now it was Brock who pushed to his feet, toppling the bench behind him in the sand. He narrowed his gaze on the deluded girl before him, and lowered his voice. "If you only knew how far off you are, kitten."

Maybe it was the slow, sure way he'd spoken, but to his surprise, as a fresh silence stretched between them, she looked like she might actually believe him. "About?" Her voice softened slightly.

"All of it. About why I want you now. And why I couldn't have you then."

He watched the slow rise and fall of her breasts beneath the skirty thing tied there. "*Couldn't* have me? What does *that* mean?"

"Let's just concentrate on now," he said, steering her back to what mattered most. "And right now, I want you because every time I see you I get hard. I want you because you're hot and beautiful—and cute as hell when you're mad at me. And maybe I even want you because I'm selfish—I'm a selfish son of a bitch who can't think of anything else right now beyond being inside you." So there it was, all the shit he'd never planned to say, but had just spewed out like a volcano erupting all over the beach. He, of course, still hadn't told her about his plan to prevent her wedding from taking place, but he'd given her everything else, and for him, that was a lot.

She stayed quiet, looking a little dazed, and he was on the verge of remembering everything she'd been through in the last day or so and feeling bad about the fact that he'd just sort of yelled at her—when she simply walked back to the table, snatched up her sandwich, and padded away toward the house.

Shit. Real smooth, Denton. He followed after her. "Wait, kitten. Wait, and tell me what's wrong."

As she reached the door, she spun to face him. "Nothing, actually. Because what you just said helps a lot."

He held his hands out, palms up. "What do you mean?"

"Being reminded that you're a selfish son of a bitch makes me want you a lot less. So thank you for pointing that out."

He watched her walk inside, the screen door slamming behind her—and realized that, in fact, that part hadn't been true. The more he thought about it, he wasn't being selfish at all. He was doing this for *both* their sakes.

But she couldn't see that, so it made the point pretty moot. *Let*

her have some space. You've rocked her world the last two days—give her some
time alone.

He headed back toward the table through the cool night sand,
righted the bench he'd knocked over, sat back down, and ate his dinner. He drank the beer he'd popped open a few minutes earlier and
tried to enjoy the evening breeze washing in from the beach, the
stark silence of being alone on an island in the middle of the Gulf of
Mexico, the stillness of it all.

But his skin still itched with wanting her. And with wanting to
save her.

Relax and recover mode—turned out *that* wasn't *this*. But maybe
he no longer wanted it to be.

He wanted to let her have her space, get herself together, calm
down—but not for too long. Because Brock knew a little something
about infiltrating someone's defenses. The Bureau had taught him
well. And if he was serious about having her—and saving her from
a lifetime of dissatisfaction—then this was the perfect time to kick
things into high gear.

After eating her sandwich while standing at the kitchen counter
listening to those seventies tunes that were starting to drive her
crazy, Kat went into the bathroom and locked the door. The tiny
room, it seemed, was becoming her spot of retreat. Odd, she'd
come to this island to be alone, but could only seem to manage
that by hiding in this miniscule space done in badly chipping
Florida pink tile.

She showered and washed her hair, then conditioned it, rinsing
for a long, long time. Turning the knob to redirect the flow of water from the upper nozzle to the lower, she sat down in the tub and
shaved her legs. Finally getting out, mainly due to pruning concerns, she stood in front of the sink and blew her hair dry. Then

worked lotion into her hands, where clay resided in the pores. Then sat down on the closed toilet seat and moisturized all over. And moisturized again.

She tried to think about useful, practical things. The idea that had hit her today on the beach—about firing sand onto her pots, transforming them from smooth to gritty, making her art a more rugged expression. And about the last few things she had left to do when she got home—a final visit to the florist to make sure the special roses she'd ordered were the exact shade she wanted; a call to the country club, reminding them someone needed to be there on Saturday when the ice sculpture arrived. Her mom was handling the rest of the last-minute details, but only she could check the flowers, and she'd forgotten about the country club call until getting here.

She tried to *continue* thinking about practical things—How was the gallery running without her? Had the kids missed her at The Kiln on Saturday? Had her mom remembered to stop by for cat-sitting duty?—but the truth was, her mind kept traveling back to the moment when she'd been straddling Brock on that car seat, and she'd realized that being with her was only about sex for him, nothing more.

Because, apparently, that was still the case.

Not that it came as a surprise.

And not that *she'd* never had sex for the mere sake of sex.

Only . . . maybe sometimes she regretted that once it was over.

The truth was—sex generally disappointed her. She had always known desire, deep passion, a yearning for everything she thought sex could and should be. But it never quite seemed to live up to the hype in her own mind.

She'd never told anyone that—hell, maybe this moment, as she smeared globs of green aloe gel across her still slightly pink breasts, was the first time she'd even admitted it to *herself.*

But maybe that was the reason she'd waited to have sex with Ian. Because in her heart, sex was supposed to be a special thing. She'd never actually *succeeded* in making it very special, but she intended to. Wedding-night sex, sex for the first time with Ian, *had* to be special. It just *had* to.

She peered in the mirror, bit her lip, and wished the notion excited her more. Then she pushed the thought away. *You're just feeling glum because Brock Denton is driving you out of your mind. Playing head games. And sex games.*

Sadly, though, sex with *Brock* still sounded pretty darn good. *That* excited her.

Easing down against the hard-on hidden in his blue jeans that night ten years ago had excited her. And she wasn't sure anything had excited her as much since.

Which was a bad, bad thought—so she tried to push that one away, too, and concentrate on rubbing in the aloe. But even *that* brought thoughts of him rushing back—thoughts of wanting the hands on her breasts to be his.

You are doomed. Just doomed.

But wait, no. She stood up a little straighter and looked at herself again in the glass. *You are strong. You are woman, hear you roar.*

Clearly, she'd been listening to too much seventies music if she was bolstering herself with Helen Reddy lyrics, but at least she'd held Brock off this long—so she could keep right on doing it.

Just focus on the "selfish son of a bitch" part and the "only wants sex" part. Yeah, that should help. Because as much as she'd wanted sex from Brock when they were young . . . deep inside, she'd wanted a whole lot more. Sex would have merely been the icing.

After she finally put back on her pale green shorty pajamas— which, frogs aside, seemed risqué, but a safer choice than the panty-and-cami set she'd brought—she quietly turned the lock on the bathroom door, hoping to slip silently out and find Brock fast asleep on the floor. It was quiet out there, after all—she could tell he'd clicked off the radio—so hopefully he'd tired of harassing her for the day and turned in.

Exiting the little room, she found the space only dimly lit, most of the lights extinguished, and assumed he'd left the last one on for her. Which was kind of polite, under the circumstances. And as always with him, it took only the tiniest act of kindness to make her decide maybe he wasn't really so horrible.

Well ready to call it a day herself, she rounded the corner toward the bed—to find him lying in it with his hands propped behind his head.

She gasped—and her pulse raced, particularly between her thighs. He wore no shirt, and the covers were pulled to his waist, so she didn't know if he was wearing anything underneath, either. "What do you think you're doing?"

"Going to sleep—what's it look like?"

"It looks like you . . . might not have any clothes on under there, that's what." She pointed vaguely toward the sheet draped just below his well-muscled stomach.

He offered not even a hint of a smile, but his eyes dripped with the usual sin. "Come and find out, kitten."

She drew in her breath and planted her hands on her hips. "You can't sleep in my bed."

He gave his head a matter-of-fact tilt, looking almost like a reasonable man—if she didn't know better. "It's like this, honey. That damn floor killed my back last night. So I'm not sleeping there again when there's a perfectly good bed here built for two. You can join me, or not. Your choice."

Kat pulled in another nervous gulp of air and hoped he didn't see. She had no idea what would happen if she got into that bed with him. Or maybe she did. She swallowed back the massive lump of desire in her throat. "You're a big, rude interloper," she informed him.

He shrugged, arms still behind his head, biceps bulging. "Way I see it is—we're in this together. Not your fault or mine I ended up here, but we have to make the best of it."

Yeah, he was trying to make the best of it, all right.

She considered her options. The bed, with Brock. Or the hard floor, alone.

On the surface, it seemed a *really* easy answer. She wasn't a "roughing it" sort of girl—she'd never even seen the inside of a tent, and she'd certainly never slept on a floor. But my God, what would Ian think if he could see her sharing a bed with another guy? Even if nothing happened.

Still and all, Ian *couldn't* see her. And this *wasn't* cheating on him. Hell, the lusty thoughts in her head for Brock were probably a way worse offense than just sharing the same space with him, even if that space happened to be of the horizontal variety.

She crossed her arms and tried to look like a woman not to be trifled with. "If I get in that bed, do you promise to stay on your side?"

"Sure, kitten," he said far too easily, same old unmistakably sexual gleam in his eye. Then he scooted over, vacating the space where she'd slept last night, and patted the mattress. "Here you go."

Kat took a deep breath and moved cautiously toward the bed. She climbed in without looking at him, finding the spot delectably warm from his body, and reached to pull the sheet up—then realized she still didn't know if he was naked or not. She darted her glance to him, his utter nearness reminding her that—oh God!— they were actually in a bed together. "You're not naked, are you?"

He met her gaze, then lifted the covers.

She didn't *have* to look underneath, but she bit her lip and did anyway—and found the same pair of gray shorts he'd worn last night. Which was a relief—except for the enormous bulge in front that nearly melted her on the spot. Her eyes stuck there like two magnets that couldn't pull away.

When finally they did, she found him flashing the most wicked look she'd ever seen on his handsome, unshaven face. She suffered all the guilt and shock that surely painted her own. "What?" she said.

"Nothing," he replied, looking annoyingly satisfied.

"Shut up," she snapped. "I'm going to sleep." With that, she turned away and brusquely switched off the lamp on the bedside table, drowning them both in darkness except for the beam from the security light outside.

She lay with her back to him, thinking—*Go to sleep. Go to sleep. Go to sleep.*

But her heart raced, her skin tingled, and her whole being ached.

And she imagined him curling into her from behind, spooning her so that she could feel that marvelous erection pressing into her, full and stiff.

It would be so easy, so dreadfully easy, to turn over, into his arms . . . to sink into hot, spine-tingling kisses . . . to slip her leg between his and feel his hardness . . . to let their bodies mingle in the dark shadows while a crisp, salty breeze wafted through the window to bathe their bodies in sweet tropical air.

Stop this. But she couldn't. God help her, she wanted him. Like she'd *always* wanted him. Time and distance and growing up hadn't changed that, much as she wished it had.

She quietly rolled over, just to look at him, study his face in shadow, watch him sleep.

She flinched when she found him peering back, dangerously near, only a mere pillow away. "What's wrong, kitten? Can't sleep?"

A jagged sensation of desire zigzagged through her chest and belly—but she flopped back over in bed to face away from him again. "I can sleep just fine, thanks." *Yeah, sure I can.*

His voice came as warm as the night, deep as sin itself. "Seize the night with me, kitten. I dare you."

The hot invitation hung in the air, sultry and sweet. She didn't answer as fast as she should have, darn it—but finally managed to say, "No."

"You don't sound sure."

"You'll have to take my word for it." *And so will I.*

He said nothing more, but she could *feel* him in the bed next to her—she could smell him, sense his presence, his very maleness.

She'd always been weak with him, *always.* Even when she knew no good could come of it. He was her greatest temptation and her worst mistake. Hadn't she learned her lesson by now?

She let out a sigh, tried to breathe evenly, tried to think of sleep.

But no matter how she sliced it, it was going to be a very long night.

A week after Kat's graduation
Ten years ago

Another half hour and she was free. At least for today. A summer job at her father's gallery had seemed like such a good idea before . . . well, before graduation and what had happened with Brock. Or what *hadn't* happened with Brock. Now, she spent most of her time on the job praying she wouldn't run into him, and so far, she'd gotten amazingly lucky. She worked out front; he worked in the back rooms, or was out running errands for her dad. But how long could that last? How long could she escape facing him?

Even now, as she stood watching the last customer of the day leave through the plate-glass door, her face warmed at the hideous memory of the seduction that wasn't. It was hard enough to believe she'd been so bold. But even harder to believe it hadn't worked. Her heart turned to ground glass in her chest each time she relived the pain.

Maybe deep inside she'd known he wouldn't want her. Maybe that was why she'd made a move so very extreme, as opposed to, say, asking him out for a burger and Coke one day after work. Still, it was hard to believe the guy had turned down a naked girl in his lap—talk about the ultimate rejection! "A guy just doesn't do that. A guy just doesn't turn down a naked chick in his lap!" That's what Nina had said when Kat had gotten her on the phone afterward, in tears.

"Maybe he's gay?" Nina had suggested the next day in Kat's bedroom. They'd been polishing off a pint of Ben & Jerry's in consolation.

Kat had simply flashed her a look of disbelief, spooned a bite of chocolate chip cookie dough ice cream into her mouth, and they'd both sighed. One look at Brock and no woman on the planet could think he was gay.

"Well, either way, guess this means he's not pendant-worthy," Nina had said.

Guess so, Kat thought now, turning toward the rear of the gallery to peer briefly at her stone pendant in its frame, before walking back toward the front door to turn the OPEN sign to CLOSED.

The sad truth she'd been trying to deal with ever since graduation night was the same conclusion she'd known all along: He just plain didn't want her. She was too much of a little girl for him. Even naked. In his lap. Oh God. Had that really happened?

A lump rose to her throat, and she had to close her eyes for a few seconds to hold back tears. She reached to the edge of one of the gallery's pedestals for balance. She might have cried herself to sleep a few nights this week over Brock Denton, but she'd just made a decision—she wasn't shedding one more stupid tear on him.

"Hey, kitten."

Her heart stopped.

Oh God, oh God, oh God. Don't turn around. Just leave.

Unfortunately, her purse was in the office, which lay behind her, which was also where *he* was. And even if she decided to leave it behind to achieve a quick escape, she couldn't avoid him all summer.

So she swallowed back the threat of tears and turned to look at him—but she wasn't friendly. "What do you want?"

She made the mistake of peering into his dark eyes, which were no less than hypnotic. With that same black stubble sloping over a strong jawbone and a gaze that seemed to see into her soul—no doubt about it, he was a god of all that was hot and sexy. "To say I'm sorry."

Well, *that* was the last thing she'd expected. Brock Denton apologizing? Even those gray eyes of his were a little warmer than she'd ever seen them before. Not that it was good enough. "Excuse me," she said pointedly, pushing past him toward the office.

Stepping inside, she grabbed up her purse and came back out, starting for the door. It was just hitting her fully all over again that he'd seen her naked without returning the favor—and that she had to get out of there, now. Without looking at him, she said, "I'm locking up on my way out, so be sure you lock the back when you leave."

"Wait, kitten. Don't go." His hand closed warm around her arm as she tried to sweep past him.

She looked up to find his eyes far too close and penetrating, her whole body tingling from his touch. He was near enough to kiss.

"Heard you got a birthday coming up."

"So?" *Whatever you do, don't start trembling.*

"Just thought I could make it up to you. We could go somewhere." He gave his head a slight, oh-so-provocative tilt. "I could give you that present you wanted. Just make it for your birthday instead."

She swallowed back the lump that had just risen to her throat.

Sex. They were talking about it the same as if it were a sweater, or a charm bracelet. But she couldn't blame *him* for that—she was the one who'd laid sex out on the table between them so bluntly.

Ideally, the offer would come with dinner and a movie at the very least, but she knew Brock didn't have money to spare—what little he made went toward taking care of his sick grandpa, out at the swamp.

"Friday night?" he asked.

"That's my birthday."

"I know."

That impressed her, just a little, that he knew the actual day, had perhaps even consulted a calendar. Frankly, she was so wild about him that it didn't take much. She so wanted to see the good in him, to believe it was there. She was such a pushover where he was concerned.

"I have a party that night. My birthday party. At the country club."

He let out a soft, low chuckle. "Don't suppose I'm invited."

She didn't know where to go with that. Her father would have a heart attack if she invited Brock, and it wasn't like he'd fit with her friends. She opened her mouth to reply, but nothing came out.

"Don't worry, kitten," he said with a slight headshake. "Not my scene anyway. But maybe you'll meet me after?"

She bit her lip. Any sane girl would tell him to go to hell. But she was getting a glimpse of something she'd never really expected—a kinder, gentler Brock Denton. If she'd found him alluring before, well, now it was all she could do not to melt beneath the weight of his gaze, the manly scent of him, the urge to press against him, right here in the gallery. "The party'll go late," she said. "But I could maybe . . . slip out for a while."

A slight nod. "Sounds good."

"Pick me up at the front gate." She knew he was familiar with the club—he'd run errands for her father there before. "Ten o'clock."

The vaguest hint of a smile made its way onto his face. "See you then."

"Don't fuck up this time," she said on impulse. She never used the "f" word, but thought it might reinforce the idea that she wasn't a little girl. "You have a lot to make up for."

The attitude earned her a grin. "Don't worry, kitten. I never make the same mistake twice."

Chapter Six

The sun beaming through the window forced Brock's eyes slowly open. He instinctively turned to look beside him—to find the sheets rumpled but the bed empty. Even the pillow was gone. A small knot of disappointment settled low in his gut.

"Oh, Kat," he called, his voice echoing through the tiny house, any letdown well disguised. "Sister Katrina of the Tiny Bikini—where are you?"

No answer. And no water running in the bathroom, but surely that was where he'd find her. Pushing up from the bed, he meandered in that direction, but discovered the bathroom door standing wide open.

Great. His seduction attempts had driven the girl right out of the house.

Feeling bad in a way he usually didn't, he located the near-empty donut box on the counter, grabbed up a glazed one in a napkin, and headed outside to find her.

The tropical morning air hit him crisp and sweet, and he suffered a brief—and weird—longing for a calmer life. Life on a deserted island with Kat? Even if she resisted his advances forever, the last couple of days had been oddly nice.

Stopping near the picnic table, he looked around—where the hell could she be? The beach lay straight ahead, and on either side of him, nothing but palm- and banyan-laden woods.

That was when he spotted something he hadn't seen before—a hammock stretched between two palm trees on the edge of the jungly island interior not more than a stone's throw away. Padding through the cool sand, he found Kat curled up in a little kittenlike ball, fast asleep, her pillow tucked beneath her head, her little green pajamas as cute as ever.

He stepped up close, then waved the donut gently back and forth in front of her nose. "Wake up, kitten," he said softly. "Time for breakfast."

A few seconds later, those sweet blue eyes fluttered open. At first, she squinted at him, as if trying to figure out who he was and where they were. Then she wordlessly snatched the donut from his hand and took a big bite.

"How long have you been out here?" he asked.

She stretched, a move that arched her breasts pleasingly against the front of her top. "All night," she said on a yawn.

Damn it. He'd not meant to drive her from the bed just by sharing it with her.

No, he'd meant to make her break a promise to the man she'd agreed to marry.

In the light of day, that seemed just about as bad. And not nearly so noble as he'd thought it yesterday. "Sorry, kitten. I didn't mean to make you so uncomfortable."

Her reply came brisk and resolute. "Sure you did. But that's okay.

It's nice out here. I'm going to sleep here from now on, until my parents come for us." She took another bite from her donut.

"No," he said. "*I'll* sleep here. You'll sleep in the bed. It's your house—I'll clear out at night so you can sleep in peace."

"Typical," she replied, rolling out of the hammock to her feet in one swift move.

"What?" They stood just a few feet apart, and as usual, he wanted to kiss her.

"You come barging into my vacation, and no matter what I do, you tell me it's going to be the opposite way. I tell you I haven't had sex with my fiancé—you insist that I should have. I tell you I'm not having sex with *you*—you ignore me and keep right on trying. I tell you to sleep on the floor—you get in the bed. So I tell you I'll sleep in the hammock, but no, now *you'll* sleep in the hammock." She concluded with a huffing breath, then started to march away, stuffing a big chunk of donut in her mouth as she went.

He looked after her, feet rooted in place in the sand. "Where are you going?"

She spoke around the bite of donut. "I'm getting dressed. And then I'm going to take a walk." She stopped then, turning to glare at him. "And if you tell me I'm *not* taking a walk, I will go into that house, find a frying pan, and beat you over the head with it. Got it?"

He stood looking at her, a little dumbfounded. "Sure, kitten," he said quietly, not wanting to fight her anymore. "Take your walk. I won't stop you."

Watching her trudge on toward the bungalow, he felt shitty. He'd been trying to protect her. In more ways than one. But maybe, in a way, he was just as bad as her dad had always been. Maybe Kat didn't *need* protecting. Even if she did, she obviously didn't like it. So maybe he'd been wrong about trying to seduce her into not getting married. Maybe it was just none of his goddamn business. And maybe . . . he just wanted it to be.

He still craved her like he'd never craved a woman before—but maybe the *truly* noble thing to do was just leave her alone until they got off this island. They still had three nights here, yet maybe it was time to just let this go.

Exhaling a tired sigh, he dropped down into the hammock she'd just vacated. He smelled the soft scent of her shampoo on the pillow where her head had just lain. He vaguely wished he'd brought one of the few remaining donuts for himself, but no way he was going back in the house right now—he was gonna put some distance between them, because he knew that's what she wanted.

A few minutes later, he caught sight of her marching down through the soft sand, headed for the beach. She wore a beige halter top and a jungle-print skirt of brown that hung to her ankles and had a little drawstring in front that drew the fabric into a sexy vee below her belly button. He suffered the urge to follow but let her go on her way.

Once she was gone, nearly out of sight at the shore, he departed the hammock for the bungalow. Truth was, *he* wanted to get away from the place right now, too, away from the little mess he'd created here.

Looking through drawers, he found more of Nina's ex's kidnapped clothing. Checking the waistband in a pair of khaki shorts, he discovered they weren't far off in size and put them on. He slipped an olive golf shirt over his head and, though it was tight in the shoulders, it would do. He even found a pair of men's water sandals with sturdy fabric straps. Funny, until now, it hadn't even occurred to him to put on clothes. Nope, until now, his whole mission here had been about seducing Kat.

Well, maybe it was *high time* for clothes. And time to forget—for the first time in almost ten years—about being on a mission. Maybe it was time to quit trying to save people or change the world or influence the outcome of things. *Just for a few days, dude, try to be a normal guy.*

And what would he do today if he were a normal guy?

The notion of going fishing crossed his mind almost instantly. He didn't do it often, just occasionally, when he needed to unwind. He didn't particularly enjoy the activity, but it was relaxing, and it always made him think of his grandfather, who'd taught him to fish when he was a kid, and he always had this crazy idea that if his grandpa could look down from heaven and see him with a fishing pole in his hand, he'd be happy.

Wondering where a guy might find a fishing pole around here, he glanced toward the closet next to the bathroom, but then remembered it was locked. Then he headed outside to the storage shed—a more likely spot anyway.

Sure enough, an old rod and reel stood against one wall, looking rusty but operational. A small, equally rusted tackle box sat on the ground beside it. Inside, only a few hooks and lures—hardly the tools of a master fisherman, but he'd never *claimed* to be a master fisherman, so it would do.

Deciding they could afford to sacrifice a slice of cheese for bait, he retrieved one from the fridge, then headed out on the trail that led to the boat dock. It was a nice lagoon, probably a decent fishing spot. Hell, if he got lucky, maybe they'd be grilling fresh fish for dinner tonight. Despite himself, he knew it would feel good if he could provide a meal for Kat, all things considered.

Stepping into the clearing, he instantly surveyed what was left of her boat—which was nothing. Any remnants remaining after the explosion had promptly sunk. Debris still scattered the ground. He'd have to see about getting the government to handle the cleanup—particularly getting the hull of the Stingray hauled up and out so the dock bay would be usable again. And for the first time, as he found a nice spot to sit—a little knob of earth that jutted slightly over the water—it occurred to him that when Clark Spencer showed up here, there'd be some explaining to do. Shit.

Pride insisted he not let Spencer think he'd devolved into a criminal who had people shooting at him. But he didn't want to let Spencer know he was a fed, either. For some reason, he'd trusted Kat with the information—but he didn't trust her father. Self-respect made him want to let the guy know he'd done all right for himself, but at the same time, it also made him feel like—*Who gives a goddamn what he thinks of me now?*

He ruminated on the unhappy parting of ways he'd had with Kat's dad as he attached a fuzzy fishing lure to the line, then hooked a small, jagged square of cheese over the hook. Had Spencer ever told Kat about that? No—she'd have brought it up by now. And *he* could tell her, if he wanted. But even as much as he hated Clark Spencer, he didn't hate him *enough* to tell Kat what the man had done to him back then.

Just as he drew the fishing rod back over his head, ready to cast his line, a gunshot blasted through the air, whirring past his head. Jesus Christ. He swung his gaze to the open water—and found a big white yacht headed his way.

Brock let the pole drop from his hand as he jumped up and lunged toward the cover of trees. Breaking through dense leaves, he landed hard on the ground. He didn't stop once he was hidden, though—he barreled over the trail, through the dense greenery, with one lone thought pummeling him. *Gotta get to Kat. Gotta get her off the beach.*

By the time he reached the bungalow, his heart pounded painfully against his ribs, and his brain was working just about as fast. He and Kat couldn't come back here, to the house—they'd be sitting ducks. They'd have to take to the interior, make this a game of hide-and-seek—it was their only chance. He had the water sandals he'd snagged from inside, figuring they'd make walking the trail to the dock a little easier—but Kat would need shoes, too, if they were to have even a chance of survival.

He stormed through the screen door, scanning the room. Shoes, shoes—where were they? He rushed to the armoire next to the bed, and voilà—Kat's pink flip-flops sat on the floor next to a slightly sturdier-looking pair of leather sandals, which he snatched up in his hand before racing back out.

Once he hit the sand, it was full throttle—he ran toward the beach like a man on fire.

Upon reaching the sand packed more firmly by the tide, he spotted her footsteps, thankful they told him which way she'd gone, since the beach stretched for as far as he could see in both directions. She'd walked *away* from the side of the island where the Morales brothers were currently pulling up to shore—thank God.

Never breaking his stride, he kept running, running, until finally he caught sight of her walking along the water's edge as it lapped gently over her feet with each rush of the morning tide. He wanted desperately to call to her, warn her of trouble, but he also couldn't risk leading the brothers to them any sooner than necessary by yelling. If they were lucky, they could hide in the woods until Francisco gave up and went away—so long as they got a head start without alerting the smugglers to where they were.

So he sprinted as fast as his feet would carry him, and it was only when a few yards separated them that she heard his approach and turned around. The look on her face said she was about to yell at him for following her—until she saw the look on *his* face.

"What?" she said, sounding as breathless as he felt.

He let his palms curve softly around her elbows as he peered into frightened eyes. "Boat's back, kitten."

Her gaze widened, saying she understood exactly which boat he meant. "Wh-what do we do?"

"We hide."

She looked around nervously. "Where?"

"Put these on," he said, holding out her shoes.

"Oh," she murmured, then hurried to slip them on her sand-covered feet.

"And come with me." He took her hand and set off in a jog toward the treed area that lay just over a small bluff above the beach.

By the time they were under cover beneath the big, shady canopy of green, Kat's heart was in her throat. How had this happened? How was it possible those bad men had actually come back?

Brock had told her it could happen, but she'd been so preoccupied—with him—that she hadn't really believed it.

The fear she'd felt the other day was nothing compared to what assailed her now. Because the first time the bad guys had been here, she hadn't exactly known about it until it was over. But now they were coming onto her island. To chase Brock down. Which meant chasing her down, too. The two of them were going to be hunted like animals.

She dropped to her knees at the hideous realization, her hand slipping from Brock's as she fell, her knees digging into the soft dirt beneath her.

"What—" he started to ask, stopping, turning, but he went quiet as she heaved, throwing up her donut.

She rested on hands and knees, breathing heavy, tasting vomit, not believing any of this was true—and yet it was. And she had to deal.

Trying to swallow back the bad taste, she pushed to her feet. "I'm sorry."

Brock's hand rose warm to her cheek, his face close, as he whispered. "Nothing to be sorry for, kitten. But listen to me, and listen very carefully."

She lifted her gaze to his, heart pounding fast.

Their eyes locked for a long moment before he finally spoke. "Anything happens to me, you don't waste time crying, or stopping to see if I'm all right. You run, you hide, you stay hidden, and quiet, for as long as you have to. Understand?"

She stood before him, not quite able to fathom how their bickering had suddenly changed into this—talk of life or death. *His* death. She swallowed.

"Tell me you understand, kitten. Tell me you get it. I need to know."

She forced herself to nod, with his hand still cupping her jaw. "I get it."

"Okay," he said. Then, "You all right now? Better?"

Better was a stretch, but she faked it. "Yeah, I'm fine. Let's go."

"Good girl," he said, and under other circumstances, she might have resented that, but his eyes shone reverent, worried, and she knew he was honestly praising her for pulling herself together and being tough enough to continue.

Grabbing her hand once more, Brock led her through the woods again, but they soon battled thick vines and undergrowth. He tried to knock them away and hold them aside, and Kat followed dutifully behind, trying to watch where she stepped. "There are probably big snakes in here," she said.

"Yeah," he agreed, but neither elaborated, just kept walking, pushing through. "Don't suppose you know your way around this part of the island at all," he said over his shoulder.

"No—my first time on this side."

"Any idea how big the island is?"

She frantically searched her memory, trying to recall. "Seems like my dad said it was around two miles this way"—she motioned crossways with her hand, indicating the length parallel to the beach—"and about a mile wide."

Brock nodded. "Know anything about the topography? Any knowledge of caves, ravines, anything that would make a good hiding place?"

She shook her head, feeling useless. "I don't know—I'm sorry."

"Nothing to apologize for, honey—just hoping against hope, that's all."

He turned back ahead and continued to lead her into the depths of the island interior. Above, thick brown vines that made her think of Tarzan hung from trees, tall pines shrouded them, and somewhere a bird made a cawing noise. Leaves and palm fronds rustled in a moist breeze.

"Where do you think they are now?"

It took Brock a minute to answer. "Depends. They've probably found the bungalow and realized nobody's there. If they take to the woods around the house, we could be safe here. But if they head to the beach and follow our footprints, they could be on our trail pretty soon."

"And . . . what's our plan? Just keep walking and hope we stay ahead of them?"

He looked over his shoulder and spoke soft but frank. "Right now, we're looking for a hiding place for you."

She knitted her eyebrows. "Not you, too?"

"Hiding together wouldn't be in your best interest."

"But then what will *you* do?"

When he peered over his shoulder at her again, she got the distinct impression he was holding something back.

"Tell me, Brock. Tell me what you're planning."

He hesitated another minute, then said, "All right, here it is. I want to find a good place for you to hide, then I'm gonna go back out and play cat and mouse with them."

She pulled in her breath, horrified. "Why?"

He blinked, still looking reticent. He'd stopped walking, so she did, too.

Finally, he looked her in the eye. "Because I'd much rather have something happen to just me than to both of us. And this is the best way to prevent something happening to *you*."

No longer giving any heed to what she might step on, she propelled herself toward him, letting her hands curl into fists in his shirt. "No!" she said. "No, no, no."

"Kitten, listen to me——" His hands circled her wrists.

"No," she said again, then began shaking her head. "Please don't do this, Brock. Don't make a target of yourself just to save me."

"Your safety is what concerns me right now. It's the best way."

"No, it's not, and I'll tell you why. You're setting me up for a lifetime of guilt and misery. If you die because you're protecting me, I won't be able to live with myself. Do you want that on my head?"

He ran a hand back through his dark hair, looking troubled, and when a bead of sweat rolled down his forehead, she instinctually reached up to wipe it away. He braced his hands on her bare shoulders. "Of course I don't. But I don't see any other way to keep you safe." His eyes were so earnest, suddenly possessing depths she hadn't known possible—and in that moment, she understood, beyond a shadow of a doubt, that he cared for her, at least just a little. If pressed, he'd probably claim this had something to do with her being a civilian, but it was more than that—she knew.

And she cared for him, too—a *lot*. Always had, always would. She hadn't wanted to let herself believe that over the last couple of days, but it was useless to keep lying to herself. "Keep us *both* safe," she offered in little more than a whisper. "For me."

She watched him take a deep breath, then peer down at her. "And just how do you propose I do that, honey? Because if it was that simple, I would. I don't have a death wish, believe me. But—"

"When we find a place to hide, just hide *with* me."

His brow narrowed. "Have you ever heard the term 'fish in a barrel'?"

"Who says they'll find us? *Look* at this." She motioned around them at the dense greenery. Besides the tall, thin pines, the island's interior teemed with clumps of wax myrtle, live oaks, and large banyan trees. "The island might seem small, but we'll be like needles in a big jungly haystack out here." She'd released her fistfuls of his shirt a while ago, but didn't hesitate to press her palms flat to his chest as she looked up into his eyes. "Besides, I don't want to hide alone. If you leave me alone out here, Brock, I'll panic. I'll do something stupid. And . . ." She could hardly even bring herself to imagine this, but she couldn't avoid it, either. "And if they find me, Brock . . ." She shook her head helplessly. "I don't want to be alone for that, either—okay? So I'm begging you not to leave me. Please don't make me be alone out here. Stay with me."

Chapter Seven

*D*amn it, no way in hell should he be letting her pleas sway him. But the words sounded so strangely familiar, until Brock figured out . . . they were his. From a long, long time ago. *Please don't leave. Don't leave us alone, Mama. Please don't go.*

His breath caught roughly. Shit. Hadn't gone there in his head in a while. And not what he needed right now, that was for damn sure.

But the fact was, he knew what it was to be left alone, frightened, not knowing what would happen. And that knowledge, combined with the look in Kat's eyes, meant he couldn't do it. No matter how much he wanted to keep her safe. He lifted one palm back to her soft cheek. "Okay, kitten," he said, low. "I won't leave you."

She reached up to latch on to his arm. "Promise?" Her blue eyes remained so reaching, desperate.

He still didn't know if it was the answer that would be best for her in the end—but what he did know was that he couldn't deny her. "Promise." Then he yanked his gaze away before he did something stupid and impulsive like kiss her, and said, "But we've gotta move now."

Taking her hand again, he resumed pulling her along through the brush and low growth that blanketed the ground. He looked for cover and saw . . . nothing. The foliage was dense, thank God, with ferns below and tall trees stretching skyward, a green roof with only hints of sunlight peeking through—but the terrain was too flat and the covering of smaller trees too sparse, despite what Kat might think. Hiding behind one would only expose them on the other side.

That's when he heard it—something besides their own noise.

"Stop," he said softly, and they both stilled in place.

Not far away, someone else waded through the low growth. The brothers had found their footprints.

He didn't make eye contact with Kat—he couldn't let himself witness her fear—and instead glanced back to see if one or more Morales brother could be spotted. No—thank God. Yet they weren't far away.

"We've gotta move, honey—fast," he said, then pulled her to the right, thinking to change their direction from the fairly straight line they'd followed up to now. Might not put as much distance between them and their pursuers—but it should help throw them off the trail.

Kat stayed quiet behind him, and moved pretty damn fast, too, despite the difficult terrain. Once or twice, her long skirt got caught on a branch, but she was quick to tear it away and continue on their path.

Just keep moving and get her safe. Get her out of harm's way. It was all that mattered right now.

"Stop," he said again a few minutes later, his rough whisper bringing them to a halt. They listened—and this time, the sounds of someone else traveling the forest came from farther away. He dared glance into Kat's eyes and found a bit of relief there. Premature, maybe, but for the moment, his emotions echoed hers.

Turning, Brock realized the island's interior had begun to grow blessedly thicker. More vines blocked his path, walking was slower. He spotted an enormous snake—a pale yellowish color—slithering around a tree, but kept walking without calling it to Kat's attention.

And then, finally, he found what he'd been looking for. A sizable rock outcropping ascending vertically for maybe ten feet. At its base, clumps of thick ferns and wax myrtle, and even a convenient cubbyhole opening a couple of feet deep into the stone. It wasn't the greatest hiding place he'd ever located, but given the landscape, it was the best they were gonna get. And at least they'd, by chance, worn the right colors today—earth tones as close to camouflage as you could get without visiting the hunting department in a sporting goods store. "Here," he said, pointing.

Crouching, Kat moved into the indention in the rock, and he followed. Being close wasn't a question now but a necessity; they sat shoulder to shoulder, thigh to thigh, knees drawn up in front of them. When he turned to look at her, her face was beautifully near. "Doing okay?"

She looked uncertain, but said, "Yeah, fine."

He gave a commending nod. "Good. You're doing great." Then he squeezed her knee without quite thinking, and their eyes met again—yet he didn't pull his hand away. She might want to fight the wild sexual attraction between them, but right now he thought they both probably needed a little human contact.

"This is gonna be okay, kitten," he promised. He had no idea if he could keep her safe, but he would try like hell, and he needed to reassure her, keep her strong.

She nodded again, and they went quiet—until he realized he could only barely hear the rustling sounds in the distance now, like maybe the brothers were moving away. *Keep right on moving, guys, keep right on going.*

"What do they smuggle?" Kat whispered when he least expected it. He supposed she was wondering what the hell was so important that they felt the need to chase him down. "Drugs?"

"Nothing that bad, actually."

She looked at him. "What then?"

"Just something valuable. And stolen."

"Like art?"

"Sort of. But not exactly."

"Why can't you just tell me? Given that I'm up to my neck in this now."

"Because it's not really all that important, and the less you know, the better."

"Why?"

Because they have *to kill me—I know* everything. *If you don't know anything, maybe they'll take mercy on you.* "Because I say so, that's why."

"Tell me." Her eyes narrowed demandingly.

"No." Then he looked down at where he still touched her knee through her skirt, and decided to change the subject. "This is pretty," he said, rubbing the fabric between finger and thumb.

"I thought I'd lost this outfit somehow, but I guess I left it out here last summer. I just stumbled across it this morning."

Note to self: To distract Kat, talk about fashion. He found his gaze moving from her drawn-up knees behind them to her cleavage. "This top does great things for your breasts, by the way."

She rolled her eyes at him. "At a time like this, you're talking about my breasts?"

He shrugged. "Gotta talk about *something.*"

She let out a disgusted breath, but he didn't mind—at least they'd gotten off the topic of smuggling.

"And for your information, that was a sincere compliment. So now that you know, maybe you want to wear this top for old Ian, give him a thrill." Although by the time he finished, he had a feeling any chances of her believing in his sincerity had been blown.

Her reply sounded speculative, like she was thinking aloud. "Ian's not really much of a boob man."

Brock blinked his disbelief. What self-respecting guy *wasn't* a boob man? "What kind of guy *is* he?"

She thought it over for a minute. "He's the kind of guy who just . . . loves me for me, for the person I am."

Damn, that was just weird. Not the loving her for her part—but add what she'd just said to the fact that she and Ian hadn't had sex, and he got a lot more skeptical about the whole relationship. A guy who couldn't appreciate Kat's beauty and sex appeal in addition to the rest of her . . . well, there was something wrong with him. "Kitten," he said hesitantly, "don't scream at me for saying this—especially given that we're trying to keep quiet here—but . . . is it possible Ian's gay?"

Her eyes flew wide, and he instinctively slapped his hand over her mouth.

Clearly realizing it was to keep her from letting out the shriek he'd seen coming, she *whooshed* out a big, warm breath against his palm, then reached up and pulled it away. She spoke quiet but cuttingly. "How dare you, you presumptuous idiot. I get what you're thinking—we haven't had sex, and I just told you he wasn't into my breasts. Which I regret sharing immensely now, by the way. But for your info, it's not as if he hasn't *tried* to have sex with me. He has—quite vehemently, I might add. So trust me—he's not gay. And come Saturday night, after our wedding, we're going to make wild monkey love all night, swing from the chandeliers naked, and do all *kinds* of things *you* haven't ever even thought about."

He worked to hide his smile, but said, "Now that I doubt. I've done a lot of stuff, kitten, and if there's anything I *haven't* done, I've definitely thought about it."

It earned him another eye roll, this one accompanied by a scowl.

He ignored both, instead opting to imagine Kat making wild monkey love—but not with Ian. He suspected the guy wouldn't even appreciate the vision of Kat swinging naked from a chandelier. Gay or not, something felt very wrong between Kat and her fiancé, no matter how hard she tried to convince Brock otherwise.

Just then, a slight rustling sound quickened his pulse. He grabbed Kat's wrist and their eyes met, his issuing a silent warning. She stayed quiet, and they both heard it again—something large moving through the woods nearby. Shit.

Brock's vantage point didn't allow him to see far, and nothing in his line of sight appeared out of place. But when the noise grew closer, he exchanged another glance with Kat, and this time slid his arm around her, pulled her close, squeezed her shoulder. He worked to make his whisper nearly inaudible. "Just stay quiet, kitten."

Her body had gone tense against his, and he couldn't blame her. This wasn't the first time he'd been on the run from a criminal, nor the first time he'd been without his weapon—but it was the first time he'd had to protect someone he knew . . . and cared about.

Closer, closer came the movement through the trees. So close that Brock would have sworn one of the brothers had to be practically standing on top of them. Looking up, he saw a dark hand push a hanging banyan vine out of the way. *Stay still as a statue, kitten. No movement now—none.* His heart pounded against his chest as sweat beaded on his forehead.

That's when Francisco Morales came into view, directly in front of them, not five feet away. His eyes glimmered with hate and grim determination—he clutched his trademark .45 firmly in one hand.

Brock could have sworn he almost heard Kat's heart beating as his grip on her shoulder tightened involuntarily.

And then, slowly, so slowly, Francisco moved on. And Brock let himself breathe again. He looked at Kat in time to see her eyes drop shut in relief.

They remained silent as Francisco waded slowly through the ferns and myrtle, leaves *shushing* around him, until, little by little, the sound faded to nothing.

Finally, Brock felt it was safe to whisper again. "You okay?"

She nodded, looking none the worse for wear, and without thinking, he leaned over and kissed her forehead, tasting the sweet, salty sheen on her skin. After, she looked surprised . . . but not upset.

How would her lips taste? he couldn't help wondering. He'd shared that one long kiss with her, a million years ago, but she'd refused him last night—and he wondered how she would taste right here, right now, beneath the heavy, draping pine boughs, the island moisture seeming to cocoon them. Her breast pressing against his side made him wonder how *they* would taste, too, and he suffered the yearning to feel her taut nipple on his tongue.

He found his gaze dropping there, to her tanned cleavage, before raising it back to her eyes. Where he saw exactly what he expected: trepidation and guilt mixed with a heavy measure of desire.

But the guilt must have won out, since she whispered, "Brock, you can't kiss me, even on the forehead."

"Shhh," he said, putting a finger to his lips almost before she'd finished talking. "Quiet, kitten."

Because Francisco's movements had only just now weakened to nothing—it wasn't yet safe to chitchat. And because he just really didn't want to hear her say he couldn't have her at the moment.

Despite the fear for her running through his veins, something else raced through them, as well: a red-hot hunger, perhaps deeper and more intense than he'd ever felt for a woman before.

Just because you can't have her, because she turned you down?

Or just because you're afraid for her right now, want to keep her safe?

It was both of those things, but it was something else, too. Something in her bluer-than-blue eyes, something in the smiles he drew from her when he least expected her to give him anything so sweet. Something in the way she looked so comfortable in those tiny little tops—until she remembered to cover them up. Something in the memory of the forbidden seduction she'd once attempted, and which he regretted rejecting more with each passing minute.

You broke the rules for me once, kitten. He wanted, more than anything, to make her break them again. He wanted to bring back the Kat who would never walk down the aisle with some schlep she didn't feel any passion for.

Not that he should be thinking about sex at the moment. He had to hope he got them out of this alive before sex could ever again become an issue between them. But it was a hell of a good motivation.

"Tell me about your life, kitten," he said softly.

Kat looked up, surprised. His eyes loomed close. "Does this mean it's safe to talk now?"

He gave a short nod. "Quietly. I haven't heard anything in a while."

Something about the simple question set her heart beating as rapidly as pursuit by mad killers. Since when did Brock Denton ask about "her life"? "What do you want to know?"

His gray gaze looked thoughtful, almost probing and sincere—although she hesitated to give him that much credit. "Anything you want to tell me about. Where do you live? With your parents? Or a place of your own?"

"I have an apartment near the shore. Dad really wanted me to get a condo—you know, invest and not throw money away on renting—but I wasn't ready to commit to something that big at the time."

"Live alone?"

She nodded, then balked slightly. "Well, except for my cat, Vincent."

"Weird cat name."

She flashed a look of annoyance. "After Van Gogh. He happens to be one of my favorite painters."

"Is the cat missing an ear or something?"

"No, his ears are perfectly intact." But she couldn't help being impressed that he knew a little something about Van Gogh. "It so happens that his fur is a yellowy color that reminds me of a shade Van Gogh was particularly fond of using."

"Well, if the cat starts acting depressed, I'd hide the knives."

She couldn't resist a small grin, mainly because *he* was giving *her* one, and it made him dreadfully handsome.

"What kind of cat?"

She blinked. "What *kind*?"

Next to her, Brock shrugged. His arm still rested around her shoulder, so she felt the slight movement all across her upper back—which sent it echoing through her chest, as well. "Just thought it might be some special breed or something. Seems like something your dad would insist upon."

She couldn't help laughing—softly, of course, under the circumstances. She loved her father, but Brock had him pegged. "He tried to, actually. But I thought it would be smarter to go to a shelter and get a kitty who might not find a home otherwise."

"So is Vincent fending for himself this week, out hunting mice, what?"

"My mom's feeding him and spending a little time with him each day so he won't be too lonely. He sleeps with me most nights, so he's probably wondering where I am."

His expression locked on to her so sexually that she felt it in her panties. "Lucky cat. Not the wondering-where-you-are part—the sleeping-with-you part."

She unwittingly slid her tongue halfway across her upper lip before she realized his gaze was parked there. She dropped her eyes to his chest and pulled her tongue back into her mouth. "Yeah, I figured that's what you meant."

"So, gonna miss your apartment?"

She gave a reluctant nod, not liking to admit she was giving up anything at all to marry Ian. Yet didn't big change always require some kind of sacrifice? "Kind of, but you can't live in two places."

"Does Vincent get to come?"

"Of course."

"Does he still get to sleep with you?"

God, she hadn't even thought about that. Ian would just have to realize that the move was going to be jarring enough for the cat without tossing him out of bed, too. "Of course," she said again, as if there were no question.

"Ian's an understanding man," Brock replied. " 'Cause me—I don't know that I'd be willing to share you."

She smirked, giving her head a tilt. "It's a cat, not a guy."

He arched one knowing brow. "But it's a *guy cat*."

She couldn't hold in a small trill of laughter, yet they both slapped hands over her mouth as soon as it leaked out—and all merriment

fled the scene as they recalled exactly why they were huddled together, crouched down against a big rock in the forest. She looked
into his dark eyes as the seriousness of the situation took back over.

Now would be a really easy time to kiss him. Because his mouth was
so close and his gaze so possessive. And because maybe it would
make her feel safe, just for a minute, as it did when they were talking, as it did simply to have his body so near.

But she couldn't do that, of course.

"Tell me what else," he said, eyes never leaving hers, voice low
and deep. "About your life."

Wanting to kiss him had her a little flustered, so she bit her lip
and searched for something significant to say. "I . . . went to the U
of F and majored in art history with a minor in ceramics."

"Ceramics?"

She shrugged. "I know, that sounds about as complex as Bas-
ketweaving 101, but I'm a potter, and it's a highly specialized trade."

Now he looked interested, which she couldn't help liking. "A
potter? Like you make pottery?"

She nodded. "That's why my hands are such a mess." She held
them out, displaying her short nails and always-dry skin. She wasn't
sure why—maybe because she was afraid he might have noticed.
Acknowledging it, explaining why her hands weren't soft or supple
like other women's, made her feel better.

He took one of her hands between his. "They're not so bad," he
said, then winked. "I'd still let you touch me with them."

She rolled her eyes, but it came—unwittingly—with a smile. "I
work with my dad in the gallery, too," she went on. "I could have
taken the art history degree in a few different directions, but like
him, I really do love art, *and* the gallery. And it also fits with my passion for pottery. I'm having my very first show there next month, in
fact."

"That's nice, kitten," he said warmly.

"On Saturdays," she felt inspired to add, "I work with less-fortunate kids—helping them learn to use the wheel and throw pots. It's good for them. And for me, too, I guess. It makes me feel like I'm . . . doing some good in the world in my own way."

She had a feeling she'd run on at the mouth again as she seemed to have a habit of doing around him, so decided to shut up. As dedicated as she was to working with the kids, she didn't want Brock to think she'd become some holier-than-thou do-gooder. Not that she knew why she even cared. Yet therein lay the problem. As much as she wanted to stay true to Ian—she still wanted Brock to want her.

"That's . . . really a good thing, honey," Brock said, and he meant it. Even if it surprised him to find out Kat knew less-fortunate kids *existed*, let alone went out of her way to make them feel special. Hell, twenty-five years ago he might've *been* one of those kids.

How might it have influenced his life—or Bruno's—if someone had taken the time to teach him some craft, something he could make from nothing? If someone had treated him or Bruno like they mattered a little?

He tilted his head to one side and looked at her long and hard. Kat, an artist. He'd thought of her in a lot of ways over the years, but he'd never imagined her working with her hands, getting them dirty, and the image appealed for reasons he couldn't explain.

"What?" she said.

"Maybe you'll show me your pots sometime," he said. Although the second he spoke, he knew it had come out sounding more like he wanted to see something else. Her underwear, maybe. Or what was underneath.

Her eyes widened, luminescent as a ray of sun sifted down through the canopy of green above to light her face. "Um . . . maybe."

Yeah, *she'd* heard the sex in his voice, too. But he didn't mind.

"Tell me about the FBI," she said.

He cast a chiding look. "That's the thing about the FBI, kitten. Can't talk about it."

She pursed her lips, clearly perturbed. "Well then . . . tell me how you got into it. Surely you can say that much."

He gave a slow nod. That he could share. "First thing I did was go to the police academy—just wanted to be a cop."

"Why?" she asked, cutting him off before he'd really begun.

"I told you this part the other day. Just wanted to do something with my life."

She nodded, and he went on.

"So anyway, one of the instructors at the academy kind of took me under his wing. Guess he saw some potential in me, but he thought I needed more than the academy. At first that pissed me off, but deep inside, I knew he was right. He encouraged me to take night classes at a community college—so I took a couple English courses, a literature class—"

For some reason, her knowing smile stopped him cold. "Where you learned Shakespeare."

He returned a grin. "Yep. Also took a speech class."

"It all shows," she said, admiration in her gaze. He at once liked that and hated it. When he'd known her before, he'd prided himself on not caring what anyone thought of him, and it was easy to go back there with her, easy to want to keep their connection purely sexual, as it had been then. But the reality was, life had taught him that people's opinions of you mattered, and it filled him with masculine satisfaction to know Kat thought he'd turned out well.

"After the academy, my instructor said he thought I had the makings of an FBI agent. Plus, the fact that I didn't have much family is a big draw for them, too. So I checked it out, did the interviews and physical tests, went through the program at Quantico, and made it in."

"And then what?" she asked.

He would have liked to have told her. Everything. Every detail of every mission he'd ever worked. For some reason, his mind flashed on the two of them, lying naked in bed, spending a whole Sunday, him just talking, telling her the things he'd never been able to tell anyone before. Pure fantasy, of course. "Then nothing. 'Cause that, kitten, is where the story ends for you."

She gave a saucy little shrug that jostled her breasts slightly. "*Fine.* So—are you in danger like this often?"

"Sometimes."

"And do you win, or do you lose?"

He flashed an arrogant grin. "I'm here, aren't I? I always win, kitten. Always."

"Kitten."

She was resting, asleep, and Brock's voice flirted somewhere on the periphery of her mind, softer than she'd ever heard it.

"Kitten, honey, wake up. Quiet now, baby, but open your eyes."

So soft and deep, that voice. She could drown in it. She smelled the musky scent of him all around her, snuggled instinctively closer against his chest.

"This is serious, kitten—wake up for me now."

Something about that particular whispered plea broke through her sleepy fog. She opened her eyes and looked at him. Remembered they were hiding in the jungle. It was *very* serious. And his expression said something was wrong.

This time he didn't make a sound, just moved his lips. *They're back. Don't move.*

All the air drained from Kat's lungs. She held herself motionless, or tried to anyway—she was still trying to get full control of her mind and body. Sleep had been too sweet.

That's when she heard the startlingly loud rustle of leaves, then the crack of a twig. God, they sounded close enough to touch. Fear shot through her, finally waking her up, but also knocking her a bit off-balance inside. Bile rose to her throat, made her want to clutch at her chest, but she knew she couldn't move a muscle.

Beneath her palm beat Brock's heart—steady, sure, his chest warm. How long had she been touching him like that? She lifted her gaze to his, let their eyes lock. Felt for him a deep affection she shouldn't, and tried desperately to push it away.

The foliage *shushed* loudly once more, then ceased.

Still peering into Brock's eyes, emotion overwhelmed her—fear and attachment and confusion—and she let out the breath she'd been holding. Then accidentally shifted her foot against a fern, jarring the fronds.

Her stomach dropped. A cannon blast couldn't have sounded any louder.

She instinctively moved her gaze from Brock upward—to find a dark-skinned man with a thin mustache looking back, a different guy than the one they'd seen earlier.

"I almost hoped I wouldn't find you, Jimmy," the man said.

"You can pretend you didn't," Brock replied, his voice persuasive. "You can keep on walking, tell him you never saw a thing."

But despite the troubled look in his eyes, the man shook his head. "No, you lied. You made a fool out of me in front of my brother. I have no choice now, Jimmy—or whatever the hell your name is. I have no choice."

"Then just let *her* go. Take me and let her go free."

Every nerve in Kat's body stood on end. *This isn't real. It can't be happening.*

"Can't do that, either," the man replied, but his expression looked downright pained now as he reached to push a sweaty lock of dark, curling hair out of his eyes.

And it was just as Kat noticed he held his gun limp at his side that Brock said, "Run, Kat."

Chapter Eight

*B*rock gave her a shove, forcing her to take flight, simultaneously bolting upright to place himself in Carlos's path. As she tore away through the woods, Carlos looked after her, then met Brock's gaze, but never made a move with his feet or his gun. Brock had suspected he wouldn't.

And now he had to bet Carlos wouldn't shoot him, either, as he took off sprinting in the opposite direction from Kat, tossing a hard taunt over his shoulder. "You'll never get me, you stupid son of a bitch."

Behind him, Carlos followed—racing through the jungly growth, and Brock thought, *That's right, chase me, Carlos. Chase me so she can get away.* And then his mind moved right back to Kat: *Run baby—run and hide and don't come out, no matter what happens.*

Turned out, though, Carlos was swifter than Brock would have guessed, keeping pace with him, damn it. So he tried to shut out everything else but the running—*don't think of Kat, and don't think of the bullet that might come ripping through your back at any moment.* He concentrated instead on not tripping over roots or brush, on not getting tangled in any of the vines dangling from above.

Shit, why are you guys even here? The more he thought about it, the less sense it made. He'd held on to a niggling concern they might return, but that had been more overzealous caution—and maybe instinct—than logic. If they'd had any real doubts that they hadn't killed him, they'd have never left the first time. Two days had passed—so what had happened to bring them back?

Omega Man? Perhaps once he'd heard what happened, he'd sent them to retrieve Brock's body since it might seem unwise to leave a dead FBI agent lying around—harder to investigate a missing agent than a corpse full of clues.

Up to now, he hadn't given Omega much credit—thought many aspects of his operation seemed amateurish. For one, even as mean as Francisco was, the Morales brothers didn't have as much hard-core smuggling experience as you'd expect for guys hired to transport millions of dollars' worth of goods over a number of shipments. For another, they'd let him into their business too easy—he should have had to work harder to earn their trust. For a third, they'd been scheduled to meet directly with Omega on the night of the pickup—and the top man usually kept a much lower profile in such situations, never letting a little guy like "Jimmy" ID him. But if Omega had sent the Morales boys back out here to get him, maybe he was a little sharper than Brock had suspected.

He could only hope he stayed far enough ahead of Carlos to get away somehow, get back to Kat somehow, keep her safe somehow. Damn, too many "somehows" in the mix here—but he couldn't think about that. *Just focus on the moment. One foot in front of the other. Move. Move.*

For some reason, his mind flashed on what Carlos had said about Brock making a fool of him in front of Francisco. It sounded juvenile—yet he knew what it was to need your big brother's approval, to want so badly to please him, and maybe for some people that never went away. He wished he could shake Carlos and make him understand: *Your brother's a piece of shit—you don't need him.*

But Carlos would never believe that. Brock wouldn't have believed it either, until long after Bruno went to jail, when he slowly, finally began to understand his brother wasn't a hero. He'd just wanted one so bad, he supposed, needed someone to believe in. So in a strange way, he knew where Carlos was coming from. Hell, plunk the Denton boys down in Guatemala and they could have *become* the Morales brothers. A sobering thought.

And this was no time for sobering thoughts—*keep your mind on business here.*

Behind him, limbs cracked beneath Carlos's feet, sounding like they were breaking right next to Brock's ears. His chest pounded, and he dripped with sweat.

That's when he tripped and went tumbling, head over heels, into a ravine that had seemed to materialize out of nowhere. He landed on his ass with a groan, then looked up to find himself in an old dried-up creek bed—only about five feet deep—which probably led rainwater to the ocean.

About the time he got his bearings, he heard Carlos fall, too, with a hard grunt. But not right next to him—farther away, out of his line of sight. Realizing the small scrubby tree growing at an angle to his right provided some cover, he stayed very still—and listened.

"Where are you, you fucking fed?" Carlos sounded madder than before, madder than Brock had ever heard him. "I'll find you, you asshole. I'll find you and kill you if it's the last fucking thing I do!"

He hadn't thought Carlos could kill him or Kat—but maybe the dynamic was shifting here. Maybe a hard run through the hot jungle had been the impetus Carlos needed to transform into his brother. Maybe calling him a stupid son of a bitch had reminded him more painfully that "Jimmy" wasn't his friend.

Brock considered his next move. He couldn't stay there indefinitely—Carlos knew he was somewhere in the ravine, so now it was only a matter of searching it. And he could run, but that would only put them back in the same exhausting chase—and if Carlos was getting more trigger-happy, might earn him that bullet in the back.

Exploring the ground around him, he spotted a small, smooth stone. Large enough to make a sound if thrown. Small enough to be cast a good distance. He curled his hand around it and looked toward Carlos's voice, then beyond the gully toward the part of the island they'd not yet traveled.

Would be a hell of a throw to try to make. About a million slash pines stood like obstacles, just waiting to stop the rock in its flight.

But the worst that could happen would be drawing Carlos to him. And if he just sat here, that would occur soon enough anyway. The *best* that could happen would be to lob that sucker way on the other side of the ravine and send Carlos *there*. Then Brock could double back and look for Kat.

Brock used his eyes like a gunsight and spied a straight path through the trees. Then he drew back his arm and took aim. *Now or never.* He let the rock go, willing its path, watching it sail, sail, sail, until finally it landed hard enough to make that telltale *shush* in the brush. Bull's-eye.

A second later, Carlos could be heard scampering up the opposite side of the ravine, then barreling forward, yelling, "I got you now, you son of a bitch, I got you now!"

No, Carlos, you don't. At least not yet.

★　★　★

Kat ran blindly, with no idea where she was going or where she'd been. Was someone behind her? She didn't know. In the distance, she heard noise, movement through the trees, but was too afraid to stop long enough to figure out if it was headed in her direction. *God, Brock, where are you? Please be okay. Please be okay. Please let this all be a dream.*

The last wish she knew she wouldn't get, but the first one—maybe.

She watched her feet to keep from falling as she ran; she used her hands to gather her skirt around her thighs to keep it from snagging on low branches or thorns.

Then—*ooompf!* She hadn't seen the broad chest until she'd collided into it, hard—and she jerked her eyes up with a start. *God help me.*

Relief flooded her when she met Brock's gaze, and she collapsed in his strong arms. She'd never been happier to see anyone in her life.

"Are you okay, honey?" he asked, eyes wrought with worry.

She nodded. "Are *you*?"

"Yeah."

She didn't hesitate to throw her arms around his neck and pull him into a ferocious hug, which he returned, and despite the hideous circumstances, she wasn't sure she'd ever felt warmer or safer.

Finally, it was she who pulled back, just enough to look at him. "I was so afraid you wouldn't get away."

"Don't worry about *me*, kitten—I always get away."

She drew in a deep breath, trying to believe, trying to calm down. "And then I worried you'd never find me."

It surprised her when he actually quirked a soft grin. "You made it pretty easy. You ran in a circle."

Heat rose to her cheeks. "Oh. Well, I guess this means I wouldn't make a very good FBI agent."

He gave his head a short shake of agreement, then pulled her hands from his shoulders and held them. "But it's good you didn't make it far, because I found a decent place to hide." He jerked his head slightly to the right. "Come on, let's go."

After all the running it felt strange to be walking at a composed— even if brisk—pace through the forest. Her heartbeat slowed as she became aware that the only human sounds to be heard were their own, and the first true sense of calm she'd felt since her stroll on the beach this morning washed over her.

After only a few short minutes, she found herself descending, with Brock's help, into a small gorge cut into the island like a seam, almost invisible until they were upon it. She slid a little on the steep bank, but he placed his big hands at her hips, steadying her until she reached the more level ground below.

They proceeded up the gully until finally he said, "Here," and nestled them both into a slight bow in the wall with protective growth around it—a small, aromatic red bay tree on one side and some plants spilling over on the other.

Brock's arms looped around her waist from behind, and she leaned back against him, too tired to resist resting her head on his chest. She was on the verge of asking him more about the people chasing them—when they both heard someone walking through the brush overhead. She tensed and felt his hold on her tighten.

No more rushing, running, making lots of noise—no, this was a quieter search, slower and more ominous-feeling. As if maybe the bad guys had just figured out what *she* had—they could take their time hunting because she and Brock had no place to go, they were trapped. The more close encounters she had with these scary people, the less her "needle in a jungle" theory seemed to apply.

"I know you're here somewhere, government man, and I'm going to find you eventually."

The voice held the same thick accent, yet sounded different from the guy who'd discovered them by the rocks. Must be that first guy they'd seen. Great. It reminded her they were being stalked from two different directions and made their chances of survival feel even more grim.

"I've got all day. And all night, too. I won't be leaving this island until I see you dead, fed." Then he laughed. "Dead, fed—rhymes."

Despite the intense heat of the island interior, a chill ran up Kat's spine. She wished desperately she could turn her head, just to see Brock's face, just to make eye contact since she knew it would make her feel safer—but she was afraid to do even that.

Finally, the creepy guy's footsteps passed slowly by and seemed to be moving on in that stalkerlike leisurely pace. She worked to remain totally still, despite the itch that had just developed on her ankle.

Of course, within seconds, the itch was driving her mad, but she could still hear light, distant movement above, so she bit her lip, then gritted her teeth and tried to think of anything but itches or ankles until she thought she'd lose her mind.

Finally, all noise faded, but she still wasn't sure it was safe to move, because she wasn't sure of *anything* anymore—so she turned her head, ever so slowly, to find Brock's sexy eyes mere inches from hers. She moved her lips. *I. Have. An. Itch.*

He leaned slightly forward until she felt the heat of his breath on her ear. "Want me to scratch it for you, kitten?"

She wanted to kiss him. She wanted to smack him. Instead of doing either, she let the slightest of grins sneak out. "I was merely asking," she whispered, "if it was safe to move."

"Ah, my mistake," he said, his mouth still way too temptingly close.

She found the strength to yank her gaze away and went to work scratching her ankle. And now that it seemed safe to talk again, she asked quietly, "How many guys are chasing us?"

"Two. The guy who found us back by the rocks, that's Carlos. He's the nice one."

She stopped scratching and flashed a look of disbelief. If the maniac with the gun who said he couldn't let either of them go was the *nice* one, then . . . She pointed up above them. "And that guy?"

"Francisco. The mean one."

Well, maybe that explained the menacing feeling that had coursed through her veins when he'd been lurking up there, sounding like a whack job. "Um, back by the rocks, why did that guy call you Jimmy?"

"My undercover name."

She tilted her head, freshly amazed at how differently Brock's life had turned out than she would have expected. "Is that weird, to go by another name?"

"Only if you ever start to forget who you really are."

"*Do* you ever?"

He grimaced slightly. "Unfortunately not."

"Unfortunately?"

He let out a long sigh, his look confiding. "I shouldn't tell you this, but . . . that's how I fucked up—they called me by my real name, and I answered to it." He peered warm into her eyes. "Sorry, kitten."

For some reason, she could barely find her voice. "For?"

"If I hadn't done that, you wouldn't be in this situation."

If he hadn't done that, she'd be safe now. She'd be sunning and tanning and reading and swimming and . . . transitioning. She'd be safe from bad guys. And safe from the temptation Brock Denton had always held for her.

If she could change it, would she?

For Brock's safety, yes. And for her own. Hell, she was a practical girl, always had been—so yeah, all things considered, if she could turn back time, she'd wish all this away in exchange for knowing she'd live to see another day.

And yet, deep inside, she also couldn't be sorry Brock had reappeared in her life, couldn't be sorry to know what it was to have him near, to feel his arms around her, to seek solace in his warmth. Even if she still couldn't have him in the way she'd always wanted him, and even if the circumstances were downright shitty, she couldn't be sorry he was here. "It's okay," she whispered.

He gave his head the slightest tilt. "You know, sometimes, kitten, you can be surprisingly sweet."

"Don't get used to it," she said, then turned back around and let her head rest against his chest once more.

The cold, hard truth was . . . if she had to die, this wouldn't be a bad way to go.

Debra glanced at herself in the rearview mirror, but regretted it immediately—that close a look always made her notice wrinkles more than any remaining beauty in her face. *It's an illusion*, she reminded herself. *Across the table, you'll look fine.*

She'd dressed carefully—pretty yet professional, summery but mature—a light blazer over a soft pastel blouse cut just low enough to remind anyone who cared to notice that she was a woman. She didn't have the same figure she'd possessed as a girl, of course, but she generally put herself in that category of women who "looked good for her age," and she knew how to find clothes that worked well on her. So all things considered—even the wrinkles in the rearview—she couldn't complain about her appearance and was actually much more concerned over what they would talk about. Sure, the last lunch with Michael had gone fabulously, but what if today was different? What if there was nothing left to say?

Calm down. You're making too much of this. For all she knew, it would be a quick meal—a few pleasantries, then a succinct chat about the book and her impending critique, nothing more. Only she was hoping for something longer.

After digging blindly for her cell phone in her purse as she drove toward the ocean, she finally managed to try Kat again—and for the third time in as many days, didn't get an answer. "Hate to be a worrywart, honey, but at least let me know you got there and all is well, okay? Call me."

She wasn't worried—*exactly*. It wasn't as if Kat had never forgotten to call her before. But never for three days after leaving on vacation.

So at the next light, she scrambled for her datebook and found Nina's cell number, which she'd scribbled there for just such a need. She succeeded in keying it in by the time the light turned green.

Three rings and no answer later, a real knot of concern began to grow in her stomach. Then came Nina's groggy, "Um, hello?"

It was as if Debra's heart started beating again. This meant they were okay. "Nina, it's Kat's mom."

"Oh. Um, hi."

She did a quick calculation—9:00 A.M. in Vegas, and Nina was still fast asleep. "I'm sorry to wake you, but I haven't been able to get hold of Kat. Can I speak with her?"

"She's . . . in the bathroom."

Worshipping the porcelain god? Given the way Nina sounded, Debra suspected serious hangovers all around, but since the old saying was probably passé by now, she gently ventured, "Sick?"

"Uh . . . yeah. So she might be in there a while."

Debra sighed. Her mother's instinct made her feel almost sick herself to know Kat was ill—even if she'd brought it on herself.

"And . . . you know how cruddy you feel when you're that hungover, so she probably won't really feel like talking much after."

Actually, no, Debra *didn't* know how cruddy her daughter felt at the moment, since she'd never gotten drunk enough to throw up. And oddly, just now, it made her very aware of how young she'd married, how little fun she'd had with her girlfriends as a grown-up, and even if Kat was miserable this morning, Debra was thankful Kat had waited so much longer than she had before settling down. "Of course," she said, as if she'd been there herself a thousand times before. "Just tell her I hope she feels better and to call when she can."

"Gotcha," Nina said, sounding somewhere between drunk and about to drift off.

"Are you girls having fun and being careful?" she couldn't help asking anyway.

"Both. Promise."

Debra smiled. "Sorry I woke you, Nina."

"No prob."

"Go back to sleep now. Bye."

After spending a few minutes of worry imagining Kat bent over the toilet, she reached Tin City, the collection of shops and restaurants that overlooked Naples Bay. Soon wending her way along the plank boardwalk toward Merriman's Wharf, she felt pleased that Michael had suggested someplace so casual, comfortable. Clark *never* took her anyplace like this, and it seemed like the perfect departure from her usual life.

Her pulse skittered as the interior of the open-air restaurant came into view and she caught sight of him, at a table next to the wooden railing that bordered the water. He was just as handsome as she remembered, and when he looked up, spotting her, she found herself immediately captured by those eyes. So human. Kind. The type of man who let you see his soul in his gaze. And who also wasn't afraid to spill it onto the page. Odd how those two things, added together, produced the illusion that she knew him far better than she actually did.

"Hello." She smiled, hoping it didn't come out in an overly beaming sort of way.

To her surprise, he stood to greet her, leaned in for a small hug. A manly, earthy scent permeated her senses along with the warmth of his quick, polite touch—which she felt in more than a quick, polite way. It sizzled through her, leaving her rather deliciously singed in every spot where their bodies had made contact.

As she sat, her eyes fell on the flat cardboard box on the table. "The book," she said, and something about its mere presence struck her as magical. She'd never read a book when it was still just someone's story on unbound paper and, despite knowing he worked on a computer, the thought drew to mind someone like Hemingway, sitting at an old typewriter, pounding out prose that would become art and legend. She felt as if she'd been selected to hold in her hand a diamond that others would only someday view from afar.

He returned her smile. "Yes." Then, to her surprise, widened his eyes in an almost sheepish expression. "My latest tome. Take mercy on it."

Self-deprecation was the last thing she'd expected from him—and she found it oddly endearing.

"Ignore that," he added, sounding more resolute. "*Don't* take mercy on it. I mean it. Be critical—that's what I need at this point in the process. Look for anything that feels wrong to you."

She glanced from his handsome face to the box, then back again. "I promise to . . . give an honest assessment, be it praise or criticism or some of both."

"Fair enough," he said, then shoved the box toward her across the small wooden table, an official handing-off, the slight gesture delivering his trust.

After a waitress arrived to take her drink order, they turned their attention toward the menus, perusing in a silence that felt comfortable that fast. A soft breeze blew in off the water, and somehow she knew this was going to be okay. More than okay. A good lunch. Easy conversation. She would go away feeling vital, noticed, respected. She would go away thinking of his eyes. She would probably go home and look at the dust jacket of his last novel too many times.

A hint of guilt nipped at her. Was this wrong? To want to spend time talking with a man who made her feel good about herself.

She bit her lip, peering at the list of seafood choices without quite seeing them. Yes, it probably *was* wrong, because she'd looked forward to today too much, and because each time she lifted her eyes to him she felt something more, something new, and because it wasn't the reaction a woman had to a purely platonic relationship.

But she also couldn't see any harm in it, either. She didn't even *flirt* with Michael, for heaven's sake—she wouldn't have the first idea how to. She certainly had no intention of acting on her crush. She was married, and so was he—he'd mentioned his wife and young daughter in their interview. So even if she felt an attraction she shouldn't, no one would ever know, not even him. As transgressions in life went, this one seemed minor. And safe.

"So, Kat's wedding is this weekend, right?" he asked after they'd given their order.

She couldn't help being pleased he remembered, and that he called Kat by name as if he knew her. "Yes, and I was so glad you could meet today, since the rest of my week is filled with last-minute mother-of-the-bride work. Kat's off for a trip with the girls to Las Vegas, so I'm holding down the fort until she gets back on Thursday."

He raised his eyebrows, looking mischievous. "Vegas, huh? Sounds like trouble."

Debra laughed softly. "A few years ago, maybe." When Kat had been younger, Debra had held her daughter's hair back after more than one of those too-much-to-drink nights and been witness to many you'll-wear-that-out-of-this-house-over-my-dead-body matches between Kat and Clark. Kat had possessed a wild streak that didn't come from either of her parents. Yet it seemed to have died . . . somewhere around the time of Ian's appearance as a suitor. "And the truth is, even as we speak, I happen to know she's suffering a brutal hangover. But she's a lot more settled now than in her younger days, so I don't have to worry so much anymore."

Since her engagement to Ian over the holidays, Kat had become decidedly more . . . staid. Still talkative, even lively. Still *herself.* Yet . . . different. And—it only in that very moment dawned on Debra for the first time—Kat smiled a lot less lately.

"Then why do you *look* worried?"

She raised her gaze to find Michael wearing a small, insightful grin, his head tilted inquisitively. She returned a conceding smile. "I guess she's been under a lot of pressure lately. Planning a large wedding is stressful, plus she's trying to prepare for her pottery showing at the same time. But I'm sure she'll bounce back to normal once all the hoopla dies down."

He looked a bit skeptical, then slightly wicked. "Myself, I always find really *good* hoopla invigorating."

She let out a short laugh, then covered her mouth as she felt eyes from other tables glance her way. "Sorry," she said softly.

"For laughing? Never be sorry for laughing, Debra. You have a *great* laugh."

She met his gaze. Felt the flirtation, the heat of it rising to her cheeks. She didn't know what to say, so said nothing, but then regretted it—because it left the flirtation hanging in the air, obvious, and them both so very married that it ate down into her marrow lightning-fast. "Let's talk about you," she said, desperately seeking a subject. "We always talk about me, but never about you."

His eyes widened. "Our entire last lunch was about me. You *interviewed* me, in fact—remember?"

Dunce. You are a dunce. Only, then she realized. "But you always politely turned the conversation back to something about me. So I know *facts* about you, and about your career, but I don't know . . . say, what *your* daughter is doing this weekend."

All hints of mirth left his eyes and she wondered what she'd said that was so dreadful. The mystery stretched further when the waitress returned to add water to glasses that set sweating on the table between them. After she departed, Debra asked, "Did I say something wrong?"

He gave his head a short shake. "No, it's just . . ." He dropped his gaze, then lifted it back to hers, now with a confiding expression. "Rhonda and I recently separated, so I only see Chloe on weekends now. I'm still getting used to the idea."

Debra didn't realize she'd lifted her hand to her chest until she felt her fingers splayed there. She couldn't have been more stunned. "I'm . . . so sorry, Michael. I had no idea. I thought . . ." When he didn't say anything to fill in the gap she'd just created, she continued honestly. "You sounded . . . so happy about your marriage during our interview."

He cast a slow, wry smile. "I was faking."

Of course. You don't air your personal problems to strangers. Which made it clear he no longer considered her one. "Do you . . . want to talk about it?"

"She . . . got bored with me, I guess."

"You're kidding!" *Drat—that might have come out sounding a little too impassioned.*

But he didn't seem to notice. "I thought we were happy. Twelve good years together, you know? But over the last year or so, we just grew apart. She tried to blame it on my career—claiming I was more devoted to the work than to her and Chloe. But I know how to be a good husband and a good father, always have. She's the one who pulled away. And I feel like she pulled Chloe with her. Especially now."

His pain radiated through his voice and she felt it deeply. "Do you see Chloe a lot?" She remembered from their interview that Chloe was nine, and sounded bright and energetic in a way that had reminded her of Kat at that age.

Sadness clouded his face again. "Not as much as I'd like. The house is pretty lonely these days. Weird, because writers like solitude—but not *that* much. I miss just hearing her playing in the next room. And it seems as if . . . well, as if Rhonda keeps finding reasons to change our schedule so Chloe sees me less. She makes plans for Chloe during the times she's supposed to be with me, things Chloe wants to do, so it makes me the bad guy if I object. I hate to say this, but it feels vindictive, like she's doing it to punish me for whatever she thinks I did wrong."

She nodded, thinking it *sounded* vindictive, too, but resisted saying it, since she didn't know the situation, or the woman.

"I should have seen it coming, I guess. She quit having sex with me months ago. But I thought it was always just coincidental—she was tired, or it was the wrong time of the month." He raised his gaze to hers. "I'll admit I've spent the last six months buried in this book. It didn't write itself. But she knew what I was about when we got married. I'm not sure what changed."

Debra didn't know what to say. Except now she was imagining him having sex. Not with the faceless Rhonda—but not with herself, either. She was simply reminded that he was a man, and he *had* sex, he *wanted* it. They all did, of course, but the open knowledge of *him* having warm, visceral desires settled low in her belly, like something intimate.

"God, I've blown this, haven't I?" he asked, then scrunched up his nose in a playful manner she'd noticed before—it made him seem young, vulnerable, in a good way. Like he didn't feel he needed to put on any sort of virile act with her.

"What do you mean?"

He sighed. "I meet a nice, pretty woman, I enjoy her company, I look forward to this lunch—and now I screw it up by throwing up my personal life all over the table. That wasn't part of my plan for today."

His plan? He had a plan? Maybe that should worry her—but, to her surprise, it flattered her instead. "What *was* your plan for today?"

He offered a soft smile. "Nothing too devious. When you agreed to read the book, I just . . . realized I was going to enjoy seeing you again. I just wanted to have a pleasant lunch—that simple."

She nodded. "Well, so you know, you haven't blown anything." In fact, she found herself wanting to comfort him . . . and something more, too. She hated the idea of him feeling sad and wanted to be the person who changed it somehow.

He looked wistful. "But I always think other people's marriage troubles sound so . . . generic, or typical maybe. They're complex when they're happening to you, yet there's so much divorce in the world that I always feel it sounds mundane. So I had no intention of boring you with it. Especially since I know you're in a perfectly happy marriage yourself." He wrinkled his nose again, just slightly, then gave another playful grin. "I didn't want to sound like one more getting-divorced loser."

"I would never think you're a loser, Michael. And . . ." Could she say this, actually give voice to it? Up to this moment, it had all been thoughts and doubts and disappointments in her head—but nothing concrete. And saying it would make it real. "Maybe my marriage isn't so happy, either."

His face fell, as if truly saddened for her. "Really?"

She winced lightly, then nodded. "It's not . . ." She swallowed, unsure what she intended to say, then pressed onward. "It's not awful or anything. I just feel . . . neglected, I guess." Then she bit her lip, embarrassed. "I'm starting to see a trend here—men who work hard and women who feel neglected."

"Except for one thing," Michael said. "I wasn't really neglecting Rhonda. It's an excuse she used because she wanted out, and we both know it. I have a feeling," he went on, looking deep into her eyes, "that you're not the kind of woman who makes things up. You seem . . . unerringly honest. That's one of the reasons I wanted you to read the book. You seem like you see the world very clearly, Debra. I noticed that about you immediately, and it's one of the things that drew me to you."

He was *drawn* to her. That should have felt like a miracle, set her heart racing like a teenager. But suddenly, already, it didn't surprise her anymore. They were drawn to *each other*, and it was no longer shocking—just a new awareness floating between them. The strange calm that came with understanding that allowed her to stick to the topic. "Clark is very . . . money driven. Which can be a good thing. But like most things in life, when taken to excess, it's too much. So I've just grown to feel . . . lonely over the last few years." Then she laughed, albeit without joy. "Lonely—what a morose word. Not a word I'd have ever dreamed of to describe myself."

"Nor should it be," he said, a light shining in his eyes. "You should never be lonely, Debra. He shouldn't let you be." That's when he reached across the table to touch her fingers where they played with the stem of her water glass. Her gaze dropped there, to their hands, together, then rose to his eyes.

He pulled back. "I'm so sorry—I didn't mean to do that."

She nodded quickly, dropped her gaze, and was glad when the waitress arrived bearing plates of food. A few short smiles up at her, pleasantries about the meal and did they need anything else, and she was gone—and they were back again, alone together. Their eyes, locked across the table, said they both recalled that something weird and awkward had just happened.

Michael let out a sigh. "God, I so don't intend to put the moves on you, Debra—okay? Touching your hand like that . . . Totally out of line, and it won't happen again. Forgive me?"

Something in her heart blossomed. He wore that boyish look once more, so sincere. "Yes, of course. And, well . . . it's not as if you committed a grand crime. I'll survive." She even managed to smile.

He returned it. "So you're not going to call off the friendship?"

She shook her head.

"Good."

And then things settled—into talk about their meals, and food in general. Her family's long history in Naples; *he'd* only moved to the area as a teenager when his father had accepted a job nearby. They chatted about the Everglades, and the book *The Orchid Thief*, and they soon discovered they shared a fondness for movies by the Coen brothers—although they agreed it was a little out of character for them both. Talk turned to Kat's work with children, and he shared that he and Chloe had just signed up for a father/daughter art class on Saturdays. That somehow led to home décor, and her fabulous new kitchen, although she admitted she wasn't much of a cook, turning the conversation back to food. He then regaled her with tales of his culinary feats, impressing the hell out of her—since she couldn't *create* great food, but she certainly enjoyed it.

"Too bad you've got such a busy week ahead or I'd invite you over for lunch," he said. Then he raised his eyebrows teasingly—temptingly. "I make a killer chicken parmigiana."

"Next week?" she suggested. "The wedding will be over and I'll have plenty of time."

He grimaced. "Leaving on a short book tour Sunday night, as soon as Chloe heads back to her mom's. I'll be gone for two weeks. But . . . if you can't make it this week, when I get back."

She reached in her purse, locating her datebook much easier now than when she'd been driving.

"Besides, this will give you a chance to read the book. You can rake me over the coals while we eat," he said with a grin.

"I could maybe do Thursday," she offered.

His eyes widened hopefully. "*This* Thursday?"

"If the offer still stands."

"Of course. Are you sure you have the time, though?"

She smiled boldly, pairing it with a nod. "I keep reminding myself lately that I should do more things just for me. And this is for me."

Chapter Nine

*H*ours passed, and Kat napped in Brock's arms. He sat still, quiet, listening to the sounds of the island—breezes ruffling palm fronds overhead, the occasional call of a bird—and felt thankful when he heard nothing more.

His arms wrapped around her from behind, same position a couple might assume to watch TV in bed or to sit cuddled against a palm tree next to the ocean. This wasn't quite as relaxed as that, but he couldn't help noticing she hadn't extracted herself from his embrace. She let him hold her. And he drank in the sweet scent of her hair, the soft curves of her body—and wanted more.

Shouldn't be thinking about that—not now, dude.

What was happening to him? What the hell kind of FBI agent let himself get distracted from his job over and over by a woman?

He knew the answer and it was simple—the kind of FBI agent who needed some time off. And the truth was, once this was all over, he'd probably be given a mandatory leave of absence.

He'd needed a leave three years ago, too, after the Reyes case in Miami. And he'd climbed behind the wheel of Reyes's Porsche, which he'd promptly bought at a police auction as a souvenir, and driven across the country. He'd seen the mountains and the canyons, the rivers and the plains. He'd stood on a lonely Oregon beach, looking out on cold Pacific waters, and he'd searched his soul until he knew it was almost time to go back. First, though, since he'd gotten his head clear and his troubles worked out, he rewarded himself by jetting to Maui, where he'd imbibed fruity concoctions from coconut shells and found a pretty hula dancer to spend a few evenings with. Then he'd finally headed back to the FBI field office in Miami and told them he was ready to get back to work.

So that's probably what he should do *this* time, too. Just get away. Soak up something besides crime and danger for a while. Refuel.

Only . . . he shouldn't have visited so many damn places last time, because at the moment, he couldn't think of anyplace else he really wanted to go.

No, at the moment, this island, where he'd found this girl who needed his protection, seemed like the only place in the world that mattered.

The second Kat awoke, she couldn't believe she'd actually fallen asleep again, but she supposed she knew deep inside that as long as Brock was there, it would be safe to rest. In fact, waking up with his strong arm looped around her from behind felt far too cozy.

Despite the thick cover of trees overhead, she could sense the sky darkening, turning everything around them more shadowy. Must be an afternoon thunderstorm brewing. Common in Florida, but it didn't bode well. If they had to run again, the ground would be slippery—it wouldn't dry under the canopy of trees as fast as in the sun.

Just then, he leaned around to peek at her. "Sleep good, kitten?"

She gave a short, sheepish nod. "Sorry about drifting off."

His expression reassured her. "Good for you to rest."

"Did I miss anything?"

He pointed to a thick trunk on the opposite rim of the gully. "See that tree? Three little green geckos have been playing around the base of it. That's been the highlight of the afternoon."

His words calmed her further. "Good."

At that moment, the first thick drops of rain began to sift down through the trees, pelting leaves. Funny, she was the sort of girl who usually ran from the rain, covering her head if she had to dash from her car in even a drizzle—but this, now, seemed like nothing, not even worthy of mention. Just one more obstacle in the day. So even as the drops fell faster, harder, finding their way through the patchy ceiling of green, and even as her chest, arms, and face slowly became covered with trails of wetness, she and Brock both just sat in the pouring rain as if it were normal, neither of them saying a word.

She looked down at his arm, spanning her stomach, his skin becoming as saturated as her own, and thought it felt as if the rain somehow melded them together, like watery glue. Still tired, she leaned her head back on his chest again, not opposed to melding some more.

A few minutes later, amid the downpour, he said, "Can I ask you something?"

She lifted her head from his chest, noticing instantly that the steady cadence of his heart no longer sounded near her ear, but resisted turning to look at him because he sounded so serious. "All right."

He spoke low. "If we were to die here, Kat . . . would you regret last night? Would you regret not having sex with me?"

Her chest tightened, and her own heartbeat sped up.

She could rail at him for still not respecting her engagement, or she could turn and roll her eyes at his insistence on pressing the subject of sex, even now that they were running for their lives. But the earnest quality to his voice kept her from it.

Instead, she thought about the question for a minute, about all the circumstances and complications, and about the fact that they were in real danger here, danger like she'd never been in before. And she remembered how she'd wanted him ten years ago, and how she'd wanted him just as much last night.

"Yes," she finally said, the word coming out raspier than intended.

He slowly, slowly leaned forward until finally his cheek came to rest moist against hers. "Kitten," he said, rough and deep. Nothing more, just that. His breath warmed the side of her face as he placed a soft, lingering kiss next to her ear.

And as that mere touch from his lips sizzled through her, nearly making the rain dance across her skin, she felt him . . . *holding back*.

He was no longer trying to seduce her—instead, he was trying *not* to.

The very air thickened around them as the hot desire that seeped from him oozed down into her pores, as tangible as the rain that continued to soak them.

He remained still, so very still. Except for the slight, tense trembling of his arm, the heavy sigh that left his mouth. Their faces still touched.

A glance down found that arm still latched firmly around her, and the tips of her breasts jutting through her halter top—from cool rain and hot arousal. She wanted him—God help her, she did. And this time it was a want that mere guilt could not assuage.

Sheer need turned her face toward his.

I love you.

Oh God, what was *that*?

But she knew. It was something old, ancient, buried inside her for a long time, ten lengthy years, suddenly unearthed.

Yet not real. Once upon a time, it had been *very* real—but not anymore. Just an old echo, a weird reaction to all this nearness. She *didn't* love him. She *didn't*.

And just because you kissed someone didn't mean you loved them. A kiss only meant passion. Passion she couldn't push away right now.

She never really leaned forward, and he never exactly moved in on her, either—but somehow it happened. A slow, gentle meeting of mouths, soft, lingering. Rain on their lips making it moister.

And then another, longer kiss. And just like she remembered from the swamp—the most delicious of her life. Swallowing, enveloping. Brock's kiss had the power to reach down inside her, deep, so deep, like being touched between her thighs.

His mouth moved warm over hers, his tongue pressing inward, and she didn't hesitate to give him entry—she wanted to take him inside her more than she wanted to keep breathing.

And then came shorter tongue kisses, but just as passionate—like taking small, hot drinks of him, sip after quenching sip. They were the most agonizing kisses of her life. The most wrenching, the most engulfing. Her body surged with moisture so that she barely knew where the rain stopped and her body's reaction to him began.

Below, his hand on her belly slowly caressed through her top. Her own arm cradled his now, her hand curling around his strong forearm, finally touching him, feeling his skin, beginning a slow exploration that set off a whole new flood of longing inside her.

As they kissed—she was lost to it now, drowning in it—his thumb grazed the underside of her breast, and she wanted to die from the pleasure. The juncture of her thighs clenched, and she realized she was kissing him harder, even delivering a hot bite to his lower lip that elicited a moan from him, making her spasm with still more wet heat.

His thumb raked over her nipple and this time the moan was hers, leaking from between her lips into his warm mouth, but he kissed it away, one kiss, then another as he kneaded and caressed, cupping her breast now, taking it full into his hand.

Oh God, how she wanted him. She'd never wanted a man this way, ever. Not even him.

She wanted to untie her top, let it fall, wanted to arch her breasts into his mouth, wanted to let him kiss and suckle them beneath the hard, cool rain.

She wanted to lift her skirt and straddle him, wanted to tear away her own panties, wanted to dig her knees into the dirt and ride him to oblivion.

She wanted to forget. Everything else.

Ian. Her parents. Her future.

Danger. Blown-up boats. Men with guns. Being chased.

Oh God. She wanted him with a force unequaled—yet something clicked on inside her then. Something important.

Stopping now was probably one of the hardest things she'd ever done, a test of pure will, yet somehow she managed to cover his hand with hers and slowly, torturously, draw it back down to her waist.

The kissing ceased, both of them panting with labored breath, foreheads pressed together—and when she spoke, her voice quaked. "I, uh, know I'd make a lousy FBI agent, but . . . shouldn't we be staying a little more alert here?"

Brock drew back slightly, hissed in his breath, closed his eyes. "You're right."

She still wanted to kiss him. Madly. She pressed her lips flat and tight together to help her resist.

He let out a sigh. "You take away my edge, kitten."

The words sent fresh warmth skittering down through her just as the rain died away, slowing to sprinkles, then nothing. Around them, the whole forest smelled lush and earthy and wet. With the trees creating an awning overhead, the place, more than before, felt like a world unto itself. Somewhere they were trapped.

The reminder washed away her passion, which was for the best, although it turned her thoughts back to why they were there, hiding in a big, soggy ditch, with a thin stream running through it now a few feet below them. "What you asked before, about having regrets if we died—do you really think we're going to?"

His face hardened. "No," he said, almost forcefully. "I shouldn't even have said that, because we'll be fine."

She sighed, still suffering doubt. "Then why did you say it?"

"It was hypothetical," he reassured her. "I just wanted to know if you'd have regrets. And now I know."

He looked satisfied, although not cocky. Acknowledgment that the truth had been laid out between them and there was no taking it back. It made her lament her honesty, even if it *had* led to the most sumptuous kisses of her existence.

Instead of responding, she simply turned back around, facing away from him again. His arm still circled her—only more loosely now. And, to her shame, she still didn't push it away.

"Tell me something, kitten," he said, leaning near her ear again. "About that virginity of yours—when did you finally lose it?"

"None of your business." Spoken not with rancor, just frankness.

"Come on," he prodded, low and persuasive. "Tell me."

"No." It hadn't been the best move she'd ever made, and he didn't need to know that. In hopes of sloughing it off further, she added, "It . . . wasn't a big deal. Nobody special."

His voice came out somber, serious. "I'm sorry to hear that."

His sympathy on this particular topic wasn't welcome. And it lodged a thought in her head that forced her to turn and narrow her gaze on him. "And I guess you think if it had been you, it *would* have been special."

He lowered his chin and flashed an arrogant grin. "I'd have *made* it special. Just on pure skill alone."

He was trying to make her smile, and it worked. He was probably also trying to arouse her again, and that also succeeded. Sadly, after the kisses they'd just exchanged, she believed him completely about the skill.

And it *could* have been special if it had been with him. But that no longer mattered. Much like their kisses just now—those didn't matter, either.

Being forced to think back to the night she'd lost her virginity reminded her of how little such events and connections sometimes mattered once they were over. And it reminded her, one more stinging time, of that moment at the swamp when he'd made it so scathingly clear that sex with her would be sex and nothing more. And that was good. Because soon *this* would all be over, too. And life would be normal again, and he'd be gone, and she'd be a married woman. Today's kisses . . . history. It was only about sex for Brock Denton.

"It's not too late," he said, voice brimming with confident flirtation. "I could make it up to you after we get out of this."

He had no idea, of course, that she'd managed to get angry with him all over again just because of a memory. He still thought they were flirting, and wanting, and that something more might happen now. But she was about to wake him up.

She didn't think he was a bad guy. Sadly, for her, she thought he'd turned out to be a pretty *good* guy. But not for her. Not for *any* woman in *that* manner, she suspected.

She hoped not, anyway, feeling wholly selfish about it. She hoped he'd never fall in love with *anyone*, hoped he'd never give *anyone* the things she'd once wanted from him—and had maybe let herself want again, just for a short, tiny moment.

She turned in his loose grasp and lifted her hand to cup his stubbled cheek. And she spoke with the same sureness and confidence she always heard in *his* voice, in hopes that he would finally hear her this time. "It *is* too late, Brock. Despite everything that's happened today—the scary stuff, and the kissing—it *has* to be too late."

"Because you're still planning to get married Saturday."

She gave a succinct nod. "Yes. Do you finally grasp that now?"

He stayed quiet, looked grim and—if she wasn't flattering herself too much—sincerely disappointed. "Yeah, okay, kitten—I get it."

Then he finally released his hold on her, making her feel a little bit abandoned—even though it was definitely for the best—so she turned back around and bit her lip, trying to dull the loss.

Whether or not Ian was her dream guy was irrelevant—she'd agreed to marry him, and no matter what happened, if you were going to be married, you had to respect the marriage, treat it with reverence, place it above all things.

As for the fact that she'd just made out with Brock for a few blissful moments that had temporarily made her forget Ian existed, she'd just have to make peace with that, forgive herself and move on. From this moment forward, her commitment to Ian took center stage.

And if she was entirely honest with herself . . . it also had to be too late because Brock had hurt her once upon a time, badly, in ways he'd never even known about and still didn't—and she'd promised herself she'd never be wounded by a guy that deeply again.

As a beam of sun angled down through the trees overhead, casting one of those ethereal glowing rays that always made her think of God, she permitted herself a fraction of a second for an ironic thought: The really great thing about marrying Ian was that he simply didn't possess the power to hurt her that much—because maybe she simply didn't love him that much.

She pushed it away as quickly as it came, not wanting to believe it was true.

Then wrapped her arms around herself as the cold from the rain finally replaced Brock's warmth and began to seep into her skin.

Kat's eighteenth birthday
Ten years ago

Kat checked her watch, then an elaborate gilt-framed mirror in the lavish room where no less than fifty teenagers stood laughing, dancing, and eating—as well as occasionally throwing—birthday cake. The whole evening so far had felt surreal, like she was watching someone *else's* party, a distant observer. She resented that a little—she'd looked forward to the party, not to mention turning eighteen—but knowing what she was going to do with Brock in a little while overshadowed it all.

Peering into the glass, she licked her freshly glossed lips and imagined Brock's reaction when he saw her. No flirty sundress tonight—instead, she'd worn a black sheath that hugged her in all the right places. Demure enough to suit her parents, but not the dress of a little girl. And instead of wearing pink lace panties, she'd worn none at all.

Only Brock Denton could inspire her to such hedonism.

Growing warm from anticipation, she was just about to slip out and start toward their rendezvous point when a male hand closed around her wrist. She looked up to find Scott Powers, quarterback of the football team and the best-looking guy in her class. She'd dated him briefly, but they'd broken up because she wouldn't have sex with him. He'd thought she was a prim Goody Two-shoes, but the truth she'd been too kind to tell him was that he just didn't do it for her. Sure, he was hot, but his kisses were sloppy and his hands surprisingly fumbly for a quarterback, and he was too aggressive, no finesse. She simply hadn't *wanted* to have sex with him—there'd been no *zing,* and certainly no emotions.

A fleeting thought assaulted her—maybe Brock had found *her* kiss sloppy, *her* hands fumbly. He'd thought her a little girl in the very same way she'd thought Scott a clumsy schoolboy. It withered her confidence just slightly.

"Some of us are going swimming now. You coming?"

It had been part of the professionally printed invitation designed by her mom—*Swimming after dinner and cake—don't forget your suit!*

"Later," she said to Scott. *Much* later. She had way better plans.

But instead of releasing her wrist, he leaned in close. She smelled beer on his breath as he whispered, "Come into the pool house with me, Kat."

She drew back slightly, more from distaste than surprise. Scott lacked the ability to frazzle her. "And why would I do that?"

Despite the dryness of her tone, he gave a grin that looked more like a leer. She couldn't help thinking how badly he was handling whatever small amount of alcohol he'd managed to smuggle into the party. "Are you still a virgin, Kat? Hmm?"

She flashed an oh-grow-up look. "And that would be your business because . . . ?"

He smiled wide, and in spite of other circumstances, it reminded her what a good-looking boy he was. "Because I thought you might want to change that. It's your birthday, you know."

She blinked, attempting to look bored, since she was. Mostly. "Yes, I'm aware."

Then he tried to go earnest on her. "I've wanted you ever since we quit going out."

"What about Nicole?" A cheerleader he'd been dating, and screwing all over town, from what she'd heard.

He shrugged. "She's okay. But it's you I really like. I've *always* liked you, Kat—you know that."

"Hmm," she said, skeptical.

In a surprisingly smooth move, he released her arm and slid his hand to her butt, squeezing lightly. "Why don't you let me show you how much?"

She looked him in the eye, wondering if he could tell she wasn't wearing panties, then took a step back. "Sorry, Scott, I don't think so. I'm into somebody else."

His eyebrows shot up. "Who?"

She shrugged and let a small smile leak out, starting to feel just a little giddy about what lay before her. "It's a secret," she said, then spun and walked away—out into the breezeway that led to the pool, but she turned in the other direction, toward the front entrance.

The humidity had lightened over the last few days, and a sea breeze had reached inland to waft over her, lift her hair slightly, and cool her rather heated thighs. She walked with confidence down the sidewalk that led from the club's buildings and parking lot, glad the distance was short, since she'd worn her sexiest strappy heels, and also suddenly glad she'd worn black so that if anyone stood lingering around the front entrance, she wasn't particularly noticeable.

When she reached the tall wrought-iron gates, they stood propped open as usual, and she stepped through, looking up and down the quiet-at-night road. Brock hadn't arrived yet, but she was a few minutes early. She sat down on a big boulder used for ornamentation, careful not to snag her dress, then drew in a deep, refreshing breath of air, still amazed he'd changed his mind about her, and apparently wanted to change even more than that.

Part of her felt foolish for agreeing to go with him tonight—he'd been so mean out at the swamp, things had felt so horrible and final. But how could she turn him down?

Because maybe this meant something big. Maybe her graduation seduction attempt had given him a chance to think, to figure out how much he liked her, and how dumb he'd been to reject her. Maybe tonight would be the start of something special between them—finally. She glanced up at the stars through the palm fronds that towered above, drank in the scent of nearby bougainvillea, and let out a feminine sigh. This was going to be the beginning of something *perfect,* she just knew it.

When she spotted headlights in the distance, she stood up and walked toward the road—only to see a sedan go speeding by. A minute later, more headlights, but they belonged to a truck. She sat back down.

By five after ten, she was miffed. Where was he?

Calm down, Kat, he'll be here. He wouldn't stand you up.

Would he?

No, definitely not. *I never make the same mistake twice.* She was counting on that.

By ten after, though, her stomach hurt—nervous fear. *Please show up, please show up.* She wanted him so much. He had to want her back, he just had to.

When another set of headlights appeared, she thought they might belong to a Mustang. Her heartbeat doubled. As they neared, she cautiously pushed back to her feet and watched, watched . . . until finally the car—an older model that glowed silver beneath the light of a streetlamp—slowed to a stop, lifting all the worry from her chest to replace it with excitement.

Glancing inside the open passenger window, she smiled. God, he was hot.

"Hey," he said quietly, leaning toward her. He wore another black T-shirt, his usual fare, and seemed to fill the car with his masculinity. She couldn't wait to climb inside.

"Hey," she said, then reached for the door handle—only to see him push down the button that clicked the lock into place.

Her heart dropped to her stomach. "What's wrong?"

"This isn't gonna happen tonight, kitten."

It was like being punched in the gut, and she had to press her palm against the car to keep her balance.

But don't panic. Maybe something just came up. Maybe he was simply postponing—in his usual gruff way—and she was misreading it. "Another night then?" she asked, trying to hide how unsteady she'd become.

He shook his head. " 'Fraid not."

She drew in her breath. *Don't faint.* "Why?" She boldly met his gaze, unable to believe he was really going to humiliate her again.

"Just not gonna happen, that's all."

"You owe me more of an answer," she snapped, then even banged the flat of her hand on the car.

He let out a tired-sounding sigh. "I'm leaving town, okay?"

She suddenly couldn't breathe. "Leaving? When?"

"Now."

She blinked. "As in . . . right now? This very minute?"

"Yep."

How could this be? "But . . . where are you going? When are you coming back?"

"Don't know. And never."

Now she *really* couldn't breathe. He was telling her she was never going to see him again? She could barely absorb it. She started shaking her head. "I . . . don't understand. What's going on?"

"Look, it's none of your business, all right."

"It *is* my business," she said, deciding not to back down just because he was being brusque. But unfortunately, her voice went softer without her permission when she added, "You were supposed to give me . . . a birthday present. Remember?"

"Guess you'll have to get it somewhere else. I'm sure you've got a whole country club full of little boys who'd love to get under that dress."

It wasn't much worse than other things he'd said to her, but at the moment, the words clogged up everything inside her, making her feel at once frozen and empty. Unable to move, and like a shell of the person she'd been just a few minutes before, all giddy with hopes for some magical summer with a guy who—when all was said and done—barely knew she was alive. It had taken stripping to her underwear just to get his attention—and even that hadn't been enough.

"Look, I have to go. The only reason I came at all was because I didn't want you standing out here all damn night." And she would have, too—probably. Pathetic that he knew that about her. Even more pathetic that, in spite of everything, she was silly enough in this moment to hope it meant maybe he cared about her in some way, just a little.

"I can't believe you're doing this to me," she said numbly, without meaning to.

"Well, believe it, kitten," he said just before the car shot forward, leaving her behind, literally in his dust.

She stood there, watching until the little square taillights disappeared, and for a long while after, too. The air around her stood still, and she could have sworn she felt the humidity creeping back in, stealing her ability to breathe freely. He wasn't coming back, which made her heartbreak and simultaneous humiliation complete now.

Theoretically, she thought she should be able to go back to the party, put on a happy face, and act like nothing had happened. She should be able to be her regular fun-loving self. After all, only she and Brock—and Nina—knew what a fool she'd made of herself. And only she—and she alone—knew that it was about so much more than losing her virginity; only she knew she'd stupidly fallen for him.

But that was enough—her knowledge alone.

She hated him.

And she loved him.

And she didn't know what to do with life at the moment, how to deal with anything.

Finally, she wandered forlornly back up the drive, toward the party. When she arrived, the pool was busy—her friends splashing about, some knocking an inflatable beach ball around, and the DJ her mother had hired was still spinning tunes.

But for her, she realized quickly, the party was over. She couldn't pretend to be happy right now, and it hardly mattered since no one had even noticed the birthday girl had gone missing.

She was trying to remember where she'd left her purse, ready to find her keys and quietly depart, when a familiar hand touched her arm. She looked up to find Scott Powers in a pair of bright yellow swim trunks. He looked good in them—his chest was a little broader and more muscular than she'd have suspected. His eyelids had gone heavy, his expression striking her as one of drunkenness or lust. Probably both. "Where's your bikini, Kat?"

Still feeling numb, detached from the situation, she pointed vaguely toward the pool house.

He let a small smile unfurl. "Need me to help you with it?"

She tilted her head, bit her lip, and thought about the fact that she wasn't wearing panties. And that Brock Denton was an idiot. And that her heart hurt so bad she couldn't think straight.

And at least *somebody* wanted her. A ton of girls would give their right arms to have Scott Powers coming on to them, after all.

"Actually," she said, "I'm not really in a swimming mood."

He cocked his head slightly. "What kind of mood are you *in*?"

She looked him squarely in the eye and said, "I'm in the mood to show you what I'm wearing under this dress."

His eyebrows shot up. "And what's that?"

"Nothing," she said, then grabbed his hand and headed for the pool house.

Chapter Ten

The smell of wet earth still pervaded as Kat and Brock sat quietly, waiting. She missed his warmth but wouldn't dare ask for it back.

Her mind replayed what she'd done the last time Brock had let her down—she'd made the mistake of giving that most important part of herself to someone who didn't matter at all, someone she didn't even like.

Afterward, she'd tried to feel so strong and grown-up, like the sexual princess she'd wanted to be. And she'd acted the part just fine, played it off cool—acted to Scott like a total vixen, utterly carefree. And when he'd asked her out the following week, she'd turned him down, playing the, "it was fun, but just a one-night thing" card as if she were mature enough to truly feel that way—when, really, she'd simply thought she'd rather stick a needle in her eye than let him put that part of him inside her again. She'd never quite thought through it so clearly until now, maybe even pretending to herself that it *had* been cool, but deep down she'd always felt a little sick whenever she remembered Scott Powers or her eighteenth-birthday party.

What a letdown it had been—to have all these sexual feelings and spend them on the wrong guy, a guy who'd left her thinking— *Eh, that was* it?

And what was a girl to do after such a letdown? Try, try again, of course. Only it had never gotten much better. *Some* better, with some guys, but no one, to this day, had ever lived up to her expectations.

Ian will. He has to. And I do love him enough. I do.

Of course, at the moment, she was leaning up against another guy and had just let him kiss her, touch her. Had imagined letting him do a whole lot more than that. Brock, just now, would *definitely* have lived up to her wishes and expectations, no doubt, and no use denying it. But she shoved the thought away before it could weaken her resolve.

Besides, what had happened a few minutes ago was just due to the heat of the moment. The danger factor. It happened in books and movies all the time—people turned passionate when they feared death. In fact, maybe those thoughts about not loving Ian enough for him to hurt her had been trauma-induced, too. Nothing that had happened in this ravine meant anything. Nothing at all.

"What are you thinking about?"

She flinched at Brock's deep voice behind her. "Ian," she answered simply, turning toward him.

She couldn't help thinking he looked a little disappointed. "Oh."

She was considering reminding him again that Ian was her fiancé, so that *of course* she was thinking about him—when Brock grabbed her wrist and lifted a finger to his mouth, silently saying, *Shhhh.*

That's when she heard the rustling of leaves, louder than before because the whole forest was wet, heavier, the dampness seeming to envelop them. She tensed, her stomach churning, her eyes locking on Brock. All had been quiet so long that maybe she'd begun to relax on some level. Now, their peril felt imminent again, and fresh fear stretched through her like a rubber band ready to snap.

As the sound of someone meandering through the wet ferns and greenery grew closer, Kat realized it was coming from the opposite side of the ravine, but she didn't look, too determined to stay still, and maybe too afraid of what she'd see.

"Mr. Government Man, come out, come out, wherever you are. I know you're here. I can smell you. I can smell your fucking fed carcass."

She suppressed a shiver upon recognizing that this wasn't "the nice one"—it was the whack job again.

"Or maybe I smell something else. I hear you got you a girlfriend, Government Man. Hot—yes, Carlos?"

"*Real* hot," Carlos answered, and—oh God—this meant *both* of them were nearby.

The whack job gave an evil chuckle. "Bet she'd be some fun on the ride back after I blow your brains out, fed."

Kat and Brock remained eye to eye, and this time she *couldn't* stop the shiver. His hand still circled her wrist, and he ran his thumb softly back and forth on her skin, clearly trying to calm her.

"You got what I want, Government Man, and I'm not leaving 'til I get it. Can't hide on this little shithole island forever, and I swear to God," he said on a strange little laugh, "I *can* smell you. You're here somewhere. Close. So close."

His footsteps inched nearer, and Kat's heart threatened to beat through her chest as she fought down the urge to vomit. *Please God, please God*, she prayed desperately, sorry she'd cursed Him for his timing a few days ago.

"So close that . . . I found you, fed." The movements stilled,

Brock's eyes steeled on the bank across from them, and Kat followed his gaze to find two dark men with guns, the whack job smiling wide as he lifted his and pointed. "Bang, bang, fed. You're dead."

Kat froze in terror, light-headed. But Brock moved, thrusting her behind him against the muddy embankment as he pushed to his feet. "What brought you back, Francisco? Need to show the boss a body?"

Whack Job shrugged. "Since it's hard to tell when you're really dead, probably not a bad idea, yes? But first, you're going to hand over what you took." Both gun-wielding men were as soaked to the skin as she and Brock, curly black hair plastered to their heads, shirts and shorts clingy and heavy with water.

Brock's gaze narrowed on the mean guy above. "What do you think I took?"

Even looking like a drowned rat, Whack Job's eyes shone with pure evil, especially when he ignored Brock's question and shifted his focus to Kat. "Send the girl up."

"No good place for her to climb the bank here," Brock replied. "Need to walk down some." He pointed in the direction they'd originally come as he took Kat's hand to lead her through the gully on one side of the rainwater now trickling through.

"Well, hurry up about it," Whack Job said, and above them, she could hear the two bad guys moving through the woods along the ravine again, although a thin row of trees blocked them from direct view.

"When we get up there," Brock said lowly, "be ready for my signal to run."

"Won't they shoot me if I do that?"

He gave his head a solemn shake. "They want you."

Her stomach twisted. "I think I'd rather get shot."

He stopped walking and drew close, speaking firm and low. "This isn't over, kitten. Don't give up on me now."

As he turned to lead her on through the ditch, the floor of it now mushy beneath their feet, his words almost stung. She knew he was talking about the hideous situation they were in. But God help her, she heard more in them, even now—she heard ten years of heartache and knew, in that second, that she still couldn't quite let it all go, no matter how she tried to move on inside.

"I need you to be tough for me," he said over his shoulder as they trudged on, then peered back at her. "Can you do that? Be tough for me?"

She nodded. She could. She had to. Because she wanted out of this. And despite her doubt, something in his eyes made her believe they could actually *get* out.

"Here." Coming back into view, Whack Job pointed with his gun toward a sloped area in the gully's wall that looked climbable. "Get out here."

Kat's heart continued to pound as Brock made his way up, then pulled her behind him over slippery mud. Once at the top with the two scary hooligans, she wanted nothing more than to throw herself into Brock's arms but knew it would be smarter to do what he'd said—act tough. As tough as possible. Even if tough, at the moment, just meant *not* letting herself look needy.

"Hot damn, my brother didn't lie," Whack Job said, his accent seeming thicker with excitement as his eyes moved down her body. "You are a nice piece of ass, *chica*."

She wanted to spit at him, but ignored him instead, keeping her eyes glued to Brock's chest and wishing her heart would slow down.

Whack Job only laughed at her—then turned more serious again. "Now march."

Kat went first, then Brock, then the two bad guys—brothers, she presumed from what Whack Job had said—following behind, guns at the ready. She didn't quite know the way, of course, but

Whack Job seemed to, instructing her at one point to bear right, and she guessed they would circle the back of the island and make their way to the dock.

As she trudged through the undergrowth, she wondered when they were going to kill Brock. Would they do it right in front of her? Probably. The image drew all the breath from her lungs. After that, it wouldn't really matter what they did to her—it would measure nothing compared to watching Brock die.

Just then, a hard *Ooomf!* came from behind, along with a crash on the ground, and when she realized one of the bad guys had tripped and fallen, Brock said, just loud enough for her to hear, "Now, Kat. Run, baby."

Part of her didn't want to—it took everything she had to leave Brock behind—but she had to do what he said, so she gathered her skirt around her thighs and took off, sprinting for all she was worth. She never looked back, fear burning in her chest as she heard a small scuffle, and she prayed again *Please God, please God*, for both Brock and herself, until she heard Whack Job say, "Get her, Carlos!"

Like earlier, she concentrated on the ground as she ran, trying to avoid roots and branches, trying to keep her skirt from snagging on anything and her feet steady—but this time she also occasionally lifted her eyes because she didn't want to run in a circle again.

Get away. Get away for Brock. She knew he'd never feel for her what she'd once felt for him, but she also knew her safety was important to him, and she yearned to do what he'd said, be tough for him, make him proud.

The only problem was, if her ears didn't deceive her, Carlos was gaining on her. She ran as hard as she possibly could, but he grew closer, closer—she heard him closing in right behind her, the sound of his footsteps like a locomotive bearing down. And no matter how she tried, her feet simply wouldn't move any faster—until he tackled her in the soft, sandy island dirt, his big body slamming her to the ground.

"Where are we going?" Brock asked over his shoulder as Francisco herded him through the jungle.

"*You* tell *me*, fed."

Brock sighed. It wasn't enough that he was worried sick about Kat, hoping like hell she could outrun Carlos, but now he had Francisco making no sense. "What?"

"Where's that key, fed?"

Ah, that. The moment the evil Morales brother had mentioned Brock taking something from him, it had all made sense—*that's* why they'd come back. They'd figured out that if the key wasn't on the boat, Brock must have taken it. Of course, he'd never admit to having it. As long as they didn't have the key, they couldn't kill him. Not unless they wanted to risk never finding it. "What key, man?"

Of course, finding it wouldn't actually be all that hard. It was still zipped into the side pocket on his swim trunks, currently tossed over the back of a chair in the bungalow. But they didn't know that.

"The *key*. The fucking *key*." Francisco jabbed the gun into his back to shove him along. "I know you've got it, fed. Now you'd better lead me straight to it, or I *will* blow your brains out in front of your pretty little girlfriend, then I'll make her eat them."

Okay, that turned even *his* FBI-hardened stomach—thank God Kat was nowhere around to hear it. But he didn't let it intimidate him. "Look, dude, I don't know what key you're talking about."

And when Francisco jabbed the gun into his back again, Brock got pissed. By this whole situation. He knew he didn't have a gun, and they had two, but they were a couple of incompetents and he should damn well be able to outsmart them. And he was tired of fucking around out here.

"Fine," he said, "you want to know where the key is? I'll tell you. It's back in the gully where I left it when you found us." He stopped, spun, and pointed in the direction from which they'd traveled.

When Francisco automatically looked that way, Brock grabbed the evil brother's gun-wielding arm, forcing it skyward, then gave him a knee to the groin, forcing him down with a deep, guttural groan.

But despite Francisco's obvious pain, the bastard didn't let go of the gun, as Brock had hoped, so they rolled on the ground, fighting for it. A shot fired, blasting upward through the trees. Francisco managed an admirable blow to Brock's gut—damn it!—slowing his momentum. "Son of a bitch fed!" Francisco yelled, once, twice, but Brock said nothing, conserving his energy as he focused on wrenching the pistol from the bad guy's fist.

When Brock finally closed his fingers around the grip, Francisco knocked it free, sending the gun flying to land with a thud in the brush probably fifteen feet away. Shit. But that was better than Francisco's having it.

Both men instinctively seemed to know they could keep beating each other to a pulp all day and it wouldn't change this situation— firepower was the key—so they both struggled to their feet. Francisco lunged, but Brock managed to trip him, sending him face-first into the dirt. Brock rushed past his fallen form and, after a moment, spotted the gun, resting deep in the fronds of an enormous fern. He started to reach for it, then pulled back upon realizing a large brown snake happened to be gliding past right next to it, but it had stopped, lifting its flat reptilian head to eye the encroacher. Damn it to hell.

Brock lifted his gaze to his opponent to see Francisco had stopped short, too.

Then he thought—*Shit, I'm going for it*, and took a smooth step past the snake, carefully watching its head, ready to dive away if need be. The snake's eyes followed him, but Brock swiftly snatched up the gun and backed away without harm.

He turned to see Francisco sprinting through the jungle away from him, with a good head start. "Stop or I'll shoot!" Brock yelled, and when Francisco kept going, he cocked the pistol and fired. But the evil Morales brother continued running, and two seconds later disappeared into the thick foliage.

Brock jogged all the way back around the island while trying to watch for trouble. He kept the gun cocked. And he thought of Kat, who, wherever she might be, was scared shitless by now. *I'm coming, kitten, I'm coming.*

Please be okay, he thought, but then he decided she *had* to be, because the brothers would surely try to ransom her when he caught up with them. And he'd trade the damn key for Kat in a second—except for one thing. Give them the key, and he and Kat were both dead, no question. No way the brothers could let him live, even *before*, let alone now. A thought that brought home the cold, hard truth: Someone would die before this was over. *Just don't let it be Kat.* He remained pretty determined not to let it be him, either.

He headed for the dock, figuring it was a likely meeting point for the brothers—and if he found no one there, he'd make the short run to the bungalow.

But as first the water, then the dock, then the big, shiny, white yacht came into view through the trees, he realized he wouldn't have to look any further. Francisco and Carlos both stood on the boat's front deck—with Kat. Carlos held a gun to her head.

Brock's chest nearly exploded in anger.

But keep cool, man, keep cool. She didn't appear hurt, her clothes weren't torn, they hadn't done anything to her. So all he had to do was get her off that boat safely. And, of course, figure out how to get rid of two thugs. Yet mission number one was getting Kat back onshore with him where she belonged.

Postponing this wasn't going to help anything, so he boldly stepped out from the trees into the first bright sunlight he'd seen since early that morning, pointing Francisco's gun at Carlos. The sun nearly blinded him for a second as his eyes adjusted, but he held the .45 steady, ready to shoot to kill.

Kat saw him first—she flinched, her eyes widening with emotion. But he couldn't concentrate on her now—his focus was on the brothers, and that damn gun Carlos held on her.

"Let her go," he said, coming closer, both hands on the pistol's silver grips as he centered Carlos firmly in the sight. "Let her off the boat and you two can just go on your way." It would never be that simple, he knew, but he had to make the suggestion.

"Not without that fucking key, man," Francisco said.

"Forget about the key and realize you're lucky to get out of this alive," Brock countered. "Let her go, then point that boat somewhere far away from here, and this can all be over."

Francisco glared at him, menacing as ever, his dark hair dried from the rain but sweaty and hanging in his eyes. "No way. No fucking way."

"Why not, Francisco? Just call it quits, call it even. You'd be getting off light."

"I'd be getting screwed. Lotta money coming my way, man, and you're not going to keep me from getting what I've worked for."

He should've known by now that Francisco was a lost cause, too bent on getting something for nothing, even if it might cost him his life—so he turned his talk to Carlos instead. "You need to let the girl off the boat, Carlos—now. Then maybe you can talk some sense into your brother and get the hell out of here."

Standing between Francisco and Kat on the wide deck, Carlos looked agitated, confused. Not good—guys with guns who were confused. "I don't know. I can't trust you anymore. You lied before—you're probably lying now, too."

"No, dude, listen to me. You let her go and our beef is over."

"Like hell it is," Francisco chimed in, then glared at Carlos. "You let that girl go, I will fucking kill you. Understand?"

Damn it, shut up, Francisco. Brock didn't have a chance reasoning with Carlos with his asshole brother right next to him.

"Listen to me, Carlos," he said, trying again. "You let her go, and this can end without bloodshed. You don't, and . . ." He sighed. "I don't want to hurt you, man." And he really didn't. But deep in his bones, he feared it was coming to that, fast. Unless he could get Carlos to listen.

"Shut up and leave me alone!" Carlos snapped, sounding more frazzled—the last thing Brock wanted. He stood darting his gaze back and forth between Kat and Brock, his mustache twitching.

But Brock *couldn't* leave Carlos alone. Because next to the nervous brother, Kat stood trying her damnedest to be brave, yet tears rolled silently down her cheeks. And Brock had done this to her. By swimming up onto this island, he'd let this happen. And she was *not* going to die, damn it. She simply was *not*.

"I know you don't really want to hurt anybody, Carlos," Brock said, trying for calm persuasion. "So I'm asking you to put the gun down."

"You put *yours* down!" Carlos demanded. His pistol was shaking now—Jesus—shaking right next to Kat's beautiful face. Brock had been trying to stay cool up to this point, but his patience was fading fast. He was gonna have to end this.

"Shoot him, man!" Francisco yelled at his brother. "Shoot that fucking fed—now!"

Brock knew what he had to do. He hated it with all his heart, but he knew. Carlos had become a loose cannon and there seemed no stopping it unless *Brock* stopped it, one way or another.

Last chance, Carlos. "I never wanted to hurt you man, still don't. I was just doing my job." He took a deep breath, aiming, aiming more carefully than he ever had in his life. Fortunately for Kat, he was an excellent shot when given this much time. "But now you *have* to let her go."

Next to Carlos, Francisco seethed, shoulders heaving, and although Brock kept his eyes peeled on Carlos, it seemed almost like Francisco knew what was coming, knew Brock wasn't gonna wait much longer. "Give *me* the fucking gun then," Francisco said. "If you aren't gonna kill him, I am."

Looking a little crazed, Carlos swung the gun around toward his brother for a fraction of a second, then turned it back on Kat.

And Brock neared the breaking point. "I don't want to bring you down, but I will. And it'll happen so fast you won't even have a chance to pull your own trigger. Now let her go!"

Clearly, Francisco could see Carlos waffling more and more—and that's when he reached past his brother for the pistol. Carlos automatically yanked it back, toward his body, to keep it from Francisco, but it took the aim off Kat long enough for Brock to squeeze the trigger.

The shot blasted through the still air in the cove and Carlos went down hard without ever uttering a sound. A shot exploded from *his* gun as it fell to the deck, skittering across it, but no one was hit. Brock ran toward the boat, gun still raised, as Kat and Francisco both scrambled for the loose pistol.

Kat ignored her horror at having the crazy man next to her shot dead, and she ignored the blood staining the front of his shirt and spreading in a large puddle beneath him. She ignored the fear still pounding through her body with every breath she consumed—and ran for the gun.

Whack Job raced for it, too, and she knew if she dove for the pistol, they'd wrestle and he'd win, so just before he made a last lunge, she kicked it hard, watching as it slid over the edge, plopping in the water below.

So he grabbed her around the ankle instead.

She kicked more, instinctively—and got him once in the face, at which point he let out a yowl—before they both heard the distinctive sound of a gun being cocked nearby. She looked up to see Brock standing at the end of the boarding plank where it stretched to the dock. Whack Job still held her leg from where he lay prone on the deck, but he froze in place, too.

Brock's voice was clear and commanding. "Let her off the goddamn boat, or I'll drop you just like I did your brother."

Slowly, Francisco released her ankle. His expression flashed more hate than she'd ever witnessed, but she didn't waste time pondering it, instead scurrying to the ramp and down to Brock and safety.

She didn't even think, just did what came naturally, throwing her arms around his neck, feeling the warmth of the man who'd saved her. One large hand curled automatically around her waist, but the other still held a gun, and it never wavered from the bad guy on the boat. "Now, *you* get off the boat, Francisco," Brock said, his voice low and menacing, "and drag Carlos with you." Kat realized Brock intended to leave Francisco here with his dead brother while they took the yacht back to the mainland, rather than forcing her to travel with them.

The awful man struggled to his feet, looking at once evil and harried, eyes crazed. He paused over his brother's dead body, letting out a small sob that Kat felt in her gut, even though she suffered no sympathy for either man. Then he rushed to the helm and started the ignition.

"Damn it, Francisco, I mean it! Get off the goddamn boat!"

"You'll have to shoot me first!" he yelled back.

Kat watched as Brock drew in a hard breath, eyes pained, gun still aimed at Francisco—but he didn't pull the trigger.

Within a moment, the yacht accelerated away from the dock—Francisco hadn't bothered to haul in the boarding ramp, so it flopped hard against the boat's side, and he began shaking his fist, yelling as tears rolled down his cheeks, "You killed my brother, you fucking fed asshole! You killed my brother! I'll make you sorry you were ever born—I'll make you pay!"

Once the rear of the boat faced them—the now-ironic name, EASY MONEY, getting smaller as the yacht departed, leaving a wide and oddly gentle wake—Brock let the gun drop to the ground next to him with a solid *phlunk*. "Shit," he said, but then he wrapped his arms full around Kat, giving her his full attention. "Are you okay, honey?"

Oh God, he was so warm, felt so good. Had he just kissed the top of her head, her hair? She wasn't sure, but luxuriated in the mere presence of his hard, solid body against hers. "Yeah—just . . ." She took a deep breath, attempting not to cry anymore. "Trying really hard to be tough for you."

He pulled back to look at her, his dark eyes earnest, relieved—somehow almost . . . sweet. "You did great, kitten. You were so tough, so good." Then he kissed her forehead and it zigzagged down through her like a tiny pinball, spreading sensation all through her tired body.

Above her, though, he sighed, and she peered up to find him watching the boat in the distance. "Damn it," he groused, loosening his grip slightly. "I should have taken the fucking boat. I should have shot him and taken the boat, and we'd be fine now."

She shook her head lightly. "We're fine now anyway—as in *alive*—and that's all that matters."

Brock's gaze clouded darkly as he peered down into her eyes and spoke slowly. "I'm just now realizing . . . maybe I'm not a very good killer."

"That's not a *bad* thing, Brock."

His expression remained grim. "For an FBI agent, it's not a good thing, either."

She couldn't help digging a little deeper, trying—as always—to understand him more. "You said you killed a guy once. And . . . you didn't sound emotional about *that*."

"Yeah. But he was . . . worse than you can imagine. A drug lord, and a really shitty excuse for a human being—way worse than Francisco. He needed to die bad." He shook his head and tossed another glance at the boat carrying the two brothers away. "Maybe I'm glad I didn't kill Francisco just now. But since I had to kill somebody . . . I wish it had been him, not Carlos. Carlos thought I was his friend," he said softly. Then he swallowed hard and looked down at her, lifting one hand to cup her cheek. "He left me no choice, though. I couldn't let him hurt you, kitten."

She got the impression he needed to be absolved. And that he might actually care what she thought of him as a person. "Brock, you did what you had to. And they're gone now—so we're safe. The bad part's over."

Yet he appeared troubled. "Thing is, kitten, I don't want to scare you—I know you've already been through hell today—but I *shouldn't* have let Francisco get away. Because he'll be back. And . . ."

His words stunned her. "What?"

He let out another sigh, looking hesitant.

"Just tell me," she demanded.

He ran his hands from her shoulders smoothly down her arms to capture her hands. "Chances are he won't come with just one other guy this time. Or just a couple of guns."

Doom settled over Kat like a heavy blanket she couldn't shake off, and she nearly crumbled in his arms.

"I'm sorry, kitten. I really fucked up."

Yet she hated hearing him say that. Because it wasn't true, not really. "Just by being a decent man."

He shook his head. "Doesn't matter. Right now, right here, I needed to be a federal agent first and screw the rest. Sometimes . . . there's no room for decency."

"I don't believe that. I'm glad you're a decent man. A *good* man, Brock. There's no shame in that."

His eyes still looked glassy, filled with emotion, as he glanced once more at the retreating boat, still visible probably a half mile offshore now, then ran his hand through his hair as he brought his eyes back to hers. "Here's what we'll have to do. Work on a good hiding place in the woods, someplace that will camouflage us. Stock it with some supplies. Be ready to go there the second there's any sign of—"

An explosion in the distance made them both flinch, then drew their gazes to the water. The yacht had just become a ball of fire, although only small bits of black smoke billowed skyward. "Jesus Christ," Brock murmured.

"What the hell?" Kat asked.

Brock slowly shook his head, still watching the yacht. "No telling. Could be that stray bullet from Carlos's gun hit something vital. Could have just nicked the fuel line or something so that it took a few minutes for any fallout to result."

Kat swallowed, considering the implications. "Do you think . . . he got off the boat?"

Brock seemed certain, giving his head a slow, thorough shake. "You don't have warning with an explosion. And besides, Francisco couldn't swim."

"What about . . . flotation devices, life jackets?"

But Brock shook his head again. "Happened too fast—no time for him to grab anything. Probably no time . . . *at all*. I'd bet he died instantly."

For some reason, the news took Kat's breath away, and she slumped slightly.

Brock caught her in his arms. "Hey, hey, hey—what's wrong, kitten?"

She shook her head, peering up at him helplessly. "I'm not sure. I just . . ." She swallowed. "Weird to think of people dying, that's all. And it's just been . . . a rough day."

At this, Brock drew her into a big, warm, consuming hug, exactly what she needed in that moment. "We're okay now," he reassured her. "They're both gone now and we're okay, kitten." They embraced for a long moment—and the truth was, if it had been up to Kat the hug might never have ended, because he felt so strong and protective, so masculine and sure, so . . . Brock.

When finally he released her, he silently took her hand and led her toward the path that would deliver them to the bungalow. Which felt like a surprisingly wonderful place to be at the moment. Where they'd been together before—before all this danger and chasing and shooting had started. In a way, it felt like going home.

Upon walking in, the comfort of the place surrounded Kat immediately. Old and still in serious need of redecorating, but at the moment, it felt like a palace. She'd never been so glad to see the antique armoire or that Formica table.

"Food," she murmured, spying the refrigerator. The clock on the nightstand said it was nearly 7:00 P.M., and they hadn't eaten since breakfast.

Brock snatched up a couple of bananas from the counter and passed her one, starting to peel the other for himself. A bit over-ripe for her taste, but at the moment, she hardly cared. She yanked down the peeling and took a huge bite.

With her free hand, she jerked open the fridge door and drew out bottles of water, which they both started to gulp, then she grabbed two of the Milky Way bars she'd been hiding in a drawer and hadn't told him about.

"Hey, where did these come from?" he asked accusingly when she handed him one.

"Secret stash. Don't whine or you won't get anymore."

Looking amused, he ditched what remained of his banana and ripped into the chocolate.

They stood in the kitchen gorging themselves like people possessed. But almost as soon as the strange, rushed dinner of bananas, candy bars, and water—supplemented with a few corn chips from a rolled-down bag on the table—came to an end, things suddenly felt awkward, and Kat had no idea why.

Now that the light euphoria of food was wearing off and the daylight starting to fade, an unexpected light-headedness struck her. Images of the day started to flash through her mind. Her and Brock kissing in the ditch. Running, running, running, her heart hurting in her chest. That gun to her head and the very real possibility that she was going to die. She let out a heavy breath and reached out to grab on to one of the kitchen chairs.

"Hey, you okay?"

She raised her eyes from the table to Brock. He looked a little shell-shocked himself standing there in damp clothes just as filthy as her own, and she couldn't help thinking they were both suffering the same *whoosh* of emotions. "Yes," she answered. Then, "No. I don't know."

"Come here," he said, but he moved toward her instead and drew her into another of his great, engulfing embraces. She went willingly because she knew it felt good there, and she also knew she needed his comfort to get through this. "You're safe now, kitten, I promise. No more danger. You're safe."

With her arms around his neck, his around her waist, they stood quietly, chest to chest, torso to torso, and Kat realized that she'd never until today understood just how vital someone's touch could be to her well-being. But not just *someone's*. Right now, no one else's would have felt nearly so soothing.

She drew back just slightly, not to end the hug, but simply yearning to see him. He stood nearly a head taller than her, but the move brought into view an angle of darkly stubbled chin, his strong jawbone, his closed eyes . . . and the lone tear rolling down his cheek. She felt that tear deep inside, like a blow to the stomach, and it forced her own eyes shut.

"Are you thinking of Carlos?" she whispered into his neck.

She felt his silent nod, the dip of his head. His pain seemed to drip onto her, and she was willing to absorb some of it for him, whatever she could do to take it away.

Still nuzzling close, she lifted a hand to his cheek and whispered low in his ear. "You did what you had to. It's all right."

Another slow, painful nod. "I know," he breathed. "But it's not just Carlos. It's you. I was so afraid . . . so afraid he would hurt you."

His grip on her tightened as he lifted one hand to the back of her neck, and then to her hair, stroking, stroking, gathering it in his hand at her nape, and she opened her eyes. His rested only a few inches away. And so did his mouth, lips parted. His look was hungry, needful. The same torrid desire filled her, too.

When he spoke, it sounded as if the words had been wrenched from his soul. "I need you so much right now, kitten."

"I know," she said softly. "I know."

He was a beautiful man in pain.

His hands possessive, his eyes dark with passion.

She closed her eyes.

And gave herself over to him.

Chapter Eleven

*H*is kiss came warm and hungry, tinged with chocolate, and deep with the need he'd acknowledged. She drank it in, licked at his tongue when it pushed between her lips, and held so tightly around his neck that she dug her fingernails into his shoulders. She needed, too.

His hands dropped to her rear, tugging her close against him so that the stone-hard column between his legs pressed into the soft juncture of her thighs, just where she longed for it most. If there'd been a shred of resistance remaining inside her, any chance she was going to stop—that killed it. A sensation so delicious she thought that, in this moment, she would have died for it.

Their kisses grew hotter, harsher, more frantic and bruising. She clawed deeper into his flesh, feeling him wince at the pleasure of just how intensely her own hunger ran. His fingers sank harder into her butt as he thrust at her through their clothes. They both moaned, and she instinctually lifted one leg over his hip, needing to be more entwined with him.

His kisses trickled warm and intimate to her neck, and she leaned her head back. His mouth dropped to the vee of her soiled top, descending onto the curve of one breast. She arched for him—*more, kiss me more*—and his teeth and tongue and lips worked over the soft flesh as she held his head there, running her fingers through his dark hair, until he could go no further. Clearly too impatient to untie the top, he simply reached for her breasts through the fabric, caressing hotly and lifting his mouth back to hers for another hungry tongue kiss.

Both panted in slow, jagged breaths by the time he picked her up by her ass and turned to set her on the Formica table. She closed her legs around his thighs, wanting to feel that beautifully solid part of him up against her again, craving it. "Oh . . ." she moaned at the contact, then drew him back into another kiss. His hands found her face, then her hair. Their tongues played intimately together, and she lifted her pelvis to meet his hard-on, needing more, so much more.

When he pulled back, she wanted to kill him, but forgave when his hands slid up her thighs, under her skirt, his fingers closing quickly on the hem of her panties. "Lift up," he said in low command, and she braced herself on her hands until he drew the undies down.

She reached to push up his shirt, let him know she wanted it off—so he ripped it over his head and flung it aside. The only sound as he moved back in was their labored breathing, and all she saw was masculine flesh and eyes that looked as if they would devour her.

Gazes locked, she reached between them for the button on his shorts, then the zipper. No underwear—something she hadn't thought about him not having—so when she reached inside, her hand closed instantly around him, flesh to hot flesh. They both groaned, and his head fell back even as his hands curled around her bottom again, drawing them together under her skirt.

Oh God, I'm really touching him there. Such heat flared inside her as she'd never known. Her chest ached, and a moan tore from her throat. And nothing else in the world mattered but getting more of him.

Releasing him below, she sank her hands into the solid muscles of his shoulders and tilted for him, almost reflexively. She bit her lower lip as his erection nudged at her most intimate place, then plunged inside.

A light sweep of pain—because of waiting with Ian, it had been a while since sex—but half a second later, nothing but pure, deep pleasure. Filling her. Brock inside her.

She'd waited so long for this moment, so long to know this connection with him. She held on to him tight, shutting her eyes against the profound emotions assaulting her and thinking—*He's in me. Finally in me.* She never wanted the moment to end.

But then he began to move, thrust—and it was suddenly okay for the moment to end, because this was a really good moment, too, in a whole different way. "Oh!" she cried as he pulled her to him, hands still cupping her rear, then again, again, so deep, incredibly filling, delivering every ounce of bliss she'd ever dreamed such a physical union could hold.

She moved with him, finding the right rhythm, then pulled back enough to meet his feral eyes, see his clenched teeth, feel all the power emanating from his body and flowing fast and hard into hers.

He was more holding her than letting her sit on the table now, and she gyrated against him, aware of the growing pleasure at her core, aware that everything inside her was moving in just the right way and that she was getting close, so close.

She rocked with more abandon, moaning in raw joy as she sought the orgasm she already knew would be the best of her life. He moved with her, thrusting in the tempo she'd set, letting her guide them.

"God, oh God," she said. Then kissed him, tongue and lips and passion overflowing, breaking the connection of their mouths only to cry her release as she toppled headlong into the deepest, surest ecstasy she'd ever experienced. It was like the sun had shattered and rained shimmering bits of light and heat all around her. It was like exploding from the inside out. She suddenly knew what people meant when they said the earth moved.

"Oh my God," she breathed, her whole body trembling as the hot pulses finally began to fade. "Oh . . ." She clung to him, her face against his neck, kissing, little kisses.

"Unh . . ." he groaned, the sound bursting forth as if involuntarily, and she felt him jerk inside her.

"What . . . ?" she whispered.

"Oh God," he said, and then he was lowering her back onto the table and driving, driving, hard, deep, his breath coming fast and warm on her neck, and she locked her ankles behind his back to let him know she wanted more. He pounded into her that way until letting out another ferocious moan, one last deeper-than-deep thrust—then collapsed gently, his hard muscles seeming to slump all around her as his forehead came to rest on her shoulder.

They stayed like that for a long, quiet minute, recovering. Through the open window across the room, she heard the crashing tide in the distance. Behind him, she caught sight of banana peels and candy wrappers strewn on the counter. She was coming back to the world, to real life. And it suddenly seemed like a better place than she'd left behind.

His voice cut through the solitude in a low rasp. "My God, kitten, I'm sorry."

She blinked, stunned, as he slowly lifted his head, gently pulled out, then reached down to zip his pants, actually looking guilty. "For?" she asked.

He released a heavy breath. "Because I meant to back off, I swear I did. And I know this changes things for you, about your marriage. And so maybe I just ruined your life."

Oh. God. Yeah, she was supposed to get married this week.

To someone other than the guy she'd just had mind-blowing sex with.

She'd, amazingly, forgotten that for a moment.

Then realized—maybe that was part of why the world had suddenly seemed so much sweeter.

Of course, the implications were overwhelming. If she was serious about her claims to Brock, serious about treating marriage with reverence and respect—she *couldn't* marry Ian now. And that meant . . . oh God, that meant so much. From canceling an enormous wedding that half the free world was involved in . . . to breaking her father's heart into so many different pieces she couldn't even count them . . . to maybe being responsible for changing her family's entire existence for the worse.

But she couldn't take back what had just happened with Brock. No, she'd just put major life changes into motion, for more than just herself, and there was no altering it—only dealing with it.

"You're right," she said, trying to be stoic. "You just ruined everything."

He dropped his gaze to the floor. "I really am sorry, kitten."

"We can't go back in time, though," she went on, "so the way I see it, you may as well keep right on ruining it."

He lifted his dark, sexy gaze. "Huh?"

She swallowed. "Because we've had sex, I'm going to have to call the wedding off, change everything about what I thought my life was going to be, and let down a hell of a lot of people. But not until someone comes for us on Thursday."

"And?" He leaned forward slightly, clearly trying to understand.

"And until then, we may as well have more sex. Lots of it."

Now it was he who swallowed hard.

"I need to be comforted," she explained, completely straight-faced and feeling just as sincere as she did sexual.

His eyes appeared somewhat glazed as her words began to sink in. "Then . . . I'm your man."

"Yes, you are," she said, a bit more softly.

Brock stepped up close to the table, where she still sat, and used one bent finger to lift her chin so he could look into her eyes. "Kitten," he said slowly, "what just happened here? What just changed?"

"I just . . . figured out what I want."

"Which is?"

You. No, that was going too far, being too honest. So she reached out to press her palm over the still-rigid bulge in his shorts. "This."

He looked pleased in that arrogant, masculine way of his, and she didn't even mind, since it somehow diverted attention from the fact that what she'd *really* just said was—*I'm willing to trade my entire future for sex with you.*

And the future almost didn't even matter. Because except for when she thought about how this would affect her parents, she suddenly felt happier and more alive than she had in . . . a long while. Months, definitely. Years, maybe. So she didn't care if it was just about sex for him. She almost didn't care if it was just about sex for *her*—although she knew, despite herself, that could never be true. This was Brock, and that meant it was about more—that simple.

But all she planned to concentrate on for the next three days and nights was pure unadulterated lust—and how best to fulfill it. She was going to live every fantasy she'd ever had of him and then some. She was going to drink her fill of Brock Denton . . . and hope that when it was all over it was enough.

But before she could *completely* focus on lust, she figured she'd better discuss something with him—she hated to bring it up, but it would just be plain irresponsible not to. "Um, are you aware we didn't use a condom?"

He tilted his head. "Didn't have one on me, I'm afraid."

"I'm on the pill," she told him, "but . . . how often do you . . . not have one on you?"

Remorse laced his grin. "Only when I wash up on islands without my wallet."

"So you're saying . . ."

"You're safe with me, kitten. Promise."

"Same for you, with me."

"Good to know. And . . . sorry we didn't discuss that beforehand."

She shook her head. "Takes two to tango. Or to do it on the kitchen table. I didn't exactly bring it up, either."

He moved his hand to cup her cheek. "And about today, I want you to know—I'm sorry you had to go through that. If there was anything I could have done to prevent it, I would have. And I'm really proud of you for not falling apart—and for kicking that gun overboard. That was quick thinking." With that, he leaned in for a warm kiss that melted all through her and ensured that the next couple of nights were going to be heaven on earth, and a hell of a good way to forget about today.

"I need to take a shower," she said. "But maybe while I'm in there, you can think of some way to reward me for my courage under fire."

He gave her a sexy-as-sin grin. "I'll reward you, all right. I'll reward you all night long." Another kiss, this one as sweet as the first, warm, lingering—and it started to get her hot all over again.

"Of course, *you'll* need to clean up, too."

He glanced toward the bathroom, just a few feet away. "We could clean up *together*," he suggested with raised eyebrows.

Slowly, Kat smiled. She'd never actually showered with a guy before. She'd had invitations from a lover or two, but something about it had always sounded a little too intimate. Like something a person should only do with someone they were really, deeply comfortable with—because, movie images aside, what if she slipped and fell, what if she got shampoo in her eye, what if it was just plain fumbly and awkward in there? But after all she'd been through with Brock today, climbing into the shower with him would feel as instinctive as breathing.

Five minutes later, she opened the bathroom door to spy Brock, naked, from behind, water sluicing down his perfect body through the clear shower door. Thank God the sound of the water drowned out the little, "Unh," that escaped her at the sight.

He'd offered to get some warm water going while she grabbed something to put on after. Now, as she looked down at the jammies in her hands, it occurred to her that she probably wouldn't *need* anything for after.

Dropping her cami and panties on the edge of the old sink, then shedding her dirty clothes, she glanced down at her *own* nakedness. He'd seen her close to naked before. And they'd just gone at it like animals on the kitchen table. Yet she'd been right—this would be more intimate than anything else they'd shared.

But that was okay. Because even as she kept telling herself, *it's only sex, it's only good, hot, wild sex,* she knew deep inside that being still more intimate with Brock would fulfill all those high-school dreams. And even if she was a little nervous, she wasn't afraid. One part of her still couldn't believe this had happened—she'd been with him now, in that closest of ways that she'd always wanted. Yet a bigger part not only believed it, but was ready for much, much more.

Slowly, she slid one of the glass door panels to the side.

Brock looked over his shoulder, his gaze meeting hers before dropping to give her body a slow, heat-inspiring perusal. "Damn, kitten."

She felt weirdly sheepish being so filthy—she'd seen the dried mud on her knees and calves, the layer of sweat-smudged dust on her arms and chest, and God only knew what her face and hair looked like at this point. "I'm all dirty," she replied.

He arched one brow. "That's what I'm counting on."

She let a playful smile leak free as she stepped into the small tub shower with him, the cool spray blocked by his large frame.

He immediately focused on her breasts, causing their peaks to tighten under his scrutiny. He made a teasing, *tsking* sound and said, "Sunburn's all gone."

She cast a questioning smile. "Why do you sound disappointed?"

"I was gonna kiss 'em and make 'em better."

The words hissed down through her body like a burning dynamite fuse. "I'll still let you kiss 'em," she promised.

And with fire in his dark eyes, he backed her against the shower wall. He pressed her arms over her head, his fingers threading with hers against the old tile, his body grazing hers from chest to thigh. His kiss came hot, long, pleasantly capturing her. She'd never felt such power flowing from any man as she did with Brock, and it was impossible not to lose herself in it.

She returned the kiss, luxuriating in the lushness of his mouth on hers, aware that her nipples raked against his chest and that— *oh yes!*—his erection was growing delightfully harder against her belly, making the small of her back ache with desire.

When he broke away, it was only to head south—he rained still more sweet kisses over her neck, down onto her chest, then her breast. When he took the taut bud into his mouth, suckling, slow and deep, the exquisite pull reached to her very core. "Oh . . ." she heard herself practically purr.

"I've been dying to get a taste of these, kitten," he admitted, then swirled his tongue around her nipple to leave her moaning.

"They might, uh, taste better after the shower," she said, somewhere between a sigh and a smile.

Moving on to the other breast, he raked his tongue across the pink bead as he gazed up at her. "Taste fine right now. Sweet. Like you." The compliment tumbled through her, mingling with heat, and she decided she'd been wrong about liking him better when he was the silent type.

When finally he finished laving her sensitive breasts, she couldn't help but glance down—because his erection had continued to press into her, and while she'd recently experienced the joy of feeling it inside her, she hadn't yet really *seen* what rested between his thighs.

Only—it wasn't exactly resting. And it was easily the most beautiful and majestic male specimen she'd ever encountered. She bit her lip, weak at the sight.

"Like?" he asked.

She lifted her gaze to find his mere inches away, not a hint of a smile on his handsome face. He was so hot she had to swallow. "A lot," she breathed.

He leaned in for another tongue kiss and she decided to prove her point by wrapping her hand around him, just like when she'd first unzipped his pants. Mmm, silk over steel. He moaned.

She glanced down for another peek—but then, oh my! She gasped upon spotting his tattoo: an angular, graphical version of the sun—right behind his stiff shaft. "Oh my God." Kat had thought she'd seen sexy things before, thought she *knew* sexy. But this was . . . oh, this was something new.

"Like?" he asked again.

This time she couldn't even answer except for another eloquent, "Unh."

Looking sensual as hell, he rewarded her with yet one more scintillating kiss, after which she tried to catch her breath. "How did, um . . . I mean . . . did this hurt?" It was located squarely between his navel and the base of his penis.

"They all *hurt*, kitten."

"But, I mean . . . how did this . . . you know, come about?"

He cocked his head, clearly amused by her bewilderment. "I've got a friend in Miami who's a tattoo artist, so I told her I wanted one someplace where very few people would see it. She suggested *this*, and I thought, what the hell."

Kat glanced down again, pushing his erection aside just enough to get another good look. "I bet she enjoyed her work *that* day."

He chuckled. "Actually, I think it was just another tattoo to her."

That sounded impossible. "Well, it's not just another tattoo to *me*." She couldn't quite get over it, in fact. And it made her want to spend a *lot* more time in that area.

"Knowing you like it so much, kitten, makes it worth every ounce of pain." He narrowed his gaze on her hotly, just before dropping it to her hips and below, as if looking for something.

Shit—she'd told him *she* had a tattoo in a private place, too. She cringed, but he was too busy searching to notice. "Where is it? On your ass? Turn around." He steadied his hands at the curve of her waist, ready to spin her away from him.

She let out a sigh, feeling like an idiot. "I have a confession."

He met her eyes. "Oh?"

She clenched her teeth lightly, feeling utterly caught. "I . . . don't really have a tattoo. I kinda lied."

He lowered his chin, looking doubtful at first, then slowly quirking a soft grin. "Why?"

"I don't know." She spread her hands and shrugged. "I really don't. I guess I just thought it seemed . . . sexy."

His eyes went sultry again. "Kitten, you don't need a tattoo to be sexy—trust me on this. You *breathe* sexy."

She bit her lip, *feeling* sexy. And sort of like she'd stepped into some kind of dream. A few days ago, she never would have believed she'd be in a shower with Brock Denton, discovering the hottest tattoo on the planet in his most private area, hearing him tell her how sexy she was . . . and then watching him reach for the body wash.

He grabbed up the fluffy, round, spongy thing she'd hung on the shower handle, squeezed some of the pearlized liquid into it, and gently began to wash her.

The next few minutes were heaven. Brock ran the sudsy sponge over Kat's shoulders and arms, her breasts and belly, her hips and thighs—and once in between, making her shiver. Facing away, she held up her hair as he washed her back and bottom, nearly melting when he gave her a warm little kiss on the neck for good measure.

Then, to her surprise, he reached for her shampoo and said, "Lean your head back toward me." When his fingers sank into her hair, massaging her scalp, she felt it all the way to her toes. She'd never dreamed a guy's hands on her head could produce such tantalizing sensation, even making her moan.

"Feel good, kitten?"

"Mmm," she replied. And after she stepped under the spray, Brock helping her rinse, she looked up into his eyes, bit her lip, and grabbed the sponge. "My turn."

Soaping up Brock's muscular body was like running her hands over every inch of a perfect male statue. She wasn't sure she'd ever taken the time to explore any guy's body the way she was slowly discovering his right now, but found herself glad she'd waited to do it with Brock. No other man would have lived up to her wants and expectations. No other man would have compared to the images of Brock in her mind from her youth—only now he surpassed those images, because he was broader and stronger, every ounce a man.

Thoroughly aroused, the crux of her thighs *burned*. She remained drawn to that hotter-than-hot tattoo, her sponge making its way there again and again. And, of course, while she was in the neighborhood, it would be rude not to swirl it around his penis another time or two. Which looked sumptuous covered in suds.

As she worked, his muscles tensed slightly beneath her touch, and his breath grew heavier. Her own limbs felt just as weighty with building passion. She rose to kiss him, and he lifted his hands to her face even as she caressed him below—finally abandoning the sponge.

Turning him toward the spray so that the soap rinsed away, she reached around from the rear to slide her hand behind his erection and over the tattoo, then leaned up to whisper in his ear. "Would you think I was a bad girl if I wanted to kiss it?"

Heat filled his gaze as he looked over his shoulder. "The tattoo? Or something else?"

She drew in her breath, then teased him. "I'm not sure yet."

He grinned. "Kitten, I've *always* thought you were a bad girl—in the best possible way."

As Kat slowly descended to her knees, her stomach tightened. This was not what she'd planned on when she'd agreed to a shower with him. But she found herself overwhelmed with desires she'd never quite experienced.

How much would it surprise Brock to know that, although she'd done this before, she'd never really *longed* to do it, never really felt the burning urge that sizzled inside her now? How much would it surprise him to know that—even though this was about heat and arousal—it also came from her heart, her very soul, from the deepest part of her, because she wanted him to know ultimate pleasure and because she wanted to be the one to deliver it?

She ran her palm slowly up his hardness. Sucked in her breath. Met his gaze above and loved the fire there. Suffered the incredible yearning to be his.

Wrapping her hand firm around him, she drew that part of him aside and leaned in to kiss that sexy tattoo. He moaned as his flesh contracted beneath her lips, and she realized with a jolt of feminine power that no one had ever done just that before, kissed him exactly there, and that he hadn't realized how good it would feel. When their eyes next met, she witnessed a new depth of passion in his gaze and wondered if he saw the same in hers.

I love you.

No, don't think that, Kat. You can't.

There was suddenly no more Ian—whisked from her mind as frighteningly easily as if he'd been but a speck of dirt on her shoe—yet she still couldn't admit such emotions for Brock. He wasn't a man who stayed, a man who loved. He'd changed a lot, but in some ways he was just the same—a dangerous loner whose heart was his own.

So she told herself she wouldn't think the words, wouldn't permit herself to—but she still knew deep inside what it was that flowed through her veins.

And it also flowed from her mouth in kisses, soft, tender kisses that spanned his length, top to bottom, then back again. Spray from the shower—just distant enough that a thin mist made him wet—left his taut skin tasting of fresh, cool water. She heard his labored breath, felt his hand rake through her wet hair, but she focused only on her task, only on the giving—and the thrilling joy it gave her in return—particularly when she slid her tongue around the tip of him, then lowered her mouth there.

"Ah, kitten," he groaned, filling her with a hot satisfaction she'd never known before. Because she gave this affection with her whole heart, feeling so much more tender, she suspected, than Brock would ever believe. Because she'd been so broken by him once upon a time. But this was no time for such ruminations. No, it was a giving time.

So she gave more, with her mouth, her hands. She gave him everything she felt inside. And he moaned and gasped above her, and it made her want to give still more, and more. "Kitten," he said, sounding heated, urgent. "Kitten, I can't . . . Stop, honey, or I'll . . ."

She almost didn't care, didn't want to stop, period. She wanted to take him to heaven. But he was reaching for her shoulders, easing her back away from him, until she peered up, wondering why. Wasn't that a guy's greatest fantasy, to come that way?

"I want to be inside you," he said. "Make *you* feel good, too."

Oh. How lovely. He wanted to give, as well. He would never *love* her, she knew that—not the way she wanted a man to love her, and not even the way Ian loved her—for sadly, she knew Ian really did and was simply going to be the victim in all this. But just knowing

Brock was a good enough man, and a kind enough lover, to want to give to her as much pleasure as she gave to him . . . mmm, the next couple of days were going to take *her* closer to heaven than she had ever expected to get.

There seemed only one logical response. "Then come inside."

Chapter Twelve

"And if you're good," she said, a sexy sparkle in her eye as Brock helped her back to her feet, "maybe there'll be more of that later."

Damn, the woman's sexiness turned him inside out and conjured every naughty instinct he possessed. "Oh, don't worry, kitten, I'll be good. I'll be *very* good."

Brock had never thought of himself as a particularly considerate lover. Not rude, not totally selfish—but if a woman wanted to give more than take, he'd let her, and he'd like her for it. And he *adored* Kat for it, yet he couldn't let her do it. And he didn't know why.

Maybe he felt he owed her somehow. From ten years ago. Hell, from what he'd unwittingly put her through just *today*. Or maybe because he'd effectively ruined her wedding plans.

All good reasons. But he didn't really think it was any of those things. The urge to please her felt oddly . . . purer than that.

Given that he wasn't an especially pure guy, he barely knew how he recognized such an emotion, but when he'd stopped her from taking him all the way with her beautiful mouth—and "all the way" had been only a couple of tempting heartbeats from happening—it had come from someplace other than guilt or obligation. He'd just wanted to make her body hum with pleasure.

"Turn around," he said and when she rotated that pretty, wet body away, he leaned in, nestling his cock at her ass and reaching up to press her palms to the wall. She shivered beneath him and he liked it. Feeling a little wicked, he leaned near her ear. "Such a hot little kitten."

She wiggled her bottom against him, excited and impatient. "Don't tease. Don't make me wait."

He smiled inwardly. Just last night, *he'd* been begging.

Part of him still couldn't believe what had happened out in the kitchen—at a time when he really hadn't been trying to seduce her but had just truly needed her to help slake the pain of their day. And yet, another part of him knew this had been inevitable. Maybe from the first moment he'd seen her lying on the beach. Her, him, together—they'd always been a highly combustible combination. And the time had finally come for them to ignite.

Gliding his palms down her outstretched arms, over the hourglass shape of her torso, then bracing his hands at her round hips, he nudged at the warm slickness between her legs and pushed deep. They both groaned at the hot entry—and damn, it felt new, like they hadn't even done it out on the table, like this was the first time he was sinking home in her soft, pliable body. "God, kitten, you're so wet for me."

She let out a soft, high moan in reply and pushed her ass back against him, taking him deeper.

"Damn," he groaned. Then began to move in her—steady, even thrusts. He loved how she met each one, loved how she looked in front of him, accepting him, meeting him, loved the passion he felt spilling from her even without being able to see her face.

Still using one hand to steady her hip, he let the other snake around, dip into her moisture. Oh God, to finally touch her there. He knew he was inside her, but pressing his fingers into that most intimate part of her ratcheted up his heat another few vital notches, whisking him swiftly toward oblivion.

Their shared passion drove him harder, harder, making them both sob their pleasure. And in an old, cracked shower in a tiny house on an island in the middle of the Gulf of Mexico, Brock let himself acknowledge—just for that one moment in time—that he'd never before felt as close or connected to a woman as he felt to Katrina Spencer.

Kat lay beside him, naked and exhausted.

"I think we'll both sleep good tonight, huh, kitten?" he asked, reaching to turn off the lamp next to the bed. She bit her lip, just thinking how nice that was, to be sharing a bed with him—without the tension of worrying about her engagement. Of course, technically, she remained engaged, but in her heart and mind, it was over, and as soon as she could see Ian, it would be over *officially*.

"Hmm, let's see," she said playfully. "A day full of running from psychos with guns, one shooting, one exploding boat—the second of those in three days, I might add—and two energetic rounds of sex. Yeah, I might be able to sleep."

She was surprised when he rolled on his pillow to face her, the security light illuminating the room enough that she could see the serious look in his eyes. "You didn't love the guy, did you?"

Apparently, they were *both* thinking about the far-reaching implications of their sex. She tried to answer as honestly as possible.

"I . . . thought I did. I truly . . ." She stopped, shook her head. "Maybe I just *wanted* to be in love. Because it made everything so perfect. But . . . I have to admit I'm not too broken up about the idea of not marrying him. The truth is, the second I realized what we'd done and that I *couldn't* in good conscience marry him, I was kind of . . . relieved."

"Good," he said, shoving one hand under his pillow. With the other, he reached out for hers. "And . . . how are you doing with the other stuff, everything that happened today? Are you okay, kitten?" He gave her hand a gentle squeeze.

"I'm . . . not thinking about it." And that was the truth. She offered a slight grin. "I'm sure at some point I'm probably going to need massive psychiatric care to overcome the trauma, but for right now, I'm not thinking about *that*, I'm not thinking about the wedding I have to cancel—I'm not thinking about anything but good, hot sex."

The corners of his mouth quirked arrogantly. "Is it? Good and hot?"

She flashed her driest, get-serious look. "Like you don't know it is. You just want to hear it, to keep your ego as big as your . . ." She glanced downward, although they'd pulled a sheet to their waists.

He arched a brow. "That's all I needed to know. And by the way, what you did in the shower, with your mouth, it was well worth the wait."

She propped up on one elbow. "The wait?"

"You couldn't have done that so well ten years ago."

She let out a trill of laughter. "How do *you* know? Maybe I'd never done it before tonight. Maybe it was my first time."

He lowered his chin, casting a highly skeptical look. "Come on, kitten."

She pursed her lips in concession. "Okay, yes, I've done that before. But . . . I've never done it exactly like *that* before."

"What do you mean?"

What the hell had she just said? She *knew* what she meant, of course. She'd never *felt* it like that before—never truly *made love* to a man that way before, never truly given up her heart and soul to the act, wanting only to please him, thereby pleasing herself. She'd never felt it so profoundly stretching through her in a taut band of desire that had spurred her on, deeper and deeper, until nothing else had existed. But she sure as hell couldn't tell *him* any of that.

"Well?" he prodded.

"I just . . . tried a couple of new moves on you, that's all."

He gave her a sexy grin. "They worked."

She pushed down a bittersweet reaction to the compliment and said, "I'm glad." Then wondered . . . "So . . . how are *you* doing? I mean, about Carlos?"

He answered with a faraway look in his eye. "It's my job, and I shouldn't have let it affect me that way. That's shit I can work out later."

"Work out later?"

"When something like this happens, I get counseling after the mission ends, but until then, I'm trained to compartmentalize it, put it out of my mind so I can stay focused on the job."

"So what happened? I mean, it obviously *did* affect you, at least for a little while."

Just when she'd started to think he might not answer, he seemed to come back from where ever he'd been, his eyes finding hers again. "Truth is, I'm not sure. But it's over. And it's fine. He was a bad guy—he had to go—that simple."

"It's not *really* that simple." His job had forced him to take another man's life. That struck her as being pretty darn complex.

"When you're a federal agent, kitten, it *is* that simple. It has to be." Then he got a familiar and delightfully naughty look in his eye. "But enough about that. I'd rather get back to you telling me how hot I am, and how big I am. And if you've got any more new moves to try out, you can consider me your guinea pig."

She smiled, even though grogginess was quickly setting in. "Afraid I'll have to wait 'til tomorrow to start conducting my experiments."

He looked just as sleepy, but said, "Hey, come here," then met her halfway for a warm, soft kiss. "Everything that happened on the table and in the shower, honey—it was *all* well worth the wait."

"For me, too," she whispered. Then drifted quickly off to sleep, aware of only the sound of the tide in the distance and the feel of Brock's warm hand curving over her bare hip beneath the sheet.

On Tuesday morning, Clark Spencer sat behind the desk in his office, talking with a young textile artist from Bradenton who'd been courting the gallery for months. After some deliberation, he'd just offered her a showing the month after Kat's, in July. She'd yipped and yelled into the phone like a banshee, which, although unprofessional, drew a smile from him, making him think of his daughter—who'd responded exactly the same way when he'd recently offered *her* a show. He hung up, pleased to feel he'd done his part to set another artist on the road to success in a very tough business.

He checked the gold clock on his desk—almost ten, time to unlock the front door. But he had another phone call to make first. Picking back up the receiver, he hit the speed dial to Ian.

"Ian Zeller," his future son-in-law answered on the first ring. Just one of the many things he liked about the young man—a sterling work ethic like his own.

"Ian, it's Clark."

"Ah, good morning, Clark. I bet I know why you're calling." Ian's usual confidence came through in his voice.

"Mr. Klinger," Clark said simply. A particularly stodgy and impatient old art collector.

"I still don't have his pieces in hand," Ian said, "but give me his number and I'll smooth things over with him." Ian had recently started acquiring some rare art—just one of many shrewd investment moves Clark had witnessed from him over the past six months—and since Clark's business *was* art, he had hooked Ian up with collectors who were interested in purchasing such finds. As a result, Ian gave him a healthier-than-to-be-expected cut of the profits, enough to make it worth his effort—and enough to keep him solvent for a while.

"Not necessary—I can do it," Clark said. Ian had never been anything but cordial and respectful to him, but given his generosity, Clark felt the need not to trouble him with such tasks.

"Listen, Clark, if you need advance payment, just say the word."

"No, no—that's not necessary, either."

"You're sure?" Ian knew Clark was having money problems, which was a little embarrassing, all things considered, but Clark just tried to be grateful Ian was so willing to help.

"Absolutely—I'm good for now. But about Klinger, any estimate I can give him?"

On the other end of the line, Ian sighed. "Afraid not—I'm still looking into the delay. Speaking of which . . . have you heard from Kat?"

Now it was Clark who sighed. "No, actually. You haven't gotten a call from her, either?"

"No," Ian said simply, but Clark felt the young man's concern and could tell he was hurt by Kat's neglect, as well.

"Not to worry. Debra spoke to Nina and apparently the girls

had had a late night and were sleeping in. I'm sure she's fine—just busy with her friends. I'm sure she'll call soon." Kat's wilder nature had kept him worried through a lot of her teenage years—but he'd tried to adjust to it once she'd reached adulthood, especially since she seemed to have her head on straight about most other aspects of life. Still, he hoped the girls were being careful.

"Yeah, I hope so. I want her to have fun, but . . . well, not *too* much fun." Ian chuckled, and Clark did, too, but he didn't think either of them were very amused.

He felt the need to put Ian at ease. "Don't be concerned, son. I've seen my daughter become . . . well, a whole new tame sort of Kat ever since you two got engaged. And frankly, if anybody's having too much fun, it's probably Nina."

Both men laughed lightly, then Ian said, "Well, in a few days, this kind of thing will all be behind Kat. Once we're married, she won't have time to be jetting off with her friends."

To Clark's surprise, his stomach flinched slightly. As much as he felt he knew what was best for Kat, and as certain as he remained that it was Ian, he wasn't used to anyone outside the family trying to dictate her actions.

But then, Ian *would* be her husband. *Definitely* in the family. And a husband had some say over what his wife did, and vice versa. And having Ian in the family . . . that was going to be very good for all of them. Ian had let both Kat and Clark know that once they were married, he planned to sink some money into the gallery—another investment.

"Totally hands-off," Ian had pointed out. Maybe there'd been a hint of anxiety on Clark's face when he'd made the offer. "No fears, Clark—I would never want to be involved in any aspect of *running* the gallery. But, as you know, I'm starting to realize the investment value of art, and besides, family helps family, right?"

If Clark believed in anything, it was family. His own had plenty of squabbles and disagreements, but overall, they were a solid unit and everything he did was for them. Without Debra and Kat, he wouldn't feel nearly so driven to succeed. So even if it was a little humiliating to have his new son-in-law bail him out of trouble, it was a workable solution that would hold everything together. He'd decided to think of it as just another little bit of glue for his family and their way of life.

When he hung up with Ian, he tried Kat's cell phone for the heck of it—only to hear the same "unavailable" message Debra had been getting. After the beep, he laughed softly into the phone. "It's Dad, sweetheart. It would do your mother and me a world of good to get a call from you. I know you're having fun, but spare a minute for the old man?" He paused, missing her, and worrying just a little. "You might consider calling Ian, too. Be careful, Kat. I love you."

He was sure she was fine—because Debra *had* talked to Nina, after all. Yet he suffered the oddest inkling that something wasn't quite as it should be.

Kat could be irresponsible, but not to call home after all these messages? Of course, Debra had theorized maybe her phone was dead, but to not call home *at all* while traveling? She knew they worried, and this wasn't like her. Hell, if Debra hadn't talked to Nina, he'd probably be booking a ticket to Vegas himself right now to make sure she was okay.

Maybe in one sense it had jarred him to hear Ian sounding as if he planned to monitor her comings and goings, but Clark would rest easier once they were married, once he knew there was someone dependable looking after her. Ian was exactly what Kat needed in her life, and Clark was only thankful she'd had the foresight to recognize that when Ian had proposed.

Just then, his computer beeped with incoming mail. He looked up to see a message from Debra. Odd—normally, she called. He clicked to open it.

> *Will you be home for dinner tonight? If not, I'm going out with Lita and Beth from the book club to the new seafood place on Third.*

He hit reply.

> *You should go. Have fun. C*

Frankly, it was a relief—it meant he could work as late as he wanted without guilt. And given that a big shot author had just asked her to read his next book, Clark figured he might get a free pass right up to Kat's wedding and maybe even after. Mr. Klinger wasn't the only buyer Clark needed to contact about the delayed goods—in fact, there were dozens of collectors who'd committed to one or more pieces, and Clark didn't want to lose any of them over a miscalculated delivery. If he didn't have much time to be with Debra right now, she'd just have to understand.

And once Ian sank some cash into the gallery, things would get better.

Of course, Ian had recently informed Clark there would be future art coming in, as well, and he would need Clark's help to find homes for it all. So, the truth was, it might take a while before the late nights were *really* over.

But it would be worth it for the money.

Brock sat in his sagging lounge chair watching Kat's ass sway toward the ocean in her little white bikini. He crossed his feet at the ankles, put his hands behind his head, and enjoyed the view. Sex had relaxed him more than he could have predicted. Here he was, on a private island with a beautiful woman on a gorgeous day—no immediate worries and nothing to anticipate at the moment besides hot sun, cool sand, and sizzling sex. Who knew—maybe he *wouldn't* need time off to recover. Maybe the next two days—and nights—with Kat would clear all his troubles away.

He'd been trying to think this was all about sex, but now he had to admit there was more at work between them. All those memories from when they were young, all those fantasies from the ten years since he'd last seen her, and . . . the way she made him feel. Not just all the passion zipping between them and the erections constantly plaguing him, but the way she made him laugh, the way he liked bickering with her, the way a mere smile from the girl turned his chest warm. Hell, just watching her move down the beach and into the water captivated him. She was wading slowly in now, letting out a high-pitched, "Oooh!" when a wave crashed over her, waist high.

He'd been scared shitless to see Carlos with that gun to her head, and he'd have given his life for hers in a heartbeat. And not just because he was FBI and she was an innocent bystander, and not just because he'd felt responsible for getting her into this mess. It had come from someplace deeper.

So . . . they had a history. And he enjoyed her company. And seeing her in danger had ripped a hole in his gut.

But hell, fantasize about a woman for ten years and she's gonna have an effect on you when she comes unexpectedly back into your life. That simple.

So it was okay if he was a little bit captivated with her for the next couple of days. As he'd already speculated, maybe he'd return to the mainland with a clear head, ready to get straight back to work.

Of course, he had no idea how he'd get to Omega Man after this. And surely Omega had dispatched more worker bees to pick up the artifacts by now. He'd blown this mission sky-high, and there was probably no saving it at this point. But he'd still have to try. And he'd have a hell of a lot of explaining to do. Shit—his boss would *not* be happy.

Just then, he reached down to the side of his trunks, patting the pocket against his thigh to make sure Francisco's key still resided there. That key was the only chance left for this case—he only had to hope it opened a sturdy enough lock on a sturdy enough door that getting through without it would be a challenge. Knowing that Francisco had wanted the key badly enough to come back to the island gave Brock a little optimism.

But was the key the reason they'd come the first time, when they'd blown up Kat's boat? No, Brock had been lying there "dead" and they didn't come looking for it *then*. So what *had* brought them to the island that first time?

Maybe they'd seen him swim ashore, as he'd assumed at the time, yet . . . he couldn't help feeling like he was missing something here—like there was more to the story.

But figuring it out would have to wait, he decided when Kat came walking back toward the beach through the surf. She was a page in a swimsuit calendar, a scene in one of those guy's fantasy beer commercials. Only she was a lot more that that. Which made him offer a slight, suggestive smile at the mere sight of her. When she smiled back, something contracted low in his belly.

As she sat down at the water's edge, facing the ocean, he suffered a niggling disappointment that she hadn't rejoined him at the chairs. So much that he pushed to his feet, soon lowering himself to the wet sand beside her as a thin, shallow ridge of water washed up under them to recede just as quickly.

"Short swim." He leaned his forearms on bent knees.

"Just wanted to cool off," she said, dragging her fingers absently through the sand between them.

"You look good doing that."

"Cooling off?"

He gave a short nod and let her see the heat in his eyes. "Kitten, you look pretty damn good doing about anything. I never should have let you out of bed this morning."

She let her grin go sexy, too, now swirling her fingers in sensual little circles in the wet sand. "Afraid you won't be able to get me back in it?"

He laughed. "No—just thinking how good your tan body looked against that white sheet." In fact, he'd been just about to roll over and kiss her good morning when she'd eased out of bed, slid one of her little strappy tops on with a pair of panties, and announced she was going foraging for breakfast since the donuts were history. She'd found some stale Cheerios, then made some toast and announced that breakfast was served. He'd joined her at the table, naked, hoping to entice her with that tattoo she seemed so fond of, but every time he'd caught her sneaking a peek, she'd darted her gaze away.

Now, she lowered her chin and cast an almost shy expression. "You don't look bad naked yourself, Mr. FBI Man." She made squiggly trails with her fingers, deep down in the sand.

Something about watching her fingers was sexy as hell. "Have you got a sand fetish or something I should be aware of?"

She grinned. "I just like the way it feels. I've been thinking about incorporating sand in some of my pots."

He knew nothing about pottery. "Sand? How would you do that?"

"I can mix it with glaze and fire it on that way. Although it might melt—I'm not sure yet. I might try putting it on the clay before firing it at all. I'm still mulling it over. Deciding exactly what I want the texture to be. Heavy and gritty, or something lighter, more subtle."

Her words made him curious. Not so much because he was interested in pottery, but because he was interested in Kat. "Why sand?"

She reached up to pull his hand down to the beach. "Feel it," she said, so he let her rake his hand through. Then she scooted up a little higher, just past the line where the sand went from wet to dry, and motioned for him to follow. "Now, touch this sand, too. Let a handful run through your fingers."

He watched the sand sift through hers, then followed suit, and even though he felt kind of dopey about it, he wouldn't deny there was something pleasant and peaceful about the act that made him pick up another handful and do it again.

"Smooth, right? And smooth on your feet when you walk through it?"

He nodded.

Then she leaned forward, scooping up a handful of the wet sand and smearing it in gentle circles on his calf. "But now it feels rough on your skin, huh?"

He nodded again. "Yeah."

She tilted her head, her wet locks curling slightly over one shoulder. "I guess I just find it fascinating—a natural thing that's . . . sort of an enigma. I mean, can you think of anything else in the world that's so smooth and so rough at the same time?"

He couldn't resist a slight, slow, arrogant smile as he glanced down between his legs. "Well, kitten, I can think of *one* thing."

She offered up a light, pretty giggle. "Do you ever think about anything *else*?"

He shrugged. "Not since I found you stretched topless across that lounge chair the other day. Speaking of which," he added, "you can take your top off if you want."

She stretched out a little, letting her toes dig in the wet sand as the tide rolled in a bit higher, coming up around their feet again. "No, I learned my lesson on that. I don't want to be tan there bad enough to risk another burn."

Holding his hand down so the next rush of the tide washed away the grit between his fingers, he then lifted his wet palm to lightly squeeze her soft, slender thigh. "I didn't mean for tanning, kitten." He leaned a little closer, near her face, and looked into lovely blue eyes. "I meant because I want to kiss them some more."

Kat's breath caught in her throat. She wasn't used to this yet. And in the light of day, she'd suddenly started feeling strangely timid with him. That's why she'd bounded out of bed and into the few clothes she could find. And that's why she couldn't quite breathe right now.

"What's wrong?" he asked, sitting up a little straighter. "Regrets?"

She shook her head quickly. That wasn't it at all. The plain, hard truth of the matter was that she wanted to fuck the man senseless.

But she also wanted . . . not to feel quite so much when she did it.

Because it was too good with him. Too hot, too perfect, and . . . too emotional.

She'd actually cried a little after they'd done it in the shower, and they hadn't been tears of sadness or worry or regret of any kind. They'd been tears of wanting more of him somehow, wanting whatever was inside him, in his heart. They were tears of . . . love.

Insane, she knew. She'd wondered ten years ago if it was really possible to be in love with a guy she didn't know any better than she'd known Brock—yet, to this day she knew what she'd felt had been real. Now, God help her, it was back, with a vengeance. She'd fought it, denying the words every time they'd popped to mind, using her engagement as a weapon. But now that the engagement was gone, she felt . . . defenseless.

"Then what is it, kitten? What's wrong?" And damn it, now his voice was so deep and gentle—it was killing her.

She let out a quiet sigh. The way she saw it, she had no choice. She knew as well as she knew her own name that Brock wasn't a falling-in-love kind of guy. He hadn't been that kind of guy then, and he definitely wasn't now. But she had two more days with him. Two more days that she could love him and know him and drink in more physical pleasure than any man had ever even come close to giving her. Or two days to pass that up and kiss him good-bye forever. The good-bye kiss would most certainly come, either way—so how could she not let herself have this time with him, emotions be damned?

"Nothing's wrong. In fact, everything's right. Because . . ." She lowered her voice to a throaty whisper as she leaned near his ear. "I want you. I want you to kiss them, Brock. I want you to kiss me *everywhere*."

"Aw *baby* . . ." he said, low and hot.

"I want you so bad," she murmured, finally letting that out, letting him know. It was hardly a secret, but she needed to tell him, needed to surrender the admission, just say it out loud.

His hands rose to her face and their eyes met, dark and intense beneath the scorching rays of the sun, just for a moment before his mouth closed over hers, firm and demanding.

And as he reached behind her to untie her top, dashing it onto the beach, as he lay her back into the soft cradle of the sand, as he leaned slowly down, dragging his tongue gently over one nipple, she heard herself saying it again. "I want you. Oh God, I want you."

He licked her, kissed her, suckled her, pulling deeply, using his hands to cup and massage her breasts, and as the exquisite sensations echoed through her accepting body, she whispered it still more. "I want you. Yes. Oh, I want you so much."

And when he urged her rear up off the sand long enough to ease her bottoms down, then shed his trunks and parted her legs and sank deeply inside her in one stroke which was, just as he'd promised, as rough as it was smooth, she still couldn't keep the words from tumbling off her lips. "I want you, Brock. I want you."

But the whole time, her heart spoke different words inside her. The whole time, in her mind, she was divulging a deeper truth.

I love you. I love you. I love you.

When this whole thing was over, it was going to be bad—her heart broken to bits. Which was maybe exactly what she deserved since she was doing the same thing to Ian.

Yet for right now, while they were alone, while the rest of her existence seemed a world away, while she could soak this up and take it inside her and let it be whatever she wanted it to be . . . it was going to be very, very *good.*

Chapter Thirteen

*K*at had offered to make what she now loosely referred to as dinner. She exited the house balancing two plates bearing sandwiches, chips, and a few cookies from a package she'd stuffed in her grocery bag on the way out the door at home. "Would you like turkey?" she asked, holding up one plate. "Or turkey?" She held up the other.

Brock, lounging at the picnic table in his trunks, and looking just as hunky as usual, rewarded her with a small grin. "Hmm. It's a tough call, but I think I'll take the turkey."

"Excellent choice," she replied, lowering both plates to the table, then her bottom to the bench across from him.

"Not that I'm dissing the turkey," he said, picking up his sandwich to take a big bite, "but didn't I see a couple of prepackaged hamburger patties in the freezer?"

"Yes, and I just moved them to the fridge to thaw. I thought since—if nothing unexpected happens with my parents and

Nina—tomorrow night will probably be our last night here, I'd save the burgers for then."

He gave a small nod, tipped back his head with an, "Ah," and Kat's stomach churned at the notion of this coming to an end. Soon it would be Thursday and they'd be rescued and her fabulous fantasy-come-to-life with Brock would be no more.

Unless . . .

No. He was not going to announce he was madly in love with her and stay.

Hell, she knew little to nothing about his life other than the fact that he was an FBI guy—but that alone was enough to keep her sure he wouldn't.

Yet . . . she still brimmed with that niggling curiosity one couldn't help feeling over a guy she was crazy about. In fact, she suddenly couldn't believe she'd wasted so much time in shock without trying to learn more about him. Of course, some of that time had also been in bliss, so she forgave herself slightly, then said, "So, tell me about *your* life, Brock."

He glanced from his plate to her eyes. "Hmm?"

"We've talked about me, me, me—a lot. Not so much about you."

He narrowed his gaze, looking a little mysterious and making her a little wet. "What do you want to know, kitten?"

"Well . . ." Instantly thrust into the throes of arousal, she lost her focus and spoke more softly. She reached for her wineglass and took a drink, letting the alcohol glide warm down into her chest. "Where do you live?"

"I've got a condo in Miami, near South Beach."

Figured. Mr. FBI was also Mr. Swanky Jet Set. It was still hard to reconcile either image with the Brock she'd once known, but it was getting less so. "I guess you hit all the clubs?" She and Nina had once gone to South Beach for a weekend and found the club scene too wild even for them.

Brock shrugged. "Not often."

Oh. Well, good. But still . . . "Probably lots of women, though."

Another careless lift of his shoulders. "Enough. Lot of girls on South Beach looking to party, but not wanting any attachments— and that works out well."

Uh-huh, of course it did. Images of a revolving door into Brock's probably stylishly retro-yet-modern bedroom darkened Kat's mind. She never should have asked about that. Not while *they* were in the midst of a hot and heavy . . . well, she hesitated to call it an *affair* for some reason, but . . . whatever they were having. If she wasn't careful, she was going to end up feeling like a Bond girl.

"How about Sister Katrina?" he asked. Behind him, the sky darkened in shades of rose and plum and the air around the bungalow grew shadowy.

Kat tilted her head. "How about her?"

"Lots of guys get into that tiny bikini?"

She'd had to start this, hadn't she? She sat up a little straighter. "Are we back to questioning my moral virtue when we don't question yours?"

Across from her, Brock looked slightly exasperated. "I never questioned it, kitten. And I don't really think you've lived the life of a nun, but that's more than fine with me—I've never been into the prim type. So just answer me without getting your bikini bottoms in a wad."

She let out a sigh. Bossy. "Why do you want to know?"

He countered with a bigger sigh. "I just wondered, okay? You asked me first, remember?"

Kat took another sip of wine, then a bite of her sandwich. Turkey and Chardonnay didn't exactly go great together, but she was getting oddly used to it. "Okay. Some," she finally said, not really sure how to quantify it. *Probably a lot fewer than you, Mr. 007.*

"Anyone special?"

For some reason, the question made her a little sad. "Before Ian? Not really." She dropped her gaze, fiddled with the stem of her glass. "You?"

She looked up in time to see him shake his head. "I told you, the no-strings girls work well enough for me."

Weird—she didn't like the idea of him having meaningless sex with tons of other women, but she was also relieved he'd never really cared for any of them. She nodded, hoping no emotion passed over her face.

"So tell me, kitten, were you really ready and willing to settle down, do the whole family thing?"

Kat drained her glass as she considered her answer. Brock reached for the bottle and refilled it, which suited her fine, since a little intoxication might be a nice distraction from this topic she hadn't quite meant to open up. "Willing, yes," she finally said. "Ready, maybe not so much."

He gave her a small grin. "That's my girl."

"I mean, I love kids," she went on. "And eventually, I want all that, sure. But maybe not yet." She quieted, chewed on her lip, then forced herself to spit out the next question burning in her mind. "Do *you* ever want that kind of life? Kids, a family?" She tried really hard to look casual about the inquiry, but wine also sometimes made it hard for her to hide her feelings.

Thankfully, he didn't seem to notice. "Nah, I'm not really a settled kind of guy." He propped one elbow on the table and perched his chin atop it to tease her. "But hey, you never know. If Sister Katrina can actually settle down someday, maybe there's hope for me, too."

Kat tilted her head. "Why do you find it so hard to imagine me settling down?" The question came out smaller than she'd intended.

He pinned her in place with his gaze. "You've got wild blood in your veins, honey."

You put it there. "What makes you think so?"

"Um, maybe it was having you climb on me naked when you were a teenager."

Oh. Yeah. That. Her face warmed, despite all they'd shared the last couple of days. She shouldn't be embarrassed—it made no sense—yet she was.

"I *like* your wild blood—you gotta know that."

What would he think if he knew she wasn't *really* so wild, that it was only him who had turned her that way? What would he think if he knew what *she* suddenly knew—that any and every hedonistic act she'd ever indulged in had somehow stemmed from him, from that night, from the want in his eyes and the rejection he'd dealt out instead.

She swallowed back the realization and asked, "Do you like anything else about me besides the fact that I can be wild?" Again, her voice had come out too quiet, laced with emotion.

And this time he'd heard it—she could see the fresh concern in his gray eyes. "I like a lot about you, Kat," he said softly.

"Because . . . I happen to be more than just a good time."

He lowered his chin slightly. "You think I don't know that?"

She let out a shaky breath, hoping like hell he hadn't caught the shaky part. "I'm not sure." She reached for the wineglass, knowing the alcohol would either shore up her strength or dissolve it further—but it was mainly an instinct, something to do with her hands since she'd become nervous.

"Well, think back to yesterday, kitten," he said matter-of-factly.

"You got to see a little more of me than most people do, and . . . well, if you look back, real carefully, you'll know that . . ."

She lowered her glass, raised her eyes. "That what?"

Brock sighed, but never broke their gaze. "That I see more than a pretty face and a killer body when I look at you."

"What do you see?"

She read the honesty in his expression. "A vibrant, sexy, alive woman—who loves art, who helps kids, who's funny and smart and . . . I won't lie to you . . . a great time in bed, kitten. You rock my body, honey. But don't worry—I see the whole package. I know what I've got here."

It was like a flower bloomed in Kat's heart. It was hardly a profession of love, but it was . . . pretty phenomenal anyway.

He knew. That she was more than sex. And his eyes said he appreciated all the pieces of her he'd just mentioned. And it was dangerous as hell to let her thoughts even go there, but . . . she almost thought his eyes said he cared for her. *Really cared.*

She bit her lip and cast a playful smile, ready to lighten things up. "We haven't actually . . . done it in the bed yet, you know."

He grinned, making her glad she'd broken the tension she'd unwittingly created.

"Unless, well, maybe the bed isn't exciting enough for you?" she asked.

Brock let out a laugh. "Anywhere your body happens to be is exciting enough for me." Then his eyes went dark, seductive, and purely animalistic. "And trust me, kitten, I'll *make* the bed exciting. I'll make the bed the best you've ever had."

When Kat exited the bathroom in a gray cami-and-panty set trimmed with pink lace, she found her man lying in bed, sheet pulled to his waist, his torso beautifully bare and well muscled, and an oh-so-sexy smile on his handsome, darkly stubbled face. A soft breeze blew a fresh, salty scent through the window, the room was lit by only a small lamp—which Brock had tossed one of her sarongs over to dim the air even more—and Rod Stewart sang "Tonight's the Night" low on the radio perched on the table next to the bed. Brock patted the empty spot next to him and said, "Here, kitty kitty."

She surged with moisture as she padded toward the bed. Over dinner, she'd let those pesky nervous emotions sneak into their passion, but now they were gone. She wasn't sure if she'd washed them away in the shower, if the wine had drowned them, or if Brock's seductive eyes had just overpowered them until they evaporated from the heat—but at the moment, all she felt was hot lust, a rampant, unstoppable desire to climb in that bed and let him keep his promise.

Of course, it might be difficult because what he didn't know was—the best she'd ever had was *him*. On the table. In the shower. In the surf.

And yet, she confidently lifted one bare knee to the mattress knowing that tonight he could, would, surpass even those marvelous encounters. His eyes said so. And her body believed.

She rose high on her knees next to him, indulging the urge to hover over him, play with him, let her inhibitions run free. She'd never exactly been *inhibited* with Brock, but now, more than ever, she just wanted to follow her instincts, just do, just feel.

Balancing on one elbow, he gazed up at her, then let his eyes travel slowly downward. She felt them as keenly as a touch, moving across her breasts, her belly, lower. She burned for him.

He answered the burn by gliding one hand from the back of her knee up to her bottom, then leaning in to gently French-kiss the mound at the front of her panties, his tongue pressing through the fabric in exactly the right spot.

She let out a shivery sigh as the pleasure rushed through her, hot and electric, and had he not had a firm grip on her, she might have collapsed to the bed.

"Time for my dessert," he said, the fire in his eyes enough to paralyze her.

"The cookies weren't enough?"

"They weren't even close to being what I'm hungry for, kitten." With that, he kissed her there again, his lips closing over her this time, nibbling.

"Oh . . ." she murmured, curling her hand over his broad shoulder for balance, reaching with the other to the headboard.

The palm on her bottom snaked inward, smoothly pulled her panties aside. One finger slipped moistly into her at the precise moment his tongue raked over her most sensitive spot in front.

She shuddered, clenching her teeth, and his voice came labored, raspy. "Ah, kitten, you taste so damn good."

Trying to catch her breath, she pressed her fingertips deeper into his hard flesh, peered heatedly down at him, and said, "Then have some more."

He released a hot groan just before sinking his mouth back to where she needed it. She bit her lip at the pleasure and moved against him, closed her eyes and thought of nothing else. And then . . . she opened them. Wanting to be aware of exactly where she was. Wanting to stamp this perfect moment into her memory. The view out the window of the picnic table, illuminated by the security light, and the shadowy silhouette of palm trees beyond. The breeze cooling her skin where he made it so hot. The sexy song Rod still crooned on the radio, its languid notes dripping over her, encouraging her yet again to relax and let her inhibitions run wild.

She moved more urgently and his fingers—two now, she thought—dove deeper, thrusting in and out. Her breath echoed heavy, and she didn't consider her response, simply let it happen, let herself ease closer and closer to ecstasy.

Closer. Closer. Yes. And then—"Oh!" she cried out. "Oh! Oh God!"

The climax crashed through her like a tidal wave, the hot, weighty pulses nearly overwhelming. She gripped his shoulder tighter, then released it and twined both hands into his hair. *I love you, Brock. I love you.*

As the waves of pleasure—and those still-startling emotions—slowly passed, she went dizzy, light-headed, weak and quivery, crumpling next to him on the bed. "Thank you," she heard herself murmur, and even as the words left her, feared it an odd thing to say, but it was certainly better than *I love you*, and she'd needed to say *something*.

As she reclined back into a pillow, he slid up alongside her, gave her a sex-laced grin, and said, "It was definitely my pleasure, kitten." Then he lowered his mouth onto hers, letting her taste the remnants of his affection, and she thought about how intimate that was—just as intimate as she'd been with him in the shower. She lifted her hands to his face, simply to feel how utterly close he was in that moment, to wish he would *always* be that close.

As his palm moved over the flat of her stomach and onto her breast, his knee slid between her legs. His kisses were deep and swallowing, and he smelled fresh from the shower but also like a man—musky, warm. His erection pressed against her hip as his thumb stroked her nipple through the cami.

She missed his kisses when they trailed over her jaw, down onto her neck, but she got over it as the scintillating delights echoed downward. She arched her neck and lifted against his thigh, unable to help herself.

His breath came raspy as he drew back to ease the strap off her shoulder. Her breasts ached with missing his touch, and she wanted to *beg*, beg for more, beg him to stop going so slow—but she bit her tongue and realized that sometimes slow was good, because she felt every nuance of every move he made so much more. His fingertips, grazing her arm. His lips as he lowered one soft, sweet kiss high on her chest. His eyes, burning into hers, then shifting downward as he lowered her top over her breasts. A long, slow moment later, he helped her free her arms until the cami rested around her torso.

He looked at her breasts the way *she* looked at a work of art, and her nipples grew even harder beneath his scrutiny. *Kiss them, please kiss them.*

But he didn't. He studied them, then brought his hands slowly up to cup their sides, his thumbs spanning the lower curves. He softly molded them, and she sighed. He raised his thumbs to rake across the pink peaks. She let out a thready breath.

Slow was torturous. But slow *was* good.

He massaged them, thoroughly, leisurely, then tweaked her nipples between thumb and forefinger, soft—again, again.

She moaned at the hot sensation such a gentle motion produced inside her, then lifted her hands to press them flat against the wooden headboard behind her. Offering her breasts up to him completely. Basking in the wonder of his touch.

Once more he kneaded her flesh in his capable hands, sinking to kiss her mouth, press his tongue between her lips, intoxicate her further with all that he was. A perfect male specimen. But not just a specimen—that would be so much easier. No, he was Brock. Bringing her to life even as he buried her.

She returned the slow, sensual kisses, her lips brushing across his mouth. But then the kissing ended and she sucked in her breath, anticipating. When he finally delivered a gentle lick across the distended peak of one breast, she released a moan that came from deep inside. And when he closed his mouth over her, his tongue still diddling the very tip of her nipple, she let out a low sob. When he sucked, drawing her deep and holding on, the small of her back contracted, sending a low ache of pleasure all through her.

Her breath seemed the loudest thing in the room. He breathed heavy, too, and she felt in perfect unison with him, no longer frustrated by the slowness, but only experiencing it with him, every tiny detail and sensation.

Below, he eased her panties past her knees and she kicked them off. He was already naked, and his arousal still hard and hot at her side. She wanted him inside her more than she wanted to exist at that moment, so she reached for him, pressing her palm across the column between his legs. He let out a short groan, then looked into her eyes, and she felt that wild blood in her veins that he'd been talking about. *All for you, lover. All for you.*

His fingers slipped between her thighs, replacing his knee, and she let out a deep, "Ooooh."

"So wet for me, kitten."

Then he pushed his way inside in one slow, deep plunge that filled her to overflowing. "Oh God," she whispered.

"So tight."

"Maybe that's because you're so big."

He flashed a lusty grin. "You know the way to my heart."

"It's true," she said between heavy breaths. "Bigger than anyone else."

He drew back with a sexy but skeptical look. "That's a real nice thing to say, but . . . probably a stretch."

She giggled softly amid her passion. "No, I just mean . . . bigger than anyone else I've been with."

"Mmm, now that I like to hear."

"Not that it matters."

"Hmm?" He was moving in her now, slow, deep.

"It doesn't matter to me how big you are." She felt each thrust to her core.

"Well, it matters to *me*. I want to fill you up. Make you feel more than any other guy ever has."

"You do, you do." She lifted against him, feeling as incredibly full as he wanted her to. "But it has nothing to do with size."

He didn't stop moving—in fact, maybe he drove even deeper now—but he looked at her, long and hard, and she peered back, at once regretting the words but glad she'd been honest, because she was getting braver and wanted him to know the strength of her emotions for him.

He never replied, only kissed her—deep, slow tongue kisses that made her feel like he was inside her in a whole different way—and she understood that what she'd always suspected was true. Sex with a man you were in love with was the most profound physical experience on earth. She'd waited and waited to have this, to know this fulfillment, and finally Brock was making it happen, taking her to an entirely different plane, filling her with more than just his body.

After a time, he withdrew, leaving her to feel empty until he rolled her to her side and entered her again from behind. "Oh," she said, amazed that the fresh intrusion could still be so powerful even after having just had him inside her.

It was only as she let her eyes open that she realized she faced the mirror on the door of the armoire. Brock dragged his teeth slowly down her earlobe as he met her gaze in the glass. They'd kicked the sheets down so their bodies were bare, although they were only visible in the mirror from the waist up.

She bit her lip when he kissed her neck, then let her eyes drift shut again.

"Don't close your eyes, kitten." He curved his palm over her hip, driving into her deep.

She opened them, met his gaze once more in the old glass. "What?"

"Look at me. Look at me while I move in you."

She obeyed the command, although it was difficult at first—she'd never realized how often she let her eyes close during sex. Every time it happened, however, Brock said, "Open them, kitten. Look at me. See me."

And then their eyes would meet, and he would thrust into her, still slow, but hard, hard, and she'd see the passion in his face, and on hers when she cried out. He was *making* her see it, forcing her to experience it raw, as it really was. She'd never undergone anything so intense. His eyes burned on her, filled with lust and heat and something deeply primal. The pleasure was almost overwhelming—she had to clench her teeth to bear it. She'd thought she'd felt close to him before, thought she'd known true intimacy with him—but looking into his eyes as he made her moan with each thrust was by far the most intimate thing she'd ever done with a man.

Fitting that it was him, she thought. The one man she'd always wanted. The man who was fulfilling all those long-ago dreams better than she ever could have anticipated.

She watched him cup her breast, stroke her between her thighs. She watched her own face contort in the sweet agony that was passion when she came. She watched his lip curl in perhaps the darkest moment of pleasure when he said, "Now, baby, now, I'm exploding in you." And it was only after those last hot strokes that they both finally let their eyes fall shut.

As Kat lay recovering, it struck her how . . . *wholly* into this she had been. Normal for most people, she presumed, but for her . . .

She let out a sigh, releasing the strange truth that, sadly, all other sex before him had somehow been wooden, an act, a masquerade of sorts. There had always been at least one moment during sex where she thought about what she was doing—considered her next move, how to touch, what to say, how to be the woman a guy wanted.

And with Brock, she just was.

In other sex, moments occurred when she somehow stepped back mentally and noticed a guy's imperfections, or her own, moments when she was keenly aware that she was *not* swept away by passion, that it wasn't perfect, maybe *far* from perfect. There were instances when she perhaps wondered what she was doing with that particular guy, or when she wished for some grander passion— but it didn't come.

Now, with Brock, the passion was grand, she was swept away, and it was perfect. This was the sex she'd waited for her whole life, the *man* she'd waited for. And she had to smile to herself, realizing she must have had damn good instincts back in high school, since even then she'd known he was the one.

The one?

Whoa. *That* was a terrifying and sobering thought.

Push it away. Don't let anything mar this perfection.

She did so, fast. Because this was too good to ruin with useless yearnings.

She turned to look at him in the bed next to her to find he'd fallen quickly asleep, as men were so wont to do after sex.

Weird, she even liked *that*. That he was such a male. And that maybe she'd exhausted him. Cuddling would have been nice, but in that moment, the truth was, she'd have loved him no matter what he did—because she just did. Love him. There was no help for it. Only a certain acceptance coming over her.

She loved him, and she couldn't stop it—and maybe it wasn't horrible, maybe it was good. Maybe it was *wonderful*.

Maybe he'd liked what she'd said about size having nothing to do with the way he made her feel. Maybe what he'd said at dinner about appreciating all of her meant . . . something.

She didn't know the answers, but she made a decision. Even though she knew Brock wasn't the relationship type, even though she knew he lived a fast-paced secret agent kind of life, even though nothing indicated he was ready to change any of that—she wasn't going to look on her love for him as an ending, a closed door. Instead, she was going to think of it as a beginning. Something good, precious. A new start.

And maybe, just maybe, something good would come of it.

After reaching up to turn off the lamp, she leaned over and sealed the wish with a tender kiss to Brock's cheek. *I love you. I love you so much. And I'm not going to run from it anymore.*

Chapter Fourteen

The next morning they slept in, but when Kat finally got up and dragged herself to the bathroom, Brock announced through the door that he'd just found some Pop-Tarts hidden behind something in an overhead cabinet. Not even expired, either!

So now they took up their usual spots on the beach, nibbling on freshly toasted blueberry Pop-Tarts and life felt more than a little wonderful. For today, at least. Only one more night on the island remained, but *last* night had been . . . the most incredible experience of her life. She glanced over at him, her stomach tightening from the memory.

"So . . . about last night," he said over the sound of the crashing waves a few yards in the distance. He flashed a sly look in her direction, and she thought it was almost as if he'd read her mind.

She gave her head a saucy tilt. "What about it?"

She waited for him to start waxing poetic about how amazingly intense it had been, how earth-moving and soul-shattering. Instead he said, "Was I right? Was it the best you ever had?"

With a small smile, she let out a conceding sigh and refused to be disappointed—that was just Brock. "Yes," she said, not quite meaning for her voice to sound so husky.

The slightly playful and very satisfied look he gave in reply made her yearn for him yet again, so she decided not to waste any time. He liked her wild blood—she'd let it flow free.

Ditching half a Pop-Tart in the sand, she pushed to her feet, walked over to Brock, and boldly lifted one leg across his lounge chair to straddle him.

He thrust his hands behind his head and leaned back comfortably. "Well, hi there."

Nibbling sensually on her lower lip, she let her hands curl around the waistband of his trunks, her eyes following their path.

He hissed in his breath slightly, but still managed to sound cool and seductive when he said, "Are you being a naughty little kitten again?"

She met his gaze briefly, then pulled down the front of his shorts, slowly, just enough to spy the sexy ink below his belly button. "I haven't seen enough of this tattoo yet."

He cast a wicked grin. "You say it's the tattoo you want, but we both know there's something else in there you like."

She rolled her eyes playfully, as if he were making no sense. "I don't know what you're talking about." Then she even moved her palms over his lower abdomen, touching here and there, at one point pressing on a delightfully hard column of flesh but pretending she hadn't, to say, "Nope, nothing here."

He arched one brow. "Funny, kitten. Hysterical as ever."

But she kept playing it straight. "I really don't know what you mean, Brock."

He lowered his arms from behind his head, closing his hands over her knees on either side of him. His palms glided slowly up her thighs until they rested at the edge of her bikini bottom, and a flutter of arousal trembled through her. "Maybe I should remind you."

"Mmm, maybe you should," she agreed. Especially since tomorrow was Thursday, her own personal doomsday, when the island fantasy would end. At the moment, it seemed wise to take all of him she could get. And easy, too, since no matter what they did or how often they did it, her desire for him never waned for long.

In reply, he pushed down his trunks, took her hand, and wrapped her fist snugly around his erection. Sensation skittered through her like errant electricity, and she let out a low, "Ooooh."

"Remember now?" he asked. No smile this time. All heat.

In fact, things had just turned so hot she could barely respond. "Uh-huh."

"I thought so."

She bit her lip against the pleasure his mere voice sent vibrating through her, and did what came naturally with him, it seemed. She lowered her mouth over him, listened to his agony/ecstasy moan—knowing it was closer to the latter, and loved the power she felt over him, the power she somehow felt them exchanging this way.

Moments later, she followed the instincts of her body and, upon releasing him from her lips, lowered her breasts there, finding he fit neatly in the valley between.

"Jesus, kitten," he breathed, and she basked in the glory of thrilling him, surprising him. He reached behind her neck to untie her top and let it fall free.

Soon after, she found herself sheathing that same glorious part of him, watching it happen, his tattoo becoming the background for it all—and as she moved on him, she forgot anything else existed and knew the most pure joy life had ever given her.

She belonged here with him. On this island. Riding him to oblivion. Everything happened for a reason—she believed that.

And Brock had come back into her life not only to show her she was making the wrong move, but also to give her the *right* one. Nothing had ever felt as safe and real and relevant to her as her union with this man who had become so much more than she'd ever expected, this man who kept her safe and made her laugh, then took her to heaven with his hot eyes and even hotter body.

She came without warning, hard and fast, her limbs quivering with the force of the climax. "Oh, oh God! Oh Brock!" She clawed at his chest, clutched at his shoulders, then collapsed on him when it was over.

His hands gripped her bottom, drawing her down tight, and his voice echoed much softer than hers. "Me, too, baby. Ah, God. Yeah." And then he was emptying inside her and holding her near, and other than the surf and the call of a seagull, there were no sounds, only repletion and peace.

They lay that way for a long time, until Kat almost fell asleep beneath the warmth of the midday sun. She figured Brock was *already* asleep, so it surprised her when he whispered, "You okay?"

Her mouth rested near his ear, so she answered gently. "Mmm hmm. Why?"

She opened her eyes to find him peering back, beautifully close. "Your orgasm seemed . . . intense."

She gave him a slow, languid nod accompanied by a sensual smile. *It's what you do to me. You move me profoundly. You make me want nothing more than you and this island, forever. You change everything inside me . . . just when I thought I knew myself so well.*

She should tell him. All of that. Everything in her head right now. She should just put it out there, be honest. *Tell him how you feel, for God's sake.*

But she couldn't. The very idea brought on the same sense of humiliation she'd experienced by the swamp ten years ago. She couldn't deal with that kind of rejection a second time. Different circumstances, but the heartache would feel the same, maybe only magnified now by all they'd been through together over the last few days. "Just that wild blood in my veins," she finally replied. Being what he wanted her to be.

But maybe that was okay, because it was also what he truly *made* of her—*injecting* that wild blood.

"I'm sleepy," he said, eyes shutting. "Let's go take a nap in the hammock."

She giggled softly. "We only got up an hour ago."

"I don't care. You wear me out. And I'm on vacation. Kind of."

Since cuddling in a hammock with Brock didn't exactly sound like torture, she climbed off him, bending to snatch up the pieces of her bathing suit from the sand—but he grabbed her hand to say, "Leave it. As much as I like you in it, I like you better out of it."

Kat's first inclination was to protest—but if you couldn't walk around naked on your own private island, where could you walk around naked? And it left Brock naked, too—a definite perk.

Leading his lover into the shade of the palms supporting the hammock, Brock plopped down into it, then drew her onto the heavy netting next to him, wrapping her in his arms. Damn, she was good. Last night hadn't been only the best *she'd* ever had—it had been pretty freaking astounding for him, too. And tomorrow was coming a little too fast for his taste. He didn't like thinking about their being marooned coming to an end—maybe that was why he hadn't wanted her to get dressed and go back over to her own lounge chair. He'd had the urge to keep on being close to her.

"Comfy?" He curled his hand over her bare hip.

"Mmm," she said, nestling against him. Her breasts pressed into his side, and the hammock curved around them like a cocoon.

"So, tell me more about this pottery of yours."

She lifted her head to meet his eyes. "I thought you were sleepy."

He shrugged. "The walk across the beach woke me up."

"Well," she said, "since you asked, I'm having my very first show next month."

"You mentioned something about that. When you were talking about your dad's gallery."

She nodded, but looked sheepish. "Don't think it's just because I'm his daughter and happen to be employed there. He made me work long and hard before he offered it to me. I've been inching toward this since college."

"What kind of things do you make?" Truth was, it was hard to reconcile the idea of Kat doing something that got her hands dirty—but maybe that wasn't fair. She'd been a hell of a trouper out in the woods, offering up not one complaint. And even though he hadn't noticed her hands not being soft and manicured, once she'd pointed it out, it had provided physical proof she wasn't the froufrou girl he'd always thought.

"Vases, bowls, plates," she replied. "Mostly decorative. I actually do a lot of different kinds of pottery, but all the work in my show was created with the Raku method, fired in a pit, then adorned with sea glass. In fact, this afternoon I thought I'd walk up the beach and *look* for some sea glass. I found a few pieces here last summer."

"Sea glass?"

"Glass that's been sort of . . . transformed by the ocean. Like, say someone drops a bottle off a boat somewhere. The broken pieces wash toward the shore, and the sand and water are like a giant tumbler. It turns the glass smooth and frosted, almost like a transparent stone. It's used for jewelry sometimes, but I've incorporated it into my pots."

He couldn't help being intrigued. "And you just find this stuff on the beach?"

"Well, less-populated beaches like this one are better. Or when the tide goes out, just like hunting for shells. And you can buy it, too, which I've done, but I really like to find my own when I can. I've found some on Sanibel, and I've also made trips to the Great Lakes because they have a lot up there, and off the coast of the Carolinas, too. The most common colors are blue and green—from bottles—and fortunately, those are my favorites and they fit nicely with the blues and greens on my Raku stuff. In fact, my show has an ocean theme—it's called Into the Deep Blue."

God, just when he thought he knew her, got her, he found out there was even more. She'd truly surprised him this week, in so many ways, and she hadn't stopped yet. "That's very cool, kitten. Really." Then he bit back something on the tip of his tongue.

"What?" she asked.

He sighed. "I almost said that maybe I'd try to make it to your show, but . . . it might not be a good idea for me to come to your dad's gallery."

She looked bewildered. "Why not?"

Shit. He'd totally forgotten she didn't know what had happened between them. "Well . . . I left town pretty quick back then. And he and I weren't exactly buddies before that, if you know what I mean."

She nodded. "I think he knew I liked you. And I don't think he was too wild about the idea."

You can say that again. "Uh, yeah. I don't think so, either."

"But my God, Brock, it was ten years ago. And I'd love for you to come. I mean, if you want to. And once he shows up tomorrow and sees that you're a nice guy, it'll be fine."

He laughed. "Yeah, he'll be thrilled to know we just spent five days together and that you're calling off your wedding because of it."

She bit her lip. "Okay, maybe I see your point. But I'd still like you to come to the show."

Her voice was so sweet, earnest—and now he felt bad for bringing it up, because he'd probably disappoint her. "It'll depend on my work, if I'm in Miami or out of town. But . . . we'll see, kitten."

She stayed quiet, and he felt like he'd disappointed her *already*. He shouldn't have said anything—he'd just been curious about her pottery. But it probably *was* a bad idea. For a lot of reasons.

"Speaking of ten years ago," she began, sounding cautious, "there's . . . something I always wondered about you."

Given that Kat didn't usually lead into questions with so much— if any—care, he couldn't imagine what was to come. "What's that?"

Peering down, he couldn't mistake the concern in her eyes. "Why did you live with your grandpa? I mean . . . what about your parents?"

Even now, all these years later, something inside him tensed when someone mentioned his parents. He hated that he still didn't have full control over that. And anyone else in the world, at any other time or place—he'd probably tell them it was none of their damn business. But he'd pried about as deeply into Kat's personal life as he could over the past days, and they'd shared some pretty close, profound moments, so a sense of decency prevented him from trying to withhold the information.

"They left us," he said simply. And he'd tried to look her in the eye as he said it, but had failed, instead finding his gaze stuck on an old coconut hull in the sand a few yards away.

Next to him, Kat stayed quiet for a moment, and he felt her fresh horror. "Left you?" she finally asked.

He swallowed back the old bitterness and sense of abandonment. "Yeah," he said. "When I was eight, my dad took off—just went out one night and never came back. He was always saying how much he hated me and Bruno, so I guess he decided he'd had enough. And it was good in a way, because at least we didn't have to listen to the two of them screaming and threatening each other anymore."

"Threatening?" she whispered.

Get ready for some real *horror, kitten.* She'd asked—and he didn't see any reason to sugarcoat it. "They were always waving something around while they screamed. A knife from the kitchen, an empty whiskey bottle, one time a hammer. Always saying they were gonna kill each other, bash each other's heads in, great stuff like that."

Her palm pressed warm against his chest, a sweet comfort—yet he wondered if his heart was beating faster than normal and if she felt it. He'd never liked letting anyone see his weaknesses. And maybe Kat had seen more than most people this week, but this was different. This ran deep.

"At any rate," he went on, "my mom held us responsible for making Dad leave. Hell, you'd think she'd have been glad, but instead it just meant she had to work to keep us fed, something she wasn't real into. Sometimes . . ." *She locked us in the bathroom when she left the house.* He could still see the old mildewed wall above the tub, the rust stain around the drain, the little window that had been painted shut, and even when Bruno had pried it open one time, they still couldn't get out. Not even a fan in there, and it had been hotter than hell on a south Florida summer afternoon. They'd dripped sweat, started taking turns in the shower, had once run water and both just sat in the tub, Bruno at one end, Brock at the other, curled up in naked little balls, trying to talk about baseball and school and their friends like it was a normal Saturday.

Then his mind flashed on the times his mother had locked him in the coat closet, Bruno in the one in the bedroom. She knew separating them made it much worse—so dark, and even hotter. And it made them feel so alone. They would yell to each other every now and then.

You okay?

Yeah. Just hot. And I think there's spiders in here.

Don't worry, she'll be back soon.

They would say that last part to each other for hours, trying to believe it each and every time it left their mouths.

They'd considered running away—Bruno had wanted to, but Brock had been younger, afraid. They'd walked the half-hour drive to Grandpa's once, but Mom had come for them that night. Grandpa had known things were bad—Brock was more willing to tell him about it than Bruno was—and he'd asked his daughter-in-law to let them stay. She'd said no. To this day, Brock had no idea why, except that maybe she'd just liked having them around to blame for her pathetic life.

"Sometimes what?" Kat asked.

He looked down to find her still nestled in his arms, eyes brimming with sadness for him, and realized he was going to edit the truth for her, just a little. There was already enough revulsion in her expression, and he couldn't think of a reason to make it worse. "Nothing," he said softly. "The upshot is, after a couple more years, my mom left, too. Sometimes she'd do that, just take off and leave us for a few days."

Thank God she'd never locked them up *then*. No, then she only left them without any food or money, so when they figured out she wasn't coming home, they'd call Grandpa and he'd come and get them until she showed back up days later, usually with some ridiculous story about someone who'd needed her help, a friend in an accident, some bizarre emergency that she would claim prevented her from picking up a phone for three solid days.

"I can't explain how, but when she left for good, we knew it. Just felt it. We sat up all night watching old monster movies on TV—some kind of marathon—just perched on the couch together, not talking, and I remember thinking about her the whole night. Part of me felt afraid," he said, remembering how long it had taken to forget that locked-up feeling, remembering the desperate pleas inside that he'd never given voice to, not wanting his tough older brother to hear. *Don't leave, Mama, please. I'll be good. Don't leave us here.* "But part of me didn't want her to come back. And she never did.

"The next morning, we called Grandpa. He picked us up, took us home with him, and we never went back to that house, ever. After a couple of weeks, Grandpa went to pack our clothes and other things. When the rent was due, he told the landlord to send everything in it—which wasn't much—to the junkyard, except for a few things we could use, like the TV. And that was it. We never heard from her again."

He peered down into her shocked eyes and said, "It's okay, kitten. It was a long time ago. And trust me—it was for the best."

"But you were just a little boy. Both of you. That's . . . the worst thing I've ever heard."

He shrugged. "Bad shit happens sometimes."

She still looked despairing, and he didn't like having unwittingly dumped his personal tragedy on her, so he decided to tell her the rest of the story. "If it makes you feel any better, going to live with my grandfather was the best thing that ever happened to me."

"He loved you," she said simply.

And he felt that love all the way to his bones, as real as if it still existed, as if his grandfather were still alive. "Yeah," he said quietly. "A lot.

"He wasn't the kind of guy who'd walked the straight and narrow his whole life. Hell, you heard what kind of son he raised. But he raised me, too, and he'd mellowed by then. As I got older, he confided in me regrets from when he was a younger man, but I'll admit I didn't care much about what he'd done when he was young—I was just glad we had him, glad he was willing to take in two rambunctious boys at a point in his life when he probably thought those kinds of responsibilities were behind him."

"He was probably glad to have you," Kat offered softly.

"Maybe," Brock allowed, then added on a laugh, "but we were pretty bad kids sometimes."

"I remember your grandpa being sick when you worked at the gallery."

"Yeah. Lung cancer. But he still kept right on smoking, right up until . . . well, I can't say 'til the day he died, because I wasn't around for that, but at least right up until the day I left." His chest tightened slightly. "That's my greatest regret. Leaving when he was dying."

Below him, Kat blinked prettily, then voiced a gentle question. "Why did you?"

I can't tell you that, kitten. He thought about tossing out the old I-could-tell-you-but-then-I'd-have-to-kill-you line, but this wasn't the moment for that. So instead he'd just have to lie. "He wanted me to." And it wasn't a *total* lie. Grandpa had told him to go when he'd found out what Clark Spencer had said to him. And this next part was even the truth. "He wanted me to go and make something of myself. He believed in me. Bruno was already into some pretty bad shit by then, already doing time, but Grandpa thought I was cut out for better things and wanted me to go somewhere and start a new life and do something good. That's how I ended up at the police academy, and then later, Quantico."

"Did he know?" she asked. "Did he know before he died what you were doing?"

"He knew about the police academy, not the FBI. But that's enough for me. I talked to him on the phone a few times from the academy. He wasn't a real talkative man—just kept saying, 'That's real good, Brock, that's real good'—but I could hear the pride in his voice. So I like to think maybe he died a little happier because he knew I was gonna turn out okay."

"I'm sure he did," she whispered, and as she slid her hand up his chest onto his face, drawing him down for a kiss, he decided to quit thinking about all that wrenching stuff so long in his past and concentrate on the lithe, beautiful girl who lay naked with him in a hammock. Hell, he couldn't even remember what had taken him down that dark road, but sun, sand, and sex were far better, so he cast his most wicked grin and said, "Ever done it in a hammock, kitten?"

A small, sensual smile reshaped her face and he was instantly glad to have drawn *her* back to the present, too. "No."

He slipped a hand between her thighs and found her delightfully dewy. "I think you want to."

Her breath came warm on his ear. "I'll do it wherever you want me to."

A jolt of masculine power shot through him, propelling him to roll on top of her and take control. He kissed her, gently bit her neck, rubbed his hardened shaft between her parted thighs, then eased inside in one long, smooth stroke.

She gasped at the impact, imparting in him still more male control, and he moved in her, smooth and warm, and listened to her pretty moans combining with the sound of the tide and the rustle of palm fronds from the sea breeze.

Damn, their sex just kept getting better and better. He didn't even know how that was possible, but it did. She was so easy to be with, in every way. At once so sweet and so sexy, saucy but gentle. At moments wild, at others completely demure. In ways, she was just like the sand—an enigma. Hell, the girly girl with pink sparkly flip-flops and the perfect tan also had clay-dried hands and broken fingernails. And yet, she was just . . . Kat. His sweet, naughty kitten. A handful of a girl. But a *good* handful.

No matter how he tried to stop, he still couldn't deny how very . . . *close* he felt to her. He wasn't *supposed* to get close to people. Never had. Had thought he never *could*.

Hell, he didn't even know how to go about it. He could joke, he could flirt, he could seduce—he could even open up his heart on rare occasions, and he'd done that a time or two with Kat, not by plan but because of the shit that had happened.

But he didn't know how to go beyond that—and he didn't think it was a good time to find out. He didn't think it would *ever* be a good time. The FBI liked his being unattached, and so did he. If something happened to him, there wasn't anybody to mourn or cry—and no one for the government to support, either. It had always seemed wise to keep it that way. And he'd never once, since the day he'd joined the Bureau, had a reason to think about *not* keeping it that way.

As for Kat, well . . . she was incredible.

But from his job to her father to every one of the zillion reasons in between, there was a lot to keep them apart. And that would be best for all concerned—for more reasons than he could name.

So he'd just enjoy the rest of their time together. Take it for what it was. Mind-boggling sex and good company and, hell, someone who—if there wasn't all this heat between them—he'd even consider a friend. Which felt pretty damn weird. Because he got along well enough with the guys he worked with, might even refer to one or two of them as a "buddy," but as for real friends, he wasn't sure he'd ever had one. Maybe that was why it had pinched so much that Carlos had called him that.

So Kat was his lover. Kat was his friend. He'd hold this week with her as something special. And he supposed the next time he got into danger and found himself escaping with a fantasy, it would be a memory instead. Maybe he'd even feel a little wistful about it.

But he was who he was. An undercover fed whose job was everything. A guy who didn't think about anything as abstract and hard to understand as relationships, or God forbid, the L-word. He'd been that guy his whole life, and he'd gotten by okay.

Just then, her hands curled around his ass, tight, pulling him deeper. He instantly wanted to kiss her, make her feel his affection—he wanted her to know he was making love to her.

But no. If you truly made love to someone, it meant there *was* love. And this wasn't that. Couldn't be. *It's just sex, dude, just sex. So don't kiss her right now. Hold something back.*

But he kissed her anyway, unable to resist. Kissed her warm and deep until he was as lost in it as he was in *all* of her, in her body, in her very soul. He stopped thinking, weighing, or worrying. He just followed his instincts and urges, let the flawless joy of the moment swallow him up, and he knew, just for those few minutes, as he plunged deep inside of her—deeper, deeper—that he was indeed making love to Katrina Spencer. Making love to her for all he was worth.

"That was perfect," she said after they'd both come and still held each other tight.

"Yeah," he admitted. "Yeah, it was."

After heating up the grill that evening, Brock opened the bungalow door to find Kat's back to him at the kitchen counter. Wearing her bikini bottoms with that same cute pink strappy top from the first day, she was shaking her ass to "You Sexy Thing" by Hot Chocolate. He'd come for the burgers, but instead crossed his arms and leaned against the doorjamb to watch. She danced her way to the sink, washing off a tomato, then moved to the fridge, wiggling her bottom enough to turn him half-hard before emerging with a couple of slices of cheese in her hand.

"I thought you didn't like seventies music," he said with a grin. She'd complained about it more than once over the past days.

She flinched, then turned toward him with a you-caught-me grin. "This one's okay," she replied, resuming slight swaying movements, which he discovered he enjoyed even more from the front.

When she danced right over to him, grabbing his hands and encouraging him to move with her, he followed his instincts, letting himself find the rhythm on the old tile floor. His hands made their way to her hips, then her rear, and he leaned closer, brushing his growing erection against the front of her bikini.

She cast a coquettish smile. "I wouldn't have guessed you for a dancer."

"Neither would I."

"What's the occasion?"

"A scantily clad chick letting me rub up against her to music. *That's* the occasion."

She leaned her head back in a soft trill of laughter, making her breasts rise slightly from her top.

"But if dancing is always this fun, maybe I could get into it. Maybe when I get home, I *should* start hitting the clubs," he teased.

She gave a haughty eye roll, as if saying it was no skin off *her* nose. "You might find other girls who let you rub up against them to music, but they won't be as good as me."

He grinned. "Don't worry, kitten—I would never expect them to be." *And the only girl I really want to rub against right now is the one in my arms.*

Good time to shut up. Because even if picking up girls he didn't know sounded damn empty at the moment, what he'd *already* said was close enough to being too much.

Even so, he was still enjoying himself when she handily extracted herself from his grasp and made her way back to the counter, still moving slightly to the music.

"Hey, hey, hey—song's not over. Where you going?"

She returned a moment later with a plate bearing two hamburger patties. "I'm hungry," she said with a playful smile, "and not just for you. So start cooking, mister."

As Brock made his way to the grill and put the hamburgers on, he wondered if he'd ever suffered as many hard-ons in a five-day period as he had since finding Katrina Spencer on this island. Hell, maybe when he was a kid. That had been torture. *This* had been torture at *first*, but had gotten a lot less horrible. God, what a turnaround he'd seen in her. From pushing him away to *having* her way with him on the beach this morning.

Fifteen minutes later, Brock flipped the burgers onto the buns Kat had brought out, then joined her at the table. The last supper, so to speak, and to his surprise, he *felt* that. They still had the night together and probably much of the day tomorrow, but he'd grown accustomed to sitting down to dinner with her at the little table in the sand. They ate chips with their burgers, and then more store-bought cookies, and he was amazed at how good such a simple meal could taste under the right circumstances.

"Thanks for walking up the beach with me today," Kat said. After sex in the hammock, they'd finally napped, then Kat had announced her sojourn for sea glass. He'd offered to go, curious to see the stuff, if there was any to see, and they'd trekked up the shoreline holding hands, still naked. It had felt at once bizarre and natural—and like an experience it seemed only appropriate to have with his wild Kat.

"We didn't find much." They'd picked up only five small remnants, all green, which they'd deposited in the zipper pocket on his trunks. Only as she'd dropped the first piece in had he remembered Francisco's key remained there, too.

"Finding *any* is like discovering treasure," she explained, eyes sparkling. "It doesn't exactly grow on trees, so I always feel lucky if I find any at all." Her expression dampened just slightly as she said, "I'll need to be sure to get the pieces from you before we . . . you know . . . part ways tomorrow."

He gave a soft nod. Maybe neither one of them was exactly looking forward to "rescue," but that was how things had to be.

"By the way," she said, still looking a little uncomfortable, "I should mention that Ian will probably come tomorrow."

He lifted his gaze from his plate to her eyes. "Really?" He had no desire to meet the guy and didn't like hearing that his last few minutes with Kat on the ride back would be spent with her fiancé. He still couldn't help wondering what the hell she'd been doing planning to marry that guy. Just to please their families? He knew Kat's parents were important to her, and he knew Clark could be overbearing, but . . . when he thought about it, he still remained stumped that someone as self-possessed as Kat would let herself be railroaded into an engagement just because it made everyone but her happy.

"By the time they come, they're all going to think something is wrong, and everyone will be mad at me for lying about where I went, and Ian's in pretty close touch with my father, so . . . yeah, it's likely."

He took a big, annoyed bite of his burger, thinking tomorrow was going to be a real drag. "Tell me something, Kat. Tell me, straight up, why you agreed to marry him."

She drew back slightly, lowering the chip between her fingers back to her plate. Maybe he'd sounded a little gruff.

"I already told you. Because . . . our families are close and I've known him my whole life and he's a decent guy who's crazy about me. It was a mistake, sure, but the only ingredient missing was the fact that I'm not in love with him."

"That's a pretty big factor, kitten," he said, trying not to sound so brusque, but still firm. They'd had this conversation before, but he still wasn't quite buying her answer.

"Well, I sort of convinced myself I *was* in love with him. Right up until . . . you." She swallowed, suddenly looking a little nervous. "I mean, I just figured out that if I wanted to sleep with you so badly, I must *not* be in love. But until then . . ."

He tilted his head, gave her a come-clean-with-me look. "You're too smart for that, Kat. There's gotta be more, some other reason besides 'our families are close.' "

He knew the moment he said it that he was right—guilt draped her face.

"Tell me why else."

Across from him, she bit her bottom lip and let out a big sigh. "You're going to think I'm crazy."

"Probably. But tell me."

"The truth is . . ."

"Yeah?"

"My family is having money trouble."

He felt his eyebrows shoot up. Clark Spencer, in financial trouble? "How is that possible?"

"The gallery isn't doing well. I mean, it does *okay*, but my dad made a lot of money dealing in art and antiquities when he was young, and that money just isn't there anymore. I guess we lived on it for a long while, but it's finally dwindled."

Brock was trying real hard to absorb what she was saying, but then stated the obvious. "Honey, your family is doing *fine* on money.

I've seen the house you grew up in. You guys *own* a gallery. Cars. Boats. You own a freaking island, for God's sake."

She looked a little embarrassed. "This is complicated. Because . . . yes, we own an island, and a big house. But the money is running out. And . . . if I married Ian, it was going to change *everything*. It was going to bail my dad out of trouble."

"First of all, I don't call maybe having to sell your private island *trouble*. But you're telling me that Ian has enough money to keep people as rich as you guys *staying* rich, while he stays rich himself?"

She nodded.

"That's a lot of damn money, kitten." An almost unfathomable amount.

"I know," she said on a slight swallow. "And I don't want to say I was marrying him for that, but . . . well, let's just say I was aware the marriage would make a lot of people happy in a lot of ways. And I know you think my family would be just fine without all the stuff we have, but you don't know my dad."

"You forget—I *do* know your dad. And I've always thought he was a greedy, selfish son of a bitch." She flinched, and he added, "Sorry, kitten, I know you love him. But even *you* have to admit he likes his money and possessions a *lot*."

It shouldn't have surprised him when she defended her father. "That's just who he is, Brock. He somehow equates his value as a person to what he owns. And it's not *totally* selfish. It's because he's always wanted to be able to give my mother and me the best of everything. He grew up poor and turned that around, and it's important to him to *keep it* turned around."

"I grew up poor, too, kitten, and I damn well understand the value of money and why it feels good to have nice things. But . . . don't you think it's a little extreme with your dad? That he needs to own a freaking island to feel good?"

"Maybe," she conceded. "It's just . . . how he takes pride in himself. Being able to give his family extraordinary luxuries. It's his way."

Yeah, Brock knew more about Clark Spencer's *ways* than he cared to remember, but only one question seemed significant now. "Did he ask you to do it? Did he ask you to marry Ian to bail him out of trouble?"

She sighed. "Not exactly."

Brock's temperature rose a little higher. "Then *what* exactly?"

She dropped her gaze to her plate and spoke lowly. "When Ian and I started dating, Dad told me how happy he was that we were together, and he . . . sort of said, jokingly, that if Ian and I ever got married, it would solve a world of problems. I knew what problems he meant, of course. And he thinks of it as *my* problem, too. I've told him I don't care about having the absolute best of *everything*, but *he* wants me to have the best, and if he doesn't feel he can provide it, he wants me to be with someone who can. Ian, too, once told me he knew about Dad's money issues and said that if he and I ended up together that my dad wouldn't have to worry about that anymore. And so, when he proposed to me at Christmas in front of both families, I . . . said yes. It *did* seem like the answer to everything."

How utterly shitty for her. "You know what? I'm really glad I came along to mess that up. And your father and Ian are both assholes to put you in that position."

"My dad doesn't mean to be that way, Brock. He just thinks he knows what it takes to make me happy."

He hated how vehemently she continued to defend him. "He *doesn't* know, though."

"You're so sure?"

Wasn't it obvious? "Yeah, I am. And he didn't know ten years ago, either."

"What do you mean?"

Shit. That was the second time today he'd nearly tripped over his words. And as much as he detested Clark Spencer—even more so in this moment than ever before—he still had no intention of telling Kat what had really happened to make him leave town so abruptly back when they were young. It would only wound her deeply, and even if he wanted to open her eyes to her dad's flaws, he just couldn't bring himself to show her how big those flaws could be. So he let out a large sigh and simply replied, "Let's just say I always thought the guy was a little too controlling."

"He tried to be, I know that. But I didn't let him."

He looked her in the eye, and saw, once more, how beautiful she was. "I know you didn't, kitten, and I'm glad."

"In most ways, I mean," she replied, biting her lip again. "Although I guess there are little things, concessions I had to make to get my way on bigger things."

He lowered his chin. "Like what?"

"Like, if it were up to me, I probably *would* have a tattoo to show you, but . . ." She went on to explain about bathing suits and swimming pools and how her dad would surely see such a thing. "It's not as if he's ever even *mentioned* tattoos to me—I just know he would object, so I never bothered. I didn't want to fight. When I was younger, we fought a *lot*—about what I wore or where I was going—and I didn't want to argue anymore. So I just learned to pick my battles and know how far I could push my boundaries."

Brock could only imagine what a handful Kat must have been as a young girl—and he could almost feel sorry for Spencer if he didn't know what an asshole the man could really be. But mainly, he respected the hell out of her for her graceful way of dealing with her dad, and maybe he also respected how much she loved the man, even knowing he had faults.

Brock *didn't* love *his* parents. And admittedly, their faults had been a lot bigger than even a jerk like Spencer, so maybe it made sense. But he'd never been the type of guy to look beyond someone's mistakes and try to forgive. That just hadn't been ingrained in him. As a result, the only people he'd ever really loved were his grandpa and Bruno. Grandpa had been gone a long time now, and Bruno . . . well, Brock still felt a nostalgic affection for his brother—you don't go through what they did together and not feel a bond—but Bruno had disappointed him so much that his affection had faded a lot until it seemed more like a sentimental thing, or maybe even an obligation.

As he sat there watching her eat, he envied her ability to love.

And he thought she could probably teach him a lot about it . . . if only he'd let her.

But for the moment, he no longer wanted to think about *could* and *couldn't*, or all the things that would keep them apart once they got back to the real world—he just wanted to be with her. "Hurry up," he said as she took another bite from her burger.

She looked up, clearly surprised by the command. "What?"

"Eat up, kitten, and then I'm taking you to bed."

Brock woke up to the sun shining in the window, but his thoughts remained stuck on the previous night. He'd kissed her from head to toe, concentrating more on some spots than others. She'd returned the favor with admirable enthusiasm. Then they'd brought their bodies together—again and again—until they were both exhausted.

He leaned over to kiss Kat a sleepy good morning—then remembered it was Thursday. Rescue day. That word had started to seem like it didn't make much sense, though. How was it rescue when you wanted to stay?

"Pop-Tarts?" she asked with hopeful eyes. "I'll toast."

"Then I'll eat." He playfully swatted her bottom as she departed the bed, and realized he didn't like thinking he couldn't do that tomorrow morning, too. He was gonna miss that bottom. He was gonna miss all of her.

"Hey," she said, slipping on a pair of panties and a little top, "can you get my sea glass out of your pocket before we forget about it?"

"Yeah, sure," he replied, rising with a yawn. He walked naked to where his trunks lay tossed over one of the kitchen chairs and unzipped the pocket. Turning it upside down, he emptied the smooth pieces of glass into his palm—along with the key.

He glanced up to find her back to him, heard her push down the lever on the toaster. Plucking the key from the sea glass, he deposited the green frosted glass on the table—along with a few wayward grains of sand—and closed the key in his fist.

"Hey, can you grab those when they pop?" she asked, moving toward the bathroom. "I want to wash my face and put on some lotion."

"Sure, kitten," he said with a wink, then watched as the door closed behind her.

As he was turning back toward the counter, though, his eyes landed on something he hadn't thought about in a couple of days. That damn locked closet. The explanation for it had sounded reasonable enough, yet something about it had bugged him, not quite rung true.

Then Brock's gaze dropped to the key in his hand.

Key. Lock.

Nah.

But as he recalled the niggling feeling that the Morales brothers had come here for some other reason, his chest tightened slightly.

What the hell. Walking to the closet, he slid the key in the lock, fully expecting it not to fit.

Only it fit.

He gently turned it and listened to the surprising click that unlocked the door.

Shit. What the hell was going on here?

Twisting the knob to pull the door slowly open, his eyes fell on a stunning array of Mayan treasures. Statues, masks, pieces of jade, chunks of stone carved with hieroglyphs. Jesus. His heart nearly pounded through his chest as he realized that *this* had been the pickup spot all along. Clark Spencer's island.

Chapter Fifteen

Holy shit. They *hadn't* seen him swim here, for God's sake—they'd been coming for the artifacts and happened to find him standing on the goddamn shore. And yeah, they'd been looking for the key the next time they'd shown up, but they'd planned to haul this stuff away the second they *got* that key.

Brock took a good look at the door—extrathick, reinforced. A mega lock—you couldn't tell that from the exterior, but it was massive from the side, at the door's edge. Which explained why they didn't just break the thing down while Brock and Kat were running through the woods. Hell, for all he knew, they'd come in and tried to—there had been hours when Brock and Kat had hidden in peace.

So this explained a hell of a lot.

But it also raised some enormous questions.

This island belonged to Clark Spencer. That meant he had to be involved.

But if Spencer was in on this, where was the money, and why did he claim to be low on income? And why hadn't anyone come for this stuff after Carlos and Francisco failed to show up with it? Why hadn't Omega Man dispatched someone else?

Shit, shit, shit. This discovery meant they were still in danger. He glanced toward the bathroom, thinking of Kat, of protecting her, and hoping like hell now that her parents showed up sooner rather than later.

Only . . . was Spencer involved or not? He wouldn't put it past the guy. But Spencer just plain shouldn't need money if he was smuggling Mayan artifacts.

Behind him, the toaster popped, and he flinched. The scent of warm pastry and blueberries filled the air. Kat would be out in a minute to eat.

Glancing down, Brock's eyes fell on an intricate little piece of smooth gray stone with some carvings on it. Small enough to fit in his pocket, along with the key—and a tidy piece of evidence to take with him. He didn't really *need* evidence, but something made him pick it up. He wished he could take more—all of it—in case someone arrived to collect this stuff before he could get a federal boat out here, but this would have to do for now. He quietly closed the door, quick to relock it, then dropped the stone and the key into the pocket of his shorts, still on the chair, just as the bathroom door opened.

She looked playfully perturbed. "I was expecting to be greeted with my Pop-Tart at the door."

"You should pack."

She looked a bit stunned—understandably, he supposed. But he wanted them to be ready to go the moment someone came to pick them up. "What?"

"You can eat first, but after that, you should get packed."

She raised her eyebrows. "Anxious to get off the island and away from me?"

He sighed, then took her hands in his. "No, actually."

"Then why were you cute, sexy Brock when I went into the bathroom only to be weird, bossy Brock when I came out?"

"Weird, bossy Brock is also known as Federal Agent Brock, and as of today, I'm back on the job. The second we get off this island, I have some serious stuff to do, people to call, that sort of thing. And that reminds me," he said, this just hitting him, "presuming your father is on the boat that comes to get us, you're to let me do all the talking—got it?"

She just gaped at him, but he didn't care. What he'd just found in the closet had thrust him back into mission mode, big-time.

"What the hell is that supposed to mean? I'm not allowed to talk to my dad?"

"You can hug him and tell him you're okay, sure. But when it comes to questions about what I'm doing here and what happened to your boat, you let me handle it—understand?"

"Sure," she said in a short, clipped, clearly angry tone. Then she stomped to the toaster, yanked up a Pop-Tart, and started to march away.

He cut her off as she rounded the table. "Don't be mad."

"Why are you suddenly acting like a jerk?"

Because this is important, kitten, so damn important, and I can't explain why. I can't explain that your dad might be a smuggler who's about to go to prison once we get back to the mainland and get this sorted out. "I'm sorry," he said, letting his arms close warm around her.

She didn't look appeased, and he wondered if she had any idea how rare it was for him to care if a girl was pissed at him. He wasn't sure he'd ever apologized to anyone just for being a little gruff. But he did it again anyway. "I'm sorry, kitten. I'm just think-ing about the case I was working on when I got here. But I didn't mean to take my troubles out on *you*." He tilted his head and peered into her eyes. "Forgive me?"

She looked aloof, then said, "A kiss might help."

He narrowed his gaze. "Where would you like it?"

She tilted her head to one side and pointed to her neck.

"I was hoping for lower, but okay," he said, then delivered a soft kiss just beneath her ear, pleased when it made her shiver.

"I might let you go lower later," she offered, sounding a little less mad.

"*Might*, huh?" He arched one brow.

"If you're nice."

"I hate to break this to you, but I'm not a very nice guy, kitten. Ask anyone."

"You *can* be," she reminded him, starting past, toward the door. Yeah, he supposed she kind of brought that out in him. At the strangest times.

Slipping into his trunks, then grabbing up his own Pop-Tart, he followed her out to the picnic table. He really hated to turn things back to work so quickly after their spat, but she wouldn't realize this was *about* work, and there was something he needed to know. "When your dad made the big bucks, back when he was young, how'd he do it? What kind of stuff did he deal in? I mean, what changed between then and now?"

She turned to face him, looking a little confused, and he realized he'd neglected a segue. Thankfully, she let it go, and answered. "Well, he dabbled in some old art and rare collector's items then, but mainly, he imported Mayan artifacts and sold them to collectors and museums. He bought them in Central America, then brokered deals up here. They were very valuable, and it was easy to make a lot of money, but then in 1983 laws were passed making it illegal to bring artifacts into the country. So after that, he switched his focus to showcasing local artists, like he still does now—but that's just not remotely as profitable."

"Yeah, I've . . . heard about that law," Brock said. And his heart broke a little for Kat—since it looked like Daddy dearest was going to be in very big trouble before this was over.

Debra should have been worrying about twenty different things. Confirming all the girls' manicure and pedicure appointments for tomorrow, as well as the bridesmaids' luncheon afterward. Her own hair appointment for Saturday. Making sure Ian's best man, who'd always struck her as a little scatterbrained, especially to be Ian's friend, remembered to pick up the tuxes on time. And whether or not Kat was all right.

Surely she was, and Debra wasn't *really* worried—actually, Clark had seemed more concerned the last couple of days than *she'd* felt. The only real niggling fear in the back of Debra's mind was that maybe Kat was incommunicado because she was having doubts. But her plane would arrive in a few hours and then surely all of Debra's questions would be put to rest. She'd find out Kat had simply been too busy having fun to call, or that she'd just wanted some time completely away from thinking about the wedding. Everything would be fine.

So instead of worrying about *any* of that, she was off to lunch with Michael. And had just located the street number he'd given her and pulled into his driveway.

Her heart beat too hard and her palms were sweaty and the sad, shameful truth was, she'd fallen asleep last night—alone in bed because Clark was down the hall working in his office—imagining what it would be like to let Michael seduce her.

Of course, it was only a fantasy. And there was no harm in that— was there?

She let out the breath she'd been holding. She'd probably feel less guilty if she weren't about to see him right now.

It's only lunch. Calm down.

The house wasn't nearly as elaborate as her own—and that was probably why she found it so charming. The bright white trim and pointed gables on the yellow stucco made the classic Florida style uniquely quaint and inviting. Although the flower beds looked a bit neglected and she supposed that had been a chore that had fallen to his wife.

He opened the door before she even knocked, and as usual, the kindness in his eyes nearly paralyzed her. "Debra, I'm glad you're here. Come in."

He stood back to let her enter, but she failed to notice much about the interior other than a general feeling of pleasant styles and tidiness—too nervous.

"Find the place okay?" His smile melted her.

"Yes—your directions were great."

"Wedding plans under control so far?"

She nodded, watching as he passed through to the kitchen.

"Need to check my sauce," he said, and she followed to find the white-on-white kitchen teeming with sweet, spicy, Italian aromas. He stirred a red sauce on the back burner, then reached to turn on the front one, holding his hand over a skillet, waiting for heat to rise.

"Chicken parmigiana, right?" she asked.

"Yes, but starting with a crisp Caesar salad," he answered like a guy who knew his way around the kitchen.

"Sounds delightful," she said. Then wondered for a moment what she was doing here, why she felt so awkward, and if he noticed how stiff and stilted she probably seemed.

But then he reached for the small wooden spoon in the saucepan and held his hand under her chin for drips as he motioned for her to taste. Just like the scent, it was spicy yet sweet—and she realized that in all her years of marriage, Clark had never once done something so simply intimate as feed her. The unpretentious act reminded her how much she honestly *liked* Michael and that he liked her, too, and her nerves began to fade.

An hour later, they were finishing their meal on the deck behind the house, at the most darling little wrought-iron table for two she'd ever seen. Actually, the whole yard was darling. Wind chimes tinkled in the breeze and small, painted birdhouses dangled from tree limbs. A circular wooden bench curved all the way around an old oak whose boughs provided shade that stretched all the way over their table.

"More wine?" he asked.

"I shouldn't." She'd already had two glasses, and that seemed enough at lunch.

He looked amused. "Is that a yes or a no?"

She sighed and thought—*Live a little.* "Oh hell, pour the wine."

His rich laughter trickled down through her chest, warm as a drink of alcohol.

A moment after he refilled both their glasses, Michael stood without warning and walked around to pull out her chair. "Come with me—I want to show you something."

She followed him down the wooden stairs to a rock walk winding through the fairy-tale yard that felt a lot more like Snow White's cottage than south Florida. Leaving the stone path, he took her hand and she let him, amazed at the mere feel of it—the touch of a man she didn't really know, and yet it felt safe, right, comfortable. She wondered as they traversed the soft, shaded grass if he felt it as keenly as she did. He wasn't a typical male. He was an artist. He noticed things. About her. She'd seen it through their meals together— seen him studying her hands, her lips, the tiny details that were her.

Approaching one of the low-hanging birdhouses—this one painted deep blue and looking like a tiny Swiss chalet in shape and trim—he looked around as if on a covert mission, then pointed inside the oval opening. It was only then that she saw bits of straw sticking out and realized there was a nest inside.

"If the mama bird sees me looking in here, she goes crazy," Michael said, "but I think she's off hunting for worms right now."

Debra peered in to spy three baby birds, looking rather unkempt, their heads no bigger than the end of her thumb. "Oh my."

"You probably think this is stupid," he said, but when she looked up, he was smiling, as if he weren't embarrassed even if she *did* think that. She liked his easy confidence in who he was.

"Of course not—why would I?"

He gave his head a light shake, peeking back into the birdhouse. "I suppose this is the sort of thing most people discover as kids. But I never did. So when Rhonda left, I started spending more time out here, just trying to . . . notice little things more, appreciate nature or something, I guess, and I found the nest. These guys were still in eggs then, but I made a project of watching for them to hatch, and now watching them get strong enough to fly."

"I never saw baby birds in a nest, either," she said softly. She'd never thought about that before, but . . . "I was sort of a rich kid. We weren't really the outdoorsy types, other than boating and the beach."

"When I look at these guys, it makes me think about . . . life." He let out another rich laugh, adding, "I don't mean to sound like such a dork, by the way."

"You don't." And upon realizing he still held her hand, after all this time, she squeezed it.

He met her gaze and she felt his look reach out inside her, like stretching fingers, touching her breasts, her belly, lower. "What I think about is how each living thing has its own life, its own unique experiences, and how short life is for some creatures and how long for others. But that it's all relative. And that no matter how you slice it, life *is* short. I think I've been worrying about . . . having regrets," he said, finally releasing her hand, then turning to walk the few steps to the bench around the oak.

She followed, sitting next to him, but didn't reply. God knew, she'd been thinking about regrets, too, about wasted time, a wasted life—but she was somehow afraid to share that, afraid it might somehow make whatever might happen between them inevitable. Because she wanted to kiss him so badly she could taste it on her lips. And at the same time, she feared she was misreading him, the only one feeling this way.

"Being alone the last few months has made me think I've . . . been too careful in life, if that makes any sense. Like maybe if I'd been less cautious, I might have ended up in a better place. I've wondered about opportunities missed, times I wanted to go for something but didn't, moments that will never come back to me." He chuckled lowly again. "I sound ridiculously morose, don't I? How the hell did that happen?"

For some reason, Debra couldn't quite meet his eyes, so her gaze stayed focused on a button on his shirt. "I wonder about things like that, too, Michael."

He took her hand again, and it surprised her enough that she raised her eyes to his without quite planning it. "I'm really glad you came today, Debra. I enjoy being with you a lot."

She just nodded. She enjoyed being with him, too. So much that it was almost painful.

So she was glad when he lightened the mood slightly. "I suppose I would be dreaming to think you'd had a chance to start the book yet," he said with a grin. Although he still held her hand.

"Actually, yes, you would be." She laughed gently, reminding him, "Kat's wedding. But you have no idea how many times I've had to struggle to keep myself from picking up the manuscript when I walk past it. It's going to be my treat to myself once the wedding is over and Kat's off on her honeymoon. Bright and early Monday morning, I'm pouring a cup of coffee and settling down in my favorite reading chair."

"Ah, so *that's* when I need to get nervous."

She gave him a chiding glance. "Why on earth would you get nervous? You know I'm going to love it."

"No, I don't. A writer *never* knows."

"Well, *I* know. I love everything you've written. I love everything . . ." She stopped herself—but then, in a split-second decision, gave herself permission to just say it, even if it came out a bit softer than she'd started. "Everything about you."

She released a heavy, *whooshing* what-the-hell-did-I-just-do breath, her eyes dropping to the wooden slats between them. Then let her eyes fall shut, wishing herself away from the situation.

But then warm hands cupped her cheeks, raising her face. She opened her eyes to see the yearning in his gaze just before his mouth covered hers.

Maybe she shouldn't have been shocked, but she was. Utterly stunned. That it was really happening. She'd fantasized about it, even *wanted* it, even come here *hoping* for it—but somehow, deep inside, she'd not really, truly *expected* it.

It was a large, engulfing kiss—nothing small or tentative—and for a split second, she tried to kiss him back. She thought to herself— *This is what you wished for, this is living, this is the opportunity you don't want to pass up.* But then the utter wrongness of it swept down through her like a black flood. She was *married*, for God's sake.

She pressed her palms against his chest to push him away.

But he didn't go, misread her touch perhaps, kept kissing her even though she wasn't returning it. She pushed again, harder, and finally he backed off.

"I can't," she said. "I *can't.*"

He simply looked at her for a long, slow, disappointed moment. "I thought you wanted . . ."

His hands had somehow come to rest on her shoulders, but she pushed to her feet and turned her back to him. "I thought so, too. But I don't."

His arms came warm around her from behind, his voice low in her ear. "I'm sorry. I didn't mean to . . ." He let out a sigh. "I just like you so much, Debra. You're everything I could want in a woman."

The words sifted down through her, dreamlike. *He* was everything *she* could want in a man.

But one thing had just become startlingly clear. She could lecture herself all day on wanting to grab life and experience it, on wanting a man who appreciated and stimulated her—she could promise herself she wasn't going to miss any more opportunities. And this was probably the most exciting, promising opportunity that would ever present itself to her. But if it felt wrong, nothing else mattered.

And Michael's lips on hers had felt like the most wrong thing she'd ever experienced, like being kissed by a dark immorality she never wanted to flirt with again.

"I have to go," she said, breaking free from his loose embrace and starting toward the deck.

"Debra, wait."

He followed, but she walked faster.

"Let me apologize. Let me make it better somehow. I don't want you to leave."

Reaching the French doors that led inside, she stopped just long enough to look over her shoulder. "No, Michael, I really *have* to go." And she hoped he could see in her eyes all she felt, including the wish that everything here was different, that it would somehow be easy to be together—but that, in reality, it would just be a whole new kind of torture.

"You're sure?" he asked.

"Yes." She nodded. Then rushed inside, found her purse on the kitchen counter, and left through the front door as fast as her feet would carry her.

Hurrying to the car, she backed out of his driveway, then sped up the street and out of his neighborhood. Only when she'd reached the main, retail-laden thoroughfare did she find someplace to pull over, a car parts store.

Sliding the car into a parking space that faced the street, she threw it into park and watched the traffic rushing past. All those people, hurrying someplace. How many were happy with their lives, their decisions? How many had secrets? How many wanted more than they had? How many cheated, betrayed?

She sucked in her breath, sad to think the answer would probably be a lot, more than she'd want to believe.

But she wasn't one of them.

She had a husband, she'd taken vows. And he was so hurtful, so neglectful, that sometimes she wanted to kill him. But he was hers, and she knew he loved her. And she loved him, too—a lot. And even if she spent every night from now until forever sitting in their big, luxurious house all by herself, at least she wouldn't feel any shame, have to keep any secrets. At least she'd still like herself.

Reaching to pull her cell phone from her purse, she dialed the gallery. Clark answered on the second ring.

"It's me," she said.

"Hey, I was just thinking about calling you."

"Really?"

"Kat's plane is due around three, right?"

She nodded, even though he couldn't see her, still numb from what had just happened. "Um, yeah. Three-ten."

"I know Nina's supposed to bring her home, but I was thinking about closing early and going to pick her up at the airport. I thought maybe you'd want to come."

"Uh, yeah, I'd like that." Going with her husband to pick up her daughter. Being with her family. Life as it was supposed to be. "I'd like that a lot."

"Everything's packed and ready to go, right?" Brock asked.

Kat lay in his arms in the hammock, trying to enjoy their last afternoon together, but he was making it difficult. "For the fourth time, yes."

"Nothing left in the house you need to take?" They'd hauled down a cooler, her weekend bag, and a sack of trash that needed to be carried back. The only thing to do before leaving was put the radio inside—which now sat perched in the sand nearby, still spewing out seventies hits—and lock up the house.

"Yes, for God's sake."

She was trying not to feel miffed at him, especially given what he'd told her yesterday about his family. She was still attempting to grasp what his childhood must have been like. She'd always assumed it was . . . less than desirable, but she couldn't have imagined the things he'd shared with her.

Nor could she quite believe *she'd* told *him* the rest of the story about Ian and her dad, about the whole money thing. Maybe, just like loving Ian, she'd never quite let herself think through the situation clearly because she'd known she wouldn't like what she saw. It shamed her to think Brock thought she'd *planned* to marry for money—that so wasn't her. Yet somehow she'd made it sound like that was exactly what she'd been doing. She couldn't help wondering if that had anything to do with why he was suddenly acting so gruff.

"When do you think they'll get here?" he asked.

She rolled her eyes, wondering why they were even lying there together. He'd invited her to—or commanded it, actually, with a "Let's go rest in the hammock"—but he didn't exactly seem in a cuddling mood.

"Well, the flight from Vegas is due around threeish. Nina drove to the airport, so they'll expect her to drive me home, probably by four or five. When they don't hear from me, they'll call her. Or . . . actually, Nina might call *them* because she's probably worried by now, since my cell's been dead all week. At any rate, I'm sure Nina will come clean at this point and tell them where I am." She let out a sigh. "I dread this."

For the first time in a while, his voice softened a bit as he gazed down at her. "Dread what, kitten?"

"All I have to deal with. All the explaining I have to do about why I'm here. And breaking Ian's heart. And canceling a colossal wedding." She shook her head at her despair, well aware she'd left out the thing she dreaded most. Leaving Brock. Leaving this time with him behind.

She knew in her heart they'd shared way more than sex—she'd

slowly started to trust him, she'd confided in him things she'd confided in no one else, and she honestly thought he felt just as close to her. And the truth was, she'd sensed that bond growing so much the last day or so that she'd continued being tempted to tell him how she felt and to ask if he'd still be in her life after they left the island.

Yet she hadn't—because she could still feel the way he'd rejected her ten years ago. And she didn't want to be that needy girl again, who wanted him so much more than he wanted her.

And now he'd turned into Mr. Order-barking FBI Man—and she was starting to get irritated. "What's your problem today, anyway?" she asked without warning.

He seemed entirely unfazed. "Problem?"

She let out a sigh, then lifted slightly to peer down at him. "Look, I don't know what's going on with you, why going back into FBI mode is turning you into a bastard—" He raised his eyebrows in surprise, yet she went on. "But I guess I'd like to think we've shared some pretty intimate stuff here, and I would really prefer if it didn't end on a bad note. Like last time."

"Last time?"

"When you left town so abruptly that you couldn't even be bothered to relieve me of my virginity."

Brock let out a low, tired-sounding sigh, then looked her in the eye for a long, lingering moment. "Maybe I didn't want to just fuck and run, ever think of that?"

She released a breath, feeling slightly cowed, but only for a few seconds. "No, I didn't. And that might actually have been somewhat noble—but I don't believe it was the reason."

"All right, it wasn't," he admitted. "But you'd have been pissed if I'd taken your virginity, then disappeared the next day."

"True. Yet I was *already* pissed and you didn't seem to care." She almost wished she hadn't started this, escalated his bad mood into what seemed like an argument now. But on the other hand, she felt them moving closer, finally, to an answer she'd wanted for a very long while.

He stared at her long and hard. "Did it ever occur to you, kitten, that maybe, just maybe, there was other shit going on in my life at the time? That maybe there was a reason for the things I did and the decisions I made?"

She lowered her gaze, suddenly going sheepish. "I was seventeen. I thought your whole world should revolve around me."

He let out a short laugh, and as always when there was tension between them, she was glad to have relieved it. "That would have been nice," he said. "But there was other stuff happening. Stuff I haven't told you."

She couldn't ignore the weight of his words. "So tell me now."

He shook his head, utterly serious again that fast.

"Why not?"

"It was a long time ago, Kat—why dredge it up?"

She swallowed hard, then confided in him one more time. She'd told him all her other secrets—hell, she may as well admit this one, too. "Because you really hurt me, Brock," she admitted quietly. "You broke my little teenage heart, if you want the truth. I was . . . *devastated*, thought I must be the most undesirable girl on the planet. In fact . . ."

His stiff, angry FBI face had transformed into something softer, sadder. "What?"

She sighed. "You really want to know how I lost my virginity?"

He blinked. "Yeah, I do."

She took a deep breath and met his gaze. It was a horrible thing to have to confess, but it would be worse if she couldn't look him in the eye. "After you sped away that night, I grabbed the nearest available jock and took him into the pool house."

His face fell. "Tell me you're lying."

She pursed her lips. "Pathetic but true."

"Not pathetic, honey, but . . ." He looked genuinely upset, ran his hand back through his hair. "Shit. I feel awful. Worse than awful."

"You should. I mean . . ." She couldn't quite believe she was telling him this, but now that she'd put it out there, she needed to keep going. "It was *my* stupid fault I did what I did. But I wanted you so much, Brock. I put myself out there. It was the hardest thing I'd ever done. And when you turned me down—*twice*—I just . . . needed to feel like *somebody* wanted me."

Brock lifted a hand to her face and she let the warmth seep into her, so glad he had stopped acting like a jerk again. Slipping his other arm around her neck, he pulled her down into a sweet, deep kiss that turned her inside out.

"You were *so* desirable, kitten, so desirable that, to this day, I have no idea how I managed to push you off my lap. And the up-shot is, I've been having dirty dreams about me, you, and that car seat ever since."

She sucked in her breath, stunned. "Really?"

He closed his eyes briefly, looking as if he regretted saying it, but then replied. "Yeah. Though, more fantasies than dreams. Just wishing I hadn't shoved you away."

In one sense, his words were the most wonderful she'd ever heard. They wiped away so much doubt in herself, so much fear that she wasn't good enough, pretty enough, sexy enough. But in another, they left her all the more frustrated.

So she asked him straight out exactly what she'd wanted to know for all these years. "Then, for God's sake, why *did* you? Once and for all, Brock, why did you turn me down that night? Why did you leave me again at my birthday party? Why?"

The day before Kat's eighteenth birthday
Ten years ago

"Sit down, Brock."

Brock didn't like being summoned to Clark Spencer's office. Never once had the guy called him in to say, "Hey, thanks for getting that delivery there in time," or "Thanks for working late last night." Nope, anytime Spencer had called him into his fancy little office behind the gallery in the past six months, it had been to bitch or complain about something Brock had or hadn't done.

Never should have taken this job in the first place, he thought, lowering himself into a chair too expensive for his dirty blue jeans. But he hadn't had a choice. The job had been there, listed in the want ads, and he'd needed it—bad.

He listened to the click of the door as Spencer shut it behind him, then walked around a mahogany desk too big for the space. He met the man's gaze and tried to keep his expression neutral. *No need to stir up trouble where there ain't any,* his grandpa always said. But he sat there waiting for it just the same.

Spencer propped his elbows on the desk and interlaced his fingers, but the look on his face told Brock he wasn't getting ready to pray. "What the hell is going on between you and my daughter, Brock?"

Spencer's eyes glimmered in threat, and a cold chill crept up Brock's spine as he wondered what the man knew. He wasn't afraid of Spencer—wasn't afraid of anybody—but he needed to keep this job as bad as he'd needed to take it six months ago. "Nothing," he lied. "Why?"

Spencer lowered his chin in doubt, and Brock knew already that his lie hadn't fixed anything. "I overheard her on the phone with a girlfriend last night."

Eavesdropped is more like it, Brock thought.

"I heard her say you and she have a date planned, for tomorrow night."

Brock sat weighing his answer. This had blindsided him, big-time. Stupid to have thought her old man wouldn't find out. Stupid, stupid, stupid. *Should have just kept your distance, no matter how hot she is.*

"It's the first," he volunteered, thinking that might help. "So . . . nothing has gone on up to now, and that's the truth." *If you don't count her giving me a lap dance in my front yard last week.*

Spencer let out a hard breath and said, "I hope to hell that *is* the truth. But either way, I can't control the past—only the future."

Brock sat waiting for him to go on, the tension building like a brick wall that might come crashing down on both of them at any second, until finally he said, "Get to the point."

Spencer nodded. "All right. You're fired."

Shit. Brock slumped in his chair and let out a long sigh. This was the last thing he needed right now, the absolute last fucking thing.

But then he sat up a little straighter. He didn't like Spencer, but he didn't hate him, either—and the guy knew about his grandfather, so maybe he could be reasoned with. "Look, Mr. Spencer, you know I need this job right now, and you know why."

Again, Spencer gave a light, almost imperceptible nod. "Your grandfather's still struggling with cancer."

Brock hated that word, hated it. He had to deal with it every day, but he didn't like to say it, or hear it. This time it was he who nodded. "I need this paycheck to make ends meet. We got a lot of bills these days. And he . . . well, I'm all he's got."

"I understand that, Brock, and I've got a proposition that I think will make things better for us all."

Something sounded damn fishy, that quick, and set Brock's nerves more on edge than they already were. "A proposition, huh?" He wasn't holding out much hope for anything good.

"Right now I'm having some papers drawn up by my attorney, Walt Zeller, indicating that I'll be responsible for your grandfather's outstanding and future medical bills."

Brock blinked. "What?"

"I'll also be arranging and paying for a home health worker to take over his care, immediately."

Okay, what the hell was going on here? He leaned slightly forward, deciding it was time to cut through the crap. "What is this, Spencer? What's the catch?"

"The catch is that you're leaving," he replied without missing a beat.

Brock pressed his lips tightly together, trying to process the guy's words.

"Tomorrow," Spencer went on. "You'll get some money for that, too, by the way. You're going to leave town and never come back."

Brock slumped back in his chair, his gaze still stuck on Clark

Spencer, his brain trying to wrap itself around the situation. "All this because you don't want me messing around with Kat?"

"Exactly," Spencer said, the mention of his daughter putting a sharp edge in his voice.

Part of Brock was almost amused, in an odd way. "You think I'm *that* bad a guy?"

"You're a lot older than her. And I don't plan on taking any chances with her future—or her present, for that matter."

A bit dumbfounded, Brock actually let out a laugh. "You're fucking crazy, man." He leaned forward again. "I mean, do you have any idea how big my grandfather's bills are? Do you know what it costs to have cancer?"

Spencer responded without emotion. "I have a lot of money, Brock. And I can't think of a better way to spend it than protecting my daughter's interests."

The two men sat staring at each other for a moment—sizing each other up—until finally Spencer said, "Take a minute and think it over. Let me know what you decide."

"You're serious about this?" Brock asked, to clarify.

"Very."

Brock swallowed slowly. Money—he was being offered a shitload of money. His grandfather was dying, no changing that, but money could make it all go a hell of a lot easier—both for Grandpa and for him.

"You said I couldn't ever come back. But what about when he dies? I need to come back for that, man. I need for him to have somebody at his funeral."

"You've got a brother, don't you?"

"He's in prison."

Spencer sighed. "Well, I'm sorry, Brock, but no go. You leave, you're gone for good. That's the deal."

Brock leaned over, resting his elbows on his knees, then ran his hand back through his hair. A funeral was one day, and Grandpa wouldn't even be there, not really. But right now, Brock wasn't able to take care of him well enough—he was alone too much, they were too poor, Brock couldn't cook for shit. The only good times for his grandpa these days were when he was asleep. The night Kat had shown up, Grandpa had been sleeping, quiet, at peace, and Brock had slipped out just to get away from it all for a little while.

"I have a couple of demands," Brock said.

Spencer quirked half a smile, almost as if in respect. "Let's hear them."

"You get him a big, fancy-ass TV delivered out to the house." Watching TV was about all Grandpa could do these days, and Brock knew it distracted him from the pain. "And you get somebody to cook for him, somebody who can cook decent, and you get him some good food—whatever he wants." Grandpa didn't eat much anymore, but every now and then he craved something hearty and homemade.

"Reasonable enough," Spencer replied. "Anything else?"

Brock thought for a moment, his mind racing, wondering if he was forgetting anything important. Finally, he said, "No. No, I guess not."

Spencer looked pleased. "Then we have a deal?"

Goddamn, that's when it hit him, what he'd just agreed to. To leave. To leave his grandpa to die without him.

But when he looked at it, he couldn't stop thinking that the gain outweighed the loss. If there was one thing in the world Grandpa didn't want, it was to leave Brock with a lifetime of debt. *Your life's already been too damn hard as it is, boy. Don't want to add to that.* He thought his grandfather's remaining days might go a lot easier knowing that burden had been lifted. Now he could tell Grandpa he didn't have to worry.

Although as he shook hands with Spencer, then walked out through the back room and into the intense Florida heat, he couldn't help thinking he suddenly knew what it was like to make a deal with the devil.

Chapter Sixteen

"Kitten, when I turned you down out at the swamp, it had *nothing* to do with not finding you attractive, trust me. It was because you were only seventeen years old, not legal yet. And I was tempted as hell, but I was afraid your dad might find out and put me in jail. Plus, I wasn't sure if you knew what you really wanted, know what I mean?" He paused, spoke slower. "And I guess I wondered if you only wanted me because you were rebelling against him—thought maybe I was just the guy from the wrong side of the tracks, a way to break the rules."

Oh God. It had been that simple? All this time? It had just never dawned on Kat. That all made so much sense, yet it had never once crept into her self-absorbed, woe-is-me, spoiled girl's mind. Despite the warmth of the day, a chill shivered down her spine.

He continued, although his voice was uncharacteristically quiet. "As for leaving town on your birthday," he said with a sigh, "shit, kitten . . ."

"What? Why did you leave? Whatever it is, I'm a big girl, I can handle it."

He looked doubtful, worried, and she couldn't imagine why. "Are you sure you want to know this? Because . . . it's big, honey. It'll change the way you look at . . . a lot of things."

She let out an impatient breath next to him in the hammock. "Of course I'm sure. Just tell me."

"It's about your dad," he said, then dropped his eyes before raising them back.

Her dad? "What about him?"

"Kitten, your dad got wind that something was brewing between us. So he called me into his office and . . . he bribed me to leave town."

She gasped, beyond stunned. "What do you mean? Bribed you how?"

"The usual way. Money. Which I needed damn bad. He offered to give my grandfather everything he needed to make his last days comfortable, and to pay his medical bills. We didn't have much insurance, so it was . . ." He looked discouraged, just remembering. "It was overwhelming. Hospitals and collection agencies calling us every day, trying to look for something to take from us, but there was nothing there. It made my grandpa sicker than he already was to heap that kind of burden on me. Even though it was an impossible amount of money for *most* people, he still felt ashamed that he couldn't pay it.

"Your dad also fired me when he made the offer, which meant we were even more screwed—my paycheck was the only thing that brought groceries and medicine into the house, the only thing that kept the electric on. Even a week or two without it while I tried to find something else would have been disastrous, and more stress and worry my grandpa didn't need.

"So I took the deal. And I went home and talked it over with Grandpa. He didn't like the idea of me leaving any more than I did, but he agreed it was the best of our options. That's when he encouraged me to make something of myself. He said he'd seen I was responsible enough to take care of him, seen I could work and hold a job—unlike Bruno, and that I had a good heart in me." Brock seemed a little lost in the memory now, peering up into the palm fronds overhead, clearly seeing something Kat never could, and she lay watching him, still aghast, trying to absorb it.

"So I left, the next night, on your birthday. And it turned out to be . . . my greatest regret, like I told you. Because I let my grandfather die without me. And even though we agreed on it, even though he saw it as a fresh start for me and it turned out to be exactly that, when word reached me that he'd died, I couldn't help thinking how alone he must have felt, even with a nurse at his side, and how scary it must have been without anyone there who loved him."

Kat wiped away the tear she felt rolling down her cheek and wanted desperately to comfort him. "But at least you made good on your promise to him."

She saw him swallow back his emotions. "Yeah. Ironic, though, isn't it? That I would turn out to be in law enforcement," he said, trying for a grin, but it came out sad, "given that my family historically spent a lot more time *breaking* the law than trying to keep it."

She attempted to return the smile, but so many kinds of sadness flowed through her in great, rushing rivers that she barely knew what to think or how to feel. "So you're telling me," she finally said, "that all this happened just because my father wanted to keep you away from me?" It sounded too horrific to be true—and yet, she knew her father. His love for her was sometimes desperate, controlling . . . and maybe even a little conniving.

Brock drew his gaze to hers. "Sorry, kitten. I never planned to tell you. Even after I found you here. I despise your dad—for obvious reasons—but I never wanted to hurt *you*, never wanted to mess up what you have with him."

She wiped away another tear. Desperate, controlling, and conniving were one thing, but . . . it was hard to think of her dad being the kind of man who hurt people in an exaggerated attempt to protect her. "He's always saying he'd do anything for his family," she began gently. "I guess he meant it. I'm so sorry, Brock. So sorry you had to suffer because of me. Because I was being so . . . pushy and aggressive with you." She looped her arms around his neck and lowered a soft kiss to his mouth.

Sorrow still laced his smile, but his dark eyes shone hot on her. "Don't apologize, kitten. You're *beautiful* when you're aggressive, and believe it or not, I wouldn't trade that memory. I told you, it stayed with me." His voice went lower, dropping to a whisper. "When I'm in danger, I think of you, naked and on top of me. It takes me to a much better place, and then I can go on, get back to work, until the next time I need you, and you're always there."

She kissed him again, deeper this time, just needing to feel that connection with him, the warmth that stretched so tautly between them when their bodies came together. She pressed her tongue into his mouth, found the moisture of his, let it consume her. Heat mingled with their sadness, and sharing it made it somehow better.

God, she still couldn't quite fathom what her father had done. He'd changed Brock's life, and hers, too—without her knowledge or permission. Without his interference, Brock would have taken her virginity—she'd have been with a guy she felt impassioned for rather than that jerk Scott. And who knew how that one single difference could have changed her from that moment onward?

Of course, it wasn't as if she'd had a horrible life. But she'd never found another guy she cared for like Brock. And she'd suffered all this time thinking he really hadn't wanted her. And somehow she'd allowed her father to keep on controlling her all this time, too. Sure, she'd had her fun, done her partying—but hell, even that, when all was said and done, had to do with Brock's rejection. At heart, she *wasn't* a party girl—all she'd ever really wanted was the right person to love, and everything else was her way of venting frustration because she couldn't find that.

And even if she *had* managed to be Crazy Kat, even under the watchful eye of her dad, in the end she'd talked herself into marrying the guy who would make *him* happy! She'd been doing it for *him*, to save his butt financially, to keep him feeling like he'd provided for his family—despite that it didn't even make any sense! Damn it!

If her father hadn't stepped in and changed the course of their lives, would she and Brock have had sex one time, or even ten times, and then parted ways—or would it have been more, bigger than that? Maybe *she* could have made him into the man he was today. Maybe *she* could have supported him through the loss of his grandfather and helped him change his life. Maybe he would have fallen in love with her, just as she'd been in love with him.

Brock's hands cupped her face now as they kissed, and their legs intertwined, his knee pressing over the swatch of bikini between her thighs. Her body needed him, as much as her soul did. And just as it had been since the moment he'd arrived here—the aching need inside her spanned ten long years.

Between kisses, she bit her lip, pressed her forehead to his, and confided her heart. "This is sort of embarrassing, but I was . . . really crazy about you then, Brock."

"I know," he said sweetly, as if trying to make it easy on her.

But he *didn't* know. He didn't know the depth of it. "No, *really* crazy." *I loved you.* "I didn't know you that well, so maybe I had this idea in my head of who I thought you were or who I wanted you to be. But I was really . . . well, just *wild* about you."

She thought he looked touched by her words, but he merely offered a small smile and said, "Well, good that you got over me."

Her heart beat too hard in her chest—with honesty. "What makes you so sure I did?"

He pressed his lips gently together, looking thoughtful. "Well, I don't get the idea you've been holed up at home all these years pining for me. Come on, kitten—I know all about your wild side, remember?" He concluded with a soft grin, clearly trying to lighten the moment.

Yet Kat only sighed. She wanted him to know, to make him understand. "But maybe *you* were the only guy I ever really felt wild for, and everything that came after, anything else wild I've done . . . maybe my heart hasn't really been in it."

His eyebrows knit slightly and his embrace tightened around her waist. The smile vanished. "Then . . . why did you do it?"

Another sigh. "I don't know." *Yes, you do. You just admitted it to yourself.* All she had to do was look at him to know. "Because of you. Because I thought you didn't want me. And . . . if the only guy you ever really wanted turns you down, why not cut loose? Why not rebel? Why not try to hide the pain by being a wild child?"

She'd spent the last ten years trying to live, find excitement, find something . . . unattainable—and now she knew what it was she'd been looking for all this time. Maybe she'd always known it. All she'd ever really wanted was one guy—the right guy—to be her wild self with. Which maybe wasn't really so wild. But that was what she'd wanted—and she'd found it with Brock the last few days.

"Ah, kitten," he breathed, their faces close, "I never meant to hurt you."

"I don't blame you anymore. I did, all this time, but not anymore." *I love you.*

Once again, she kept herself from saying it, thank God, and kissed him instead. Thinking how she loved the responsible man Brock had become just as much as she'd ever loved the wayward boy he'd once been.

"I want to make you feel good, baby," Brock whispered, letting his hand glide down over her ass, pressing their bodies more snugly together. The first enchanting notes of Styx's "Lady" sprinkled the air around them as Kat lowered her lips back to his, letting her body move against him, creating a perfect friction that drew soft moans from them both. His hands slid inside her bikini bottoms, molding over her rear just as her fingers curled into the waistband of his trunks.

They exchanged still more gentle but smoldering kisses as she pushed his shorts down to reveal the magnificent erection she'd become so well acquainted with these past days. But the wonder she experienced upon seeing it, closing her hand around it, still felt new. "I love this," she purred, letting her gaze linger on the hard shaft before she lifted her eyes to his. As close to *I love you* as she could possibly come.

His small smile was sexy, penetrating. "It loves you, too."

Oh. God. Pretty damn close to *I love you*, as well, and she knew that wasn't what he'd said, but the very word *love*, passing between them, in any capacity, felt relevant and powerful in her heart.

He lowered her bikini bottoms and she kicked them off, over the edge of the hammock to the sand below. As she moved up over him, lifting her knee over his hip, he pushed the triangles of her top aside to mold her bare breasts in his hands. "*I love these*," he said before lifting a gentle kiss to first one pebbled pink tip, then the other. The sensation whirred through her like bottle rockets on the Fourth of July.

She arched toward him instinctively, lowering one breast to his welcoming mouth as she rubbed her moisture against him below. He licked her beaded nipple, then drew it in, suckling, suckling, so deep, good. The pull reached clear to the center of her desire as the romantic song filled her senses still more. *I love you, I love you, I love you.* She longed to say it, to tell him. She almost didn't even care how he responded—just needed for him to know.

Yet she held it in, because rejection still lingered a heartbeat away. And even though she knew now that he hadn't wanted to reject her all those years ago, the harsh hurt still remained near, and she couldn't risk ruining this moment.

She continued to move over him, let the juncture of her thighs hover and play, rubbing gently, until he released her breast and said, "Kitten, I need inside you." He pressed her hips firmly downward and they both groaned at the impact, then kissed, moved, touched—slowly, slowly.

She rode him in hot, grinding circles, letting her arousal heat her flesh from the inside out. He watched her face, her breasts as they swayed with her movements—then let his gaze drop to where their bodies connected. She moved harder, pressing her palms to his well-muscled chest. She bent toward him, lowering one breast back to his warm mouth, where he captured it, tight. She twined her fingers through the thick white netting at both sides of his head as his hands splayed over her ass, kneading with her slow, rhythmic grind, adding to her deep, expanding pleasure as he seemed to pull, parting her, opening her to him even more. "Ah, God," she sobbed as fresh ribbons of sensation spiraled through her, taking her closer, closer. She bit her lip, heard her own labored breath, shut her eyes, and tumbled over the edge.

"Yes," she managed on a hot sigh, then simply let the pleasure consume her, own her, until the hot, sweet pulses finally drifted away.

She opened her eyes in time to see him peering up at her as if she were the most beautiful creature he'd ever seen. Then he swiftly, gently, rolled her onto her back in the big hammock until he was on top and sliding back inside her, deep. "Yes," she said once more, then whispered, "I don't like it when you're not there."

He rained hot kisses over her neck and said, "I'm back now, kitten."

He was. Back in her life. Where she'd never thought she'd have him again. A miracle.

She locked her legs around his firm ass and he laced his fingers with hers, pinning both hands over her head. He moved in slow, deep, powerful strokes that made her cry out at each and every one. She'd never before thought she could *like* being controlled, but right now, she couldn't have imagined anything more perfect than being beneath him, completely within his domination.

His eyes fell shut as his groans grew hotter, more guttural, and she used her legs to press him deeper, deeper. "Oh God, baby, I'm coming. I'm coming in you."

She met those final strokes, lifting her hips, wanting to take him inside her as much as humanly possible. *I love you, Brock. I love you so much I can barely breathe beneath the weight of it.*

Afterward, he lowered a soft kiss to her forehead, another to her lips.

Hot, intense—but it was also the sweetest sex they'd shared. Because she'd opened her heart to him in so many ways. And she'd felt his response in his lovemaking. He would surely never use that word, but she'd felt it—he'd made love to her in that hammock as surely as the sun would rise tomorrow morning.

Of course, when the sun next rose, it wouldn't come up from

behind the palm trees that shrouded the bungalow—they'd be somewhere else, and life would be a hell of a lot more complicated than it felt in this perfect, serene moment. She hated remembering that—and she knew that when her parents arrived, she wouldn't be able to speak freely, so she had to speak now. "What happens tomorrow?"

They lay side by side in the netting, faces close. She drank in the musky scent of him, loved his nearness. "Tomorrow?" he asked.

"Will you . . . head back to Miami right away, or . . ." She sighed. "Will we see each other, Brock?"

He didn't answer, and she suddenly hated herself for asking. Hated her need for this man. She'd just thought . . . It had felt so . . .

She let out the breath she'd been holding. "I don't want this to end. And I know *this*—the island—*has* to end, but I don't know why *you and I* have to end. Because I thought we were . . . having fun together." More than fun. Deep, abiding passion. "We're good together, Brock. I know you feel it, too."

He remained quiet as Cat Stevens began singing "Wild World" on the radio, and her heart started to crack in her chest.

"Of course I feel it, too," he finally said—only his tone had turned brisk again. "But I have a dangerous job, kitten, that takes up my whole life. I'm not around most of the time. And even if I were . . ."

She swallowed, her stomach sinking. "What?"

"Haven't we already talked about this? I don't . . . *do* relationships. I wouldn't have the first idea how. I'm just not that guy."

Sitting up next to him, Kat pulled the triangles of her top back into place, then rolled out of the hammock to grab her bikini bottoms. She accidentally dumped him on the ground in the process—she heard him *plunk* in the sand with an *Umph*—but didn't even look, didn't care. She just wanted to get some clothes back on, get herself covered.

"Kitten, what are you doing? What's wrong?"

She still didn't glance back, couldn't face him, couldn't stand to peer into those sexy eyes right now. Her heart beat too fast, and she felt naked—in a *vulnerable* way. She had no idea what she'd been thinking, trying to believe Brock Denton could want her for anything other than sex, but somehow, somewhere along the way, she'd let herself be deluded—and now hurt consumed her. A hurt much worse than what she'd suffered at seventeen, because as real and as painful as that had been, she'd shared so much with him now—her body, her heart . . . her freaking soul, for God's sake. And he didn't want *any* of those things.

"Kitten, don't be mad. It's not that I don't care for you—it's that my life just isn't . . . that kinda life."

After hurrying back into her suit, she grabbed up the sarong she'd tossed aside earlier, too, securing it around her hips. She sensed him getting to his feet behind her, and when she yanked the radio up from the sand and started toward the house, he followed.

"What the hell is so wrong?" he snapped behind her.

She finally turned to face him, still feeling just as alone as when she'd been ignoring him. His dark eyes were painfully beautiful. "Maybe my dad is right! Maybe I should just marry Ian! At least *he* wants me. You never have, and you still don't."

He slowly began shaking his head, and the shock and disdain in his gaze gave her strength. "You're kidding me, right?"

But she wasn't. Because Brock had just reminded her of one of the big reasons she had agreed to marry Ian. Money aside, lack of passion aside, Ian was *crazy* about her. And that felt so incredibly nice, secure, compared to *this*. "No, I'm not. In fact, I think I've just come to my senses."

He stood gaping at her in pure disbelief as the song on the radio warned her there was a lot of bad in the world and that she should beware. At the moment, she just couldn't be sure if she was looking at the bad or running back to it—everything was so confusing.

Snapping it off with a click, she marched into the house, deposited the radio on the nearest table, grabbed up the keys as she slipped on her pink flip-flops, then locked the door. Without ever making eye contact with Brock, who still stood looking bewildered, she started through the woods on the path to the boat dock.

"Kitten, wait, damn it," he said, hurrying to catch up on the sandy trail.

She kept walking.

"You can't do this. You can't marry that guy. You know that, right?"

She spoke over her shoulder. "Maybe I just know where I belong. And it's obviously not with you."

"You don't love him, remember? You told me that."

But she couldn't *hear* that right now, couldn't let herself. She stopped and turned to face him in the shade of the jungly overgrowth. "It's none of your fucking business, Brock!" Then she stormed on.

As she emerged from the tree cover onto the grassy ridge above the dock, bits and pieces of her boat still scattered across the ground, she peered out over the water, praying to see her family coming for her. Only the horizon met her gaze, but they'd be here soon—they had to be.

She plopped down on the grass and wrapped her arms around her knees. Brock sat down a foot or so away.

When he spoke, he suddenly sounded very calm. "Can you tell me why you're doing this?"

"Doing what?"

"Acting like you hate me and telling me you're gonna marry a guy you don't love."

She kept her eyes on the water, the late-day sun creating a sparkling line across the rippling waves. "I don't wish to discuss it."

"I thought you didn't want things to end on a bad note."

"I didn't. But that seems impossible now, doesn't it?"

"Not if you'd act sane and tell me what the hell is going on."

How dense *was* he? Then again, he was a guy, and when it came to matters of emotion, Kat had found the male species could sometimes be extraordinarily thick. Even so, if he didn't know what was wrong, no way was she humiliating herself any further by telling him. *I wanted more with you. So much more. I wanted forever.*

"I don't want to talk anymore," she finally said, her voice too soft.

"Kitten, this, us—it was amazing, okay? I loved it. I'm sorry I'm not into the relationship thing, but I don't see why that has to ruin this."

"You wouldn't," she muttered.

"What?"

"Nothing. I told you, I'm tired of talking. I just want to sit here and be quiet and wait for my mom and dad. Okay?"

Next to her, he let out a sigh, sounding disgusted. "Fine. That's how you want to play it, go ahead. I don't give a shit."

Obviously.

"But listen to me, Kat. When they get here, you still have to let me do the talking and go along with whatever I say, understand?"

She jerked her head around to meet his gaze. Was he serious? "Why *should* I?"

Brock narrowed his gaze on her sharply. Damn it, he couldn't believe this—none of it. How the hell had things turned to crap so quickly? One minute she's naked and riding him to orgasm and the next she's stomping away and talking crazy, and now apparently threatening to—frankly—defy the order of a federal agent.

He'd been iffy on what he was going to tell Clark Spencer before he'd stumbled across the Mayan artifacts—but now that he'd found them, no room for honesty remained. No way could Spencer find out he was FBI. And it wasn't gonna be easy pulling that off, but Kat *had* to go along with him; there was no other way.

"We've discussed this before," he said pointedly. "The more any of you know, the more danger you're in. Do you *want* to endanger your mother and father?"

Looking insolent, she shook her head.

"Then you can't let your parents know I'm a federal agent— it'll only create questions I can't answer, and if I know your dad, he'll go digging for them. I can't have that, and neither can you. So you let me handle this—got it?"

Just then, the sound of a boat engine cut through the stillness, and they both shifted their eyes to the water. In the distance— around the spot where Francisco's yacht had sunk—a pristine white cabin cruiser plowed through the ocean toward the island. Kat's back went rigid, and her eyes filled with mixed emotions— enough to tell him it was the boat they'd been awaiting.

Still looking pissed, she turned to him and said, "I have one demand."

"Name it."

"Whatever you tell them, you can't let on that anything happened between you and me."

"I hadn't planned on it—that's your information to share if you want."

"Well, I don't."

He gave a short, disgusted nod, assuming this meant she was still persisting in this idiotic plan to marry Ian.

As the boat grew nearer, leaving a wide wake in the otherwise calm water, Brock said, "I really am sorry you're mad at me, kitten, because being here with you really *was* . . . a special time."

She met his gaze, her eyes glassy, but she never replied. Just looked back out at the approaching boat, pushed to her feet, and started toward the dock in those sparkly pink flip-flops.

Chapter Seventeen

*H*ell. He wasn't quite sure how, but somehow he'd ruined this.

And as the cabin cruiser eased up to the dock, Brock's day managed to get even worse. Because the cleaner-than-clean-cut guy who stood on the deck, too damn good-looking for Brock's liking, had to be Ian. Brock hated him on sight. And it was more than just jealousy, or worry for Kat's future—there was just something about him. Nobody was that perfect.

Clark Spencer was parked at the captain's wheel, his hair grayer and his face more wrinkled than when Brock had last seen him, but he still carried himself like the confident, wealthy man he was—even if he defined wealth in far different numbers than Brock did. His wife—Debra, Brock remembered—looked equally well-groomed and sophisticated in a gauzy blouse and tailored blazer. Another woman stood at her side, and Brock didn't recognize her right off, but he'd bet it was Nina.

Great, the entire freaking cavalry had come to save Kat from his clutches. Or that's how it suddenly felt anyway. He was pissed as hell at Kat, but he didn't know what he could do about it, so for the moment, he could only hope they'd make it through the next few minutes without things getting any shittier.

No one seemed to notice him at first, which suited him fine. He hung back on the shore and let Kat run to greet them all. "Oh my God, thank goodness you're safe!" her mother said as she moved toward her.

"Kat, what the hell?" Nina asked. "I've been trying to call you *forever.*"

"Forgot my charger," she said, and everyone groaned loudly enough that Brock knew it was a typical problem.

Mr. Perfect was busy tying off the boat after it slid gently into the dock's second slip, just as any good, responsible son-in-law-to-be would. Fortunately for Spencer, it wasn't the one where the hull of Kat's Stingray rested just under the water.

Kat's mom and friend raced out onto the dock to hug her, her mother saying, "I was worried sick. It was bad enough when we didn't hear from you, but ever since we met Nina at the airport and she told us you came out here by yourself . . ." She stopped and sighed, then hugged Kat again.

Which was when Ian moved in for *his* hug. Brock's chest tightened, his blood boiling. The only bit of satisfaction came from knowing he'd been where Ian never had. Well, at least not yet. Shit—not so satisfying to know the jerk probably *would* be there in a couple of days and have a lifetime of her.

"What the hell were you thinking coming here by yourself without telling me?" Ian snapped at her. "Are you out of your mind?"

Brock's back went rigid as his hands curled into slow fists. Now he *really* didn't like the guy. Brock knew he was brusque sometimes—it was his nature—but Ian sounded like a father reprimanding a child and, given what he knew about Kat and her dad, that seriously rubbed him the wrong way.

"I just wanted some private time, that's all. No need to make a huge deal of it." _That's right, kitten—don't let that jackass talk to you like that._

"I'd say there is," Ian replied in an all-knowing manner. "_Anything_ could have happened to you out here. Nothing happened, did it? I mean, no one bothered you here or anything?"

She cast a glance toward Brock, but Jackass still didn't notice him. Nina, on the other hand, did. "Um . . . who's the dude?"

All eyes turned his way as Ian groused, "Who's this?"

Clark Spencer, who was just now stepping out on the dock, squinted long and hard in his direction. "Brock Denton? Is that you?"

"Yeah, it's Brock," Kat said softly.

Nina gasped and said, "Wow."

"Who's Brock?" Ian asked.

Spencer's eyes widened in pure horror. "What the hell are you doing on my island with my daughter?"

"And . . . where's your boat, Kat?" asked her mother.

Shit. Well, here went nothing. "Good to see you, too, Spencer," Brock said, starting slowly toward the crowd. "Damnedest thing— I had a little boat trouble a couple of days ago. Was out when that big rain hit and it stirred up some monster waves and sank my Chris-Craft. I happened to see this chunk of land and was trying to make my way toward it, but didn't get here before the boat went down—had to swim for it. Imagine my surprise at finding Kat here, after all these years."

It wasn't a great lie, but it would have to do. And this next one was a doozie, too—but it was all he had. "Once the rain stopped and the water calmed down, Kat was going to drive me back to shore, but . . . her boat caught on fire as soon as we started the engine."

"*Fire?*" Spencer boomed. "How the hell did it catch *fire?*"

Unfazed, Brock held out his hands. "No idea. But we got the hell off it and it's a good thing—because the damn thing blew up."

Brock's explanation seemed to draw their attention to the pieces of debris scattered on the ground.

"Dear God," Spencer said as Kat's mother lifted her hand to her chest.

"Who *are* you?" Ian asked pointedly, looking disgusted that no one had answered him yet.

"He used to work for my dad, a long time ago," Kat replied, meeting Brock's eyes.

"I'm damn surprised to see you, Brock," Spencer said, clearly trying to intimidate him with a cold stare. *Yeah, right. Those days are over, old man.* "I didn't think you lived around here anymore."

Brock met the man's glower with one of his own. "I'm over in Miami. But I go wherever I damn well please." Which didn't make sense to half the people there, but Brock couldn't have cared less. He'd kept his deal with Spencer for far too long and it was done now.

Spencer appeared surprised by his tone, and everyone else went quiet, obviously sensing the tension between the two men, until Kat finally said, "Um, Dad and Brock never got along very well," to Ian.

Who replied with, "Well, I'm just glad we're here and can take you home now."

Like Brock was some big threat to her. *If you only knew, asshole.*

"I've missed you, sweetheart," the guy said then, pulling her into a close embrace.

"I've . . . missed you, too."

Brock's stomach churned at her lie. *Don't do this, kitten. Don't throw your life away on this doofus.*

As she wrapped her arms around Ian's neck, her eyes met Brock's—just for a moment before she looked away.

Why was she doing this? Why had she made this ridiculous switch? Well, okay, he *knew* why, but . . . damn it, why couldn't she understand? Hell, if he were *gonna* be with a woman . . . well, she'd be the woman. But that just wasn't in his blood. Why couldn't she accept that and be glad for what they'd shared, like he was?

When he couldn't stand watching Kat with Mr. Perfect for one more second, he shifted his gaze to Clark Spencer, looking for any worry, or fear. After all, Kat had been on the island for five days and if the artifact pickup had gone as planned, she'd have been in harm's way when the Morales brothers arrived.

But Spencer's expression didn't give much away other than general dismay at the whole situation. Given worry over where Kat had been and the fact that her boat had blown up, and of course that she'd been forced to share her private getaway with *him*—the scourge of humanity as far as Spencer was concerned—the grimace on his face wasn't particularly telling in terms of whether he was involved in the smuggling operation.

Yet no matter how Brock looked at it, Spencer had to be in this up to his neck. It was his island, his house with the locked closet. And he had a history with Mayan artifacts. It all fit.

"Well, let's get your stuff on the boat and go home, little girl," Spencer said, and Brock cringed at the endearment. Damn it, wouldn't the guy ever realize she wasn't a little girl anymore?

As Ian hauled the cooler on board and Spencer grabbed Kat's bag, Brock hefted the plastic trash sack over the side onto the deck, thinking there was something absurdly apropos in that, since that's exactly what Clark Spencer thought he was—trash.

As Spencer maneuvered the boat back out of the slip, then aimed for the south Florida coast, everyone continued spewing questions and reprimands at Kat—leaving Brock thankful. Not that he liked seeing her harangued, but it kept him out of the spotlight in a group where he definitely qualified as the odd man out.

Her mother still questioned her on why she'd lied about going to Vegas, and Nina was apologizing to Debra Spencer for keeping it from her, and Ian remained angry and harped on all the terrible things that could have happened to her on the island by herself. Brock stood at the opposite end of the boat, peering toward the mass of land that grew smaller with each second, where his fantasies had come true.

Glancing down at the cabin cruiser's large motor trolling through the seawater, Brock caught a glimpse of the boat's name— KAT'S MEOW. Apt . . . but still odd, he thought. Kat seemed to be *everything* to these people—yet they beat her down so much and probably didn't even realize it. Hell, no wonder she'd decided to marry Ian—she'd likely been browbeaten so long that she couldn't make sense of things anymore.

It was when talk turned to the wedding that Brock couldn't stand to listen any longer, so he quietly meandered belowdecks, where he stretched out on a built-in upholstered bench to wait out the ride. He'd been in a lot of crazy situations, so this should be nothing, yet something about it felt surreal, and he saw no reason to endure it when he could escape down here and get his thoughts together.

As soon as they reached shore, he'd find a phone, call headquarters. Job one: getting some agents and possibly some local lawmen back out to the island to retrieve the artifacts before Spencer or anyone else could. Brock wasn't sure why no one had come for them before now, given that the Morales boys had failed to deliver five long days ago, but time remained of the essence. Next, he'd have to launch an investigation into Clark Spencer. One part of him delighted in that idea—*How smug will you be when I bring you down, Spencer?* But when he thought of Kat, the idea of putting her father behind bars wasn't nearly so appealing.

Just then, a shadow blocked the sunlight streaming through the narrow doorway. At first, he thought the female figure descending to join him was Kat, but it turned out to be Nina. "Hey," she said. "I don't know if you remember me, but I'm—"

"Kat's friend, Nina," he finished for her.

She smiled that he knew, then took a seat across from him on the opposite bench. "Listen, I know this is none of my business, but . . . you showing up on the island, was that . . . really just a coincidence?"

He'd actually thought so at first. But finding the artifacts had changed that. "Yep. Amazing but true."

Nina didn't possess the same natural beauty as Kat, but her angular features and long blond hair, combined with a saucy attitude he'd seen immediately, made her attractive. She leaned back and studied him with a suspicious twinkle in her eye. "I know this is totally out of line, but . . . I also know you and Kat sort of had a thing way back when, so . . . tell me, Brock Denton, did anything happen between you two out on that island?"

She posed the question with suggestive amusement, but he felt the need to remind her of the obvious. Glancing upward, where the rest of the party remained, he said, "In case you hadn't noticed, she's engaged."

She didn't miss a beat. "Yes, but she was way into you in high school, and even though that was a long time ago and things have changed . . . I still can't quite believe Kat could be alone with you for that long without something happening." She dropped her gaze to his left hand. "I mean, unless things have *really* changed. Unless you're married or something."

He gave his head a short shake. "No, not married. Or something."

She raised her eyebrows, prodding him. "So? Tell me."

"You'll have to ask *her*," he said, but he supposed it was enough of an admission, since Nina's expression softened, looking pleased. "Now *you* tell *me* something. Why are you hoping your best friend cheated on her fiancé?"

She tilted her head, pushed a lock of long blond hair behind her ear, and looked like she was about to share a secret. "I hate him," she said, then glanced upward.

Brock blinked. "Really?" This was getting more interesting.

Nina sighed and cast a dry expression. "Well, maybe hate is too strong a word, but he's a *drag*, and he's *so* not right for Kat. I hate that she's marrying him."

"I'm not too wild about the idea myself," he admitted, having unexpectedly found an ally. He suddenly recalled Kat claiming Nina was surprisingly sensible on her good days, and now he believed it. "She told me she doesn't love him."

Nina gasped. "I knew it!"

He was probably taking this too far, sticking his nose in way too deep—especially since he kept mentally harping on how everyone tried to run Kat's life—but he felt he had no other choice. "If there's anything you can do to stop the wedding," he said, lowering his voice slightly, "you should."

Yet she shook her head. "I've been trying to derail it for months."

"Ask her about the island," he said. "Ask her what happened out there."

Just then another shadow blocked the doorway, and Debra Spencer's voice filtered downward. "We're coming in to the marina. Brock, do you need a ride someplace?"

He'd rather walk all the way to Miami on hot coals. "No— thanks, I'm good. I'll call a friend." A friend named the Federal Bureau of Investigation.

In a few hours, the Spencers' private island—his and Kat's se-cluded hideaway—would be crawling with cops. And Kat would be anticipating her wedding. Their lives would be separate once more, going right on as usual, almost like they'd never even crossed paths.

More or less, that's what he'd wanted.

So why did it leave an empty feeling in the pit of his stomach?

Late that night, Kat sat alone in her apartment, surrounded by boxes packed to move, hugging her kitty on the sofa, and watching David Letterman. There were a million things she could be doing—among them sleeping. She was exhausted, and tired eyes wouldn't make for a pretty bride.

Yet she couldn't quite seem to close her eyes on the day.

Because when she woke up tomorrow, the island and Brock would seem so much farther away. The next day the distance would be even greater. And before long, it would be almost as if it had never even happened.

Of course, maybe that was a good thing. Any *sane* person would certainly be trying to push the whole episode from her mind. But lately Kat was beginning to wonder if she fell under that heading.

Too much. There was just too much going on.

She had the urge to go to The Kiln, right now, and throw a pot. The feel of the smooth, wet clay beneath her hands, the mesmeriz-ing spin of the wheel—nothing relaxed her like her art, and right now it would be extremely welcome to concentrate on nothing more complicated than shaping a lump of clay into something new and beautiful.

Only it was far too late. She had keys to the place, but she didn't think Renee, the owner, would appreciate her coming in that late—someone would probably call the cops or something. And it wasn't really a practical idea anyway. Tomorrow at 10:00 A.M. she was getting a manicure. And pretty much every moment of her time from then on would be devoted to some wedding preparation or another, and then . . . she would be married.

Odd. Her wedding was in less than two days, and after that she'd be jetting off to a fabulous Tahitian honeymoon—and the thing she was looking most forward to at this moment was the solace of making some new pots in a few weeks when she got home.

She hugged Vincent to her, smiling to herself as she remembered Brock's joke about watching the cat around knives. "But you're not a psycho, are you?" she cooed to the kitty in baby talk. "No, of course you're not. Your *mommy's* the psycho."

Because there were beaucoup things she should be thinking about, and instead her mind lingered on Brock. The incredible sex. The intense intimacy.

Her mind flashed to the horrid moment today when they'd all exited the boat at the marina, and Brock had said, "Bye, Kat."

Simple as that. Like nothing had happened.

He didn't have a choice, she knew—everyone had been standing there, and she was the one who'd changed gears this afternoon—but it had seemed like the most anticlimactic instance of her existence. "Bye, Brock," she'd said, wondering if anyone realized that she'd had trouble getting the words out, could barely breathe in the face of knowing it was the last time she'd see him. Probably ever.

"Take care," he'd said, and she'd been trying to summon a *You, too*, but before she could get it out, he'd turned and walked away. Surrounded by her parents, her best friend, and her husband-to-be, she'd never felt so alone.

For some reason, the memory of that emotion made her feel guilty about Vincent. "I'm sorry, buddy, but I have to leave again in a couple of days. Mom will look after you, though, and you know she's a good kitty-sitter, even if you like to act all aloof and bored with her. And when I come home, guess what—we're moving! To a big, brand-new place where you'll have lots of new stuff to explore." And it made a hell of a lot more sense to focus on things like her cat, her upcoming move, and her wedding than on a guy who'd flitted out of her life as quickly as he'd flitted in.

As for why she'd done an about-face and decided to marry Ian again . . . well, there were a *lot* of reasons. Ian loved her. He was smart and a good provider. Her family adored him, and she was equally fond of his. Their similar backgrounds made them highly compatible. Wildly successful marriages had been built on less.

And as for the love part, it was true—she wasn't "in love" with him. But she really believed that could grow. In India, they still had arranged marriages, and she knew just such a couple, who owned a cafe a few blocks from the gallery, and the wife had once told her they couldn't be happier. Kat believed it was all about attitude—and despite her little detour on the island, she was committed to having a long, happy marriage with Ian.

The wedding was going to be beautiful, the day she'd always dreamed of, with all her friends and family around her. Then she and Ian would jet off to the South Pacific, where she would luxuriate on the beach, soak up the rays and the serenity, and let people bring her umbrella drinks and spray cool mists over her whenever she felt the urge. She'd *planned* to relax and luxuriate on her family's island, but turned out she needed a vacation from her vacation.

Which brought a certain hot, sexy FBI agent back to mind—of course.

You have to stop thinking about him. You have to banish him from your mind—now. He was . . . a nonentity in her life. A blip on the radar screen. Soon, the whole island affair wouldn't even matter.

As for keeping it from Ian, she wasn't proud of herself for that. And having wild, mind-numbing, screaming sex with her old crush for the last three days didn't seem like a great way to start a marriage. But she was chalking it up to temporary insanity. And telling Ian would serve no purpose. She was committed to him—that was what mattered. She was going to make this work.

On Saturday afternoon, Kat stood before a mirror in a private room in the same quaint-yet-regal Port Royal church where her parents had married nearly thirty years ago. Pearls and sequins sprinkled her pristine white gown, her dainty bouquet lay clutched in one fist, and her veil flowed down behind her, making her feel the full measure of being "a bride." Her hair hung in pretty ringlets, and a glance at her hands revealed a perfect manicure that could almost leave one not knowing she was a potter. Everything was perfect.

Except for the butterflies in her stomach.

But that's natural—all brides get them. Don't they?

She took a deep, cleansing breath and told herself to be happy. Because practically speaking, this was as good as life got. Not everyone could have grand passion. Maybe she should just be thankful she'd gotten to experience it for a few brief days, since lots of people probably never did. But life went on, and a girl had to be practical and sensible. This was the right thing to do. This would make everyone happy.

Across the room, the door opened and Nina appeared behind her in the mirror, looking lovely in her pale yellow dress, a flowered wreath nestled in her curling blond locks. "You look beautiful," Nina said, but Kat could see that her best friend's eyes brimmed with sadness.

"You, too," she said, trying to smile. "I knew the yellow would be perfect for you."

Nina stepped up beside her. "I've been trying to pin you down for two days."

"Huh?"

As Kat turned toward her, Nina took her hand and led her to a small sofa nearby. "I couldn't get you alone during the manicures yesterday, or at the bridal luncheon, or at the rehearsal dinner. And you haven't been answering your phone—cell or home."

True enough, she hadn't. For this very reason. She loved Nina, but she'd been far too persistent in her protests. "I'm trying to rest and recover from the whole island ordeal. And I didn't need anyone harassing me—still don't. So if you're going to make one last plea to cancel the wedding, forget it."

Nina spoke calmly and quietly. "What happened on the island between you and Brock?"

Kat had been staring at her hands, her bouquet, but jerked her eyes up to Nina's. "Nothing. Why?"

Nina pursed her lips. "Kat. Come on. I know better."

Kat grimaced slightly. "What do you think you know?"

"That he's hotter than hell, that you never got over him, and that you were alone with him in a very secluded setting. It's pretty easy to do that particular math."

Today of all days, Kat had been trying to *forget* what had happened with Brock. Which made lying about it seem natural. Only she'd never blatantly lied to Nina about anything before, and given that she felt close friendships were just about as sacred as marriage, she had no choice. Although she kept her voice low when she replied. "Fine, yes, we did it—is that what you want to hear?"

Nina blinked. "And you're still going through with this?"

"Look, I'm not proud of what I did, but it was just a temporary lapse—something I . . . needed to get out of my system. And it's out now, so I can move on with my life."

"You're glowing," Nina said.

"What?"

"You're thinking about what you did with him and you're glow-ing. You're radiant right now."

"Maybe it's because I'm about to get married, ever think of that? I'm a bride. We glow. It's a rule."

"No, it's Brock. You're just as crazy for him as you ever were." She said it matter-of-factly, as if there were no question.

Which pissed Kat off. She was getting married in a few minutes, for God's sake, to an entirely different guy than the one they were discussing. "Is there some reason you're trying to ruin my wedding?"

Again, Nina's voice stayed uncharacteristically calm and sure. "Yes. Because I love you. And this is wrong."

A lump grew in Kat's throat. "I can't believe you're doing this to me." She dropped her gaze back to the bouquet in her lap.

"I'm sorry, Kat, I really am. I just couldn't in good conscience let it happen without trying one more time to make you see reason."

Kat let out a sigh. She'd never felt more dejected—or confused. All she knew at the moment was that beyond the door sat a churchful of people waiting to see her take vows, a man who loved her, and a well-planned life waiting to begin—and nothing Nina said was going to change it. It hurt like hell to have her best friend tell her she was wrong, even now, when it was too late to do anything about it anyway.

She lifted her gaze to Nina's. "Are you going to stand beside me today, be my friend, and support me in this?"

Nina let out a breath, looking sad, and also maybe as if she felt a little guilty, which Kat thought warranted. "If you're sure this is what you really want, Kat."

"I do," she whispered.

And the next time she said those words, it would seal her fate.

Brock's Porsche 911 Turbo Cabriolet purred from Second Street onto Galleon in Port Royal, where large, stately homes lined the coves and inlets, and every crisp blade of grass stood polished and in place. He eased down the quietly elegant street until the car prowled slowly past the Trinity-by-the-Cove Church, where millionaires came to pray. "I'm Not in Love," an old song by 10cc, played low on the radio—on that same seventies channel they'd listened to on the island.

Judging from the parking situation, the place was packed, and he wasn't surprised. Kat's wedding was probably *the* social event of the season in Naples.

He wasn't sure why he was here. If he had any sense, he'd be at home, with the blinds pulled, getting some sleep. On Thursday night, he and various law enforcement officers had returned to the island and retrieved the artifacts, using Brock's key after easily picking the lock on the front door, and now the island remained under surveillance to see if anyone showed up looking for them. That night, he'd traveled home across the Everglades to Miami, where he'd promptly been debriefed. He'd recounted everything that had happened on the island—other than copious amounts of sex with Kat, because that was none of the FBI's business—and shared his suspicions about Clark Spencer's involvement in the smuggling. Given that Carlos and Francisco were dead, Spencer was vital because he was now all they had to go on. And Brock wanted like hell to be the guy to bring Spencer down, but as he'd suspected, his boss had immediately ordered him to take some downtime, then put someone new on the case. Brock had gone through a mandatory counseling session the following afternoon before being sent home to take a month off, whether he liked it or not.

When he'd found himself packing a small bag, getting in his car a few hours ago, and making the trek back across south Florida's Alligator Alley, he'd told himself it was about his grandpa and old times. He'd decided he needed to go back to the swamp house—for the first time since he left ten years ago. He needed to figure out if he wanted to fix it up and sell it, have it leveled and sell the property—he needed to see if there was anything left there he might want. He should have done this a long time ago, but he hadn't quite been ready to face it—until now. Somehow, talking with Kat, telling her everything that had happened with his family—which he'd never told *anyone* before—had finally given him the guts to do this. Coming clean with her had helped him begin to make peace with his past and maybe start forgiving himself for taking Clark Spencer's bribe.

Yet when he'd gotten off the expressway, then glanced at the clock on the dashboard, he'd found himself headed *here* first. Before parting ways, Nina had mentioned to him the time and place of Kat's wedding, and maybe arriving in Naples just before the two o'clock nuptials hadn't been purely coincidental. God knew the girl had been on his mind ever since he'd left her at the marina with that other guy.

He wasn't sure why he'd come, though. Was he planning to stop the wedding?

Nah, not his style. And not his business if this was what she really wanted to do.

Maybe he just wanted to see if she'd truly go through with it. Damn, he hated to think of her becoming some Naples version of a Stepford wife. As he slid the convertible into a parking spot, he could only sigh. *Why are you doing this, kitten?*

The classic white church was at once quaint but opulent, the architecture sporting just the tiniest hint of Caribbean flair. The immaculate grounds, dotted with tall palms, increased the grandeur. Or maybe it was all the guests' cars, most just as expensive as his. No one lingered outside the building, and for the first time it occurred to him he might be late.

He'd wanted to time it close—he didn't need to have anyone who might recognize him see him slinking in—but shit, what if he was *too* late? What if he'd missed it? Didn't matter, really—yet he'd wanted to get here before she actually said *I do*. Maybe he needed to see it to believe it.

Jogging up the steps in jeans and a button-down shirt way too casual for the occasion, he eased the door open just a couple of inches. The foyer appeared empty, so he stepped inside. A guest-book rested there unattended, and it gave him a jolt of wry amuse-ment imagining if he just wrote his name down and slipped back out. Just to let her know he'd been there.

But no, that wasn't why he'd come. It was growing clearer with each passing moment. He needed to see Kat do this—because if she made a mistake this huge, well, maybe she wasn't the strong, independent woman he thought her.

When the rustling of fancy dresses filled the air, he automati-cally went into low-profile mode and stepped back into an alcove. A procession of bridesmaids in gowns that matched in color but not style paraded to the door leading into the sanctuary. He recog-nized Nina at the rear of the pack. She either hadn't tried to stop the wedding or, more likely, had failed.

The gentle, regal notes of a harp echoed around him, and the bridesmaids began their walk, one by one. As each girl started her journey, it drew Kat's trip up the aisle closer and made his heart beat faster.

When finally Nina clutched her bouquet tight in both fists and took that first step, he shut his eyes and tried to swallow back the pain. Why the hell did this hurt so damn bad? It was Kat's mistake, not his. Her lifetime of unhappiness, not his. He didn't *think* it was his anyway.

Clark Spencer then came walking from the same direction the

bridesmaids had, all decked out in black and white, looking like the perfect father of the bride. Brock hated him in that moment as he never had before. For ripping him away from his grandfather ten years ago. For cajoling Kat into this marriage. For endangering his family—particularly her—by storing smuggled goods on that island.

But then a vision in white drew his gaze across the vestibule.

Damn, she looked like an angel floating across the floor, and the mere sight of her stole his breath.

The angel looked up, and their eyes met.

Chapter Eighteen

For a split second, Brock imagined taking her hand and running from the church, Dustin Hoffman style in *The Graduate*.

But as quickly as the image passed through his head, Kat switched her gaze to her dad, they exchanged warm smiles, and Clark said, "Ready, sweetheart?"

She gave a slight but sure nod, then gently hooked her arm through her father's. Brock's blood ran cold as he watched his kitten walk up the aisle toward another man.

He moved up to the door, unworried about being seen now. Every eye in the place focused on Katrina Spencer, princess and soon-to-be high-society wife. A lump rose to his throat as the profound wrongness of this union washed over him.

For the first real time, he thought about stopping the wedding. About stepping through the door and speaking up when the minister asked if anyone had any reason to object.

Could he really do that? And was he going to tell them *why* he objected, what Kat had done with him on the island? The things she'd shared about her feelings for Ian?

Kat would hate him forever. But maybe it would be worth it.

Brock stood watching, waiting. He wasn't the sort of guy who stuck his nose into other people's business, but he thought he was about to become one. He tried to plan his words—enough to stop this travesty, but as little as possible that would hurt Kat.

Hell, what was he thinking? No matter how he said it, she'd be severely wounded. So maybe he should just spout out the brutal truth. *She doesn't love him. She just spent three days making wild passionate love to* me. *She's only marrying him to bail her father out of financial trouble, and because I wasn't willing to commit.*

But by the time he had it worked out in his head, he realized that they must have cut that part of the ceremony—since he never had a chance to say *anything* before the minister asked, "Katrina Spencer, do you take Ian Zeller to be your lawfully wedded husband?"

Kat stared at Ian's chest as the minister went on with, "To have and to hold, to love and to cherish, in sickness and in health, in good times and bad, from this day forward, so help you God?"

So help her God. Why had she never really heard that part before? She might have been rolling her eyes at God out on the island when Brock showed up, being dangled before her like a bit of cheese to a hungry mouse—but she actually held God in high reverence.

And it suddenly hit her, hard, that here she stood, in a church, about to marry a man she knew she didn't feel the right way for. She could *try* to love and cherish him, but could she *promise*?

And somewhere Brock was watching. She could feel him, still here. When she'd spotted him out in the foyer, her heart had nearly burst in her chest. With love. And hurt. And strange hope—because why had he come?

But that didn't really matter, because he hadn't dropped to his knees, declared his undying love for her, and begged her to come away with him—and that's what she wanted, *demanded*, from a man.

The kind of love and cherishing the minister was asking of her right now.

The kind she couldn't give Ian.

Because it just wasn't in her heart, no matter how much she might wish it was.

The minister cleared his throat; she'd taken too long to answer.

God, what the hell was she even doing here?

"No," she said meekly.

"What?" the minister and Ian both spat in unison.

Tears threatened, making her eyes burn, clogging her throat. "No," she managed again anyway. "I . . . can't. I'm so sorry."

With that, she turned, lifted the skirt of her dress slightly, and ran for all she was worth back down the aisle. She heard the rustling of the fabric with each frantic stride, the low gasp that echoed from the crowd, and the stunned silence that followed.

Sprinting through the foyer, she looked for Brock despite herself, and tried not to be crushed when he wasn't there. Still, her heart plummeted.

She burst through the front doors out into the blistering hot sun. Still no Brock, just pristine palms and lines of shiny cars, but she wasn't really looking for him anymore so much as seeking escape. Damn it, why hadn't she gotten married at night? She yearned for some darkness to blend in to. And cool air—some cooler air would be welcome at the moment since she feared she might soon pass out.

Directly before her at the end of the walk sat an elegant white horse and carriage—a startled driver in a top hat looked up from his cigarette, clearly surprised to see the bride quite so soon, and by herself. Where was a getaway car when you needed one?

And then, as if by magic, an iridescent jade green Porsche convertible pulled to a stop just beyond the carriage.

"Kitten. Get in."

She sucked in her breath at the sight of Brock behind a pair of Ray-Bans in a killer ride. She absently yanked the veil off her head, letting it flutter away behind her as she hurried around a smelly white horse and wide-eyed driver to leap into Brock's passenger seat.

As the car squealed away, she looked up to see Nina and her mother and father all scurrying out onto the front walk. Nina was smiling.

And for a few short seconds, her world was perfect. Her own personal Prince Charming had rescued her, and now they raced away from imminent disaster with the wind in their hair and the sun on their faces.

"Where the hell did you get this car?" An odd question at the moment, but it was an impressive vehicle—and not one she'd have imagined the average FBI guy could afford.

"Belonged to a drug dealer I brought down a few years ago. Bought it at a police auction."

She nodded. "Nice."

"Where do you want to go?" he asked as they wound through the well-manicured, water-lined neighborhood.

Where do you want to take me? She let out a sigh. "I don't know. My place?"

"Tell me how to get there."

She gave him directions and realized her heartbeat still hadn't slowed from the moment she'd exited the church. She should probably be thinking about Ian, about all those people, about the colossal mess she'd left for her parents to clean up—but instead all her attention focused on the man to her left. Who now drove with the same single-minded purpose she'd witnessed on the island when he got into work mode. And though a few days ago she would have phrased this more delicately, this seemed no time to mince words. "You aren't here to tell me you've changed your mind and want to take a shot at us being together, *are* you?"

Easing to a halt at a stop light, he turned to look at her, but she couldn't see his eyes behind the sunglasses. "I came to see if you'd really go through with it, and to stop it myself if I had to."

She blinked. "For someone who planned to stop it, you let me get awfully damn close."

He let out a long sigh. "You cut out the part asking if anybody objected."

"It seemed prudent."

"Well, it blew my plan to hell."

"No backup plan, Mr. Secret Agent?"

"It was a last-minute idea—no time."

As the light changed and the car *vroomed* forward, she said, "Answer my question."

He didn't pretend not to know which one. "Kitten, I'm just glad you made the right decision. I'm proud as hell of you."

But she didn't need his pride, she needed his love. And she knew she wasn't going to get it. She really wasn't sure why he'd bothered showing up at all. If he didn't love her, didn't want her, what was the point? She stayed quiet, just wanting to get home, put on some comfy clothes, and curl up with Vincent. How comforting to have someone in her life who couldn't ever ruin things by talking.

"Don't be mad at me, honey."

What do you care? She kept her gaze steeled on the road before them. "I'm not."

"I think you are."

"Why does it even matter?" She hated how immature she must sound, but Brock had that effect on her. He made her want what she wanted, *now*—the rest of the world be damned.

"You seem to be under the impression that I don't care about you," he replied pointedly, "but for your information, you couldn't be more wrong. If I didn't care, kitten, I wouldn't have shown up at that church, would I? And I wouldn't have gotten you out of there."

A lump rose to Kat's throat as she looked at him long and hard, then quietly said, "Turn here," at the entrance to her apartment complex. She didn't quite know how to respond, which was just as well, since she doubted she could squeeze any more words from her clogged throat. He was telling her he cared. Which, in one sense, helped. But if he cared so much, why was he willing to walk right back out of her life and never see her again?

As she pointed toward her building and he parked, her chest tightened painfully. He might claim he cared, but if he didn't want her, why should *she* want *him*? And now she had to say good-bye to him yet one more time. She was beginning to feel like that's all her relationship with Brock *was:* a never-ending series of good-byes.

She couldn't bear to look at his handsome face as she opened the door and said, "Thanks for the ride."

"I'm coming in."

She looked over to see him getting out, too. "Why?"

He'd ditched his sunglasses, so she could see his eyes now. "Just want to make sure you get inside okay."

"I'm a big girl, Brock."

"Duly noted."

"And it's not like the police are chasing me or anything. My dad, maybe, but him I can handle."

"Just the same, I'm taking you in," he said, then rounded the car, grabbed her hand, and led her toward the private-entry door as comfortably as if it were his place and not hers.

That's when it hit her. "Damn, I don't have my key—everything's at the church."

"Not a problem," he replied, then reached in his back pocket, drew out a well-worn brown leather wallet, then an American Express card. He slid it smoothly down the edge of the door with one hand, gently turning the knob with the other, and the lock clicked open.

She looked up at him, slightly aghast. "*That's* reassuring."

He shrugged as if to say, *That's reality.*

"Is this a skill you learned in the FBI—or before?"

He cocked her a quick, chiding look, then opened the door and placed a hand at the small of her back, ushering her inside. The a/c hit her like a blast of heaven. Odd, the heat hadn't bothered her at all on the island with Brock, but just today she'd started finding it oppressive. Maybe it was her *life* she was finding oppressive.

Vincent came trotting to greet her, and she bent to scoop him into her arms. "Hey, kitty." Rising back up, she ran a hand back through his thick fur. "Guess what—we're not moving anymore, this is still home." How good that sounded to her. She smoothed her fingertips over one declawed paw, soaking up the comfort a cat could so easily provide, then turned to Brock, who'd stepped in and closed the door behind him. "This is Vincent."

He nodded. "Glad to see he still has both ears."

"Pet him hello."

Brock shifted his weight from one foot to the other. "I'm not really into cats."

She cast a look of warning. "I'm in a bad mood, Brock. Pet him."

"Fine," he said, then reached out to swipe his hand over the cat's head. Vincent looked perturbed, and Kat could understand why.

She rolled her eyes at Brock's pathetic effort, then lowered the kitty to the floor. "I'm in," she said, "so I guess you can go now."

But instead of going, he turned to face her, effectively pinning her to the wall of her foyer. "Kitten," he said, lifting one large, warm hand to her face, "I just want you to know, back at the church, when you didn't say 'I do' . . . well, now I can sleep tonight, that's all."

Her whole body tensed beneath his touch, electrified. As always. But she tried to hold her mental ground. "So glad I could help you out."

He ignored her sarcasm, leaned in, and melded his mouth to hers in a slow, lingering kiss that she felt all the way to her toes. Her body instantly ached for him.

"What was *that*?" she asked when they parted.

"A kiss good-bye," he said, warm and dark, but the predatory look in his eyes didn't give her the impression he was quite ready to go. "Here's another one."

She nearly melted to the floor beneath the weight of her desire as his hot mouth closed again over her willing, acceptant one. He slid one hand to her waist, and with the other covered her breast, his thumb stroking over the sensitive peak through the lace of her bodice. His knee lodged between her thighs, and her whole body weakened further at the shock of pleasure. Her hands rose to his chest, neck, face. She drew him to her tight, kissing heatedly, drinking in this unexpected gulp of him, and relishing the hard evidence of his arousal against her hip. Their breathing quickly grew labored as they moved together instinctually.

The hand at her side began gathering fabric, more and more, as he tried to work his way beneath her wedding dress. Finally, his palm found her thigh, gliding swiftly up her stocking until he encountered the lace top and let out a small groan that fueled her with the same knowledge clearly exciting *him*—no pesky panty hose lay between them.

Which meant in mere seconds he could be back inside her, where they both clearly longed for him to be.

But oh God—what was she thinking, doing? She was about to have sex with Brock in her wedding dress!

Collecting all the remaining bits of strength inside her, she pushed at his chest, ending the kiss. "Stop." She couldn't do this. Not any more than she could have married Ian today. It was all suddenly, painfully, clear.

He looked shocked at her rebuff. His words came low, raspy, near her ear. "Why, kitten? I want you."

Her breathing remained thready, but she managed to answer, even as his body still grazed hers. "Because I can't do this anymore. I can't do this knowing it means nothing."

Their eyes met in the shadowy entryway. "Who said it means nothing?"

She pulled in her breath, trying to read him. Was there more than passion in his gaze? She didn't understand a man who said he cared, who wanted to take her with such heat, who implied maybe it did mean something—but still wanted to say "So long" and never look back the moment it was over. She swallowed the lump in her throat and let herself be brutally honest. "It doesn't mean to you what it means to me—what it's *always* meant to me—or you wouldn't be able to leave. Ever."

Brock finally pulled back, releasing her thigh, her breast, his eyes looking pained. "Honey, I've explained to you. I'm just not a—"

"Relationship kinda guy—yeah, I know," she cut in dryly. "But I *am* a relationship kinda girl." Maybe not always. *But with you—yes, always.* She dropped her gaze to her white skirting. "I think you should go."

He stood still before her, and she grew aware of how hard her heart pounded.

"Please," she said. "I mean it. Leave."

Still staring at her dress, his shoes, the hardwood floor, Kat finally heard his long, slow sigh. One bent finger lifted her chin until she met his gaze. "Take care of yourself, kitten," he said, then kissed her chastely on the cheek and disappeared out the door.

One more painful good-bye.

An hour after Kat's departure from her wedding, Clark Spencer rang his daughter's doorbell. Debra and Nina had both come along, but he'd asked them to wait in the car. His heart was bending in his chest—felt on the verge of breaking. He simply didn't understand what had happened and he needed to get to the bottom of it. He and Kat had always been close, and he just wanted a few minutes alone with her to see if she would open up, tell him what was going on inside her.

She swung the door wide, clutching her cat in her free arm. Her long hair remained in the fancy—albeit windblown—curls she'd worn earlier and her makeup remained in place, making her eyes look large and her complexion luminous. But she'd shed her hand-sewn gown for light blue stretchy pants with a stripe down the side and a small white top with thin shoulder straps.

"Can I come in, sweetheart?"

She simply stood back and let him enter, then shut the door behind him.

Moving into the living room, he found the curtains drawn, a plate of brownies adorning the coffee table, and an open bottle of wine next to them.

"Brownie?" She motioned toward them as they both took a seat on her sofa. "They're left over from the luncheon yesterday—I had thought Mom might like to nibble at them when she came to feed Vincent. Or would you like a glass of wine? I actually didn't bother *using* a glass, as you can see, but I can get a couple out if you like."

Clark shook his head lightly—he hadn't come here to snack or have a drink, although he wouldn't begrudge Kat either indulgence. "No, but you go ahead."

She obligingly snatched up a brownie and took a bite. When a few crumbs fell to her lap, the cat quickly relieved her of them. She stroked the cat's back, and Clark realized that behind the bridal glow, his daughter looked very tired.

"Do you feel like talking? Can you tell me what happened back there?"

Slowly, she met his gaze. "I don't *really* feel like talking, but that's okay, because I'd rather get this over with. And besides, I owe you an explanation. I know the wedding cost an arm and a leg and that we really don't have cash to blow right now and—"

"I don't care about any of that, Kat." He reached out to give her elbow a light, loving squeeze. "I just want to know what's going on with you. Is this just . . . some extreme case of prewedding jitters? Too many people, too much fanfare? Because if it is, we can fix that. Ian loves you, and he'll understand. We could have a much smaller wedding, just family, if you'd prefer."

His daughter let out a sigh, and even before she spoke, he realized this went much deeper. "Dad, I'm sorry to tell you this, but I just don't want to marry him. I don't love him. It was stupid of me to try." She gave her head a short shake with every sentence.

Her words left him even more confused. "But then . . . why did you say yes when he proposed?"

Another deep, tired sigh. "Because he asked me in front of

everyone? Because I knew it would make you all so happy?" She stopped, dropped her gaze back to the cat, then raised it again. "Mostly for you."

He blinked. "What? What do you mean?"

Kat looked troubled, like she was about to say something difficult, but maybe, deep inside, he already knew what it was. He'd just never allowed himself to really think about it before, because it was too awful.

"Because I knew he had money. And because the gallery isn't exactly raking it in these days. And because I know that's really important to you. And I . . . well, I just thought if there was something I could do to help you . . . if it was within my power to make you happy, Daddy, I wanted to do that."

It wasn't so much what she'd said as what she'd called him that made the lump rise in his throat. He didn't think she'd referred to him as Daddy since her childhood, and now she seemed wholly unaware she'd just said it. He remembered lamenting the day she'd stopped, the day he'd become Dad.

And it ripped his heart in two to realize with horror that his little girl had thought she had to marry someone she didn't love just to keep him happy. And to realize with even *more* horror that he'd pushed it along, willed it to happen.

He'd thought she loved Ian—that's what had made it okay to accept that her marriage would be fortuitous to him. Okay to think that since they were becoming one big happy family, there was nothing wrong with letting Ian's money solve some of his problems. Hell, he'd let this engagement pull him in directions he'd never have gone in otherwise. And all this time he'd been telling himself it was okay, but now the look on Kat's face told him it *wasn't* okay. None of it.

"Kat," he whispered, but his throat was closing up. He didn't quite know what to say, how to make something this enormous up to her. "Kat," he managed again, and that was all. He simply drew her into his arms, sending the cat pouncing to the floor.

They both stayed quiet until he said, "I'm sorry, sweetheart. So sorry."

She lifted her head from his shoulder. "*You're* sorry? For what?"

"For ever making you feel you had to do something that massive for me. For . . . maybe pushing you at Ian. I didn't realize you didn't feel the right way. But maybe I was just . . . too blind to notice. Sometimes, Kat . . ." He looked down at his tuxedo pants, ashamed. For things that went beyond the last six months. "Sometimes I'm afraid I love you too much. And that it comes out in ways that . . ." Ah, hell, he didn't even know what he was trying to say, so he started again. "I guess I always think I know what's best for you—and maybe sometimes I don't."

She sat up, leaving his embrace, and in that moment, he knew she knew. The very thing he'd just been thinking of. Hell, he'd been surprised Brock wasn't here when he'd arrived. But he wasn't surprised that Brock had found occasion to tell her the rotten truth about her father.

"I know," she said, "what you did to Brock."

He nodded shortly, and his voice came out small. "Believe it or not, it felt like the right thing at the time. I wanted to protect you—can you understand that?"

"Yes, but I'm afraid I *don't* understand the lengths you went to. You made him leave his grandpa when he was dying, for God's sake. Brock was all his grandfather had, and he still feels guilty about it. Even though *you're* the one who should feel guilty. And I've been so screwed up the past couple of days that I haven't really let myself think through this until now, but . . . how could you, Dad? How could you do that to him?"

Clark leaned over, putting his head in his hands. *He* hadn't allowed himself to think about it often, either. He'd told himself back then, whenever a sliver of guilt embedded itself, that it was Brock's fault, that he shouldn't have been messing around with a young girl, that he'd had the choice of staying and facing the music and would have if he'd been more of a man—but deep inside, Clark had always known he'd put the boy in an untenable position. "That's what I mean," he finally said, lifting his head, "when I tell you I love you too much."

Next to him, Kat appeared resolute. "You've got to stop, you know. You've got to stop it right now. I'm an adult—almost twenty-eight years old. And I know my mind far better than you've ever given me credit for. For the last six months, I allowed myself to be deluded, but prior to that, and from this moment forward, I've known and *will* know exactly what I want, and I need you to promise me, right now, that you'll respect that and never interfere again. Can you do that, Daddy?"

Again, Daddy. Ironic, since clearly, she *wasn't* his little girl anymore and apparently hadn't been for a long time. And he had no other choice but to respect the hell out of her. "Yes, Kat, I can. I will. I promise."

He swallowed. He usually felt so strong—money made him strong, and even the pursuit of it had kept him strong these past couple of not-so-great years. But right now he felt weak. And it wasn't because he no longer had the promise of Ian's financial backing. It was because *she* was so strong, and *he'd* been so foolish. "Can you forgive your dad for being an idiot, sweetheart?"

She nodded without hesitation, and he loved her all the more. But then instantly tried not to feel it quite so much. He had to learn to love his daughter in a . . . more distant, respectful way, and he had to start right now.

"So about you and Brock," he began, unable to help it—he had to ask. He had no idea where Brock had ended up in life, had no reason to wish him ill—yet old habits made him want to shove the guy right back out of their lives. He'd been stunned to see Brock Denton on that island when they'd floated up, and wished he'd been more surprised to see him *today*, helping Kat escape her own wedding.

Kat sniffed, and he realized she was on the verge of getting weepy. "You don't have to concern yourself with Brock. I don't expect to ever see him again."

A rush of relief washed through Clark's body—but he still forced himself to say the right thing. "Well, if your answer had been different, I would have . . . accepted it. For you."

She nodded. "Good."

"Where'd he get that car, anyway? What does he do now?" Sheer curiosity made him ask. Ten years ago, the kid hadn't had two nickels to rub together.

Kat's eyebrows knitted slightly. "I'm . . . not sure what he does. He . . . wasn't clear on it."

Clark nodded. Wheels like that and no education? Drug dealing, he'd bet.

But he couldn't feel guilty about that, too. Nope, he'd given the boy enough money to get a good start on a new life, and if Brock hadn't capitalized on that in a positive way, that was *his* problem. This just made him all the more relieved Kat was shed of him—hopefully once and for all.

Just then a small knock came on the door, and he remembered. "I left your mother and Nina in the car."

"Oh," Kat said, leaping up to answer.

A moment later, the ladies paraded in, Nina still in her yellow dress, his wife looking lovely in a warm shade of coral brocade. To stall any further questions, since he thought Kat had probably endured enough interrogation, he said, "Kat doesn't love Ian. So the wedding is, indeed, off. And that's all right." He glanced to Kat, who was plopping back down on the couch. "I've told her we'll all support her in whatever she wants to do."

Debra rushed to Kat's side, dropped Kat's forgotten purse on the sofa, and pulled her into a wordless hug before finally saying, "You should come for dinner tonight. We'll make whatever you like, just name it. Or we'll go out somewhere. Whatever you want."

But Kat was shaking her head and Clark realized he wasn't the only one who coddled Kat, and that she looked well tired of it. "I don't think so. I just want to stay in tonight and veg."

"What about me?" Nina asked. "Am I banished from your life tonight, too?"

"No. *You* may come over. And you may bring pizza and ice cream. And DVDs of *Thelma and Louise* and *Chocolat*."

"Got it," Nina said.

"And frankly," Clark said, pushing to his feet, "if you're really all right here, your mother and I should probably go back to the church and tend to things there."

Guilt he'd not intended to inflict flashed across Kat's face. "I'm so sorry. About that part of it. Maybe I should—"

"No," he said. "At some point, you should talk to Ian, but we'll take care of everything else."

She bit her lip. "He's crushed, I guess."

Clark tilted his head. "Of course. But I'll talk to him. He'll be all right. And so will you. We'll get through this, sweetheart."

At this, she got to her feet and gave him a hug, warming his heart deeply. They *would* get through this. As for the money issues, well . . . he'd have to rethink the situation, see how certain things washed out. But for today, he refused to care about anything but Kat and what was best for her. What was *really* best for her—not just what *he* thought was best for her.

And as he, Debra, and Nina piled back in the car, he realized that it felt . . . bizarrely liberating to suddenly let go of control over his daughter's choices.

His heart felt strangely lighter than it had in years.

Brock lay in his old bed at his grandfather's house, staring at a water stain on the ceiling. Driving out here this afternoon after leaving Kat had felt surreal, and the truth was, the closer he'd gotten to the swamp, the more tempted he'd been to turn back—but this was at least one of the reasons he'd crossed the state today, and it was high time he faced those demons.

The house had been empty for ten years—although he'd kept the taxes paid on it and had even hired the nearest neighbor lady, half a mile up the dirt road, to come in once every few months and give the place a light cleaning. But then she'd moved away a few years ago, and he hadn't bothered making new arrangements.

He'd been pleased to find that the house had remained locked— and glad he'd always saved the key, always kept it on his ring, more as a keepsake than a practical object, but it was practical today. Upon stepping inside, he'd found the furniture neatly covered with sheets, which helped cut down on the dust when he went around uncloaking it all.

The place, he'd discovered, was like a museum to his life ten years ago. Same cheap dishes in the cabinets. Same rust ring around the drain in the kitchen sink. Same old couch with the rip Bruno had managed to put in it with a pocketknife, and same faded curtains framing the small windows.

In the room he'd once shared with Bruno, the same two twin beds sat parked against opposite walls, the same ancient chest of drawers stood in between. Clothes he hadn't taken then—mostly black T-shirts sporting the names of rock bands—lay folded inside.

The only thing different had been his grandfather's bedroom. A big-screen TV—now outdated, but then state-of-the-art—filled the wall that faced a hospital bed.

The place had smelled musty as hell, so he'd opened the windows. Even the hot, humid south Florida air was an improvement. Then he'd reached for his cell phone, dialed information, and called to have the electricity turned back on, after which he'd let all the faucets run until the well water went from brown to crystal clear. Later, he'd go out and buy some cleaning supplies, a fan or two, and maybe a little food.

He hadn't come here exactly planning to stay, but now that he was here, he found himself not really wanting to leave. There was something comforting here. Time. *Another* time—when life had been far from great, but his grandpa had loved him, and this had been home.

So very different, he couldn't help being reminded, from *Kat's* home. Such vast differences were the main thing that had separated them ten years ago. Spencer could say it had been age, and Brock was sure that was part of it, but this was most of it. Water stains on the ceiling. Rust rings in the sink.

When Kat had come back down that aisle today, a huge weight had lifted from Brock's chest. *That's my girl*, he'd thought. Maybe without realizing, or letting himself remember, until they were back at her apartment, just how much she still wanted to *be* his girl. She'd looked so beautiful riding next to him in that gown that maybe he'd been tempted, just for a second, to keep on driving, somewhere far away, maybe over some imaginary bridge right back to their island where the rest of the world didn't matter. Her family, his job, all gone—just the two of them making love in a hammock, or in the surf, or in the sand, everywhere, natural and hot and free.

But just as quickly, seeing her with her cat, being so instinctively loving and sweet and pure, had reminded him that Kat was the whole package, more than just the hot girl who made his head spin when she was pleasuring him, more than just the sweet girl who rescued cats from shelters and taught troubled kids to make bowls. She was a little bit of everything, and that turned him inside out. She was truly a kitten, but also a tigress.

I wish I could be what you want me to be, kitten. A boyfriend. A husband?

Yet the very idea made him shiver. He couldn't be a husband, ever. Why couldn't she get that? Why couldn't she get that he just didn't have what it took?

He knew he'd hurt her, and he felt like a jerk for following his instincts in her apartment. Bad timing on his part. But at least now maybe he understood how much she really felt for him. So much that the passion didn't make up for what he couldn't give her. Her passion was boundless, and that meant her feelings for him were . . . even more powerful. A notion that gave him chills despite the stifling heat.

And what was he going to do now? Send her beloved father to prison. She'd really be crazy about him *then*.

But he had no choice. He still didn't know all the whys and hows of it, but Spencer was undoubtedly a criminal. And Brock's job was to bring criminals to justice, make them pay.

Hell, even if justice wasn't important to him—and it was—and even if his professional pride wasn't important to him—and that was, too—he couldn't deny that putting Clark Spencer behind bars was going to deliver a ton of satisfaction. The vindictive kind. He wasn't necessarily proud of that, but he wanted to be there, wanted to see the look on Spencer's face when none other than wrong-side-of-the-tracks Brock Denton brought him down.

It would kill Kat. He'd known that from the moment he'd found the artifacts. But he was an FBI agent—he'd learned a long time ago to block out that kind of emotion when it came to his job. Maybe he hadn't always done a great job of blocking it out on the island, but this was different—it had to be. It wasn't his fault the guy was breaking the law. Brock was just doing his job.

Kat's heart be damned. Unfortunately.

He let out a sigh. Everything else aside, he still remained so very proud of her. He could still hear the minister asking her today if she took Ian Zeller to be her husband. And that long, blissful hesitation that had filled him with hope—then the blessed refusal.

Something caught in his mind then. Zeller. Ian Zeller.

The last letter of the alphabet.

Just like Omega was the last letter of the Greek alphabet.

Chapter Nineteen

*K*at hit the power button on the remote, darkening the TV screen. They'd watched *Thelma and Louise* over pizza, then quite appropriately watched *Chocolat* during dessert. Nina had brought their old favorite, Ben & Jerry's Chocolate Chip Cookie Dough, for that portion of the evening.

"Feeling more like yourself? Back to normal?" Nina asked.

Kat shoved the very last spoonful of ice cream in her mouth as she glanced over. "Yes. No. I don't know. It's been a whirlwind of a week."

Nina's mouth curved into a small smile. "That's not exactly what I meant. I was thinking that you really haven't seemed quite like *you* since you got engaged to that bozo at Christmas."

"Oh." Hmm. "Maybe not." True enough, the whole pastel-beach-mom thing had nearly taken her over, and it just really wasn't her—or at least not yet.

"I figured that was why we were watching movies about defiant women—to get you back in your groove."

Until that moment, Kat hadn't realized that, automatically, she'd requested movies that fit that description. She'd mainly been thinking about a young Brad Pitt in a cowboy hat and a sexy Johnny Depp in a ponytail. And even now, realizing Nina was right, she still argued. "*Strong* women. I'd prefer to think of them simply as *strong*."

Nina rolled her eyes. "Whatever." And Kat knew the pampering period was officially over, which suited her just fine. Nina wasn't quite Nina without the occasional eye roll. "You know what you have to do now, don't you? You have to celebrate your new independence by doing something really defiant, something Crazy-Kat-like."

"I thought I already did. A few hours ago? At the church? Think back and it'll come to you."

But Nina was shaking her head. "That's not what I mean. That took strength, sure, and was pretty defiant, but it was also about self-preservation. Which, incidentally, I'm glad finally kicked in. But what I'm talking about is doing something totally for you, without giving a damn what anyone else thinks. Think like Crazy Kat."

"I'm not sure I *am* Crazy Kat anymore. Honestly, I'm not sure I ever was."

Nina raised her eyebrows in rank skepticism. "Oh, come on, sure you are. At least a little. I know you too well. Now, what are you going to do to remind yourself exactly who you are?"

Maybe Nina was right. Though she suspected this whole ordeal had forced her to grow up in a way she hadn't before, maybe she truly did have a wild side—under the right circumstances. And as Nina headed to the kitchen for another bottle of wine, Kat knew exactly what she would do to express it. It might be a little like tossing her bikini top off on a deserted beach where no one could see, but as long as *she* knew, that was all that mattered.

★ ★ ★

Keith Nichols was an FBI agent of twenty-three who looked even younger, like the quintessential beach boy, and when Brock had first found out he was the guy assigned to the artifact case, he'd been pissed. Nichols's inexperience could blow the whole thing.

His irritation had quickly subsided, though, when he recalled that *he'd* managed to blow it once already with *tons* of experience behind him. And actually, he liked Nichols—they got along well, and the young guy looked up to him.

And fortunately, Nichols had been smart enough to call Brock as soon as he arrived in Naples a few days after Brock had officially been taken off the case. Which was helpful, since it kept Brock from having to track him down.

In a coffee shop, Brock had told him everything there was to tell, leading right up to the Spencer connection, and further, to the possible Ian Zeller connection—something that had felt like a lightbulb clicking on above Brock's head. "I'm telling you, man, I really think he's the kingpin." Despite not being at the top of his game lately, Brock felt this one in his gut.

Nichols had—ironically—gotten Clark Spencer to hire him to work in the gallery's warehouse and run errands, the same job Brock had held ten years ago. Nichols had claimed to be a college kid, home for the summer. Given it was almost June, it fit.

But now Brock had talked Nichols into taking a completely different strategy—risky maybe, yet it would cut to the heart of the matter. Thankfully, Nichols trusted him—otherwise, no longer being on the case, Brock's hands would have been tied. As it was, the young agent was being man enough to let Brock sit in the unofficial driver's seat and call most of the shots—and as long as Nichols kept quiet, Brock's superior would never know he'd broken an order by getting involved again.

The two men walked down pristine Fifth Avenue South, flanked by flower boxes and tidy sidewalks, toward The Spencer Gallery. It was after hours, so there wouldn't be any customers and hopefully no Kat. His bones ached at the very thought of seeing her, but not now, like this. Her father was going to jail, and the fact that it would devastate her had been playing over and over in Brock's mind—she certainly didn't need to see him be taken down.

Of course, something ate at him as they walked past the other ritzy neighborhood galleries and cafes. That same thing that had been eating at him for a day or two now. The idea that maybe he possessed the power to keep Spencer from *going* down.

If Spencer's answers were the right ones.

And if he could bear to do it.

After all, it seemed more than a little insane for him to even think about letting this guy off the hook. This guy who'd bribed and blackmailed him out of his own life ten years ago. This guy who was willing to let his daughter marry for money in order to save his own ass. This guy who seemed pretty damn deep into smuggling illegal goods into the country.

Although if his hunch was correct and Ian was Omega Man, there was a lot more to the story than Brock knew right now. All he knew for sure was that Ian had "investments" that resulted in a lot of cash, and that—according to Kat—he'd been spending a lot of time with Spencer these past months. And when the "rescue boat" had arrived at the island, Ian had seemed a lot more frantic about Kat's safety than Spencer had—like he knew she might have been in danger. And via Spencer or some other route, how hard would it be for Ian to have access to that island bungalow? In fact, it suddenly seemed like the perfect drop-off point for someone who wouldn't be at the direct end of a pointing finger if the location were discovered. Perfect, that is, if Ian forgot to take into consideration that Spencer might lead authorities to *him*.

What it all came down to, though, was this. Whether or not Ian was Omega, Brock could nail Clark Spencer to the wall. Given the goods found on that island and Spencer's history with Mayan artifacts, it was almost a done deal. This was the first time a case had ever overlapped with his personal life, and he still suffered the intense need to make Spencer pay—for *all* his crimes, against the Guatemalan government, against Brock, against Kat.

Unless he found it in his heart to cut him loose.

In one way, that was damn hard to imagine. He finally had a legal reason to punish Spencer, to ruin his life the way he'd once ruined Brock's, to keep Spencer from hurting anyone else.

But then he thought of Kat. She might be angry at her dad right now, but if he went to prison, it would tear her apart. And that was almost enough to make Brock's very hardened heart crumble to pieces in his chest.

"Ready?" Nichols asked, and Brock realized they stood in front of the gallery he'd last set foot in ten years earlier.

He wasn't sure yet what would happen here, but it was high time to bring all of this to an end. "Damn straight."

Nichols gave a brief nod. "Let's go."

The dim lighting illuminating the interior of the gallery indicated it was closed. But Nichols had a key, so he let them in. Both men felt sure Spencer would be working in his office—it was just after six, so even on an early night, he'd still be here.

Having heard the door, Clark Spencer appeared from the back, standing beneath a spotlight that made him look a bit spectral. He spotted Nichols first. "Forget something, Keith?" Then his eyes shifted to Brock. "Denton?"

"We need to have a talk, Clark," Nichols said.

The man looked understandably confused. "What kind of talk?"

"It would be best done in your office so no one passing by can see."

Spencer blinked, looking even more wary. "I don't understand."

At this, Nichols reached in his back pocket and whipped out a badge, which he flashed in Spencer's direction. "We're FBI, Clark."

Another blink, this one more startled. "Both of you?"

"Surprise," Brock said dryly, then flipped open a leather case revealing his own federal ID.

"Shit."

"You're waist deep in it," Brock informed him.

"Why don't we step into your office," Nichols suggested again.

Spencer silently turned to head in that direction, the other two men following. When Brock took a seat in one of the chairs across from Spencer's desk, a hint of *déjà vu* washed over him. But that changed when he realized Spencer was sweating bullets.

"Just so you know," Brock said to him, "I'm not officially on this case any longer, but I wasn't on the island by accident. And it was a damn good thing I was there when those two thugs showed up or else your daughter would probably be dead now."

Watching Spencer's face very carefully, Brock caught the genuine shock, followed by a look of illness. "Thugs? When Kat was there?"

"Are you saying," Nichols asked, "that you don't know about these guys? They weren't on your payroll?"

Clark Spencer now officially looked flabbergasted. "I have no idea what you're talking about." Then he looked back to Brock. "Kat was in danger?"

"*Serious* danger," Brock informed him, not caring in the slightest how upsetting that might be. Whether or not he was *directly* responsible, he needed to know what he'd almost let happen to his daughter.

"What can you tell us about the stash of Mayan artifacts found in the home on your island?" Nichols asked.

Again, Spencer blinked, and Brock thought the man might collapse right there on his desk. "In the house? They were *in* the house? On *my* island?" If Brock had to judge, he'd say he believed Spencer was truly as surprised to learn about this as he himself had been upon discovering the goods.

Nichols tilted his youthful blond head. "You're denying knowledge of that?"

"Hell yes, I'm denying knowledge of that."

"Do you think Ian Zeller might have arranged that particular hiding place without filling you in?" Nichols asked.

At that, Spencer went quiet, his face pale.

Brock leaned comfortably back in his chair, crossed his arms, and eyed the older man. "You don't want to lie to this guy. You do and you're going to jail."

Spencer leaned over, resting his head in his hands, looking as though he might throw up. Brock didn't much care.

Until he imagined if Kat were here. Seeing her dad like this.

Lifting his head, Spencer swallowed visibly. "It sounds as if I'm going to jail anyway."

Brock studied the man, long and hard. He truly believed, in his heart, that Clark Spencer deserved to suffer for his crimes. He was a rich man who felt entitled, and he used that entitlement to do whatever he damn well pleased.

But as had been the case ever since parting from his kitten, her face entered Brock's mind. He'd seen her smile, heard her pretty, trilling laughter. And he'd seen her cry. He *hated* to see her cry.

And whereas he figured she'd get over him quickly enough and move on with her life, this situation with her dad—well, if Spencer went to prison, she wouldn't *ever* get over it. Even just the stigma. Brock knew what it was to have a family member in jail. He knew that people looked at you differently when they found out.

So even as much as he would have enjoyed seeing Clark Spencer in an orange jumpsuit, he heard himself doing the impossible—trying to get the guy off. "I'm not on this case, so I have no say in this, but . . . could be that if you come completely clean that Keith here might try to get a commitment from the U.S. Attorney for a light sentence, maybe just probation—hell, maybe even immunity if you've got enough information to ensure we nail Zeller." He shifted his glance to the other agent. "What do you say to that, Keith?"

Keith hesitated only slightly, then gave a short nod. "I could see my way clear to do that."

Then Brock looked back to the man who had taken him away from his grandfather ten years ago. "What do *you* say, Spencer?"

Spencer's voice came out small, not at all like the powerful Clark Spencer whom Brock had always known. "Yeah. I have enough information."

Debra didn't know what to make of it when Clark invited her to meet him at Clam Pass, the beach by the pier. The act was so out of character that she half wondered if he was going to ask her for a divorce. Maybe she deserved that kind of karmic irony, given her recent near mistake, something that continued to haunt her almost as badly as if she'd really gone through with it and had an affair. Although she'd found closure by promptly mailing Michael's manuscript back to him, with a note saying she didn't feel it appropriate to see him again. The whole ordeal had made her realize how much she loved Clark, despite all his faults—and there were many. But the love prevailed.

After finding street parking, she followed the mangrove-shaded boardwalk until she reached the beach. She shed her sandals upon stepping down into the sand, leaving her feet girlishly bare below beige shorts and a white sleeveless blouse. Something about easing her way through the cool, soothing sand reminded her of when she was young. She and Clark had come here often then, for sunset picnics and romantic walks. Once they'd made love on the beach after dark, wrapped in a sheet. It was the wildest thing she'd ever done, and as she peered out over the horizon toward the setting sun, she felt glad that the one and only wild moment of her existence had been shared with her husband.

She spotted Clark on a blanket near the shore. The stretch of sand was quiet and empty other than a few early-evening beachcombers and him. He wore khaki pants and a golf shirt, tucked in as neatly as ever. The bucket of chicken perched next to him made her laugh—she couldn't remember the last time they'd shared a meal so simple, and she thought it sounded delicious and perfect. But as she grew near enough to make eye contact, she tilted her head with playful skepticism and said, "Who are you and what have you done with my husband?"

He smiled, but his eyes looked sad. She wasn't surprised to find this was something more than a romantic gesture, but the knowledge forced her to panic.

She dropped gently to her knees on the blanket and said, "Whatever it is, Clark, just tell me, okay? Don't break it to me gently—just give it to me straight."

"You should sit down first," he said evenly, confirming for her that this was indeed serious.

She sat, then looked him in the eye. "Okay. Let me have it. Do you want a divorce?"

His jaw dropped. "God, no. Where the hell did that come from?"

Relief washed through her. "I don't know—I just had the feeling something big was coming and that's all I could think of."

Her husband sighed, looked tired. "Something big *is* coming, Deb. And *you* might want a divorce after I tell you."

She drew in her breath tightly, but didn't let it back out. "Then tell me."

Clark stared out over the water, sparkling bright beneath the sinking sun, then drew his gaze back to her. "Ian has been smuggling Mayan artifacts in from Guatemala. I've been helping him find clients to purchase them—contacts from the old days." He stopped, swallowed. "I didn't know the details, didn't want to. I knew it was illegal, of course—but he was offering a lot of money, and I couldn't see the harm in it.

"The only thing is . . . I didn't know he was using our island as a drop point. He must have had a key made for the bungalow from Kat's, and even installed a heavy door and big lock on that closet by the bathroom—that's where the goods were being dropped. And there was a pickup scheduled for last week—when Kat was there. And . . ." He looked weak, near tears. "Kat was in real danger, Deb. But—are you ready for this? Turns out Brock Denton is an FBI agent now, and he was working undercover on this—that's how he really ended up there. So at least he was with her. He asked her not to tell us any of it, claiming it might put us in danger, too.

"Now the FBI is onto Ian—and to me. They came to see me this evening, and they're probably arresting Ian right now. I've promised to testify against him in exchange for a light sentence. They say it's possible I'll get immunity, but there could be jail time." He sighed, clearly trying to absorb it all—as she was. "Brock has been . . . decent to me. More than he probably should have.

"So that's it. You're married to a criminal. And maybe a convict. And I'm so damned ashamed, Debra, so ashamed." He looked down, shook his head. "I don't know what I was thinking—except that I just wanted to fix our money problems, keep our life the way it is." He lifted his gaze again, his eyes reaching out to her. "Can you understand that at all? Can you possibly forgive me?"

Debra stayed quiet for a long while. Her throat had gone dry, so she reached for one of the soda cups next to the chicken. It took a few minutes to fully grasp all he'd told her, but she tried very hard not to let it overwhelm her. She tried not to focus on the idea of Kat's being in danger, and she tried not to want to kill Clark for somehow indirectly letting that happen.

But he *hadn't* let it happen, not really. Even if he hadn't been working with Ian on this, Ian still would have used the island without his knowledge. So she tried to concentrate only on hating Ian, something that suddenly came very easily.

As she thought through it, she knew just one thing for certain. She would stick by her husband. He needed her, and she would be there. Because that's what families did, what marriage meant. It was the same reason she'd been unable to sleep with Michael. She'd thought about Clark and their history, their long years together. And she'd realized that, all faults and mistakes and arguments aside, they had a bond that went deeper than anything else she could think of. She'd feared that maybe she was the only one of them feeling that bond; but even that hadn't mattered, because it made the bond no less viable and real. Now she knew Clark was feeling the bond, too, and just hoping it was strong enough.

She didn't make him wait any longer to find out. "I can forgive, yes. And I'll be here with you for every step of this. But as for understanding . . ." She sighed. "Clark, *you* need to understand something, once and for all. How much money we have . . . it's not important. Having a private island or the biggest house in the neighborhood, that just plain doesn't matter. And what I've been trying to get through your head lately is simply that I miss you. I'd rather have a smaller home and more time with my husband than the opposite. You need to loosen up, quit running people's lives, and quit obsessing about money if you want us to be happy. Can you finally get that now?"

He let out a caustic laugh. "I'd say it's a safe bet we're gonna have a smaller home, sweetheart."

She reached up to stroke his face. "That's fine with me. I just want *you*."

He dropped his gaze. "Well, if I don't go to jail, you'll *have* me." Then raised it again. "Every night, home by six. I promise." He covered her hand with his. "I want to be a better husband, Deb. I want to show you I *can* be."

She smiled, feeling his words in her heart. "I want that, too."

Next to her, he let out a long, low breath. "Do you think I pushed Kat toward Ian? Do you think that's my fault?"

She looked down at her knees, pursed her lips. "I will admit I'm a little disturbed that you wanted her to marry a man who was breaking some serious laws."

He nodded, looking contrite. "I don't know how to explain that. It seems so clear to me now, so impossible. I guess I just got caught up in it. Ian kept talking about 'easy money that didn't hurt anyone.' But knowing now that Kat almost got hurt . . ." He stopped, shook his head, closed his eyes, and a tear rolled down his cheek.

Debra fought back her own, shutting her eyes against them. She could cry about that later. For now, though, she didn't want to be sad anymore. "We should eat," she said. "The chicken's getting cold."

"Is it okay, having fried chicken?"

She just looked at him. "You silly, silly man."

"I just . . . always like to give you the best."

"This beach, this sunset, this chicken, this man—I can't imagine anything better."

He cast a sheepish grin. "Might be better if I wasn't going to jail."

To her own surprise, she laughed, then reached for his hand. "After we eat, let's walk on the beach like we used to, holding hands. Would you like that?"

Her husband smiled. "Very much. And maybe if we stick around until dark . . ." he said, playfully raising his eyebrows.

"What?" she asked, giggling.

"We have a blanket. And we haven't made love on the beach for a very long time."

The truth was, they hadn't really made love for a very long time *anywhere*. But if Clark wanted to do it on the beach, she'd be happy to once again share this wildest move of her existence with her husband, her lifemate.

Brock drove north on I-75, letting the harsh expressway winds off-set the even-harsher tropical air that came on thick and strong this time of year. Summertime had arrived in Florida with a vengeance.

He'd spent the last two weeks doing exactly what he was supposed to be doing—taking time off. Out of professional courtesy and friendship, Nichols had kept him updated on the case, but he hadn't been directly involved since the night they'd gotten the truth out of Spencer. Much to his surprise, turned out that was fine with him. All he'd really wanted in the end was the truth, and knowing it was enough. That and seeing Ian punished.

Nichols had also finally found out why no one else had ever come back for the artifacts the Morales brothers had failed to get. Plain and simple, because Ian Zeller aka Omega Man was an incompetent. He'd been smart enough not to risk showing his face anywhere near the goods, but dumb enough that Francisco and Carlos were the only guys on his payroll, and once they'd vanished, Ian simply hadn't known—according to Nichols—how to proceed.

He'd never feared the brothers had stolen the artifacts, delivered there by their cousins who lived in Guatemala, because he didn't think they were savvy enough to sell them on their own. But he finally *had* begun the process of looking to hire new smugglers when Nichols had placed him under arrest. What it came down to in Brock's mind was simply that Ian hadn't been slick enough to run this sort of operation. He'd seen hints of an amateur all along, and turned out that, when it came to high crime, that's exactly what "Omega Man" was.

The U.S. Attorney had promised Spencer immunity for his testimony and, once the trial rolled around, good old Ian would be going away for a long time. Brock couldn't have been happier about that. It still horrified him to realize how close Kat had come to marrying him, but things had worked out, so that was all that mattered. And she wouldn't have to see her dad behind bars. Letting Spencer off had been one of the hardest things Brock had ever done. But the moment he'd done it, he'd felt a weight lift from him, and he knew that he'd done the right thing—for Kat.

With all that under control, Brock had spent his time off doing something constructive—he'd started fixing up the old swamp house. And the more work he put in on it, the more he realized he didn't want to sell it. It wasn't a great place, just a little old house, but it was home—*still* felt like home—so maybe he'd just head there from time to time when he needed some peace and quiet. He'd been staying there since his very first night back, in fact, and he found the quiet—not to mention the memories of his grandpa— comforting.

The truth was, all that work—ripping up linoleum, putting in new sinks, starting to paint—had been not only a good time killer for his mandatory vacation, but a good distraction from what he *really* found himself missing. Which wasn't FBI work.

For the first time in his life, he missed a woman. He wondered how she was and hoped she'd put the whole wedding fiasco behind her. He hoped she was handling the situation with her dad okay— even though Spencer wasn't going to jail, he'd still committed a crime, and would still have to testify to that fact in public. He hoped she'd forgiven her dad since he knew how much she valued that relationship.

The further truth was, his body ached for her. Some nights he fell asleep remembering her on the table, or in the shower, or in the hammock, and some nights he couldn't sleep *at all* until he took matters into his own hands. Fortunately, he'd discovered hard work was good for deterring that, too—at least a little.

She'd had another effect on him, as well. Talking to her about his life had made him realize how much he'd neglected the things that were important to him. There wasn't *much* important, but he needed to tend to it. Maybe that was why he'd come back to his grandpa's house. And he knew for certain it was why he was driving to Gainesville right now.

Making your way into a prison was never fun, and seeing your life-wasting brother on the other side of a table was even less so. So he didn't go as much as he should. He hadn't been there since Christmas, and that visit had been strictly obligatory, out of holiday guilt, and Bruno had probably known that.

In an attempt to make up for his absence, Brock had even called a friend in the warden's office and obtained special permission to bring his brother a few gifts, and to bypass the usual application process he had to go through prior to each visit. Being a federal agent had its perks.

So he'd bought two cartons of Marlboros and a dirty magazine and hit the road early for the nearly four-hour drive to the center of the state. Less-than-classy gifts, but when he thought of what his brother would most like to have, those were the items that came to mind.

He also, on a lark, had bought a mystery novel. He didn't think Bruno read much, but maybe if he was bored enough, he would. Bruno had a good mind, Brock had never forgotten that. He'd always been able to figure out TV detective shows before the end when they were kids. So maybe he'd like a mystery to take him away from reality. Hell, maybe that was why Brock had become a federal agent.

Lastly, he'd tucked into the bag a couple of pictures he'd found at the house—one of their grandpa, another of them together as kids.

After Brock arrived and got ushered through security, he was shown to one of twenty or so tables in a stark, industrial-looking room. Around him, he saw women visiting their men, in some cases whole families, and felt a little bad for Bruno that he was all his brother had. One more reason he should get here more often.

Bruno walked into the room escorted by a guard, his eyes brightening with surprise when he saw Brock. "What the hell?" he asked cheerfully.

Brock grinned. "Figured you were probably missing me, man."

As Bruno sat down in the hard chair across from him, he shook his head, eyes narrowed. "Nobody told me." Usually, after the visit application was approved, Bruno was notified and called Brock to tell him he could come.

Brock shrugged. "I pulled a string or two. Doubt I could get away with it often, but it worked this time."

His brother's eyes dropped to the plastic bag sitting between them, then he looked inside. "What's all *this* for?" He immediately extracted the two old photos Brock had popped into cheap frames.

Brock drew in a deep breath and allowed himself to be honest. "I guess it's 'cause *I* miss *you*."

They never said things like that to each other—ever. So Bruno stayed quiet for a moment, looking down, still studying the pictures. Finally, he lightened things up, lifting his gaze back to Brock. "You still Mr. Big G-Man, out there being all James Bond and *Mission Impossible*?"

"Yeah," Brock replied, then spoke one more truth he hadn't quite allowed himself to realize until this very moment. "But I might give it up soon."

"Yeah? Why?"

Brock swallowed back the emotions his admission had just made him feel. "Just tired, I guess. Ready for something new." There were a lot of reasons, actually, all tumbling through his head and gradually getting smoothed out, just like Kat's sea glass. It was about growing weary of bad guys, about shooting Carlos, about endangering Kat. But mostly the last one, if he was honest with himself. He wasn't sure he ever wanted to risk endangering anyone again.

Bruno's mouth cut a grim line across his face. "Guess it's pretty fucking embarrassing to be an FBI man and have a brother in the slammer."

Yeah, sometimes it was. It had made it a little harder for Brock to get into the Bureau, in fact—despite his ultimately fitting the perfect FBI profile in every other way—but he'd never told Bruno that. Now, he said, "It makes me sad. But that doesn't have anything to do with my job. I just wish you had a better life. I wish you . . . knew what *I* know."

He realized he was shocking the hell out of Bruno with all this serious talk, but his brother didn't bail on him by making a smart remark or changing the subject. "What's that?" he asked quietly instead.

"That life can be pretty damn good without breaking the rules."

Unfortunately, Bruno didn't look like a believer. Finally, he replied, "I don't mean to do it. I just don't know . . . what else to do. You know?"

"You get a place, a job," Brock told him. "You try living like other people."

"A job, man? You know I never had much of . . . what did Gramps call it? . . . a work ethic."

Brock smiled wryly. "True enough. But you could change. I could help you."

"What are you saying?" he asked, eyes narrowed.

And Brock told him what he'd been thinking about for the last part of the drive up here. "Next time you get out, man, I want to help. I'll help you find a job you can live with. All you have to do is promise me you'll try. Try really hard."

When Bruno said nothing, he went on.

"Because it's worth it, man. There's good stuff out there."

"Like what?"

Kat popped to mind. But he didn't want to give her so much credence in his head, so he said, "Just . . . having your own place, nice things. Having your own *life*. Freedom. And . . . there's always women, sex." He grinned.

Bruno grinned back. "Women. Now that I could get into."

"If you could do anything you wanted, live anywhere you wanted, what would it be? And don't give me some shithead answer like you want to live in a mansion and sit by the pool all day. If you could have something—something simple but good—what would you pick?"

For a long while, he feared his brother would come up with nothing, that his life was so lost, so far gone, that he had no more dreams anywhere inside him. When finally Bruno answered. "Remember those pictures you showed me, of the mountains, and the buttes, the stuff you saw out West?"

After that other mandatory vacation three years ago. "Yeah."

"I'd like to go *there*," Bruno said. "Go . . . someplace far away from here. Someplace where it's not so damn hot. Someplace cooler, someplace green." He sighed. "Sometimes I watch TV shows about different places, and I think—maybe I wouldn't mind being some kinda park ranger or something." He stopped, let out a laugh. "Stupid, huh? But . . . maybe I could do something *else* someplace like that. They need other people at those places, right? People to clean up, fix the roads, other stuff. Maybe I could do *that*. In a big park somewhere."

Brock started to nod, seeing a little spark of hope and ambition in his brother's eye for the first time . . . maybe ever. "We'll work it out, dude, figure it out together. Soon."

Brock left the Gainesville Correctional Institution feeling a sense of cautious hope. For all he knew, Bruno would get out, then rob him blind. If not that, he might just disappoint Brock—again. But Brock suddenly believed people could change. He'd changed once upon a time, and was going through other changes now, again. Who knew—maybe even Clark Spencer could change. So it wasn't impossible for Bruno to change, too. All he knew was that he had to try to help him do it, had to give his brother another shot at life.

As he hit the road toward home, he decided he'd do some research on what it took to be a park ranger. And he'd find Bruno some books about some of the big parks out West and mail them to him, so that for now he could at least go there in his head.

Kat turned one of her favorite Raku vases just a little to the left, so that the light shone more intensely through the row of sea glass at the top. She'd come to the gallery early—just after closing, but before the special dinner with her friends and parents to celebrate her opening tonight—in order to make last-minute adjustments to the displays, and to just sort of soak up the glory of her first real showing, her initiation as a real, live *artiste*.

She tilted her head, looked at the vase, and smiled.

Which felt good, since the last weeks had been no less than crazy.

She'd been just about to contact Ian and make her official apology when she'd heard the whole unbelievable story that *he* was the big smuggler Brock had been after!

Only then, after learning of her dad's involvement, did she really understand just how *unfathomably* important money was to him. But she thought he was handling the situation well. He'd lost his best friend, Ian's father, but other than that, so far the fallout had been small—and the reward actually pretty great, from what she could tell.

Because her parents now seemed even closer than she'd already thought them. They kept taking late-night strolls on the beach, and every time she walked into her dad's office, she found them on the phone or busy exchanging flirty e-mails. She rolled her eyes at him a lot but secretly thought it adorable. And the way her mother had stuck by him through this from the start actually gave Kat a little hope that *she* might still someday find a man worthy of her.

Of course, it was difficult to even think about romance right now. Not because of her farce of an engagement—something that already seemed like a distant nightmare—but because of Brock. The hurt wasn't fading—at all. Every time she thought of him, her heart felt like it was shattering all over again.

You stupid, stupid man, she thought now, adjusting a pair of matching bowls set on a wide pedestal. *You don't know what you're missing.*

But the bad part was, he really did know what he was missing. Which meant maybe she wasn't really all that great. She sighed and pushed that unpleasant thought from her mind.

She'd been trying to work through it the way she always worked through problems—by making pots. Uncomplicated pieces mostly, using simple glazes. Soon she'd start experimenting with the sand ideas she'd brought home from the island, and maybe after that she'd work up the courage to make a piece incorporating the sea glass she and Brock had collected together. She knew such a piece would forever remind her of those glorious days, the glorious sex, and the glorious . . . love. One-sided, of course, which made it considerably less magical. But she would always connect those pieces of sea glass with that time.

Satisfied that everything was perfectly in place for her showing, she found herself meandering to the back of the gallery, to the framed pendant stone still hanging on the wall there. As a little girl, and even as a teenager, she'd never realized it was of Mayan origin. Only recent events had led her father to mention that it was one of the last pieces he'd gotten before importation became illegal. He'd explained that he'd given it to her because it had suddenly seemed special, knowing there wouldn't be any more. He'd told her how much he regretted letting Ian change that—that he wished the little broken piece of stone had been the last Mayan artifact ever to enter his life.

Just then a glint of late-day sun on chrome flashed through the front plate-glass window and drew her eye. Oh God. A jade green Porsche had just pulled to the curb outside.

Her heart revved as her body went tense with longing and a whole host of other emotions. *I love you. I hate you. I need you so much I almost can't breathe.*

What the hell did he want? Why was he here? And why did he keep coming back into her life every time she thought he was gone?

Chapter Twenty

She stood up a little straighter, girding herself. They made eye contact through the window, but neither smiled. He looked as good as ever in a pair of well-worn jeans and a dark T-shirt that hugged every muscle in his chest, which, of course, made her want to *touch* every muscle in his chest.

Though it was different now than when he'd first come back into her life, washing up like Poseidon in the flesh—he was no longer forbidden. But she knew if she did what she'd done at her apartment that day, allowed herself the pleasure of touching him, or kissing him, that it would only hurt all the more when he left.

"Hey, kitten," he said, stepping inside, voice low.

"If you're looking for my dad—"

"No. You."

She swallowed. "How did you know I'd be here?" Her dad was the only one renowned for working after hours on a regular basis.

"Saw the sign in the window about your opening tonight.

Thought you might be here getting ready." He took a moment to peruse the room. "Is this your stuff? Your pottery?"

She nodded.

As he took a moment to study one particular bowl, the expression on his face touched her artist's soul. "I didn't know pottery could look like this, kitten. And you made it? From nothing? This is amazing."

She felt oddly shy—she hadn't expected his praise. "Thank you."

"I mean it. It's beautiful, Kat." Their gazes met, held, and the juncture of her thighs quivered—some things never changed, and one of them was that Brock Denton could make her wet with just his eyes.

She needed a tension breaker, fast, before she pulled him into her dad's office and had her way with him, then wholly regretted it. "So what are you doing in Naples?"

"I've been spending some time out at my grandpa's house by the swamp—taking a little time off."

She tried not to be wounded to discover he'd been only a short drive away yet still hadn't felt the need to see her. It stung anyway—sharply. But she wasn't going to dwell on it because this was her big night, her night to be happy. "I, uh, know you had a hand in getting immunity for my dad. He may not have said it, but he really appreciated it."

"I didn't do it for him. I did it for you."

Stupidly, her heart fluttered. *Stop it.* But she heard herself utter another shy-sounding "Thank you" just the same. "And needless to say, I was pretty stunned to find out about Ian."

He nodded. "I'm just glad you got out of that before it was too late."

"Me, too."

"Listen," he said when things went quiet, "I have something to give you."

She blinked, taken aback, watching as he reached down into the front pocket of his jeans.

"When we were on the island, I found the artifacts, but couldn't tell you. And for some reason, I picked this up to take back as evidence. Forgot to surrender it when we turned everything over to the Guatemalan government, and when I contacted the appropriate guy, he told me to keep it as a token of their appreciation." Withdrawing his fist from the denim, he uncurled his fingers so she could see what lay in his palm. "I thought maybe you could use it in a piece of pottery, like you use the sea glass."

Kat stared in awe at the intricately carved chunk of stone in his hand, and her heart began to beat erratically. She'd never actually seen it before, yet somehow she still recognized it. "You got this from the artifacts Ian was smuggling?" She feared she sounded a little manic.

"Yeah. Why?"

She let out a heavy breath and suspected she looked pretty freaked-out—because she was. Taking the piece from him, she strode briskly toward the rear of the gallery.

"What's wrong?"

"Nothing," she tossed over her shoulder, then used her free hand to lift the framed pendant from the wall. Tearing the backing away, she snatched the piece out and held the two together.

"Oh my God," she breathed when they fit perfectly.

Brock had followed her and now peered over her shoulder, watching. "Where the hell did you get that other piece?"

"From my father, when I was little," she explained. "It was a keepsake, a gift."

"I didn't realize *my* piece was part of something bigger—it looked whole to me on its own."

She studied the two parts of the pendant, understanding his assumption. The break was neat, occurring along a crease carved into the rock. Brock's piece appeared stunning enough by itself, but its beauty multiplied when put with the rest of the sizable pendant.

Utterly amazed that the long-broken pieces had suddenly been brought together this way, she turned to look up at him, finding him closer than she realized. It was insane, but she had to ask . . . "Why did you pick up this piece in particular?"

He gave his head a short shake. "I don't know. Even though it was small compared to some of the stuff, it's the first thing that caught my eye. Why?"

She shouldn't tell him. She just really shouldn't. She'd appear desperate—he might even think she was making it up.

"Well?"

She let out a sigh. "My father got the other part on a trip to Guatemala, bought it cheap from a woman selling artifacts along a roadside. So cheap that when she told him there was a legend attached, he figured it was a bunch of hooey, but he told me the legend anyway."

Brock tilted his head. "Which is?"

"It was broken on purpose—two lovers were being separated, so the woman broke her pendant and gave the guy the other half. They never found each other again, no one knew where the other half ended up. The legend is—bring the halves together and the lovers' souls are reunited for eternity, and those who *bring* them together are united for eternity, too." Feeling her face redden at the implication, she pulled her gaze away and rolled her eyes. "So much for legends, huh?"

A hint of anger glittered in his gaze as it hardened on her. "Listen to me, damn it. I *love* you, kitten—I just can't *have* you."

"What?" she gasped, flinching. Her heart beat triple time.

"I'm an FBI agent, Kat. That means I'm in danger all the time, and it means people I care for could be in danger if I make a mistake. Which is exactly what happened on the island. Agents do better without attachments, and that's why I can't have any."

So he was saying he loved her. Her heartbeat pulsed through her whole body.

Yet she somehow also heard the implication that she would just come running now if he decided he wanted her.

And it was only in that shocking and sobering moment that she realized the truth: She *wouldn't* come running—not anymore.

Which meant that maybe she was stronger than she'd ever thought.

She swallowed back the tears suddenly floating behind her eyes and let her own anger out. "Well, that's good to know, but it just so happens I'm *glad* you don't want a future with me. And do you know why? Because there's *always* something more important to you than me, *always* something standing in the way. Your grandpa, that I get—but it's a pattern, Brock, and I deserve better. I deserve someone who puts me first, above everything else. I deserve someone who would give up *everything* for me."

To her surprise, he looked appropriately cowed. She'd never seen *that* on Brock Denton before. "You're right, you do."

"And you're not that guy. And I'm not even sure that guy *exists*, because the truth is—there aren't that many *great* guys out there. Good guys, maybe. But not great ones, who would give everything. But that's okay, because I'd rather be alone than be second-best to someone, especially you."

"Kitten," he said, looking sadder than she'd ever seen him, "if I could give you everything you deserve, I would. I swear."

"But you can't. We both know that. So you should go."

He sighed, didn't answer. Just gave her a long, hard look, as if maybe he were trying to engrave her into his memory—then turned and walked out the door.

Which she'd just demanded he do. So why did she suddenly feel so horribly alone without him already? One more thing that never changed.

"You think my mom will like it?"

Kat glanced up from the sink at The Kiln where she stood washing clay from her hands. Ten-year-old Andre stood next to her, cradling in his arms the small bowl he'd been making these past few weeks.

"Of course she will. It's beautiful."

Andre peered down at his creation, a strange color combination of orange, green, and purple that struck Kat as somewhere between garish and funky. He looked like he was seeing garish. "I don't know. Maybe it's ugly."

Turning off the faucet and drying her hands, Kat lowered herself into a plastic chair from a nearby table, bringing herself closer to his eye level. "You know, when I made *my* very first piece, *I* was afraid it was ugly. But I gave it to my mom for Christmas and she loved it. It's still on display all these years later in her china cabinet. And when I see it now, I realize how unique it is, and that only I could have made it, and that no other piece in the world is quite like it. I promise your mom will love it. And you want to know a secret?"

Andre leaned slightly closer, eyes curious.

"I'm seriously thinking of stealing your colors for the next piece I make."

A smile lit up the boy's face. "Really?"

"Yep. And I don't steal just anyone's colors. So don't tell the other kids, okay?"

He nodded. "Okay."

As he turned to go, Kat said, "See you next week," and hoped she really would. Sometimes kids didn't show back up—ever. And she never found out why—just knew it was family stuff. Stuff like Brock had probably dealt with as a child. She hoped her kids' lives weren't *that* bad.

It struck her then how well Brock had turned out, despite his past. Rough around the edges at times, definitely. Unable to have a normal relationship—that was a drawback. But he'd turned out to be a good man—undeniably so.

Which kind of made her want to cry—yet she reminded herself what she'd figured out last week, that she was stronger than she used to be, so she held the tears at bay.

Now that the studio was empty, she walked to a table on the far side of the room where just-finished pieces sat, waiting to go home. She studied her own latest creation, a mottled green vase adorned with the few bits of glass she and Brock had found on the island. It wasn't her most-polished-looking piece, probably not something anyone would pay a high price for, but it possessed a rustic, genuine quality, something that made her want to touch it, hold it.

When Brock had given her the chunk of stone that completed the pendant, she'd at first wanted to do what he'd suggested, use the whole pendant in a pot. But she hadn't done it yet—even after using the sea glass. And the longer she mulled it over, the more she didn't think she would—because it just seemed wrong.

The pieces had been reunited, but love hadn't grown from it, no matter what he'd said to her on the night of her opening. For all she knew, he didn't even know what love was. Maybe she didn't believe love was real unless you acted on it, embraced it, let it own you. And maybe that was what had made her strong enough to send him away that night.

Somehow, after he'd gone, she'd managed to block the whole incident from her mind for a few hours. Her opening had gone swimmingly—lots of pieces had sold and continued to do so—and the night had been all she had hoped. She'd known she'd become what she'd always wanted to be—a true artist. And the pride in her father's eyes had been the icing on the cake.

Of course, later that night, the encounter with Brock had all come careening back. Along with everything they'd done on the island. It had been tempting to indulge herself and believe in his profession of love. But the fact was that one "I love you"—as amazing at it had sounded coming from him—wasn't enough to negate the facts.

They'd had a whirlwind affair.

It was over.

And he didn't do relationships.

And the further fact was—she wanted to *kill* him for saying he loved her.

Listen to me, damn it. I love you. She could still hear the words, his deep voice chiseling them into her heart.

Her job now was to scrape them away somehow.

Furthermore, she was sorry she'd accepted the stone piece from him. Even if it—incredibly, almost magically—brought the long-separated pendant back together, she feared that as long as it stayed in her possession, she'd never get over him.

There was so much to be happy about right now. Her work was

being noticed, Ian was out of her hair, and certain aspects of life—
like coming in to work with the kids today—were starting to feel
almost normal again. But she knew that before she could truly
move on, she needed to get Brock Denton out of her system once
and for all.

Just then, her purse trilled, and she jogged back across the room
to grab up the cell phone from inside. "Hello?"

"Hey, what time tonight?" It was Nina.

Kat glanced at the clock on the wall—4:15. She needed to go
home, shower and change—and then . . . run an errand that might
help her begin to get Brock out of her mind, even if only symboli-
cally. The idea had just occurred to her, and there was no time like
the present. Then she could meet up with Nina and their girlfriends, and they could go to dinner for Kat's birthday. "Let's say
eight at Tommy Bahama's."

"Eight?" Her friend sounded disappointed. "That means we
won't even get to the first club 'til after ten." Birthdays for Kat
traditionally included lots of barhopping. And Nina seemed determined that Crazy Kat would make an appearance tonight, even if
she had to pour shots of schnapps down Kat's throat herself.

Kat, on the other hand, wasn't particularly anxious for that portion of the evening to commence, and was half-considering claiming
exhaustion after dinner and bowing out. "Quit complaining—they
have big drinks at Tommy's, so you'll survive. I have some stuff to
do first."

Like rid myself of a certain pirate and his treasure.

"Here's 'Fooled Around and Fell in Love' by Elvin Bishop," said
the DJ on the seventies station Brock had, for no particular reason, kept right on listening to ever since he and Kat had left the
island.

"Shit!" he yelled when he dropped a heavy wrench on his hand at the first notes of the slow, bluesy song.

His whole day had been going like this. No, his whole week.

Hell, if he was honest, nothing had been right since he'd last seen Kat. He'd left the gallery in a bad mood, and it had gotten steadily worse from that point on. The improvements on his grandpa's house were going well enough, but no matter what he did, he just wasn't happy.

Truth was, he had no idea where the hell that *I love you* had come from. Especially given that those weren't words that had ever fallen from his lips before. Since he had no intention of acting on them, it had been a stupid thing to say.

The further truth was, he now feared that they hadn't been just words, that he really did love her. She was all he could think about. And work on the house was proving less of a distraction all the time. Hell, right now his whole hand was throbbing like a son of a bitch and what was he thinking about? Kat.

Another disturbing revelation: His mandatory vacation time was almost over, yet he didn't feel the slightest inclination to return to work. Maybe killing Carlos had killed something inside *him*. Or maybe he was just plain tired of the job, like he'd told Bruno.

Or maybe he just didn't want to leave Kat. Even though he wasn't *with* her, as long as he stayed here he also wasn't exactly *away* from her—and for some reason, he couldn't quite bring himself to get any *farther* away.

Not that the last part made any sense. Because if he was here— why couldn't he just be with her?

Picking the wrench back up as the pain in his hand started to subside, he couldn't deny the overwhelming sadness that washed over him. He couldn't be with her because . . . he didn't know how. To love somebody. A woman. Or anyone.

That simple.

Damn, that was sobering. He set the wrench back down, then plopped his ass on the hardwood floor he'd just laid yesterday, resting his arms on bent knees.

He'd always thought he'd overcome his past. He'd thought it was all just a clump of distant memories. He'd even had the nerve to feel proud of himself on occasion.

But this was the first time he'd ever faced the one wound that hadn't ever healed. Hell, maybe his FBI work had just been a big Band-Aid covering it up all this time.

He swallowed, hard. What kind of a man didn't even know how to love a woman? And despite having told her he did, having said that word, he knew deep down that all he'd done was hurt her. Going to the gallery had been purely selfish—because he'd just plain needed to see her, even if only for a few minutes.

He thought of his grandpa, even glanced up at a photo of the two of them together that he'd recently pulled from an old album and put in a frame. If his grandfather were here now, what would he advise? What would make his grandpa proud, show him that Brock had become a worthy man? Not just a federal agent who could bring down the bad guys—but a truly worthy man *inside*?

Letting out a sigh, he decided he was done working for the day. In fact, he needed a beer. Pushing to his feet, he headed for the fridge and pulled out a cold one, then headed outside, toward the old swamp, where maybe he could think a little more clearly.

Chapter Twenty-one

Kat drove up the gravel drive that led to the swamp, nearly wrecking the car when she saw Brock sitting next to the water in that same exact bucket seat from ten years ago. My God, how was that thing still here? Then again, given that his grandpa had died not long after he'd left and no one had been back since, she imagined not much had changed. Probably someone had stuck it in a shed or something, and Brock had pulled it back out.

He tipped a beer bottle to his mouth, watching as she exited her Lexus coupe. She felt overdressed for the surroundings in a suede miniskirt, high-heeled slip-ons, and a beaded cami.

He, on the other hand, wore jeans with a rip in one knee and a gray T-shirt with the sleeves cut out. He looked hot and sweaty— and good enough to eat.

But she had to ignore that and do what she'd come to do. In her fist, she clutched the stone pendant—both pieces.

He opened his mouth to speak, but she decided not to let that happen, to just get to the point of why she was here. "I came to give these to you."

"Give what to me?"

She was holding them out, but he wasn't taking them, so she dropped them on his stomach. "I don't want them. Give them back to Guatemala."

The chunks of carved rock had bounced off him into the grass at his side, but he just peered up at her. "Why don't you want them?"

"Because when I see them I don't think of them being one now, I still think of the separate pieces. Instead of thinking of the lovers' souls being together, I think of them dying alone, apart."

He stayed quiet for a long moment, then finally spoke, his voice low. "Maybe it's real. Maybe we brought their souls back together somewhere, somehow."

That he could utter such words, let alone believe in them, stunned her, but she ignored that. "I still don't want them," she said, then turned to stomp back toward her car, even though it was a little hard to stomp over the uneven ground in heels.

"Wait, kitten, don't go."

She spun to face him, feeling a surprising sense of rage. "Quit calling me that!"

For the second time in the last two occasions she'd seen him, he looked hurt. "But . . . it's what I call you."

And that tore at her heart a little, yet she couldn't let herself care about that any more than she could let herself feel how good he looked sitting there in that old vinyl seat. "You don't need to call me *anything* anymore, since I hope never to see you again."

She turned to leave once more, but he got to his feet in a flash, closing the distance between them to grab her wrist. "Wait, kitten—Kat. Stay and talk to me. I miss you." When she said nothing in reply, he added, "I *love* you."

The last time he'd said it, she'd been too utterly shocked to let herself fully absorb it—*that* sentiment coming from *this* man—but this time, the words moved through her like slow liquid heat, settling in all her most sensitive places.

Even so, she said, "Not enough. It doesn't matter."

"Please," he said, turning her to face him, taking both her hands in his, "please listen to me."

She let out a sigh, sorry to hear her breath come out ragged. Oh God, the effect he had on her—still—no matter how strong she'd come here determined to be. "What?" she said. "What do you have to say that changes anything?"

"Look at me," he said, and she realized her eyes had been planted firmly on his torso, not wanting to face him. She forced her gaze upward and met those dark, delectable eyes that always held her captive with just a glance.

"I've been . . . miserable," he told her, brows knit, face wrenched. "Miserable without *you*." It had sounded like a sadder version of *I love you*, and she could have sworn she almost heard his heart breaking.

Her voice came too small. "Really?"

"Kitten, do you have any idea what it took for me to get your dad off from those charges? Inside me, I mean? If that doesn't prove I love you, then nothing does."

She swallowed, her chest tightening. While she'd appreciated Brock's efforts on her dad's behalf, she really hadn't thought about how it must have affected him personally—that he'd *sacrificed* something for her, something big.

"And if you could have looked inside my heart out on that island, when there was a gun pointed at you—you would have seen that I was dying inside, Kat. Dying. The idea of losing you was worse than anything else I could imagine."

She'd been so terrified that day that she'd blocked much of it out, but she could still remember the look in his eyes, the determination in his voice.

"Give me another chance, honey, and I promise I won't let anything keep us apart this time—you'll be first now. But not just now. From now on."

She wondered if she could possibly be hearing this right. "Now on?"

Another short nod. "I'm thinking forever."

It was as if someone had just pumped air into her heart, inflating it.

Brock squeezed her hands in his, letting out a sigh. "I don't know, maybe that pendant really united our souls—but the truth is, I think it happened on the island. I fell in love with you, and even though the smuggling operation still seemed important, I actually forgot about it for a while. Which I never do. And then we came back and the ends got tied up, the bad guys brought down, and all it left was . . . you. Normally, I'd be ready for the next case, the next challenge, but all I really want to challenge me now is you, kitten. So challenge me, please."

She peered into his eyes. "How?"

"Show me how to love somebody."

"What?" She didn't understand.

His eyes dropped, but he held her hands more tightly. "The only person who ever really loved me the right way was my grandfather, Kat. And I think he and Bruno are the only people *I* ever loved."

"Not your parents?"

He lifted his gaze, shook his head. "I'm not one of those guys who loved them despite what they did. If anything, it . . . turned off something inside me. I've just . . . never let myself get close to people. Until now. You."

She shook her head, thoroughly bewildered. "What happened? Why . . . me?"

"Maybe . . . you're like the sand and I'm like the glass." He cocked a slight, sheepish, thoroughly endearing grin. "I tumble around with you enough and it changes me, rubs away my sharp edges."

She smiled at the analogy, too, then bit her lower lip, thinking of "tumbling around" with him.

"Can you forgive me, kitten? For being blind and stubborn and selfish and God knows what else?"

"Bossy," she added softly. "You have a tendency to be really bossy."

He leaned nearer, bringing their foreheads close. "I'm sorry I ever hurt you, baby. I won't do it again if you'll forgive me and let us start over."

When she looked up at him, their mouths were only inches apart. "Today's my birthday," she whispered.

He cast a soft grin. "Happy birthday, kitten."

"And . . . you still owe me a present from ten years ago."

He arched a brow. "Can't exactly take your virginity anymore, can I?"

She tilted her head and gazed into his eyes. "You never know. Maybe there's a little bit of it left. The part I saved."

"Saved?"

"For whoever showed up with that other half of the pendant. For the sexy guy who worked for my dad and turned me all tingly inside. For the man who would promise me forever. I know you may think I'm a little wild—but all I ever wanted, Brock, was to find the right guy to be wild *with*."

"Lucky for us that I happen to be all of the above."

Kat's heart soared. This wasn't a dream. Or a fantasy. This was Brock Denton, in the flesh, giving her his heart, his love. And she couldn't help thinking it was a much greater gift since he'd never given it to any other woman before her.

But then she remembered. "Damn it."

"What?"

"I'm supposed to meet Nina and some other friends for dinner."

"Well, you're gonna be late." Pure heat dripped from his eyes as the sun began to sink behind the trees in the distance, turning the air dusky. And that heat seemed to reach inside her and grab hold of her, all of her—the girl who'd wanted him so badly ten years ago, and the woman who was about to have him.

Pressing her palms flat against his chest, she walked him backward over the dirt, into the grass, then pushed him down in the car seat. He gazed up at her in hot anticipation as she straddled him, just like once before. Of course, she had clothes on this time. But they wouldn't get in the way for long.

Their bodies melded perfectly, her softest spot meeting with the incredible length of hardness behind his zipper. They both released small, hot moans, and Brock growled, "Damn, I've missed you."

"I've missed you, too. Missed *this*." Lifting her hands to his stubbled jaws, she lowered her lips onto his mouth, then pressed her tongue inside. His hands roamed her hips, waist, breasts. She sighed, "Oh God," between kisses.

"I want you, kitten," he murmured, pushing her top up over her chest to reveal a transparent flesh-colored bra. "Damn," he said again at the sight, then nibbled at one stiffened peak through the filmy fabric.

Part of Kat wanted to go slow, savor this moment, but most of her wanted to go much faster, because it had been too long—and Brock seemed of the same mind.

He locked the fingertips of both hands into the cups of her bra and pulled them down, freeing her. She reached between them for his zipper and the button on his jeans. Pushing beneath her skirt, he drew her panties aside and she sucked in her breath as a shockingly cool evening breeze washed over them, making her nipples pucker even tighter beneath his ministrations.

Both of them breathed hard by the time she lifted, lowered, and sheathed him with her body, and they both groaned at the slow, hot connection. And she clung to him, her arms around his neck, his wrapping warm around her back. Because she'd never felt closer to another human being in her life, and this had seemed so impossible just an hour ago, and now here they were, sharing the most profound intimacy she could imagine. "I love you," she whispered in his ear, unable to believe it was the first time she'd ever said it out loud.

"Ah, kitten, I love you, too. So, so much."

And then they moved together, hot and sweet, until she came, a pure joy she'd never experienced before rushing through her—because this was real, and it mattered. He loved her, too.

"Oh God," he said as she wafted back to earth. "Watching you do that just pushed me over the edge, baby." And then he was thrusting up inside her, hard, deep, powerful, groaning, groaning, until they went still in one another's arms, just holding each other.

It was a few, long, languid, glorious minutes later that they were readjusting their clothes and she realized Brock's gaze had dropped to her navel. She knew what had caught his eye—the thing she'd done for herself when Nina had told her she had to do something defiant. A small tattoo set to the left of her belly button—a slightly prissy, feminine-looking cat, underneath it in fancy script the word *kitten*.

"Believe it or not," she said, "I never expected you to see that."

"It's almost as adorable as you," he said, studying it for a long moment.

"And just so you know, it doesn't say 'kitten' because of you or anything."

Lifting his gaze, he cocked his head to the right, looking doubtful. "Then why does it say it?"

"Because I *am* one. A sex kitten."

He leaned his head back in a laugh. "That you are, honey."

"A sex kitten for my big, sexy secret agent man," she purred, returning to the afterglow of passion to exchange a long, lingering kiss that left them both sighing when it was over.

"One thing, though," he said. "About me being a secret agent. Would it bother you if I quit?"

She blinked. "Are you kidding? That would *thrill* me." She felt a little selfish as soon as the words left her, but didn't recant, since it was true. She hated the idea of him being in danger like they were on the island.

"Good. Because I've been giving it a lot of thought, and everything inside me feels . . . done with the secret agent biz. I'd still like to stick with investigations—it's about all I know—but I was thinking about trying to make a PI business float. And if I decide that's too iffy, I can look into staying with the Bureau in another capacity. I'll explore the possibilities and find the right path."

Still sitting in his lap, she slid her arms back around his neck. "That's exactly what I want for you. And I know whatever you pick, your grandpa would be just as proud."

"I think you're right," he said, sliding his hands back up her outer thighs. "All he ever wanted was for me to make something of myself and be happy. I made something of myself. Now I want to be happy."

She gave her head a coquettish tilt. "I'll see if I can help with that."

"Wanna make me happy, kitten? Call Nina and tell her you've got other plans tonight."

Kat knew she shouldn't do it. Nina would be livid. And rightfully so, since it was probably as hard to have a birthday party without the birthday girl as it was to have a bachelorette party without a bride.

Unless, of course, she explained that it was because she'd just had wild, writhing sex with her own personal FBI agent and island lover, and was about to have a lot more of it. That Nina would definitely applaud. "Okay, you talked me into it."

He grinned. "And then after that, you can tell me what *I* can do to make *you* happy. 'Cause I'm on a whole new kinda mission here—keeping my little kitten happy and satisfied."

Kat bit her lip, remembering the very first moment she'd seen him walking up onto the shore of her island, and said, "I think we need to get you an eye patch."

He raised his eyebrows, understandably surprised. "Oh?"

"I've got a serious pirate fantasy. And Dad will probably have to sell the island soon, so we don't have much time."

He laughed, leaned in to lift a hot little kiss to the spot just below her ear, and while he was there whispered, "Avast ye lusty wench."

Kat giggled, letting her eyes fall shut with fresh pleasure, then forced herself up from his lap to find her phone and call Nina. But then she paused, remembering the pieces of stone they'd let fall into the grass beside the car seat, and stooped to find them. "I wonder . . ." she said, holding them in her palm, then looking to Brock. "Do you believe in that kind of thing? Legends?"

He tilted his head and flashed a sexy look. "This started long before I found that pendant, kitten. In fact, I think it started right in this car seat ten years ago. But if those bits of stone gave us the help we needed to get here, then sure, I believe." He swatted her bottom lightly. "Now hurry up and make that call so we can go inside and play lusty pirate games."

"We don't have the eye patch yet," she reminded him.

"Don't worry, kitten. I can ravish you just as well without it."

TONI BLAKE's love of writing began when she won an essay contest in the fifth grade. Soon after, she penned her first novel, nineteen notebook pages long. Since then, Toni has become a multipublished author of contemporary romance novels, as well as had more than forty short stories and articles published. She has been a recipient of the Kentucky Women Writers Fellowship and has also been honored with a nomination for the prestigious Pushcart Prize. Toni lives with her husband in the Midwest and enjoys traveling, genealogy, crafts, and snow skiing.

TONI BLAKE